THE ALASKA VIRUS

TO KILL COCAINE

BY GLENN ALLEN

ISBN: 1-4782-2190-9
ISBN-13: 978-1-4782-2190-6

PROLOGUE

Any reader, scientist or not, will immediately ask: "Could this really be done, and under such non-laboratory conditions as described in this story?" The clear answer is certainly yes. But now that the idea has been placed center on the table, this is not as likely to happen as it would have been before. In some ways this novel stands as a gift to the cocaine cartel which could have been a target for such an engineered cocaine virus. As the story will eventually spread and be read by many, any group or laboratory which might engage in such plant engineering would have a much harder time hiding their work and disguising their intentions than prior to the publishing of this story.

While the Manhattan project required massive efforts of thousands of scientists and the construction of huge uranium enrichment plants at Oak Ridge National Laboratory, biological engineering can be carried out under, by today's standards, rather simple laboratory environments in particular if those engaged have access to standard technology such as the synthesis of short single strand DNA (termed primers for PCR), sequencing of DNA, amplification of DNA by the PCR process, and access to imaging by light or electron microscopy. In this story the two central figures are highly trained scientists studying viruses (virologists) and they both have their own laboratories with all of these technologies at hand. What drives this story is the inner fire of a red-headed woman intent on seeking revenge for the drug-related death of her brother.

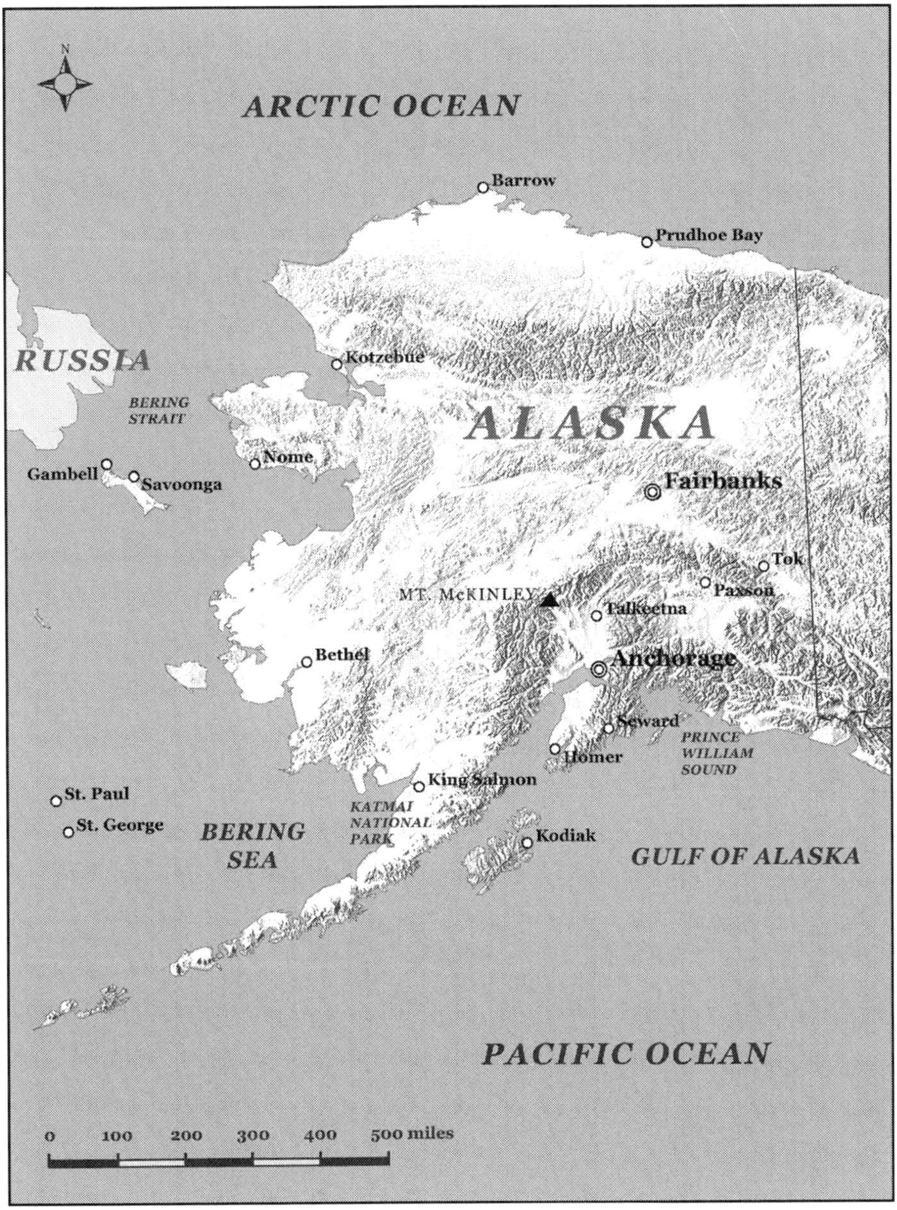
N
ARCTIC OCEAN
Barrow
Prudhoe Bay
RUSSIA
Kotzebue
BERING
STRAIT
ALASKA
Gambell
Savoonga
Nome
Fairbanks
Tok
Paxson
MT. McKINLEY
Talkeetna
Bethel
Anchorage
Seward
PRINCE
WILLIAM
SOUND
Homer
King Salmon
St. Paul
St. George
BERING
SEA
KATMAI
NATIONAL
PARK
Kodiak
GULF OF ALASKA
PACIFIC OCEAN
0
100
200
300
400
500 miles

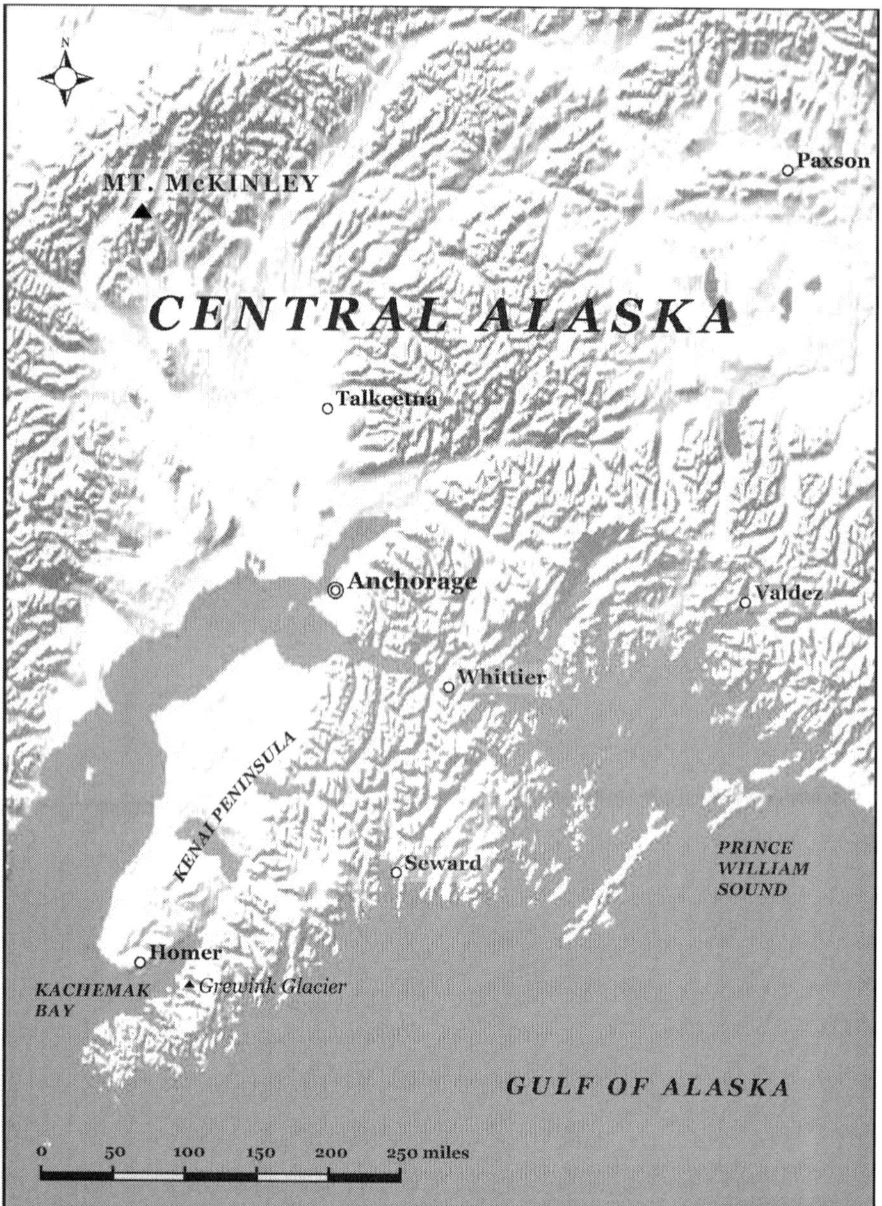
N
MT. McKINLEY
Paxson
CENTRAL ALASKA
Talkeetna
Anchorage
Valdez
Whittier
KENAI PENINSULA
PRINCE
WILLIAM
SOUND
Seward
Homer
KACHEMAK
BAY
Grewink Glacier
GULF OF ALASKA
0
50
100
150
200
250 miles

CHAPTER ONE

WINTER IN COLLEGE FJORD

The Alaskan winter daylight spanned only four hours and the world was a variation of white. The face of Cascade Glacier which was less than 500 feet away towered twice that distance above Dr. Matt Lynx as he approached in a fragile fiberglass kayak. The air was 20 degrees, with the wind creating chill factors much lower. Previous storms had cleansed the air of dust and haze, leaving it so clear that distances appeared highly compressed. Thus a mountain which Matt knew to be over 50 miles away, looked to be an hour's paddle at most. The glacier seemed on top of him.

He dared the glacier to crush him. Even in the winter when the glaciers are relatively quiet, they can still calve building-sized ice bergs that renounce their parent and plunge into the ocean to slowly drift, melt, and rejoin the cycle. These icebergs create waves big enough to capsize even the most skilled kayaker, and in these waters of Prince William Sound at this time of the year, this would be lethal. Matt believed that if he was quiet and did not disturb the glacier god, he would be allowed this close approach to the altar of ice. This was, he realized, a bit difficult to defend since the winds blowing over the glacier face created a roar that would hide a bellow from a herd of sea lions. He sat quietly nonetheless, letting the tide carry him closer to the face of the glacier and then the opposing currents move him away. He had paddled from the summer fish camp on the outlet of the Coghill River on College Fjord Cascade Glacier. This glacier begins at sea level with a 1000 foot vertical ice face. Above the face are 4 miles of crevasses and ice falls as it rises 9638 feet to the top of Mt. Gilbert.

Unseen by Matt, a twin engine Grumman Goose amphibian aircraft approached the glacier at a low altitude. Its presence was shielded from Matt by the roar of the wind. The tiny white kayak spotted, the Goose circled once to pick an area free of icebergs and then set up for the landing.

Matt was alerted by the cloud of sea gulls leaping from the water, scattering in all directions. Turning around, he saw the Goose skimming over the water at him. Paddling away from what appeared to be the point of certain collision, he had no time to wonder what this large, ugly, left-over aircraft from World War II was doing out here in a place and time when no other humans were supposed to have been within miles.

The pilot had indeed miscalculated and nearly cut the kayak in half before stopping. Matt's blood pressure rose as he imagined that this would certainly unleash several large icebergs to sink the Goose, the kayak, and their offending humans.

It was in this frame of mind that Matt paddled to the side door of the Goose as it opened. The pilot offered a silly smile and hand. Just as Matt was about to pull the pilot into the water, the passenger in the Goose, a man whose presence did not surprise Matt, appeared and pushed the pilot aside.

"I thought I would find you here," said Roland, a somewhat chubby fellow dressed in the best that some Washington D.C. outfitting store had been able to offer.

"Right! So you tried to drown me! Lets get the hell out of here before the glacier drops a few hundreds of tons of ice on our heads. The noise of this airplane could trigger a massive ice dump!" shouted Matt.

The kayak was pulled into the Goose and Matt settled into the copilot's seat as they flew 5 miles to the fish camp. They stopped 100 feet off shore.

"We'll tie up here and I will ferry you to shore. The beach is too rough to pull up to," Matt announced.

As the pilot, a fellow named Kent, stepped out of the 2-man kayak near the shore, he slipped on the wet rocks and fell backwards into the water.

"Oh God-God-God I can't breathe! Help me!" gasped Kent in short exhaling gasps.

"Right, now see what you almost did to me! You have 43 seconds before you pass out," stated Matt quietly and then extended a hand, pulling him out.

Indeed, falling into water this cold, one can suffocate in less than a minute as your chest muscles contract and refuse a breath. Matt helped him to the cabin where he was given a blanket and chair in front of the wood stove. Bringing Roland back, Matt took the long way around, pointing the kayak at this glacier and that, letting it drift, and then bringing it back again to take another glimpse of what may be the most spectacular sight in all of Alaska and possibly the earth– the head end of College Fjord.

Tide water glacier Prince William Sound

“Roland, my friend, you are looking at the battle ground where the ocean and mountains collide in the most abrupt manner. It’s right here that in 1964, the tectonic forces fought to create the greatest earthquake yet recorded in North America! Over there is Radcliffe Glacier. You are looking at a two and a half mile high ice wall rising all the way to the top of Mt. Marcus Baker.”

Matt continued his monologue while wondering why this Washington D.C. bureaucrat had invaded his hide-a-way where for 2 weeks a year, he disappeared to think, write, and renew his roots.

“OK, I am scenically challenged. It’s beyond my imagination, now please, let’s go in so I can warm up and see if I need to radio for a dry pilot,” said Roland, as Matt seemed lost in thought and drifting.

"I assume you are not here for a weekend of chasing ice worms on the glaciers, my friend."

"We'll discuss that when you take me in," replied Roland.

"And besides how did you know where I was?"

"Well, sleuthically speaking, I knew you were at your cabin, and you told me countless times about Cascade Glacier and what it is like on a clear day."

Matt was just shy of 50, 6 foot 1, 180 pounds. His straight black hair and light brown/hazel eyes were the result of some Tlingit Indian blood mixed with a good deal of Russian, Dutch and French. With sharp angled features, high cheekbones and a muscular face, he had been described as Harrison Ford with a grin. Typical of a middle distance runner or mountaineer, two sports dabbled in, Matt's build was lean and very muscular. People generally commented about his smile which was broad and genuine, or his eyes—which were large and when he was talking with someone, were always focused on the other person indicating interest and pleasure. Matt's hands were generally a mess. Either stained with some blue dye from the lab, or sporting grease and cuts from mechanical work, Matt's face was always tanned. His voice also added to the mixture of signals since it was quiet, soft, and low. His hair didn't do much to solve the contradiction. It had no part and flopped in all directions.

Another unusual feature was Matt's chin. He had a deep cleft in the center. Now that in itself was not uncommon, and most women found it attractive. Matt however had a 1 inch deep scar running directly across and at right angles to the cleft creating an X when he dropped his chin to talk. Many people had tried to get a straight answer as to its origin, but answers ranged from aliens, to fights with large animals, or that one of his sisters did it with an electric knife at Thanksgiving.

Over the years Matt explored a variety of attire. He did not envision himself as a Western cowboy type and thus blue jeans, wide Western belts and flowered shirts were out. He certainly had no interest in being thought of as a Yale or Harvard graduate with their suits and ties. Thus he had settled on a mixture of signals: cotton slacks, his wide leather belt with its Alaskan gold nugget buckle, and a dress shirt in the winter or knit tennis shirt in the summer. Always close at hand was a brown rough wool sports coat. Most days he wore black Tony Lama or Luchesse boots. He had several pair. Ties, either Western string or classic cloth were avoided at all costs. He felt they made his eyes bug out. Always present in a pocket or nearby was a bolted and screwed together jumble including a wire cutter, knife, a fork-like object with sharp edges, and different sized screwdrivers. He would tell anyone asking that this was the first Leatherman multi-purpose tool ever made and that if he had thought to patent it, he would be very rich. It was in constant evolution.

Matt was born several hundred miles to the north, in the town of Talkeetna, which for years had only been served by the Alaska railroad until the road to McKinley was pushed through. Matt's father was born on the coast of southeast Alaska, in a small village where everyone either fished or processed salmon. His father claimed 1/2 Tlingit Indian blood depending on the listener and the truth was likely in between. The common mixing of Indian and Russian genetics led to a tall, light complexioned people with straight black hair and high cheekbones. The family name was Tlingit heritage translated to the English word for the large Alaskan lynx cat. His father was the only member of the family who sought higher education, spending 4 years at the University of Alaska in Fairbanks studying geology. After several efforts to mine gold around Talkeetna he had turned to guiding and flying in the summers and working with the US Geological Service in the winters.

Matt's mother was born into an old, rather genetically exhausted elite Boston family. The admitted lineage was inbred Dutch/French but with enough scoundrels of unknown origin mixed in to keep the family tree from losing all of its leaves. She attended the Emma Willard school for girls in upstate New York and then Swarthmore college where she studied romance and Slavic languages. Sickened by the thought of a life filled with meetings of the Junior League and worse, the Daughters of the American Revolution, she traveled extensively in Europe and then drove to Alaska one summer as a whim. There she met Matt's father who was the least expensive– and at that time, the least experienced mountain pilot willing to fly hikers and climbers from the tiny town along the Susitna River to the great glaciers from which an attempt on the summit of McKinley could be made.

Growing up in Talkeetna, winters were spent learning all that his mother and father could impart. His mother taught him the multiple languages she knew, something he later came to appreciate greatly. His father taught him some geology but was more interested in relating the traditional Indian stories and beliefs which he felt were an essential part of his heritage.

At this time in the transition of Alaska from a territory to a State, the US government was still helping fund schools and the teachers were well paid, fresh from college, and were anxious to spend extra time with an unusual and gifted student. That was years ago, and two semesters were spent as a freshman at the University of Alaska before transferring to Stanford where he ran the 440, read a great deal of classic literature, and obtained degrees in physics and geology. He moved on to Caltech to obtain a Ph.D. in molecular biology.

Now, however, the only thing that mattered was why was Roland here? Roland was the one man able to transform Matt's life from that of an eccentric molecular biology faculty member at Johns Hopkins University Medical school into – for short periods– a life of adventure, and for longer periods, continued funding for his own research.

Roland Epstein was an odd combination of ex-CIA spy, somewhat overly rotund federal bureaucrat, and Jewish rabbi. He was 48, weighed at least 190 pounds, stood at most 5 foot 6, and was half bald. His body was a series of spheres and ovals. In contrast to his hair which had mostly disappeared, his eyebrows were so long and bushy that they seemed to have stolen hair from the top. He wore glasses and this mass of fur was squashed against his face and poked out from the rim of the glasses. Roland's jargon drove Matt nuts. He loved to invent words or to toss long words in whether or not they made sense. The effect of peppering his talk with long out of place words forced listeners to focus carefully to what he was saying– almost as if he was hardly able to speak English and one was helping him struggle from one sentence to the next.

Roland was able to walk and talk his way through the most inner circles of the federal machinery that interwove agents from the CIA, DEA, DOD and many multi-lettered agencies. Roland was formally attached to both the CIA and DARPA, a difficult to define agency of the Department of Defense charged with funding developmental projects considered to be of immediate concern to the national defense. For Roland, DARPA provided a means of funneling small sums (in units of 100-250 kilo bucks per year) into projects where only he and the DARPA director had knowledge about what was being accomplished.

For Matt, DARPA had funded his research on the molecular biology of viruses, not because this was of immediate importance to the national security, but as an ongoing trade for special services rendered on projects where Matt's combination of skills and knowledge were unattainable in any other person.

Matt handed Kent a glass of whiskey.

"You were lucky, a bit longer in the water and you would have suffocated. Of course that's if the killer whales hadn't gotten to you first. When we paddle back to the Goose they will be watching for you. Your scent washed off in the water. Here — take a slug. Roland and I have some catching up to do." Matt walked out suspecting that this visit would entail the offer of yet another adventure involving molecular biology and James Bond exploits.

Matt had been lured into the DARPA trap some years before when he was running out of National Institutes of Health (NIH) funding for his research laboratory and began asking about for possible funding sources out of the normal shark-infested waters patrolled by the major research laboratories. His probing had taken him to DARPA via a friend who was funded by them for what Matt felt was work no more worthy than his own. After a number of disinterested replies to his research summaries, he had been asked to visit D.C. and DARPA. There it became clear that they were far more interested in his unique upbringing and talents that included multiple languages, knowledge of several sciences, skill as a pilot and back country traveler in some of the least pleasant countries. The trade was laid out to him. In return for occasional projects the agency would support his research at a reasonable level if he continued to publish in respectable journals. Over the years, Matt had become used to this trade that allowed him to ignore the usual deadlines and re-submission dates for grant applications to the NIH. Besides, Roland's adventures had kept his life at an interesting pace.

It didn't take Roland long to get to the point. He was not comfortable away from his Washington D.C. environment, or from his array of electronic gadgets that kept him continually linked to every one else's gadgets. A hotel with free WiFi was, he felt, the minimal accommodation he deserved. The fish camp offered just a short wave radio that was turned off unless Matt felt some need to communicate with a passing airplane. Roland carried a GPS SPOT locator and was constantly updating his position. The only time he actually could recall its being of use was in Washington D.C. when he used it to find his car in the parking lot of a large mall at Christmas. He also had a satellite phone tucked away in the Goose and it could be linked to his cell phone if he wanted to chat or go face-to-face with Skype.

"Situationally speaking, this one is complicational. Matt, we need your help in a matter that requires your expertise in molecular biology, stealthology, and your ability to keep yourself and a few others alive. Indeed this one is particularly in your kitty litter box and has the potential of cutting the cocaine trade to nil, of getting people killed, or both. What I can offer is two things, the usual continuation of DARPA support for your research at Hopkins, and further in this case —all of the country and motherhood that you can choke on. There are few instances in life that one becomes patriotically challenged —–"

Matt thought to himself: "Gag me with a spoon Roland" and he cut this drivel off by firing his .44 Smith and Wesson through an open window at an empty fuel oil barrel 200 yards away. The thump echoed across the water of the sound. Matt was particularly fond of this pistol, a silhouette target pistol sporting a 10 inch barrel and firing the largest commercially available pistol cartridge. It gave him a sense of security due more to its weight than its power, since it was still less powerful than the old .30-.30 rifle cartridge, a caliber that no Alaskan in his right mind would consider as security against anything other than an angry bartender.

Roland's god-and-country lecture properly abbreviated, they allowed their ears to recover and watched Kent run in from the other room dragging his snoopy blanket to view an imagined wounded grizzly.

"O.K. Roland, we know I need your research support and I get bored in the lab after a few months of day and night work. What is the scheme this time to rid the country of the boogie men and make you all happy, fat, bureaucrats?"

Roland got up and paced back and forth on the uneven wooden floors for what Matt realized would be a lecture involving multiple replenishments of whiskey before it was done.

"You've heard the profligate numerology, Matt, the flow of cocaine into the US is greater than ever, and interdictionally we are negative. The number of drug related crimes is exponential. Mexico is in a civil war amongst the drug lords and this is spilling over the border." He continued:

"What I find shocking demographically is the effects of drugs on the small towns of America. Ten years ago, drugs were mostly isolated to the large cities and their surrounds, to the poor blacks and Hispanics, and– for cocaine– to the well off. Things are very different now and the trend looks ominously luminous."

"The last time we went over this I recall you were predicting out right class warfare if drugs continue to increase. Any change in that cheerful outlook? asked Matt.

"That's a negative-negative. The rate at which drugs have become a major industry of the lower classes is frightening. The drug industry has slowly developed from a poorly organized operation to a major part of our society. Now days you see well-to-do white kids graduating from top 4 year colleges to become secretaries. If this is the case, think about some poor kid who is unlikely to get through high school. For these kids there is only one clear path to money and that's drugs."

"And Matt, my friend, I can tell you that there is a stratospheric market for drugs like cocaine in the pressure cookers of yuppie Washington D.C, and the other big cities. Kids of yuppies see their parents doing drugs and turn a deaf ear to the drug-free lectures they hear in school."

"Ultimately this reflects societal displacement and the loss of secure jobs. All of this needs to be addressed, but the CNN News level problem is that these lost jobs are being replaced by the Cocaine Cartel. If we cannot break this industry soon, it will become too big and powerful for any of us to deal with."

Roland continued: "There are some of us who are morally pushed over this situation and once every few months a group of us, from the DEA, and other agencies, get together and mindstorm for a weekend over novel approaches to interdiction and eradication of drugs."

"Descriptively speaking, there is the old Plowshare group with their atom bombs for peace who want to nuke the hell out of Colombia, Chile and a few other neighboring countries. There are generals with surplus aircraft from the Iraq war who want to fire bomb the growing areas, I suppose following total nuclear scorching. The Navy guy wants a cable just under the water that will stretch over our entire coastline and will somehow sense drugs– but not fishing boats, I guess."

"Well, like constipation, there was nothing new. At the end of the meeting one of the people from drug enforcement took me aside and told me that he had been approached by a scientist, a woman from North Carolina. She had come to him suggesting a rather amazing idea of creating a virus that would kill the plant that cocaine comes from. This was too far out for him and he had no hidden funds. Suggested she circle my wagons."

"Ah, so Kemo Sabe, I hear my favorite word–viruses. So who is this lady? Not I hope, like that 200 pound Aeroflot stewardess you made me baby-sit the last time," asked Matt, finally having his interest raised.

"No, no. A brilliance, pertness personified! I've met her several times and I must admit she is driven like a Ferrari 430 at LeMans. She made a very good case for her plan to create this virus– but I need your input before I will spend my cookie money on it. I need to have you refresh my memory about viruses. Let me bring you up to date with what I remember from college biology."

"More about this lady– then I'll listen to your college recollections. Where is she, how did she get this idea, what are her credentials, who did she train with in graduate school? I assume she has a Ph.D."

"Affirmative to the third power–Of course, of course." Roland sighed.

"Well,– her curriculum vitae: Kiren Moore is a bright as hell, mid-thirties assistant professor at Duke University. She's in the Plant Pathology department. Did graduate work at Harvard and postdoctoral studies at the Rockefeller University. Is that candy sweet enough for your palate?"

"I wouldn't spit it out. East coast science though, not the clear incisive thinking we Westerners are used to."

"Right, when you sober up from your tequila fizzes! Well, Kiren has been working on this virus which she calls a Gemini virus for some time. Apparently she found some in South America that infect coca plants, and came up with the idea."

"Why is she bent on eradicating coca plants? A cute idea, but not likely to get her the Nobel Prize. In fact, if she is successful, it could make her very very unpopular."

"I was suspicional myself until our second visit when she opened up and told me her story. I'll leave the details for her to relate but suffice to say she had a brother she was very close to. The brother went from top student to cocaine addict to dealer to dead smuggler killed in a plane crash. She is so hot over the issue and our lack of being able to deal with it that she told me she would risk her life if it made her feel that she could consummate her vengeance."

"Now revenge is my kind of motive, Roland. It's one a man can relate to. Nothing fancy or touchy-feely, just kill the fuckers. Sounds as if I might like her. I assume you want me to check her out."

"Yes and if you legitimize her science I'll need your help for a few months to shepherd the project. There are a number of things down the line involving scaling things up and testing the virus that will be beyond her. And she may need a bit of protection. I've got a mild case of poison ivy over the whole thing. It's a non-committee idea but one that may be our only shot."

"So, so, so, another little project that is going to obliterate months of my time and likely get me killed. And what's in it for me?"

"Matt -Matt -Matt, saving the world from the bad guys of course. That's all."

"Screw you. My ass does not come free. I have tenure at Hopkins as you recall, and I can— if I desire, retire and raise show gerbils on my farm. I assume you will extend the funding for my current project a number of additional years?"

"Would I have reenacted Byrd's march to the North Pole and then suffered you playing Dr. Zhivago-in-Siberia unless I was willing to make it worth your while a few more years?"

"Now Roland, you get your money's worth from my research. If I do come up with the cause of Alzheimer's disease I will give you and your secret four letter agency full credit."

"We don't want credit." Roland snapped.

"No share my Nobel prize, huh?"

"You take the prize, I'll take the chocolate. Top up my glass and let me get my notes about this project. We will refresh my mind about viruses. There may be some glitch that is so transpondent to you that we don't need to go farther."

Matt added more wood to the large free standing wood stove, and sat back to listen.

"OK, now from the mouth of the biologically challenged. As I recall, for all living things from bacteria, to animals, to plants, there are unpleasant little parasites called viruses. We know about viruses that infect us, but in the biosphere, the greatest number of viruses are found in the ocean infecting bacteria, and on the land, attacking plants. Viruses are tiny spherical particles, containing molecules that code for genetic information. The shell of the virus is made from proteins and sometimes they have a fatty membrane coating. How's that?"

"Yahoo, an A minus. Sounds as if you are great at memorizing. Let me add a few things. Viruses are biologic but have not been considered to be alive since they are fully dependent on their host organism for their reproduction cycle. Following infection they take over the normal machinery of the host cell to make more copies of the virus's genetic material, and later in infection, the virus shell. Sometimes they are oblong shaped rather than balls."

"Right, I'm pleotrophic on all of that, but I get a bit fuzzy over the details of the genetic information. Give me a boost."

"So, let's see, at a Roland level: the genetic information, well, it is stored in the form of very long molecules called DNA– which most people have heard of, or a different form called RNA."

"Right now retread my neurons on how the information works- – at my level please."

"I like to think of a cell as a tiny factory controlled and directed by a central computer. The programs for the computer– its memory, are stored on long rolls of magnetic tape. In fact think of it as being on about 2 dozen very large separate rolls. We can call the rolls chromosomes, and the tape is the equivalent to the cell's DNA. For commands to be sent out to the rest of the factory, copies are made from the information on the master rolls onto small tape cassettes. The information on these cassettes directs all of the functions of the factory from how it makes things to where things are put in the factory. These copies are the equivalent of the cell's RNA message molecules. Since this kind of information is used for different purposes, it doesn't last all that long. One can imagine that the cassettes are frequently used up in the process of being read."

"O.K., but where I got lost was in the details of how the information was stored, or is that important?"

"Of course it is. The DNA or RNA molecules are long, long strings made from four different small chemical molecules called – for short, A, C, T, and G. They are similar to each other but different enough so that the cell can tell them apart. I find it amazing that all of the information needed to make us work can be read from a language that has only four letters as contrasted to verbal languages with two dozen."

"So how do you tell DNA from RNA?"

"You've heard of the DNA double helix. The big difference is that RNA has only one strand of the "tape" while DNA has two strands – each one containing a copy of the information and the two strands are wrapped tightly about themselves, forming a double helix of DNA. Because DNA must remain as the central storehouse of genetic information, it is important to protect this information against any change. Having two strands to check one against the other provides a redundancy that keeps us from acquiring changes that would make us all mutants in a few generations. There is one more difference. The letters that are used to make RNA are marked chemically to allow the cell to tell the difference between the basic storage molecules –DNA, and the molecules that direct things –RNA."

"So for the moment at least, I can follow the TV news on DNA. Lets get back to viruses for a moment. Here's the notes I took from what Kiren told me. Let me read."

"Well, as I said, she works on plant viruses she calls Gemini viruses and she claims they could be engineered to kill or stunt coca plants. These Gemini viruses are transferred plant to plant by insects called White Flies and both White Flies and Gemini viruses are plentiful in the tropical areas where cocaine is produced. Reading my notes here I see she said that Gemini viruses are major pathogens of food crops in the tropical and sub-tropical areas. Here in the US, Gemini viruses nearly eliminated the sugar beet industry a number of years ago. If this engineering was successful, the entire cocaine trade might collapse and the Cartel would never recover."

Matt should have seen this coming but had turned his brain onto half power while listening to Roland. He now stood up smartly and laid the .44 S&W over the open window sill. Slowly with a very even beat, he placed the five remaining shots into the barrel 200 yards distant. Their ears were deaf– the shots being fired from inside the house. Matt was now in his own world, free from Roland's babble as he considered the proposal.

The basic idea was clear, straightforward, and might work. Matt's mind ran to the more essential questions. What would be needed, what were the logistical problems? And then the biggest problem: how would you accomplish all this without having every coke sniffing doper hunting your head?

"Why not have the DEA do the work at the Frederick facility in Maryland? It has high security and could handle such work."

Roland had a few additional complications.

"Speaking out of my normal federalese envelope, I have a feeling that this magic bullet might just work, but there are a number of factors that will force me to disavow any work on the project. There are forces against us. If the Cartel learns of this, they could try to stop it by hitting the people doing the work. Also they have a lot of money that could be used to create a flood of adverse "environmental" gaff– which brings me to the next problem."

"A crowd that could engulf us in politically bad press are the "Greenies". The "Greenies" as I call them are the coalition of groups that defend any species against all intelligent thought. They would have a shit fit if there was any suggestion that the federal government was going to eradicate a species intentionally with prejudice. Never mind that this species is responsible for a very large number of deaths each year. If the Greenies get hold of this they will make such a fuss that not only will there be no element of surprise but I can promise you that the coke using yuppie bureaucrats of D.C. will use it as an excuse to scuttle the project."

Matt walked back to the window from the stove and stared into the distance while fondling the Smith and Wesson, a maneuver that kept Roland quiet and ready to cup his hands over his ears. Matt had little fondness for the radical environmentalists, but did respect their stance and had found that at times these crazies were useful in making sure that the forces of money accepted a reasonable environmental posture. He turned to Roland shaking his head:

"I'm going to have to think this one through, recall you and I agreed at the outset of our arrangements that if I did not feel comfortable with what you were asking me to do that I retain the option to beg off. I'll go along with you for now, but I must admit this sounds as if it has very far reaching ramifications, possibly beyond ridding the world of the drug of the day. To my knowledge molecular biology has yet to be used as a weapon and we may need to be sure that we are not taking on something bigger than we are."

Roland broke in: "Jesus H Sea Otter! I guess Prince William Sound was the wrong place to bring up anything to do with the environment. You've been breathing too much Bald Eagle guano."

Roland and Matt both stood up understanding a break was needed.

Matt pronounced that it was not a bright idea to fly the Goose out at night. He had a good supply of moldy sleeping bags to choose from. Dinner would come.

Matt's ravens were annoyed at the shooting but not alarmed as none of them had ever been harmed. The noise was part of the package that included an evening feeding. The Arctic Raven is nearly twice the size of the smaller continental raven. They greatly surpass all other birds in intelligence and curiosity. Thus Roland and Kent were to be investigated. This was done on foot by hopping through an open window '*en troupe*'- a gaggle of ravens arriving jabbering, letting it be known that dinner time had arrived.

Matt seldom brought his dogs, it was too dangerous to let a domestic dog roam. Thus the ravens were his pets, but more so as they were also his totem animal and his Indian blood caused him to believe deeply in their wisdom.

As dinner was being put together– caribou sausage for starters, a baked salmon and the usual potatoes and blueberries, each raven took its station for a handout.

"Never bit me very hard, these guys," Matt commented. "It took a couple of years to warm them up to me, but they are my friends and now seem to pass this info on to their off spring. They are jealous however, and can be nasty to any other bird that may come by for food."

As the dinner progressed, the ravens became bolder and discovered that Kent was terrified of them. This resulted in the entire gaggle surrounding him screaming until being rewarded with bits of salmon. Matt made only minor efforts to calm the clamor until one raven alighted on Kent's shoulder, snatched his piece of salmon and ran off pursued by the rest. This allowed Matt to shut the window leaving them outside to argue over the prize.

With calm restored, talk returned to the topic of the visit. Matt was still unclear as to where he fit into the picture.

"Assuming that I don't find any scientific snags in this project, where exactly are you going to need my help?"

"Kiren has been molecular biolizing for some time. She seems to think that shortly it will have to go to the next phase in which plants will be grown and selection started. We need to work out ways of ensuring that the test viruses do not wipe out plants like corn, wheat, and tobacco. All this is going to be dicey to keep quiet. I have information that our opposing Feds and Greenies may be suspicionially inclined. It's going to be your job to keep the whole show together."

Matt broke in: "Roland, tell me about the drug guys, do they have any idea of what is going on?"

"I changed my diapers a few times before I put the lid on things. Talk may have spread a bit too far. Who knows who she babbled to about killer viruses before she and I got together. I've never met a scientist yet who didn't want to tell everyone about their bright ideas. The drug agent who steered her to me has been brought in and will keep quiet. If I get pushed, I may have to admit to having talked with her but will deny giving her any aid. But the Cartel has a lot of cash to pay for information that relates to their welfare. We have no idea who may exist within their golden envelope."

"I suppose that as long as she stops talking about it now and as long as there is no clear proof of what she is doing that's the best we can do."

"Right." Concluded Roland turning away to check on where he was to sleep.

They had a quiet night. Matt, feeling remorseful over Kent's fear of the ravens, closed the windows to keep them out. The stove was filled to provide warmth. Matt curled up in his sleeping bag, thinking about Roland. "What a funny round little guy. Why do I let him interfere with my life? Excitement, I guess, maybe he gives me something different. One day he will get me killed".

The next morning over coffee and oatmeal Roland looked around and noting piles of Xeroxed papers, asked Matt:

"So my geographically-stressed friend, exactly what are you doing here? Looks like you are set to read an entire Xerox copy of the Encyclopedia Britanica."

"Yah, I seldom get through it in the two weeks I'm here, but I try. Fact is that when I am in the laboratory at Hopkins, there are so many distractions I never have time to do any reading or thinking. I came up here a few years ago in the winter to do some work the buildings needed and found it so relaxing and such a great get-a-away to that I've come back every year since. Over the year when I see an interesting paper I print it out as a hard copy. That makes it seem more real than a PDF on my Mac laptop. Also I can scribble notes on the paper."

"Do you take it back?"

"No leave it here as fire starter."

"Why so hard to get to? I know a great little place in the Berkshires outside New York City."

"Gag me with a spoon, Roland! If I had been born in New York that might do just fine, but for me, I need to go to real extremes to create my hide-a-way."

"And you just sit around and read?"

"Yup. And think. I love doing science, but ninety-five percent of my time at work is spent meshed in the paperwork to keep my show running rather than thinking. I know this seems a bit much but I always come back with great new ideas and perspectives on what I am doing."

The discussion was broken by a curse from Roland. His GPS transponder had gone off and he explained that this could only mean that someone was trying to put a trace on him. He turned it off quickly.

"If they track me to you then the whole project is lost. If they know you are involved they will no longer be willing to accept my statements we have scuttled the project and that nothing is being done."

Matt was confused. "Who are they?"

"The guy who put me on to Kiren in the first place told one of his friends at the Department of Agriculture. This dolt is some third rate scientist who feels that if anything is going to be done he should be the one to do it. He and some of the higher-ups at the Department of Agriculture have been keeping track of me even though I keep disavowing any interest in the project. His boss has told him to lay off but if he can implicate me in it, he will tell everyone and then the Greenies will arrive on their sea horses and slime the entire project."

Matt broke in: "Woh, Tonto, are you sure this project has blessings at the highest levels? I sure would hate to get involved in something that was to become an embarrassment to the administration. There is a bloody history of projects that were begun in good faith by one agency only to become a lead weight that nearly garroted the President and all his men."

Roland showed his impatience at this line of discussion.

"That's my bureaucratic sand box, not yours! But I promise you this project has been kissed by the highest and most politically advantaged, and if we can pull it off, it will save more lives than anything any of us can imagine." He continued:

"My problem is how to avoid being seen arriving back in Anchorage in the Goose which they might track to Prince William Sound and then put two and two together and come up with you."

"So what do you need, Roland?" Matt questioned.

"What I need is to appear nicely dressed at Elmendorf Air Force base in Anchorage with no damn Goose, that is what I need, and we need to get away from here as soon as possible!" Roland countered.

Matt was delighted. This was exactly the kind of problem he enjoyed solving, and formulated a plan that seemed not only reasonable, but had the chance of allowing him to extract a few more hairs from Roland's already thinning top.

"O.K." Matt explained to Roland and Kent.

"Here's the plan. Kent, fly the Goose along the coast stopping to pick up samples of water and relics of the oil spill. End up in Seward at the small boat harbor and chat up a lot of fishermen about their feelings as to the level of long term damage. Then you mosey back to Anchorage. Call in a lot on the radio so anyone keeping an eye out for you will be sure to know you are coming and observe you arriving alone. Assuming you guys slipped out quietly, no one may have known that the Goose left with a load of two."

Ice wall on Mt. Marcus Baker

I'll fire up my Cessna and fly Roland back via a route no one else could possibly trace. I can drop Roland close to Elmendorf."

Matt had flown from Anchorage in his modified Cessna 185 on wheel-skis. He landed the 185 on the snow covered beach below the fishing camp house. A Cessna 185 is a 4 seat single engine airplane popular with Alaskans for its sheer power, ability to carry heavy loads and its short take off and landing characteristics. His had a 285 horsepower Continental engine, and extra slow speed modifications including vortex generators and gap seals that allowed him to fly in and out of short landing strips. Matt had named his airplane "The Moose Gooser" after a famous Alaskan railroad engine and his delight in buzzing moose. All small aircraft in the US have call signs beginning with N and a string of numbers or letters. The FAA had, on his request, assigned him N186 followed by MG. Someone else had 185MG and Matt considered his 185 to be a bit better than a standard 185, hence 186 worked for him.

As the Grumman disappeared from view, Matt loaded Roland into The Moose Gooser. Roland rolled his eyes to the sky, stroked the Star of David around his neck and tightened his seat belt.

Matt snickered to himself: "Roland, now I'm in charge. Let's see how loud you can scream, fat one!"

The take off run down the beach was brief as the 185 leapt into the air pulled by the engine cutting the dense, cold air. At an alarmingly slow speed, Matt put the craft into a steep turn to avoid the cliff at the end of the beach and then flew 50 feet above the water as he coursed along the shore, trying to be as difficult to spot as possible. As they approached Mt. Marcus Baker, the 185 was placed in a nose high attitude and they flew S turns climbing from sea level up the Radcliffe Glacier ice wall to 9000 feet where he could clear the pass and start the descent down Knik Glacier.

Matt stayed as close to the ice wall as possible and Roland's face took on the same white cast as ice.

Clearing the top by the narrowest margin that Matt could calculate, the Cessna dove into a wild ski run down the back side of the mountain. The Knik Glacier is a large valley glacier 40 miles long and 5 miles wide. Here the terrain is relatively smooth, being covered by hundreds of feet of fresh snow each year. This was, in point of fact, much more dangerous than flying feet from the glacier ice. There the glacier provided edges, shadows, and relief that gave Matt precise depth clues allowing him to keep the airplane a close but safe distance from the ice. However, skimming 100 feet above the featureless snow of the Knik Glacier, these visual clues were lacking and there was a serious danger of flying at full speed, into the snow. Such an event would be —as Matt put it, as lethal as jumping into a beet dicing machine. To avoid such a mistake, Matt rapidly scanned his eyes to one side and then the other as his mentor bush pilots had taught him. All that was clear to Roland was that the airplane seemed to be flashing over the snow at enormous speed giving them the feeling that a deep powder skier must feel on a virgin mountain.

As the Knik Glacier flows down, it cuts off a valley and rams into a 6000 foot mountain ridge known as Mt. Palmer. Doing so, it forms a natural barrier across the valley. The lake thus created, Lake George, once filled to over flowing and then every few years would force its way free in an explosive rush of water that flooded the land below. However since the 1964 earthquake, the glacier has shifted position, and now the lake drains continually through a deep chasm known as "The Gorge" cut into the glacier by the river. The Gorge is 10 miles long, and curves and twists to follow the rock walls. Thus one side of The Gorge is formed by a steep rock wall hundreds of feet high, and the other side is sheer blue glacial ice. The Gorge is just wide enough to fit a single engine aircraft. To fly The Gorge coursing back and forth below the level of the glacier was considered nearly suicidal by most local pilots.

Matt announced that there was little chance of avoiding some other aircraft spotting them if they flew out over the glacier and that he would have to run The Gorge. Matt went on to say that although he had never done this before (not true, it was his favorite run), that Captain Jack, one of the best and bravest Alaskan bush pilots, had talked him through it several times over a whiskey.

Roland's grip on the seat brace of the 185 could have strangled a python, but the run was spectacular, and he later realized that this was possibly as close as a human could get to the episode in Star Wars in which Luke Skywalker flies his fighter through the trench in the enemy Death Star. The Gorge was run with 20 degrees of flaps to provide more lift, as the 185 was slowed to 80 knots. For Matt, the challenge was keeping the aircraft below the level of the glacier, thus inside The Gorge, and 50 feet above the bottom, which in the winter, was a frozen mass of ice bergs. He had to turn rapidly back and forth to follow the twisted course of The Gorge. There was the possibility that around the next turn they would encounter a massive piece of ice which had fallen from the glacier across The Gorge, barring the way. Such a barrier– if not avoided by an instant pull up– would have surely thrown both of them through the windshield as the 185 disintegrated into the ice.

These facts in the back of his mind, Matt was able to use his eyes as a camera, capturing the deep blue ice face to his right, and the ragged rock wall to his left. Each ice face was different, and often deep ice caves were glimpsed. At some places, the water had undercut the glacier so that the ice overhung the frozen river. Matt would veer and dive toward them, making Roland think that he was going to fly under the ice ceilings.

Grumman Goose

The Gorge navigated, Matt flew low over the snowy Knik river bed to a small airport at Birchwood not far from Elmendorf where he raised the skis above the level of the wheels and landed on the paved runway. He had a mechanic friend drive Roland to the base.

Roland was able to slip quietly back to D.C. Unknown to Matt and Roland, people high up in the drug trade had already been altered to the possibility of a “doomsday coca virus”.

CHAPTER TWO
RAUL

The contrast between the ice covered beach of Prince William Sound and the warm sand cooled by the froth of the waves working their way toward Raul's beach chair could not have been greater. Raul slowly collected his belongings and walked back to the villa overlooking the beach south of Cancun, Mexico. He was hosting one of the most powerful members of the Colombian drug cartel and a half dozen of his associates along with a lawyer who worked with Raul to move his moneys into safe accounts.

The "Colombian" who Raul referred to as the "idiot of Bogota" had flown to Mexico to discuss several very large cocaine shipments along with another problem that he had not been willing to talk about on the phone.

They had enjoyed a day of drinks at the beach, and entertainment by the finest ladies that could be purchased in Cancun. As usual, much time was devoted to the ongoing argument as to the most efficient way of bringing drugs into the US. Raul strongly favored aircraft. They were quick and there was an infinite number of places they could leave from and make their drops. Ships were too slow and left too many chances for slip ups that could result in the seizure of a very large amount of cocaine. The Colombian finally agreed to several large air shipments and then turned to his associate from Chile whom he asked to explain another problem that was bothering him.

The Chileano mentioned that several sources in The States had called them with rumors of a "doomsday virus". He went on to say that this information came from the Washington D.C. area. The rumor was that some scientist was planning to create a virus that would eradicate coca plants.

The Colombian was unable to deal with such an idea. Viruses, he felt, were only things that people get. Animals, plants, and mechanical things don't get viruses. The issue of computer viruses was raised and one of the group stated that computers caught viruses from people.

Raul sat back during this discussion with a flat angry look and finally broke in.

"Shut up you fools! At least one of us studied biology. Yes -yes-yes it could be done. Whether you know it or not, there are a lot of things around us already that have been changed— so I read— for the better by this kind of gene engineering. Those are nice things. Nice little genetic changes for nice little fat Americans. This idea is not nice, but you fuckers are not nice either. Bad genetics for bad people. Fuck yes, it could be done. One of these days someone is going to figure out how to make a virus that only kills Chinese or Koreans— or Chileanos." Raul finished sneering.

"No way man." The Chileano replied.

"Bull shit. Already done. The viruses that Europeans were immune to allowed the Spanish to kill millions of Incas without having to fire a single flintlock. If these guys make a virus that hits coca plants we will all be trying to make our livings selling roasted chestnuts on the streets. And with no more money coming in to buy our protection, you can bet that the wolves will eat every one of us up. The big question is not so much whether it can be done but whether there is someone crazy enough to try it and whether the US government would sanction such a project."

The group was quiet until The Colombian said:

"Nothing I hate more than stuff make me sick. So who do we kill?"

"What we don't do is go out and kill every fucking scientist working on viruses. What we do is track that rumor down first and then see what is the minimal action needed to get this thing stopped. I don't have any contacts in The States who know much about viruses. Can anyone else help?

"I think I might have just the man to do a bit of work for us." Responded Raul's portly American lawyer.

Henry Leblank, from New York, worked with Raul and was responsible for much of the money changing and interfacing with large banks in the big Apple.

"My college roommate is on the faculty at Boston University and he works on viruses. He did pot and acid when I knew him and I heard from some mutual friends that this habit has moved to coke. From what I know he deals on the side, moving maybe $20,000 per year. Gets his drugs from one of our middle level New York City dealers."

"Carrot and stick him." Raul suggested. "Carrot him with a free 6 month supply, and stick him with the knowledge that we could cut him off totally, or if that doesn't work, that he might find the Feds up his ass."

Raul continued. "I'll be in charge of this fucking project since it is clear I'm the only one who knows a virus from a wart on your ass. Henry, lets talk after the meeting and get plans straight. You can have your old roommate relay any information to me. Is that OK with everyone?"

Each nodded in turn and then left except for Henry who filled his wine glass and sat back asking:

"Never been able to figure you out. Told me the other day you were born in Mexico City but you speak English as well as I do and I detect an American twang in your Spanish. Am I prying too much?"

Raul laughed, "No, you flippin New Yorker, your English is Bronx at best. My parents were Americans living in Mexico City. Kept assuming they would move back to The States at any moment and not only didn't they let me learn Spanish, but they sent me to boarding school in New England. I finally learned Spanish in high school so I could screw the girls who kept the house."

"And you went to college in the US. What made you major in international pharmaceutical transportation if I might ask?"

Raul snickered and shook his head.

"Flippin lucky break. Learned to fly, flew across the border enough times to discover that if I didn't announce my location to the US approach controllers and I did a few other things like flying at night six feet off the waves there was no way in hell they could track me. Did it a lot for fun and then discovered that I had perfected a very useful technology."

"And that is that. I guess."

"Oh, other lucky breaks. College friends into dope, I'll bet your steps were different but the path was the same."

"Scares me now. Am always afraid for my family, relatives. I've been sending money to accounts in Switzerland and other places, but haven't figured out a way to back out safely. Not that I plan to quit. Don't take me wrong."

"Fuck no–know what you mean. Some time ago I discovered I had climbed too high on the ladder to jump off without going splat. Problem is that as long as you are with us and making a lot of money you can buy protection and the rest of the wolf pack will leave you alone. If I quit right now a lot of people would become very nervous over what I might say. Even all the money I have couldn't protect me from that wolf pack. So, enjoy the good life, Henry–you are in it till the end."

"Well, Raul you certainly are living the good life. Looks to me as if this villa must have set you back a few million, and your boats would make the Prince of Monaco jealous. How many servants if I might ask?"

"Shit if I know, current girl friend keeps trading one more exotic sex ritual for my hiring another relative. Thought she'd have run out by now. Next time you are here let me show you the car collection. I've managed to corner the market on some really gorgeous Italian art. Have one of the first 10 Ferrari's made, and had one of the 39 GTO 250s made. Paid a mil and a half a number of years ago; just sold it at auction for six. Safe way to make money I would say."

Henry shook his head and turned the topic back to the question of the doomsday virus.

"Remember a while ago we were all upset that the US government was going to make a vaccine against cocaine. Now this. Is this the same thing?"

Raul shook his head. "No, I researched that one myself and it appears to me it is in the works. They think that by blocking the spots in your brain where cocaine acts that they can stop a person from using cocaine. Frankly I don't care on that one. That is not going to cut into our trade for the near future and that's all I care about. This virus thing on the other hand could cut us where it hurts."

"See what you mean. Can't force every kid in the country to take a vaccine if its not against some disease. This virus thing just seems too preposterous to me. I'm willing to see what I can do with Brian, my old roommate, but he may or may not be willing to help. What do you have in mind for him?"

"If he's a coke head he'll help. Should poke around Washington D.C. – that's where the rumor came from. Since he is a virologist, he should be able to talk to other virologists. Maybe he could go to the Feds and suggest that he could create such a virus and see what kind of a reaction he gets."

"Hum, seems like a good start. Any suggestion as to what Feds to start with?"

"That is his fuck'n problem. Just keep in touch."

Henry left that evening and decided to travel to Boston as soon as possible to get what he considered a stupid rumor and waste of time out of his hair.

Brian Radloff had joined the Army in trade for college money and ended up in the military police as a guard at Gitmo in Cuba. There was a lot of easily obtained coke and a lot of boredom– the combination hooking him for life. Brian had a problem with stuttering since childhood particularly with words beginning with B. That, Henry had commented, was why his parents named him Brian, and he went to Berkeley and lives in Boston.

Brian finished at Berkeley then moved to Boston as a graduate student. He remained in Boston as a postdoctoral fellow in a laboratory studying viruses, in part because leaving Boston required more energy than staying. Also, by then, he had made very useful contacts in the local cocaine market and was beginning to deal in small amounts for small sums, but sums nonetheless, that were significant relative to his postdoctoral stipend. His work had gone well, and he was offered a tenure track position at

Boston University, one of the many teaching/research universities in Boston.

That was nearly 10 years ago, and Brian had struggled through tenure (obtained), marriage (lost) and numerous relationships. The pressure of obtaining and keeping research grants in the fast moving field of virology had taken him back to the one thing that he had confidence in– cocaine. As his use grew, he found that by dealing a bit and cutting the cocaine he passed along the chain, he was able to keep his habit going and keep a slightly better life style than his faculty colleagues. There were many professionals anxious to buy from another professional rather than some street kid, so his market was stable and seemed limitless.

As Henry left the cab for the research labs he wondered about the kind of person he would find after 20 years of not seeing each other, and a dwindling numbers of letters or cards at Christmas. Henry imagined himself as portly, but rather dashing in a middle aged way. Would Brian have changed or would he be the same thin radical kid who ran wild in college?

It was likely that neither of them would have recognized each other had they met by accident in the airport. Each made the obligate statements that the other had not changed a bit, but the loss of Henry's hair and his enlarged waist line was not something Brian had anticipated. Neither had Henry guessed that Brian would appear so gaunt and would have short cropped hair that was a gray/black mix as contrasted to the shoulder length hair of the Berkeley days.

They went to lunch and time was passed discussing marriages – one for Brian, two broken ones for Henry, and two children. Henry described his current life style of flying from Mexico, to Paris, to New York, and around the circuit with delight, making Brian wonder how he could be in demand so many places.

Henry offered the carrot. He explained that some of his clients were not in the drug business directly, but that their funds would be adversely affected were the drug cartel to fall into hard times. For this reason, he, Henry, had been asked on occasion to look into rumors that promised future trouble for the Cartel. Of course he himself had no direct connections, he was a mere information gatherer.

Brian listened with curiosity not realizing where he might fit in. Henry went on to explain.

"Several months ago there was a rumor running around Washington D.C. that some scientist was offering to engineer a new plant virus that would wipe out coca plants. Whether this has gone anywhere we don't know. Would like to find this person."

"This" Henry emphasized, "would be of grave concern to my clients, if such a project was underway." He continued:

"I doubt it, but there is enough concern that my clients are willing to pay the right person a significant sum to look into it and to find out who might be involved. I knew you, and they were interested in obtaining your help. All on the up and up, all they want is information."

Brian pushed away from the table realizing that he was being asked to work for a group that he assumed must be on the edge of the law, but which edge, he was not sure. Trying to bide time, he ran over what Henry had said, trying to fill in some details in his mind. He commented:

"Hum, ra ra ra rather creative idea. Of course, lots of problems bo bo bo– both at the level of the virus engineering, selection of the appropriate strain, and some major bio bio bio biological problems with the plants themselves. Viruses have bi bi bi been around for some time, and plants have worked out ways of neutralizing them. But damn, using viruses as weapons is an idea that must have crossed the mind of everyone working on them – but no one wants to be the first to do it. Scary thing is that while it took huge factories and thousands of scientists to make the first A-bomb, the right person could make a killer virus all by himself in a small lab." He continued:

"What surprises me is that our government with all of its environmentalists would consider it. Once one has let the genie out of the ba ba ba bottle, it's hard to cram it back in. Sure, I can see a clear rationale for getting rid of the cocaine trade, but wha wha wha what next? If we decide that chewing gum is ba ba ba bad for kid's teeth are we going to eradicate all the gum trees? Rather heavy issues, seems to me. I'd like to think that the folks up there can see a bi bi bi bit beyond the problems they created."

Henry felt this was the time to make his request. "Right, so if this thing is in the works, finding out would be to the benefit of all of us. What do you say, Brian, can we get your help?"

"Nope, I don't know the plant virus crowd and I wouldn't know where to start. Be be be besides, this seems a bit shady." Brian said.

Henry decided it was time for the carrot.

"Understand. But I was told by my people that they are aware of your small discrete dealings and that they would be delighted to continue supplying you at the current level, no cost, while you are working on this."

Brian stood up and looked out the window, realizing that the hook may have been set a long time ago when he began dealing in a small way with his New York connection. However, the thought of possibly ten thousand dollars in free cocaine– if he could do this one favor and likely find nothing– did make him ponder.

At that moment, seeing Brian waver, Henry decided to offer a larger carrot and a bit of a stick –or he though to himself– a twig.

"If this goes well, and you trace this rumor down, the New York group will help you step up to a larger, discrete trading operation.

But of course if you wish to beg off, I can't promise that you current connection will remain intact."

Brian turned farther away to stare out the window of the small cafe toward the Charles River. He felt cold inside, as if all remaining humanity had just been cut out. He understood that he had two choices, run, or buy in, and hope that he could ride the wild ride long enough so that he could quit science, and buy the proverbial sailboat on a lake in Minnesota.

"Sure why not, bu bu bu but I will decide if I want to sell or not, mind you my intention is to sta sta sta stop all together."

"Right," Henry said quietly.

"I suggest you spend a bit of time in Washington D.C. since that is where the rumor came from. If you can't dig anything up, one of our people thought you could go to some of the Feds who might be interested and tell them you could create such a virus–for money of course. See what reaction you get. Hopefully they will say it had been suggested but was nixed. But someone might say – oh, yah, it's being done by so and so already. We just want some more information that's all." He gave Brian hiscard, and instructions on how to check in.

Brian assumed this would be a one time trade for favors. Little did he realize how intertwined his fate had just become with that of a very bright woman with an intense obsession.

CHAPTER THREE
KIREN

Roland strapped the seat belt around his pumpkin-like middle and watched with squinted eyes as Matt tapped each of the instruments on the panel of the Moose Gooser as he went through his check list. The weather forecast had promised clear spring weather and Roland had been pestering Matt to find time for the two of them to meet with Kiren. Matt had yet to promise his support, and wanted to hear what she had to say before committing. Matt offered to fly himself as it would provide more freedom and an excuse to view some nice countryside at Roland's expense. Matt took a longer route that passed over Charlottesville, Virginia, then along the ridge of mountains, finally turning south. This put them considerably behind schedule. In the taxi from the airport Matt began quizzing Roland about Kiren.

"So, this young assistant professor. Give me a description again, and if she turns out like that last monster you set me up with, you are going to walk back."

"I may fly back commercial anyhow, my ephemerally curious comrade."

Matt squinted his eyes. He pushed again.

"You said she is mid to late thirties, skinny, bookkeeper type. Very serious. Right?"

"Well, I'm in a waffle iron there. Mid thirties– Yes. Very serious, certainly."

By the time they arrived at Duke, located the Plant Pathology Department, and then waited until a student came by with a key to open the front door, as it was Saturday, it was an hour and a half past the time Roland had told Kiren they would arrive. Roland's fidgeting signaled to Matt that he was not totally at ease with Kiren.

Kiren's laboratory consisted of an 800 square foot room with benches, centrifuges, and DNA cloning equipment. As they entered, there was a door to the far left that opened to a small office. Sitting at a desk facing away was a person, but of what sort and whether this was "Kiren" or not, Matt had no idea. Roland cleared his throat and Matt's first impression as she turned around was that he was facing a character from Alice in Wonderland.

Kiren was wearing a giant floppy hat which fell down in all directions hiding her hair and half her face. It also hid her eyes if she tipped her head down slightly. She was shrouded in a white lab coat that could have been tailored for one of Duke's basketball players giving the impression that there might not be a complete person inside. Staring at Matt, Kiren tossed her head back to allow her eyes to clear the hat brim. In turn, Matt stared back, transfixed at what seemed to be the largest pair of very very gray eyes he had seen. The color of her pupils was not that much darker than the surrounding "whites" of her eyes. It was as if she possessed the eyes of a snow leopard, capable of holding her prey transfixed. Her face was thin and the other feature that stood out was her nose, which was very sharply chiseled. Kiren did not move, but after a moment of peering at Matt, she turned to Roland.

"Did we change to daylight savings time last night or are you almost two hours late?"

Roland looked down, trying to appear like a large, soft, chocolate rabbit.

"Very sorry, Dr. Moore. Matt here, ah, Dr. Matt Lynx, flew his own airplane and we were inattentiatively delayed."

"Which translates to you got lost! Well! I should have guessed the government would keep me waiting. I have to leave soon. We'd better get started. If we need more time, you two can come along and we can finish later this afternoon."

Kiren nodded to a pair of chairs on the other side of her large desk which was piled two feet high with journals, papers, and exams for one of the classes she was teaching.

"So this is the Hopkins Professor who you said would help me if you– or he, approves of my proposal. Well, Dr. Lynx, let me say right now that I can do it all myself and I am going to run the show. What I need is money from Mr. Epstein."

Matt still unsure of where he fit in Roland's scheme replied:

"Fine with me. Trust me, I'm no expert on plant viruses. As I understand it, Roland wanted me to hear what you have to say, and then if he takes the project under his wing, it was my understanding that I might be needed down the line."

"Well, of course I did a Pub Med search on you—you have no clue about plant viruses. You are here to approve or disapprove of what I proposed to Roland, is that it?"

Roland broke in: "No, no! Dr. Moore, Matt has worked with me on many projects. He knows a lot about molecules and DNA, and I trust what he says. The decision is mine but I did want him to hear what you are planning since you are going to need some help, speaking in a logistically round about way."

Kiren tipped her head back to stare at Roland for a moment and then shoved things on her desk aside to clear off a space for a pad of writing paper. She relented a fraction.

"Well I might use some help." She turned to Matt tilting her head back to stare at him. With even more hidden by the desk, the tent-like lab coat, and her hat, she had become no more than a giant pair of gray eyes.

"I assume Roland gave you the basic idea, but got the details Waring Blendored. So let me start at the beginning. My plan is to create a virus disease of coca plants that will be so specific and rapid that in a few seasons, it will severely stunt the major coca crop – the plant from which cocaine is extracted. It's a project I have been working on part time for the last couple of years. But to make it work I need research support and access to coca plants. Further, what I plan to do is create the virus, not grow it in large amounts, or spread it around the coca fields. That's up to you guys." She continued:

"I took the idea to a number of agencies in Washington D.C. and got nowhere till I talked to Roland here. He seems to feel that he wants to get your blessing on the science and he keeps bringing up vague Sunday school questions of ethics. In terms of ethics it's crystal clear. You could create a mountain out of the bodies that have resulted from cocaine– ODs, shootings, and people on welfare, and this mountain would be higher than any created from the last war. It's just begun, unless we can do something."

Matt, still pondering the ethical issues tried to broach the subject gently:

"There's no question in my mind that the world would be a hell of a lot better off without cocaine, heroin, LSD, or any of a dozen psychoactive chemicals. But each time we find that some plant, animal, or insect synthesizes such molecules in their own bodies are we going to sanitize the planet by eliminating that species? What if we do and then find that they also make some potent anti-cancer agents? Recall, cocaine was the first topical anesthetic ever discovered by mankind. I'm not saying that you are wrong to do this, but since you and I know more about the science and the long range ramifications than Roland does, it seems to me that we need to be open to the ethical side and not shut it out."

Kiren tipped her head back and sliced Matt into one inch cubes with her eyes. She said nothing for two minutes while Matt looked to the left, the right and finally turned away. Roland sat still.

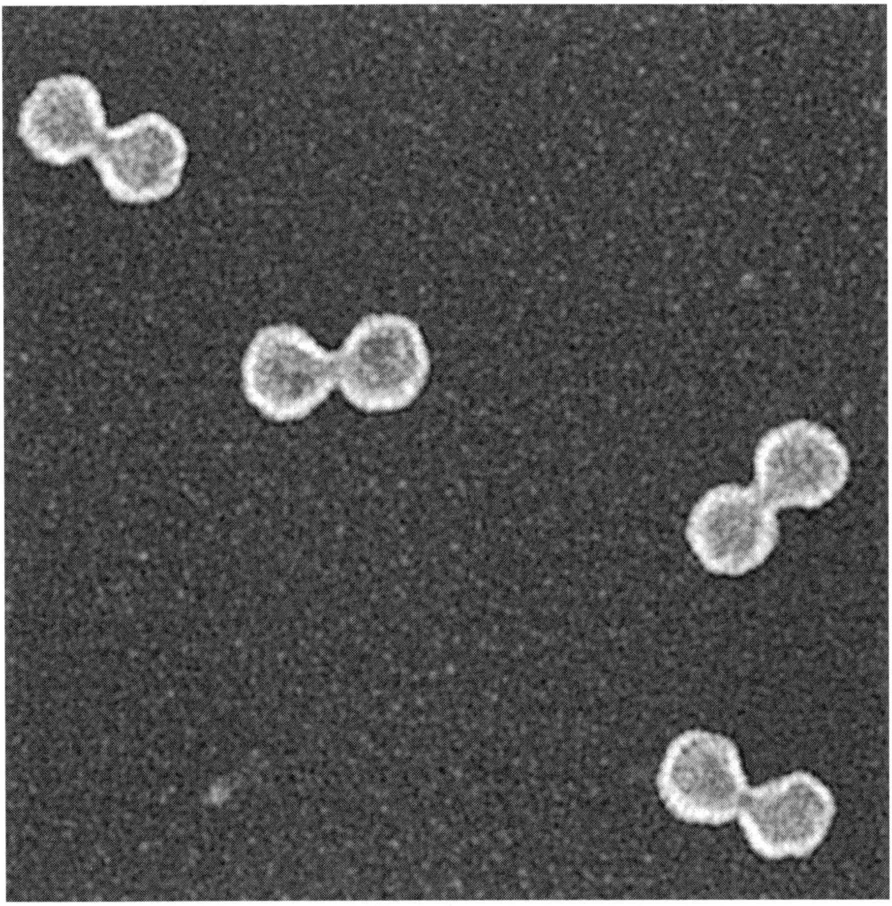

Gemini Virus

She finally broke the silence: "I have the strongest personal reasons to hate cocaine and all those involved with it. This is a one time– one virus project. I am not going to get side tracked by vague Hopkinsesque arguments over ethics. I have dealt with it in my mind and I feel that this is one opportunity for me to make a major improvement in civilization. Either you are with me or against me. Tell me now."

Matt sighed and replied:

"Fine, I'm here, am I not? Give us the run down on the science. If we get involved in this, and I don't like how things are progressing I will tell you and I reserve the right to bail out. Roland and I already agreed to that."

Kiren launched into the project. It was clear from the fact that she turned to Roland and began at a simple level, that she wished to make sure Roland understood.

"Let me refresh you on viruses. Animals have so many holes in their bodies that it is easy for a virus to gain entry. For animal viruses, there is no restraint on their size– they can be quite large and still are carried by the cells of the blood stream which takes them to every part of our body. Things are different for plant viruses."

"Plant viruses are much more restricted. Plants have extremely thick cell walls created by cellulose – wood fiber. Also plants do not have openings like throats."

"So how do they get in?" asked Roland.

"Plant viruses must be much more specialized in how they gain entry. Some wait until the plant is wounded, but many utilize insects with strong jaws or mosquito-like appendages to break through the thick cell walls. By attaching to the insect, the virus is able to gain entry as the insect drinks juice from the plant."

"But that is only half of the story. Plant viruses are also greatly limited in their ability to move from one cell to another in the plant. Plants do not have blood streams. Each cell has a very thick wall with very small pores between the cells that allow fluids to move from one cell to the next. Thus for a plant virus to travel and create damage, it must be small enough to slip cell-to-cell through the pores linking the cells together."

"You're saying that giant viruses like the Herpes viruses that infect us are absent in the plant world?" Matt asked. Kiren turned to him.

"Absolutely. You and your friends working on bacterial and animal viruses have been able to engineer your viruses at will. Plant virologists like me are a lot more restricted due to the smaller size of our viruses and the inherent problems that plant viruses themselves face in getting around in cells."

Kiren stared at Matt who had been taking notes in a brown notebook.

"What are you writing? I didn't give you permission to take notes!"

"Ah, no. But I always take notes at seminars and scientific discussions. Then I can reflect on what we said and add new thoughts —that's all."

Kiren looked displeased but then turned to the clock above her and cursing mildly, announced:

"You guys were supposed to be here a lot earlier. The one thing as important to me as my work is my horse, and I'm damn well not going to miss my dressage lesson for you. I assume that you don't know anything about horses– Roland told me you were from Alaska and they eat horses there. I suggest you two come along, I can continue filling you in– that is unless you guys are afraid of large animals, or getting your clothes dirty."

Matt smiled and was about to comment that indeed, he liked horses very much, knew something about dressage, and owned a horse, but Kiren had disappeared. Roland turned to Matt.

"So what do you think?"

"God, little Miss "try to get a word in edgewise"! Weird looking person hidden in that hat and lab coat. I really don't know. So far seems pretty intense."

The person who reappeared was so different from the one who had been peering out from under the hat and lab coat that Matt would not have guessed the two were the same had it not been for the gray-gray eyes and saber-tipped nose. First, Kiren seemed taller, Matt guessing five foot five. She was very trim, possibly 110 to 115 pounds. Her most astounding feature now was her very short cropped hair, at most one inch long all around– whose shade of red, darker than apple red, but not bronze, suggested a whim or some slight chemical mis-balance in the potion applied by her hair dresser. It was a color he had seen a lot in Prague in 1999. Kiren was dressed in tight fitting riding breaches, off-white, with extra sewing at the stress points, knee high black leather riding boots, a short sleeved shirt and was holding a handful of riding crops. Matt felt that the Alice in Wonderland –comic-looking character had become transformed into a model for Country Life magazine.

They were led to a brown Jeep Wagoneer– one of the large older models that was known for its pulling power, 4 wheel drive attributes, and extreme lust for gasoline. The Wagoneer contained a large array of horse equipment: saddle pads, reins, and an English dressage saddle.

Kiren seemed to relax as they drove away from the laboratory and toward a small town of Apex, North Carolina.

Feeling for the first time able to make small talk, Matt asked about the origin of her name, asking if it was Scandinavian.

"No, I'm a WASP's WASP. My mother had an older sister named Karen and she named me after her. When I was three, my brother Ralph liked to call me Kiiii- ren just to tease me. I liked it and called myself Kiren. I hated that fat aunt Karen who would grab me and stuff my little face into her giant sloppy chest suffocating me. So by the time I was in grade school, my parents had given up and in high school as a present, they formally changed it to Kiren. We actually had to go to court and all that. Ralph was rather proud and I was happy pleasing him."

Kiren went on to explain that North Carolina and Virginia were possibly the best places in the US for Eastern style riding, particularly in the event known as dressage. She had her own horse stabled nearby in Apex, North Carolina.

Matt started to explain that he too liked horses but was again cut off mid sentence.

"Actually Kiren, I'm a horse fancier–"

"Fancy, yes, I know about you, Roland said you were brought up hunting big game. I'm really against that –I have to tell you. I can't believe how someone could do that! Bet you would have shot a horse if there was an open season."

"No–no, and I don't hunt any more. So how long have you ridden? And I really like horses."

"Bullshit, trying to make me like you. Ridden since I was ten. Unlike most girls who fall in love with horses until they discover boys, I continued riding through college and graduate school. Postdoctoral work at the Rockefeller in New York slowed my riding to a weekend endeavor, but now I am in North Carolina, I'm back at it seriously again."

"So what kind of a horse do you own?"

"You wouldn't know anything about these breeds. It's not your typical Alaskan pack horse, or Western cow pony."

"Try me."

"Well, when I started riding here, I borrowed more money than a starting assistant professor should spend –upwards of $30,000, for what's called a school master. He's an older horse, nearly fifteen. He's a German breed, called a Hanoverian. When he was younger, he won several major Grand Prix events. That level of competition is hard on their legs, in particular the rear ones and I have to be careful not to overwork him. Nonetheless he should allow me to compete at the highest levels given the time I have available."

"Actually dressage is something–"

"Roland, I am sure that this is out of your bureaucratic realm but you and Matt will have a chance to see some very fine horses."

Matt realized that for now it would be impossible to convince Kiren that he did indeed know something about horses and just sat back and enjoyed looking at the farms along the way.

At the stable, her horse was readied and as Kiren waited for her lesson to begin, she returned to the discussion of viruses.

"As I was telling Roland earlier, plant virologists are limited in how we can engineer our viruses. The one I work on is a small virus that contains DNA and is called the Gemini virus. In terms of plant viruses it is relatively easy to engineer."

Matt started listening with more intensity, as it was clear that Kiren was moving into area he knew little about. She continued.

"Gemini viruses cause a number of very severe plant diseases in the tropics, southern United States, and South and Central America. The diseases have funny names like corn streak, African cassava mosaic virus, tomato leaf curl, and beet curly top. Funny names, but these diseases can create enormous economic havoc. Beet curly top virus disease nearly wiped out the US beet industry. The African cassava disease reduces the size of the fruit by

75%. World wide, these viruses have been one of the major causes of crop losses in important staple foods such as corn, grains, and fruits."

"How big are they?" asked Roland. Matt was not surprised at the question since Roland could always be counted on to ask how big, how far, or how much money. Drawing on the ground with her riding crop, Kiren continued:

"Small. The structure of the Gemini virus as seen in electron microscope resembles two paired spheres, hence the term Gemini, or "twin moons". The viruses I work on contain two separate chromosomes, we call A and B. Each chromosome is a strand of DNA 2700 bases long arranged into a circle." (Matt knew that the term "base" referred to one of the 4 different DNA building blocks called A,C,G, or T that are strung together to form long DNA threads. Thus each chromosome of the Gemini virus was formed from 2700 of these bases attached one after the other with the first bound to the last to create a circle).

"Gemini viruses have been around for a long time. Symptoms of a Gemini virus disease are described in a poem by the Chinese Empress Koken written in 752 AD."

"Which one do you work on?" asked Matt.

"The Bean Golden Mosaic virus. It contains two DNA circles. Each circle is single stranded. Having only one of the two normal strands of DNA saves space in the virus and makes it possible to put more genetic material into a small particle. In the cell, the single strand of DNA then is converted by the cell's proteins to a double stranded form. Transmission of the virus particles begins with an insect called the White Fly sucking juice from an infected plant. The virus in the plant juice is taken into the fly's gut where it then is passed to the saliva ready to be injected back into another plant. The viruses can remain in the insect for the bug's lifetime."

"My research group has been studying the replication of the Gemini virus, and what makes it pathogenic to the plant– that is, why its replication causes so much trouble. In some cases Gemini viruses cause severe diseases while in other cases, they do not seem to cause much trouble. We are on the verge of being able to predict what makes these viruses kill or stunt plants. Further we are learning how to change some of the virus's genetic material and add some new information."

"I'll go into the cocaine project after the lesson," Kiren informed them as her instructor motioned to her.

"You guys can watch, or walk around, my lesson will take about 45 minutes. I will be working with one of the greatest trainers in the US, and he is helping me work on some specific moves before a series of shows in Southern Pines and Raleigh."

Matt enjoyed watching women ride horses. It was, he felt, a superb way to inspect and critique a woman's physique, while at the same time appearing to be admiring the horse –which pleased the woman. The trot was Matt's favorite gait, allowing an anatomical analysis while nodding and pretending to be noting the fine details of the horse's moves.

Why, he had often wondered, do otherwise intelligent people place themselves on top of nearly three-fourths of a ton of livestock and then guide this herbivore over jumps, and through detailed antics? It seemed a bit beyond him. Why horses and not cows? Cows have a certain charm, are clearly as bright as horses, if not more so, and being closer to the ground, would be safer, warmer in the winter with their long hair, and finally, if one got tired of the cow–. Further, the most intelligent animal in the livestock category was the pig. The thought of Kiren in her expensive riding outfit, mounted on a pig and guiding it through a dressage test made him chuckle and get an odd look from Roland.

Matt knew enough about dressage to follow her lesson. Indeed Matt had had lessons in dressage feeling it was the best way to become an accomplished rider. For him there never had been any pretense of competitive showing. In the US, dressage is dominated so much by women that it is rare to find a man riding and the intense estrogen-driven women at the shows frankly scared him. Kiren was clearly leagues above him, and was working with her trainer on a movement called a flying lead change. In essence, when a horse (or dog for that matter) is moving at the canter, one front foreleg leads the other, and if the horse is turning, the leg on the inside of the turn will lead, as if it is reaching out into the turn. Now if the horse changes from turning to the left, to now turning to the right, then it must switch leads. That is, the horse must now reach out with the right front leg rather than the left. This could be done by stopping the canter, but if the horse is running in the field with no rider, then it will switch leads in the canter employing a dance-like movement at the moment when all 4 feet are in the air. This can be accomplished by a very good rider and well schooled horse but only with a great deal of training for both. Kiren was working on flying lead changes and Matt realized that given her ability to do them every three strides of the canter that she and her horse were competing at a high level.

As the dressage lesson continued, they were joined by a tall thin woman holding a thoroughbred.

"How long have you known Kiren?" the woman queried.

"Oh, Roland has known her a while but I just met her today. She seems really intent on her riding. You're also a plant biologist?"

"No, a clinical psychologist. Ph.D., not MD. Have my own practice in Raleigh."

"How about that! Rosalind, my alpha female, is a shrink; MD type —but the same business. So tell me about Kiren's obsession with riding."

"She's an odd one. She has a bad case of riding addiction. From what I know, every extra cent she has goes to riding and she put off buying a house to get her horse. I can see her take on an air of happiness and relaxation the moment she is in sight of Mr. Copper, her horse. It's an amazing transformation. But I am not sure that's bad. Kiren is highly motivated and has little time for anything that is not going to help her get to where she wants to go. She just seems to have shut out everything around her other than a few things —her work and her horse."

"Any relation to the departation of her brother?" Roland asked.

"You know about that. Yes, certainly. I'm not giving you any client/patient information there. She seems obsessed with his death. She talks about it a lot when we drive to horse shows. Funny, the only time it seems to be off of her mind is when she is with Mr. Copper. Almost as if riding transforms her into a different world."

"Sad. I guess in time the loss will fade away. Odd isn't it, her brother was addicted to drugs and she is addicted to horses."

The woman bid herself ado and Kiren appeared shortly. After some time involved with telling Mr. Copper good bye, and stuffing carrots into his mouth, they got into the Wagoneer and headed back toward the lab. Matt picked up on the earlier topic.

"Kiren, Roland mentioned that you had strong personal reasons to rid the planet of cocaine. Something about the death of your brother."

"That is not a topic you have my permission to discuss! If we get to know each other better, maybe. But not now."

"Fair enough, but tell me how you got from your studies at the Rockefeller to coca viruses. That's a big jump."

"Not really, I went to Colombia a number of times after my brother disappeared. I happened to stop by the University in Bogota and met some of their plant pathologists. Step by step I learned about the Gemini viruses that infect South American crops and realized that there were very few scientists working on them here in the US. So by the time I got my job at Duke, I had already established a good project."

"On coca viruses pray tell?"

"No, of course not! The NSF is not going to fund that. I had been working on the Bean Mosaic virus. It grows on a variety of bean plants that are easy to grow in the lab and is a good model for the Gemini viruses in the wild."

"But Roland indicated that you had made some headway on viruses that do infect coca plants."

"Right, during one of the trips to search for traces of my brother, I was hiking in the mountain area where coca plants are abundant and noted that the leaves of some of the plants had a mottled pattern not unlike that caused by very mild forms of the bean virus. I took some of the leaves back to the University in Bogota, did a crude extraction of the tissue and brought the extract back. Well, a quick look in the electron microscope showed typical Gemini virus particles. That was the big step."

"I guess the next step was deciding to engineer them to wipe out coca plants." Roland commented.

"Hell no! That had been in the back of my mind for several years."

"And is Roland's offer of three to five years of research funding for your lab a consideration? He has, I must say, been very helpful to me." Matt nodded to Roland.

"Yes, but I would be doing this— funding or not. If Roland is willing to keep my show going after my start-up moneys run out, that's fine with me. He has given me a promise for enough funding to pay for my supplies and two graduate students, and a few other things- for three years– if you tell him that I am legit. That's a lot more than my department chair is able to come up with, and is getting close to a real grant from the National Institutes of Health, or the Department of Agriculture." They drove on for a moment and then Kiren continued.

"There are of course things that I can't do, like growing the virus on a large scale, or spreading it in South America. So as I see it, I need him and he needs me. But the money will pay for my lab and I am not going to turn that down."

Back at the lab, Kiren got down to the details of the project after having returned to her garb of the floppy hat and white tent.

"Here's where we are. I succeeded in isolating the Gemini virus that grows on coca plants in the wild. It also has two circular chromosomes — A and B. We have created maps of both chromosomes and have determined the order of the DNA bases, around both chromosomes. This has taken the last year. One of the oddities of the coca plant Gemini virus is why it doesn't cause much of a disease."

"The DNA sequence information provided the answer! Near the spot where the replication of the DNA circles begins is a series of DNA bases that regulate the expression of the viruses' genetic material. We discovered that the signal created by the bases in the natural coca virus was very weak. Based on this discovery, we have begun to alter the signal to make it a lot stronger. This should make a virus able to create a much more severe disease. This new virus strain should take hold and outrun the ones that are present on the coca plants now. In addition, I plan to add a major time bomb to the virus, but I'll tell you about that later."

"So what's the time table for this operation?" Matt asked.

"So you don't think I am some fruitcake and are going to give Roland the thumbs up so he can send me some money?"

"I'm impressed, Kiren. Roland what do you say? The science seems sound to me, but I am a bit hazy on what happens after she gets her killer virus made."

"Kiren, consider yourself conscripted into our special team. Now financially speaking, the funds will take a couple of weeks at the most to arrange. Matt, your job will be to help her get what she wants and to make sure that no one gets in her way. Also I am going to rely on you to tell me if you think that Kiren has become mired in crazy glue. You two are what I call the phase one team. Phase two team will be involved in growing the virus on a larger scale and phase three team will spread it in the coca fields. Kiren, we will need a bit of help from you for the transition from phase one to phase two, but both of you will be back at your lab benches long before phase three team begins their work. At some point I will introduce you to Vitz. He is in charge of phase three and is in the Delta force.

Matt nodded and Kiren looked a bit lost. Matt turned to her:

"I'll translate for you later. Are there any things that I can start helping you on now?"

"Well, yes. First, there's a lot of hard core molecular biology that I still need to do. I figure that we have several months of hard work before I have the final virus constructed with a destructive bomb in it ready for testing on real coca plants. We have done some preliminary studies in plant extracts and tissue culture but the only test is the real test –and that is where I am going to have to get help from you guys."

"In what way?" asked Matt.

"Well, recall that the infection cycle of the virus involves the White Fly. It spreads the virus from one plant to the next by drinking infected plant juices and then injecting some of it into an uninfected plant. In the real world of the coca fields we are going to have to rely on the White Flies to spread the virus after we have dusted the virus over the fields in a crude way."

"I don't see yet where I come into this." Matt queried.

"Simple, once I have engineered the virus the best I can in the lab, I am still going to have to do the final selection and growth of the virus in real life coca plants. The virus concoction that I will give the plants is going to contain a lot of ineffective ones and my job will be to select only the most virulent ones for growth and use in South America. For that selection I will need to grow about 100 coca plants."

"Oh Jesus, you want me to become a dope farmer! Where pray tell are we going to grow that much coca without being discovered?"

Roland broke in. "Problematically speaking we have only started."

"Right. I'm not comfortable with the possibility that some of these viruses might also infect our local crop plants." Kiren commented.

"And how would that happen?" Matt asked.

"You see, in the earlier stages of selection, we will create many, many different viruses and it is possible that some of them might also harm food crops or plants other than the coca plant. Once we isolate a number of different engineered viruses that will kill the coca plant, we will go back and test them on other plants to be certain that they are still specific for coca. Problem then is in the early engineering. If one of the little White Flies got out after contacting an infected coca plant, and was carrying a virus that could infect tobacco for example, it might flit over to a tobacco plant and off we go with a very unpleasant problem."

"Tell me again that the plant that makes cocaine is different from the one that we get chocolate from. If there is any chance that this might kill chocolate plants, I could become the most hated man in all of human history." Roland fussed.

"Am I going to have to go through my lecture on plant taxonomy every time we meet?" Kiren snapped. Matt grinned and broke in.

"You would be boiled in chocolate if that happened my friend. Yes, they are very very different, but I am still lost. Where do I fit in this? You must have some thoughts on this otherwise I wouldn't be here."

"Right, Kiren and I conferenced this and decided that the final selection needs to be done where no plants related to coca grow and where it freezes long and hard over the winter—to kill the White Flies– that should be good enough environmental security."

"I see, so we need some place out in the boonies with a minus 20 degree Christmas."

"Information content correct." Roland nodded, continuing. "Your job is to find such a place. I can get 100 plants delivered where you want. I suggest that we involve our end-stage man. He can be helpful in some of this."

"One more thing." Kiren said sounding anxious. "You asked me how many people I had told about my idea. I've shut up now, but there were quite a few people I talked to in Washington D.C. Do you think that they could do something?"

"Could be nasty. I'd reconsider one more time before going farther." Matt said in a counseling voice.

"Ya Ya, everything is copesetic. I've put the lid on it and as long as you deny things and don't grow coca plants in your lab they can only guess," Roland said loudly as if to shout over any discussion to the contrary.

They parted company; she was off to a date with her boyfriend and Matt and Roland called a taxi for a ride back to the airport. In the air, Roland turned to Matt.

"So molecularly speaking what do you think about her?"

"Well, she's certainly different from Olga the Aeroflot stewardess. Very dramatic. I'll bet she did theater some where along the way. Her science seems very good. I'm amazed she has been able to do so much. Those viruses are hard to work on and she is just getting her students and technicians trained."

"Think you could get attached to her? She's about the right age for you."

"Roland, give me a break! I've got a nice romp in bed with Rosalind lined up for tonight, and while Ros may constantly analyze my head, I'm getting used to that. Kiren is damn scary."

As Matt headed home in the airplane and his evening with Rosalind, his thoughts kept returning to Kiren. When he talked with people, he liked to look directly at them, and to wash them gently all over with his eyes, as if he was giving them a pleasing shower with warm water. Kiren with her giant gray eyes on the other hand seemed to be pointing a pressure washer at him. It left him with an unsettled feeling inside. "If it wasn't for those eyes" he thought "the rest of her is quite nice." The Delta Force entity, Vitz, whom he would meet shortly, would add further complications.

CHAPTER FOUR

VITZ AND THE RIBOZYMES

The flight home was uneventful and Matt landed at a grass strip near his home where he and a few others with the "right stuff" kept their single engine aircraft. Matt lived an hour's drive from his laboratory in the rolling hills outside of Frederick, Maryland. He didn't enjoy the drive, but it allowed him to live in greater seclusion than his colleagues who resided in urban Baltimore or Washington D.C. He had bought an old farm and sold some of the land to people who wanted 1 acre plots and a house. He kept 30 to have a modicum of seclusion, and slowly in his spare time (which Roland made sure was not great), had restored the large barn, creating a garage for his cars in part of it, and was now working away at the farm house, the central part of which dated from before the war– the only war that is, that mattered to true southerners – of which he was not.

Rosalind was expecting his call and appeared shortly with a bottle of vintage wine. She was in her early 40's, 5 inches shorter than Matt and by his description was very sexy, in particular when she was dressed in a tight fitting skirt and a jacket, her usual attire for dealing with her psychologically challenged patients. She had extremely fine features and a striking mix of very dark, although not large, eyes and very white skin. The acne gene had never invaded the chromosomes of her sire or dam and her skin was soft, reflecting the fact that she spent most of her days indoors in subdued light, playing shrink. Rosalind was slim for someone who did not engage in routine sports. She had joined a health spa and taken aerobics classes for a while but found it boring. Her medical training convinced her that being overweight would certainly shorten her lifespan but she strongly believed that while many many people had died jogging, riding exercise bikes, or playing tennis in the hot sun, there were no recorded cases of people dying while refusing a second piece of chocolate cake. Taped to the mirror in her bathroom was a reminder "if you don't eat it, it can't end up on your butt."

Ros's hair was jet black. It was thick and naturally curly, and she had cycled between having it straight, curled more, keeping it up, or allowing it to frizz out. Matt refused to be drawn into a critique of her hair since any comment would be "used against him in a court of beauticians" he would tell her. Currently she was keeping it straight and curled slightly under as it just missed touching her shoulders. This was not Matt's favorite, as he felt that with her hair this way and garbed in her tight skirt, jacket, and giant black rimmed glasses she resembled the movie script librarian who becomes a sex symbol when she gets a make-over. On weekends visiting Matt, Ros would wear jeans and a flowered blouse. He discovered that if he kept buying her fancy hats she would wear them to please him and in turn he didn't have to have to look at her librarian haircut. A number of times he had suggested in a side-ways manner that she might think about keeping it short just for a change.

Rosalind spent a great deal of time concerned over what signals she sent to others, in particular in the form of what she wore. Each piece of attire was capable, she felt, of independent communication. To create the wrong mix of a skirt, blouse, and, god forbid, jewelry, was to do harm to all around her. Thus at least an hour was spent each morning after she arose and showered in adjusting and readjusting her attire to create a single coherent statement for the day. This drove Matt bat-shit. It was also why Ros seldom stayed over with Matt if she had to go to work the next day since it was virtually impossible for her to decide ahead of time on her voice-of-the-day.

She had not been able to take the blood and gore of the usual MD track and had opted for the couch– as Matt put it. She was extremely verbal, typical of her New York Jewish upbringing. He had been seeing her for the past 2 years with a number of short breaks for one or the other to retreat to their respective cocoons. As a scientist friend of Matt's put it, "Rosalind has 1000 nerve endings for personal feelings and one nerve ending for logic". For Matt, it was the exact opposite.

Rosalind hated Roland's projects for Matt and had informed Matt that if they were to get married one condition was severing his relation to Roland. This demand had at times seemed attractive and at other times impossible. Rosalind frequently provided deep insight into personal interactions among his lab people. They in turn were always surprised at the degree of insight Matt exhibited after an evening of "thinking it over" –which meant that Matt had run straight to Rosalind with a story of petty jealousies or competition for the hottest new project.

Rosalind was upset over the possibility that Matt was about to embark on yet another adventure. He had done his best to soothe her anxiety by cooking a salmon filet and presenting her with several CD recordings of different pianists playing the Bach Goldberg variations so that she could compare and pick her favorite. Through dinner and much of Rosalind's Riesling, he managed to keep the conversation away from his trip and on some of her recent patients and their craziness. Finishing dinner, he offered her coffee in the sun room which was warm and poorly lighted. Matt embraced Rosalind as they walked to the room but she shoved him away stating:

"You stink of airplane gasoline. I am not worth a 10 minute bath? My feelings are trashed as always."

Matt covered his eyes. Indeed he had gassed up the Moose Gooser after returning and had spilled just a bit. He made a lame try to repair the damage.

"Well I was so anxious to see you I didn't have time, and besides I wanted an excuse for us to relax in the hot tub."

"The hot tub is not a bath tub. Go shower and we'll discuss the hot tub. You have managed all evening to avoid telling me about this woman you visited in North Carolina or anything about your latest involvement with Roland. I'm not doing anything until you spill it all."

Doing as he was told, he exited the bathroom by the back door onto the porch where the hot tub resided overlooking a splendid view of the farm land behind the house. Matt sat naked in the dark, submerged to his shoulders for what seemed a long time before Rosalind appeared, fully clothed, with a new bottle of wine in hand. Matt picked up the omnipresent "Leatherman Model One" as he called it and used the screwdriver with a hook to pull the cork.

She sat on the edge of the tub and began her interrogation.

"So tell me about this woman. What was she wearing?— always Ros's first question. How old is she? Is she beautiful? What are your feelings about her? Did she give you a testosterone rush?"

"Get into the tub and I will tell you all."

"Fuck you!"

"That's what I had in mind thank you."

"Double fuck you! Tell me now or I will take your clothes and lock the doors to the house. I want to know what you are getting involved in. Now!"

"O.K. really, Ros, I'd be delighted to have you meet her, her name is Kiren. She is absolutely not my type. She is the exact opposite of you. You are soft and sexy (Matt tried to pull Rosalind to him but his hand was pushed away). She is cold and hard. You are extremely gorgeous— she is plainer than I could possibly imagine. You are elegant, and she is dull. What more do you want to know?"

Matt could have continued, but knew that each statement would be remembered in exacting detail. Rosalind had a computer memory when it came to his descriptions of other women. He also knew that Rosalind would find Kiren very "avant garde" and "hard edged" and that each fabrication now to the contrary would cost him dearly in the future —if the two were ever to meet.

Matt turned Rosalind around so that she was facing away and began unbuttoning her dress as he continued:

"Really I think she has some psycho-personality disorder, maybe of the first kind. She's clearly frigid— she found me totally uninteresting (Rosalind reached behind her and rebuttoned several buttons). She has a steady boyfriend (Rosalind allowed the buttons to be unbuttoned again). He's a Brit. (Matt was losing ground on the war of the buttons). She spends nights with the boyfriend; I'd guess marriage at any point."

Realizing that something major was needed to break Rosalind's focus on Kiren, he floated into total invention. "I told her about you and she was very anxious to get your advice on how to be intimate."

Rosalind allowed the rebuttoned buttons to be unbuttoned. Matt had soaped the edge of the hot tub and gave her just enough of a tug so that she slipped backwards into the water. Much screaming ensued during which she was held with only her nose and lips out of the water while Matt alternately kissed her and made it appear that he was applying artificial respiration. Finally Rosalind quieted down and he allowed her to come to the surface while he removed her clothes, wet piece by wet piece flinging them skyward.

Rosalind had quit pretending to fight Matt and the two began interacting more and more below the water line in the hot tub. Matt's legs were strong and he was able to hold Rosalind, who was lightly muscled, in a firm but not unpleasant grip. Using his palms, he massaged Rosalind's back and shoulders as he kissed her with increasing intensity. Finally Rosalind, aroused to an extreme point, managed to place herself on top of Matt who entered her while simultaneously struggling to keep his nose out of the water.

After a period of allowing Matt's engine to cool down during which Rosalind accepted a back rub, the two adjourned to Matt's closet to see what clothes she might have left from some previous visit. She had an appointment in Baltimore at 7:30 AM and dressing would require her complete wardrobe.

As Rosalind departed, Matt mused that he would appreciate her insights into Kiren, but he also did not want to pay the price that would be extracted if ever the two were to meet. Besides Rosalind might not find Kiren attractive. Men clearly are capable of major delusional thinking as Rosalind had commented on numerous times.

The following Friday Matt picked Roland up at Dulles airport and they headed for Southern Pines to meet "Vitz of the Delta Force" who was to run phase three. While phase three was some

her marriage but also her faculty appointment as their whole family was now marked by the KGB as undesirable and would be watched and harassed.

Along with Vitz and his sister, they traveled to Bratislava in the Slovak region. Bratislava is the sister city of Vienna, Austria and is located 40 miles down river on the Danube. During the Austro Hungarian empire which lasted nearly 800 years, Bratislava and Vienna traded off playing the role as capital city, depending on the druthers of the current rulers. The attraction of Bratislava was its proximity to the Austrian border and possibility of escape to the West which included Austria. Relying on friends in the underground, they waited for a particularly nasty winter night when a mix of sleet and snow was falling making it most unpleasant outside. They were hidden in a forward compartment of an old river barge that daily made the run between Bratislava and Vienna. The boat owner hated the Russians and was more than happy, for a sum, to take the risk. He had gotten used to providing a bottle of Schnapps to the communist border guards in return for their not taking his barge apart every night. This night the two bottles and the miserable weather was enough to eliminate a careful search and Vitz, his mother and sister were let out alone with only a few photographs and Czech crowns to make a new life in the West.

The following years included living in Spain and Portugal where his mother taught languages and piano before she met a American who fell in love with her and the two children and took them to the US. Vitz finished high school and then attended a military college where his sole goal in life was to be accepted into the Green Berets or Delta Force as an officer so that he would have the best opportunity to kill as many Russians, preferably in hand to hand combat as he could. The idea of being in the Air Force did not appeal as he would be unable to see them die face-to-face.

His single minded obsession did land him in the Delta force, however his linguistics abilities often took him elsewhere. Not only did he speak Russian, German, Czech, Slovak, and Polish among others, but also Spanish and Portuguese. His ear for languages, perhaps a genetic handoff from his mother, was acute and he was able to take on a local accent in each language that allowed him to easily pass himself off as most any nationality. The large population of Germans in Uruguay and Paraguay, left over from WWII, and his ability in these languages had recently kept him out of the Middle East and eastern Europe and involved in covert projects in South America designed to watch over both the drug cartel and the FARC rebels in Columbia.

Vitz was clad in his running shorts. They were cut high and loose so that one was a bit uncomfortable looking at him from certain angles when he was sitting with his legs propped up. Vitz wore running shorts much of the time and it seemed almost a badge of courage to wear them when it was raining or cold. Vitz had a set of legs that many present day athletic women would have killed for. They were well muscled, long, and tapered in such a way that they created a long smooth line from his hip to his ankles. They were simply very attractive legs. Vitz of course knew this, and knew that the combination of his size, bare legs, blonde hair and eyes were enough to cause serious multi-cart wrecks in the supermarket in Southern Pines when he wandered through in search of beer. He had been known to help an attractive victim of such a crash, and then be seen shortly afterwards leaving the supermarket with her, the cart left near the beer stand.

"So, Roland, I'm not sure about this little assignment of yours. I've got the last part sketched out. We'll drop in on the coca fields at night, off the clowns with crossbows and knives, spread this stuff of yours and then hike out to pick-up locations where the choppers will be waiting. I figure groups of 5 to 6 are best. Have some good men I can get. But you said that I was going to have to learn some science and look like a university professor for a while. I would be spotted faster than a naked hooker trying to sell girl scout cookies."

Roland seemed amused and Matt had not said a word the entire time. Roland responded.

"Vitz, all will proceed to maturation. If you want some blood and guts you are going to have to pay the price at the beginning. Tomorrow morning we will take you back to Duke to meet Kiren. She will give us a summary of the science. I don't expect you to follow it all, that's Matt's job, but I'd like you get some idea of what's going on."

Vitz nodded and blurted out:

"The Hole. We need a couple of hours at the Hole."

Matt nodded, not knowing what to expect and was frankly not sure what to think of Vitz. He had been around a lot of military types before, but Vitz was very large and seemed to have the ability to dominate everything around him. They drove to the outskirts of Fort Bragg, 20 miles away. Matt was not surprised when they turned in to a bar sporting a large sign "The Hole". It was not associated formally with the Army or Marines, but was run by two former Green Berets who had retired, but couldn't live –they felt –away from the continual comradeship of their former buds. The club catered to the Green Berets, and the even more elite Delta Force.

The Hole was truly unique even for Fayetteville (often referred to as Fayette-nam due to its proximity to Fort Bragg which had been one of the reentry points for Marines returning from Viet Nam). The Hole was a private club meaning that to belong, one had to sign a sheet giving up all rights to sue the owners for any bodily harm that occurred in The Hole or its proximity.

The Hole could be calm and verge on respectable. Earlier in the evening was ladies hour, a time when the members were allowed to bring lady friends to The Hole. The code demanded extreme deference to a comrade's lady, even if the comrade could not recall her name. For Vitz the attraction of The Hole was that they were willing to keep a running tab as long as he didn't get too far behind, and they had yet to cut his drinking off for reasons of insane drunkenness – but, they had yet to do this for anyone.

They followed Vitz from table to table where Vitz engaged in mock or not so mock fist fights with other equally rough looking fellows. These greetings made, Vitz pushed and pulled friends to make room for them to sit down.

"Great place, huh, rank doesn't cut a fart around here! Only things that matters is if a guy has done real time killing people. We try to keep the young guys– the killer wannabes —out. They can get dangerous. Don't know when to stop."

"Good idea." Matt shouted, noting that most everyone there seemed to be a good bit older than the typical recruits that fill up such bases. Eventually Vitz had enough and they drove back to the hotel in Pinehurst where Vitz dropped them off for the night, and Matt mused to himself that this was the first time he had seen Roland fail to utter a peep for at least two hours.

They stayed overnight in Pinehurst and the next morning over breakfast Vitz gave the first indication that there might be something on his mind beyond beer, killing, and bedding women.

"Matt. I worried all evening about talking to this Doctor Moore. I called one of my MD friends and asked him to explain DNA but I couldn't understand a word he said and I'm not sure he knew what he was talking about. Can you give me a quick run through before we meet her?"

Matt laughed.

"An MD understanding DNA? About as likely as Lassie being able to read the contents on a dog food can. Where do I start, Let's see." Drawing on the paper tablecloth he gave Vitz a simple description of DNA.

They finished and the three drove to the Southern Pines airport. This time Matt landed at a small airport serving Chapel Hill which was close to Duke. He tied the 185 up in the grass next to a fiberglass Grob 109B German motor glider, sporting a 4 cylinder Porsche engine on its nose. This was an unusual blend of a glider and airplane. Matt wondered if it could be put on floats– his basic test for any airplane of worth. Probably not, but each to his or her own. The IFR instrumentation in the Grob suggested that this craft might be the toy of someone who was close to having "the right stuff".

The meeting had been arranged by Kiren so that they could talk at length without being interrupted ad nauseam by students pestering her for extra points in the last exam. Kiren was dressed in a very severe black suit, skirt cut below the knees, and large shoulder pads. Her shoes were black. A black scarf was tied around her head partially obscuring her carrot red hair. She was wearing very large black rimmed glasses. Matt couldn't help but ask:

"Ah, Kiren, black becomes you, but may I ask if you are planning to attend a funeral?"

Kiren engaged Matt for a long time with her deep gray eyes. She thought to herself: "good looking guy— rock solid— probably good in bed— but he's worth more to me alive than dead. Perhaps when I am through with him." She turned to the topic replying:

"Yes, this afternoon."

"Someone on the faculty?"

"Yes, a good friend. My boyfriend and I are being forced to attend. It's a wedding but no different from a funeral in my book. The guy is a goon."

Vitz stared, looking intimidated, while chairs were arranged in the laboratory near a large blackboard. Kiren turned to them, pulling the glasses down so that she could peer out over the tops of the rims.

"As I explained before, there is an additional engineering project I want to do with this virus before I let it loose."

Kiren poured a mug of coffee, black, and wiped the board clean. She wrote the word, "ribozyme". Matt smiled, and pushed his chair back to listen.

"One of the most important discoveries in molecular biology was made when it was found, totally unexpected, that certain small RNAs have the ability to cut themselves apart. A faculty member at the University of Colorado discovered that an unusual RNA from a small single cell organism that lives in pond water has the ability to cut itself at very specific places. For some time no one even believed this. RNA was not supposed to do this. The importance of this discovery was recognized by the Nobel Prize committee a few years ago."

Matt broke in. "You see, Roland and Vitz, these little RNAs that can cut themselves or other RNAs up are called ribozymes. You can consider them as having two parts, one is a pair of jaws that does the cutting and the other is a recognition domain that looks for the specific sequence of RNA bases where the cutting occurs. When an RNA chain is cut, that generally kills it."

"Thank you my erudite and ignominious professors, clearly you both like your little molecules but what does this have to do with coca plants, and the Cocaine Cartel?" Roland asked.

Kiren took a sip of coffee and continued. "I'm going to add a ribozyme bomb into our Gemini virus to give it a second punch against cocaine. One of the most dramatic uses of ribozymes has been in cutting up the RNA of the AIDS virus. Using genetic engineering it was placed into a virus that will infect human cells without killing them. The domain on the ribozyme that guides it to its target was tailored to seek out a segment of the HIV virus RNA. These workers found that when this virus containing the anti-HIV ribozyme was placed in the cell, then HIV virus production was dramatically shut down."

Matt cut in: "But there they knew what they were targeting. Here you seem to be shooting in the dark. How do you know what RNA in the coca plant to target?"

Kiren peered over the glasses rims and responded:

"Correct. For HIV, the people knew the sequence of bases in the HIV RNA molecule. Here I don't know much about the RNA molecules involved in the synthesis of the cocaine molecule in the plant leaves."

"Major problem don't you think?" Matt asked as Roland looked concerned.

"I think there is a way around that. It's a shotgun approach. I can isolate RNA molecules from the leaves where cocaine is made and use that RNA to create a very large number of possible targeting sequences that will target the ribozymes to knock out these different RNAs. I can then let the plants help select the ones that do the most harm."

Matt shook his head. "There are a lot of steps here: engineering the virus, putting the ribozyme in, attaching these targeting segments. Do you think you have the hands and expertise to do all of this?"

"For an aging full professor, it would be insurmountable. But for a young assistant professor who has to do everything herself, not really. Besides we have done a lot of this work in our bean virus system already and in addition, we have some excellent colleagues at Duke and UNC who can help us with this work."

Vitz rubbed his face with his large muscular hands and exhaled.

"I'm sure that you two are really good at what you do, but wait a dog fart moment. You are talking about making some very sophisticated weapon that is going to change the world and its just Dr. Kiren here with some help from our pilot. You dudes expect me to believe this? Anything I've ever seen of this magnitude took a whole Army base to it pull off."

Kiren thought to herself: "Blonde Godzilla talks– shit, am I going to have to deal with him and Matt too?" She turned to Matt who broke in before she could verbally abuse Vitz.

"Good point. And a lot of people who haven't been around molecular biology labs would think the same thing. You are used to space and nuclear science that requires big teams and big instruments to do much of anything. The good but scary thing about molecular biology is how much can be done by one or two people with not a lot of fancy stuff. Oh, sure you have to be able to grow cells and viruses, make small DNAs, sequence DNAs and cut and paste DNA back and forth, and be up on the state of the art methods. But, in my lab and a lot of labs, we do all of this with no more than what Kiren here has available. And one person can do a lot. I have a graduate student from Korea who worked all by himself on a project and after a year and a half had cut up a new human virus, had mapped the genes and then transferred them into a virus that infects insects cells. He has been able to make grubby worms that fill up with this virus. Now if that virus had been one that is deadly to people, and if he had used mosquitoes instead of grubby worms — well you get the idea. That's what's scary to me about this whole field. We're training a hell of a lot of people who have some potentially very dangerous skills. So the answer, Vitz, whether you believe it or not, is that Kiren has all of the tools she needs to carry this out– with a little help from her friends"

Matt and Kiren turned their chairs around, and backs to Vitz and Roland talked rapidly, discussing each step and the relative merits of one approach over the other. Vitz broke in again.

"Ah, pilots, you have lost your passengers."

Kiren was not interested in walking Vitz and Roland through the complex steps. She turned to Matt.

"Vitz is your charge. Give him some more science lessons or send him out to sniff around the undergraduate women."

"Now, Kiren, that's a no- no. When I was just starting at Hopkins my department chair told me that until I got tenure I was to keep my hands off the undergraduate women and the Chancellor's son. I guess you need to keep your paws off the undergraduate men and your chairman's daughter."

"God, American men disgust me. You could learn a lot from my British boyfriend. He's an extremely successful chemist, making over $150,000 per year synthesizing compounds that are put in cosmetics and gets a lot of funding from industry. Francis is a sophisticated Englishman who is far more cultured than any American scientist I have yet to meet."

"Bugger" muttered Vitz.

A portly fellow cleared his throat, attracting attention. Kiren went to him with a blush on her face and turned to introduce him.

"Guys this is Francis."

Matt suppressed a giggle. Francis looked back and forth at Matt, Roland and Vitz wondering who these men were.

At this point an older man, tall and fit, appeared in the doorway and knocked loudly. Kiren shook her head and turned to him.

"Enough science for the day. This is my dad, Ben. You've met Francis. These other guys are here for a bit of remedial plant virology. Matt is a faculty member at one of those decaying urban schools up north and Vitz is a local from Ft. Bragg. Roland is from the D.C area. Can't say more than that. You were in the Air Force for 35 years. Now I can finally tell you this is on a need to know basis and you have no– to use your favorite term, no damn need to know. I am going to take my leave of the lot of you. Francis and I have this awful thing to go to and then I have my dressage lesson later this afternoon. Francis and I have plans for the evening. Matt how's your time tomorrow?"

"There are a few more points I'd like to go over with you. Roland has friends in Raleigh he wanted to see. I can hang around, and get together just after lunch tomorrow if that's OK. The weather is nice and I could fly over to the coast – see the Wright Brother's museum at Kitty Hawk and spend the night at Ocracoke or Beaufort."

He was greeted with a near bear hug from Vitz: "Well let's get our butt holes in gear so we don't miss the good flying light."

Ben, Kiren's dad, piped in. "If you can handle this hunk I assume you're not here in a Luscombe or Cub. I've got a few thousand hours flying right seat. My little daughter seems anxious to get rid of all of us."

Matt relaxed. At least he wasn't going to be left alone with Vitz for a day and felt that he might learn more about Kiren from Ben. Roland called a cab to the RDU airport and took leave of them. The rest drove back to the airport and piled into the Moose Gooser with Ben in the right seat. He would learn much about the fire inside Kiren.

CHAPTER FIVE

OCRACOKE AND RALPH'S STORY

The flight east over Raleigh Durham airport toward Kitty Hawk would take an hour and a half and Matt flew visually (VFR) at 3500 feet to provide a better view of the coastal area. Once past Raleigh's airspace, he handed the controls to Ben and sat back to chat.

"So Ben, you learned to fly in the Air Force I suppose, what birds did you handle?"

"Yah, actually learned in a J-3 cub in high school; went to The Academy. Those were the days after the Korean war. Did get to play in one of the last commissioned P51 mustangs; was assigned to the early jet fighters. By the time Viet Nam came along, I was considered too old and valuable for fighters so was given a B52 squad for a while.

"Ben. Tell me about your sharp-nosed little daughter. I'm impressed over her research and she is very single minded. I can't tell you any details about this project but if I knew more about her brother it might help me keep an eye on her."

"Yah, your job– is to work with her or be her body guard? What is this Delta Force hulk's role? I don't like the idea of Kiren being involved in anything needing a creature his size and training."

"Don't worry Ben, Vitz-the-hulk is mine, not hers, and I can assure you that if anything even smells of danger I will pull the plug and leave her on your doorstep." Matt swallowed knowing that he had not been totally honest, but he also did not want Ben snooping around either.

"Ben. Can you talk about your son, Ralph?"

"Yah, a couple of years ago would have been hard but now it's OK. What did she tell you?"

"Not a lot, brilliant student who got more and more involved with drugs. Died mysteriously 5 or 6 years ago."

"Yah, that's the summary. Ralph was the focus of my life. We were living in upstate New York– Ithaca, where I was teaching at Ithaca college. In high school I taught him to fly. We had a Cessna 152 and later a Decathalon. Flew it to every airport in 200 miles. Later he got his multi-engine and commercial ratings. All before he started college. He was tops in his class in high school, interested in science, played soccer– accepted early to Princeton. Mother and I were so proud. Guess we overlooked Kiren a bit."

"Impressive, so what happened?"

"Yah, looking back now, I can see the signs of drugs even in high school. But when you're flying as he was flying you ignore any sounds of a rough engine."

"I can understand that. My folks were baffled over the things I was interested in. I was one of those super achievers too and that bought a hell of a lot of suck up points with my folks relative to my sisters who did more usual girl things at that age."

"Yah, we sent Ralph off to Princeton feeling we were on the top of the world. Of course cost an arm and a leg and we had to mortgage the house."

"So when did things start to come apart?"

"Nah, not for a while. The first couple of years were great. Had a friend Phil, who started a flying service in Kingston, Jamaica. Ralph spent summers flying for him and building multi engine time. But Christmas of his Junior year he came home– looked awful. Had lost weight and seemed distracted. Shifted from one mood to the other; didn't want to talk much about college. Ma and I assumed he was just hitting the wall being forced to compete against others brighter than he was."

"What did Kiren think about this."

"Yah, funny. Ralph was the most important person in her life. She was a junior in high school. Kept a scrap book listing everything he had done. Was filled with photos of him, newspaper articles. But that Christmas she came to Ma and me and made a sideways suggestion he might be playing with drugs. We nearly tore her head off. Pretty cold Christmas."

"So he went back to college?"

'"Yah, for the rest of the year. Summer he went back to Jamaica to fly for Phil again. Well, mid-summer Ralph called. He had been fired but decided to stay on the islands till the end of the summer. Called Phil mad as hell. Phil told me that Ralph's flying was erratic and had nearly trashed a couple of planes. Suspected Ralph was on drugs."

"So you began to catch on finally?"

"Yah, but still couldn't believe it. Hoped that when he came back before returning to college we could fix the problem. Funny, our biggest response was to sit on Kiren and watch every move she made. Of course she was only interested in her horse."

Matt broke the discussion to point out Edenton and some of the small quiet fishing towns along the Pamlico River which was several miles wide and beginning to open up into the Atlantic ahead.

"You were telling about Ralph's return at the end of the summer."

"Yah, well he came back looking like another person. Couldn't keep his mind on things; alternately depressed and elated. Gone most nights till near morning. I tried everything but he just kept saying that yes he had tried some cocaine but that he was clean and was just having trouble getting settled down. Well, time came for him to go back to Princeton and he seemed more like his old self. Just as we had done other years, we transferred $35,000 to his account in New Jersey from which he was to pay tuition and room and board for the year."

"A lot of trust and a big lure for a coke head."

"Yah, too much as it turned out. Kept calling back all semester giving us one story after the other about how well he was doing. Finally just before the term was over I got a call from his student advisor asking why he had dropped out and taken a tuition refund. Ma and I were real hurt. Ralph didn't call for months. Kiren really took the brunt of our anger this time. Ma even followed her to the horse lessons and hid in the car just to keep watch on her."

"So what did Ralph have to say for himself?"

"Yah, well he returned at the end of the spring — he was a different person. He seemed to be talking to us through a filter that removed all of his old zest and humor. He admitted he had been hooked on cocaine and spent all of the money Ma and I had given him for school. He seemed really sorry for hurting us and we checked him into a day treatment center in Ithaca."

"And how was Kiren doing through all of this?"

"Strong. Never lost her love for Ralph. Spent a lot of time with him, talking about old times, about her plans for the future, took him to help with the horse. She reacted as if he had, Jesus I don't know, leukemia, I guess."

"The treatment center helped?"

"Yah, well, Ralph gained weight and looked better after a few months but was still distant and seemed to have lost his interest in finishing his last year at Princeton. He spent a lot of time in the coffee houses in Collegetown near Cornell. I pushed, talked, threatened. Nothing seemed to get through. He finally agreed and asked if we could let him use Ma's new car to drive to Princeton for a week and arrange things."

Ben stopped talking as if what next was hard to get his courage to continue and stared out of the window of the Cessna at the swampy mass of ponds and river-lets that lay between them and Kitty Hawk. Matt broke the silence.

"He didn't finish I gather."

"Only saw him once again. After several weeks of no word we got the police to trace Ma's new Buick. It was found in a used car lot in New Jersey where Ralph had sold it for cash. After that, yah, it was a couple of years before we saw him."

"He didn't even call?"

"Nah, not to us. Kiren had been accepted at Harvard, but we insisted on her going to Cornell where we could keep a close watch on her. Well, it seemed that Ralph was keeping in touch by phone with her. She finally admitted that to us but claimed she had no idea where he was living. Just that he would call from one place or the other. Sometimes she felt he was really doped out and sometimes he seemed fine.

"When did you finally see him?"

"Yah, well, Kiren was a junior at Cornell. He appeared out of the blue one afternoon and called from Tompkins County airport. Kiren and I drove out immediately. He was smartly dressed and looked good. Deep tan as if he spent most of the time on the beach. He handed me a roll of bills, saying that it was partial payment for Ma's car and tuition. Explained that he had sorted his life out. He had started working as a pilot for a company based in Caracas, Venezuela that bought and sold high end business aircraft. His Princeton training allowed him to take over the bookkeeping and now he was a partner. He was flying a real slick twin engine Aero commander. We took it for a run around the area. Odd thing about the plane was that it had no seats other than pilot and copilot's and the interior was a mess. Ralph claimed that it was being refurbished."

Matt was anxious to hear more but they were less than 4 miles from Dare County airport and they needed to wake up Vitz before landing at Kitty Hawk which lay another few miles beyond. Matt radioed his location as they passed over the county airport and all three watched the scenery as they flew a few hundred feet over the sand dunes and condominiums as they headed toward Kitty Hawk. Matt's landing was not one of his best, nearly doing a ground loop after catching a crosswind gust.

"Jesus Christ Matt, you said you had flown a tail dragger before. Trashing your aircraft at the feet of the Wright Brothers would be most embarrassing I would say."

"True, true. That was just an Alaskan spin-around stop —we always stop that way."

They walked up the grass slope and spent a half hour looking out over the ocean before walking to the museum. Vitz and Ben strolled along together while Matt strayed off by himself.

"Hey, Vitz, what do you think about Matt? He seems to have a good sense of humor, and I thought he was a cracker jack pilot until that landing back there. What's his involvement with my little daughter?"

"Just met Matt yesterday. He seems straight. Never trust guys with doctorates but he seems a touch bit better than the rest. I don't get the feeling that he has any interest, nookie-wise in your daughter. Mostly what we talked about yesterday was Alaska, airplanes and cars. Your sweet daughter is a bit of a snip mouth if I might say so, and it seemed to me that she had him scared to death. I thought she had a cute ass myself."

"Vitz, you touch her and you get a one way flight in a B-52."

"Oh, sorry just commenting on the genetics. My prod is being cared for by a rich horse lady in Southern Pines and she has told me that if I am caught putting it anywhere else she will tie it to her stallion and take me over an event jump."

"Hey! He has no interest in Kiren at all? He isn't a squish is he?"

"God no!"

"Good, at least he would be better than that damn Brit. If you decide Matt is OK, you have my permission to garrote the Brit and point Matt her way."

"Brits aren't worth the mess."

"Nah, I guess not."

Matt hailed Ben and Vitz and they walked back toward the Cessna. Vitz was wearing a rough knitted wool cap, dark green, that looked as if it had been with him for a long time. Ben asked about it:

"Wool cap looks like it came from your Green Beret days. Am I on track?"

"Sure is. Don't leave home without it."

"Distinctive. One of your girls make it for you?" Matt asked.

"Shit no, knitted it myself– and the last guy who made a crack about that had to become a dentist just to pay his bills."

"No complaints here." Ben commented as he and Matt exchanged smiles.

Matt wanted to fly on to Ocracoke, a charming town on the coast some 50 miles to the south where they would have dinner and spend the night. The flight was a delight. Matt and Ben traded flying as they stayed 100 to 200 feet above the beach and a few hundred feet off shore. In that area, the Outer Banks of North Carolina are a mile wide, with sandy beaches on the Atlantic side and marshes on the inland side. Approaching Ocracoke Matt tipped sharply so that Vitz and Ben could watch the wild ponies that lived in the marshes just north of town. On final approach to the strip at Ocracoke Matt announced to Ben:

" Wheel landing, left wheel only — all the way to a stop."

They touched down on the left main wheel and were nearly motionless when the Cessna finally dropped to the right, then the tail and came down. Ben clapped and Matt smiled, feeling that he had in some way made up for his earlier landing. They walked the mile to town and checked in to their rooms at the Inn. Later that evening they sat around the bar over beer and shrimp and Matt brought the conversation back to Ralph and how he had ended up dying.

"Ben, you were telling me about Ralph and the last time you saw him. Said he was buying and selling airplanes."

"Yah, well. You can guess. After he left, Kiren and I counted the cash. Nearly fifty thousand in thousand dollar bills. It took at long time before I was willing to deposit it. Apparently it was clean but we all knew it was drug money."

"And you never saw him again?" Asked Vitz.

"Nah, Kiren got calls for a couple of years and now and then he would send her some very expensive present. Then for 3 years we heard nothing. I started making inquiries. Nothing. Then out of the blue, when Kiren was in graduate school, he called her and explained that he had been in jail in Venezuela for a couple of years. Trumped up charges he said, but I found out later that he and some others had been jailed for cocaine smuggling but that they had apparently bought their way out. Ralph called me and I exploded. I told him that he was never to call us or Kiren again and that I would rather that Ma think he was dead. He hung up and I never heard from him again."

"He's still dealing dope?" Asked Vitz.

"Nah, it wasn't more than a few months after that we got a call from a government official in Colombia. Apparently a King Air being flown by Ralph from Lima to Bogota had gone down in the high mountains in a storm. They had received radio transmissions from him that he had lost an engine and was trying to find a way through the passes since the one engine left was not enough to allow him to clear the peaks. Airplane was never found. Kiren made a number of trips there but never found a thing."

Ben finished his beer. "Hit me hard. Seemed I was responsible for his death. Taught him to fly, got him the job in Kingston where I'll bet he made his first serious drug connections. Took a lot of soul searching."

The next morning in good spirits the three walked back along the beach. Ben and Matt walked together and Vitz rolled his pants up and walked knee deep in the water.

"Funny guy, Vitz, I wonder what he does when he does not have a beer in his hand. As they took off, Matt headed south and flew just a few feet above the beach. After refueling at Beaufort, Matt climbed to 6500 feet for the hour flight back to the Chapel Hill airport. After they had been in the air for a half hour Ben looked back at Vitz whom they had not heard from for a while. Vitz was fast asleep again but had a paper pad on his lap. Ben took it and after looking at it for a moment, handed it to Matt. Matt turned to Ben.

"Music, he writes music!."

Thinking back to their discussion of the previous day, he asked Ben,

"Ben, I know a lot more about what happened to Ralph and can understand why Kiren is so cranked up about cocaine. Tell me more about her. How did she handle the whole affair?"

"Kids are smart. She knew what was up and spent more and more time with her horse. When he came back and told us he was addicted she was the only one who was supportive and not angry. Funny –Ralph had been gung ho on a career in biological research and when he dropped the ball, she picked it up and has been running with it ever since."

"So she is doing molecular biology for him?"

"Yah, well, yes and no. If he hadn't gotten into cocaine I'll bet she would be doing something very different today. It's as if she felt we were counting on him to be a famous researcher and if he couldn't do it, she would do it for him. But now it's her thing. When she calls us she will say – if only Ralph were alive– he would be pleased to know that she had published this paper, or found something out."

"I get the impression that Kiren only does a few things at a time with great energy."

"She has a soft side. Loves animals of all kinds. She was always bringing some cat home from the pound, feeding it for a month and then spent days making enormous efforts to find it a home. I'll bet she saved nearly a hundred stray cats. Of course she had girl friends, all girls do. Most of them were doing horses and they would sleep a half dozen to a motel room when they went off to a show."

Vitz had awakened and leaned forward:

"So she actually was a little girl once?"

"Yah, very much. When she was in grade school she spent all of her time with stuffed animals. She even invented one. Called it the Bad Easter Rabbit. As I recall her story, its mother was a rabbit and the father was a raccoon. It had a body like a rabbit, but a raccoon face and tail. Its role in life was to do mischievous things. Oh, yah, at Easter time, it stole Easter eggs from the rich kids and give them to the poor kids."

"Sort of a Rabbit Hood." Vitz joked.

"But no serious boyfriends?" Matt asked, still trying to complete his picture of Kiren.

"Yah. She had a real steady boy the last two years she was at Cornell. We liked him. She went off to graduate school and they continued seeing each other. Ma and I were guessing marriage. He was nice. Just about that point, Ralph died and she just shut this guy out. She moved her horse to a farm outside Boston and refused to come back to Ithaca except at Christmas. I think it was just too hard for her to see all the things that reminded her of Ralph."

"What about the Brit? Marriage?"

"God I hope not, this guy has the personality of a waste can at a wart clinic."

Matt turned to Ben.

"Oh, one odd thing about your fire breathing daughter. Her eyes. They are— very large and have the most unusual color. Gray, really gray. And she just cuts into me with them. It makes me feel very awkward. Has she always done this?

Ben shook his head. "Oh, you are in real trouble, sorry about that."

"What the hell does that mean?" Vitz broke in.

"Well, yes she has very big eyes. From her mom's side. But she only uses them that way on men she either really likes or dislikes. They've all complained about it."

Vitz reached forward and slapped Matt playfully about the head while Matt put both hands over his eyes and muttered: "Bad Easter Rabbits and giant cat eyes, god help me."

Matt radioed Raleigh approach for vectors and flight following through their airspace to Chapel Hill where they landed and drove back to Kiren's lab. Ben bid them ado and headed off to the golf range.

Kiren arrived clad in jeans looking like a cow girl. She had Francis in tow and looked more relaxed, which to Matt, indicated that they had been together since they were last seen going to the horse facility. Francis appeared moderately displeased to see Matt and Vitz waiting, and tried to engage them in conversation designed to find out who they were and why they were back again to see his lady. Vitz took hold of the situation and started a mock fist fight with Matt while reciting how many women he knew named Francis. Francis fled and Kiren turned to Matt, smirking and commented:

"OK school boys, you've had your fun. Roland called. He had to go back to Washington last night and said he wanted to be here when we go over the details of the ribozyme work."

In a more hesitant voice she continued.

"Matt, before you go, did Roland have anything more to say about security and who might want to stop this project?"

"Not a lot, I gave him the list of people you talked to before you met him and he promised to do his best to give them reasons to believe he had convinced you to drop it and that he, Roland, felt it was a very bad idea. Beyond that, no more boogie men. In terms of the Department of Agriculture people, and the Green guys, I'm sure they are in the dark otherwise they would be screaming like babies in a hornet's nest."

"Good, thanks. Really, I mean that. I'm not afraid of getting hurt but I sure don't want to have anything happen to my students because of me, and if something did happen to me, my folk's lives would be ruined, having lost us both to coke."

"Well, that is the best reason I've heard yet for dropping this thing right now."

"Forget it."

Raul was much closer than either realized.

CHAPTER SIX
RAUL CATCHES UP

Brian wasn't sure where to start, whether LeBlank's people would be happier with a 'yes' or a 'no' or whether someone was working on a doomsday cocaine virus. He called the few plant virologists he knew, being circumspect, asking only if they knew of anyone who might be engineering South American crop viruses. Although he heard nothing positive, he learned more about plant viruses and came to the conclusion that there were only a few viruses that might be used for such work and thus there were also only a few laboratories that could be involved. Relating this to LeBlank, he was rebuffed and urged to visit Washington D.C. as soon as possible to look into the rumor first hand.

Brian's trip to Washington D.C. left him with the impression that no such work was being done. He visited a plant molecular biology laboratory run by the Department of Agriculture and met a staff Ph.D. who he had known at Berkeley. They had lunch and Brian cooked up the story that he was a consultant for one of the environmental protection groups based in Boston which was worried over rumors of plant viruses being used for warfare.

"So John, these friends in ba ba ba Boston have the very best credentials. One might call it a consortium of the best blu blu blu blood and best minds in the East. They meet now and then to talk about long range projections of the environment, where fund raising efforts should go and so on. Senators— old blu blu blu blood, and all of that. They heard a rumor third hand that someone was threatening to engineer some plant virus that would knock out food crops in countries that we might want to hurt, ah, like Cuba. Sounds pretty nutsoid, but as their consultant on viruses, I promised to look into it. Anything going on that you know of?"

"Jesus, not that I have heard. Would be major tabloid news. A guy could pick up ten grand just putting a newspaper on the right track. If I hear of anything I'll let you know, but it seems unlikely to me. Certainly an agency like mine is far too open and sluggish to do anything undercover. Also I can't imagine why anyone in a university would get involved, nor any biotech company either, unless they were being slipped money by the Army."

"No, you're right. The problem with being their consultant for molecular bi bi bi biology is that I have to take everything seriously including suggestions that farts can be harnessed to run automobiles."

They laughed and Brian returned to Boston and called LeBlank who seemed satisfied and called Raul to report the outcome.

"Raul, Henry here. My fellow Brian-the-stuttering virologist from Boston visited D.C. and talked to a number of plant labs in the area. They assured him nothing is in the works. Sounds as if we can put this one to rest."

"Fine, but I need more. There's something about this that makes my shit run wet. Tell your guy that I'll personally guarantee $10,000 of best grade coke if he will go back and do what I asked in the first place. I want him to pretend he is a plant virologist offering to do this and see how far he gets. If he gets nothing I promise you this whole thing is history."

"O.K. with me, I'm just the middleman. But why don't we track all of this down from who ever it was you heard the rumor from?"

"Already been tried. Cold trail— fuck all nothing. Pushed hard but nothing."

"I think that's where we are going to end up too, but I'll call Brian."

It was a week later when Brian had a few days free. It was unclear where to start, but he assumed that anyone else in this position would have been equally baffled. He decided to make a list of a dozen different offices or people he would talk to and if he got nowhere, that should satisfy Henry. Presenting himself as a Ph.D. virologist with long experience in plant viruses, Brian wandered from office to office for two days giving the same spiel– that he might be able to engineer a virus that would eradicate dope plants but that he would need support. At each office, from the Department of Agriculture to the DEA he got the same polite response of no interest, and please go away. Finally at the end of the day, as he was giving his abbreviated talk to a receptionist prior to asking to chat with her supervisor, the woman joked:

"This must be the week for killing plants with viruses. There was a young reporter here a few days ago asking about the same thing."

Brian was stopped cold. Catching his wits he replied,

"Reporter! Can you tell me who he is? Perhaps I should talk to him first before ba ba ba bothering your boss."

"Her not a him, and cute too. She left a card, Here it is, a Miss Cathy Hilldorf."

Brian copied the phone number and retreated to think over this shred of information. It seemed that a frontal approach might be called for and he phoned Miss Hilldorf immediately. They agreed to meet for coffee at one of the shops near Georgetown.

"So, my name is Bri bri bri Brian, I'm a Ph.D. virologist in Boston." He gave his phony spiel. "A secretary at the DEA gave me your name as someone who had been asking about people making plant viruses. Any chance that you can tell me what you know?"

"Well, Brian, not a lot. A friend of mine is an administrative assistant at the DEA. A few months ago a woman appeared out of the blue telling them that she could engineer a virus that would eradicate the coca plants. You familiar with that?"

"Not first hand, bu bu bu but some idea. Go on."

"Well, this woman apparently got the interest of some higher ups. Then, suddenly nothing. No lady no more, no one knows anything. Zipo. That caught my curiosity, but try as I have, I've not been able to get any more dope on her or who she is."

"No name or information as to where she came from?"

"Nope."

"Damn, sure would like to know who she is. Young, old, white – must have some description at least. Who knows, I might know her. Maybe she was one of my bench mates at Ber ber ber Berkeley."

The chance that Brian might know her was enough to lever the needed information out of Cathy.

"Well, my friend thought that she was from the East, a WASP, maybe 35 plus or minus, medium build, really pretty, extremely sharp features, huge deep gray eyes, and the most bizarre short cropped hair dyed bright red. Ring any bells?"

"Sorry, all the women virologists I know are round, dull and the only gray is in their hair."

Brian thanked her and flew back to Boston. He called Henry who taped the phone call and then phoned Raul.

"Heh, Raul, Apparently there is some truth to the rumor of a doomsday virus. Someone was in Washington D.C. suggesting that it could be done. Whether one of the agencies picked it up or not we do not know, nor do we know who this person is. Let me play the tape for you so you can hear exactly what Brian told me."

Henry played the recording which ended in the description of the red-haired woman. Raul exploded.

"Oh fuck! Damn, god-damned it! Son of a bitch! Jesus H Christ, why of all the two billion fucking people in the fucking world does she have to decide to take this on! Shit! Now what the hell am I going to do!"

"Sounds like you know this person." Henry interjected, being astounded at the intensity of the outburst from Raul.

"Shit yes. Ahhh, she is the sister of one of my former associates. Before he died he made me promise to keep an eye on her. I've pulled her sweet butt out of the fire before. But this time, fuck if I know. She's in over her head by a mile."

"So what do we do? We can't kill someone just because they have some crazy idea." Henry commented.

"Anyone touches her and I will have my surgeon amputate their limbs one by one and feed their parts to my dogs while they watch. Is that clear?"

"Absolutely."

"Right, so from now on, Brian reports directly to me. I'll find out whether she is working on this thing or not. Maybe she quit—no money. If she is, maybe I can convince her nicely to stop."

Henry shuddered several times that night thinking about Raul's dogs fighting over some fool's arm or leg while the victim looked on. Ugh. Well, at least it was out of his hands.

Raul called Brian. He explained that Kiren was the sister of a close friend who had died and he, Raul, was anxious that she not get into anything that might bring her harm. Thus, he, Raul, was watching over her and the rumor that she might be concocting some coca virus had disturbed a number of people. They discussed how Brian might poke around Kiren's lab at Duke to find out what she was up to.

"Brian, what's the chance that if you broke in at night and read their notebooks or looked at their samples that you can find out what they are doing?"

"The problem, Raul, is that it would be ha ha ha hard even for an expert to know what to look for. An engineered DNA that contained coca virus sequences probably would be named some number. Bu bu bu but too, I am a tenured faculty member at a well known University. I do not break into people's laboratories."

"That's reasonable, but there must be something that you can find out. Money always gets answers. Now, I'll send you a pile of airlines tickets from your place to Duke. I'll also toss in another ten thousand dollars. You go down and offer her some free samples or something. Send me the bill. Chat her up couple times a week. You figure it out. If you haven't found out anything in a month, give up, the money is yours and we call the whole fucking thing a dry well."

"You're on!"

Brian concocted a fake company letterhead, business card, and brochure for a start-up plant molecular biology company that would be offering special enzymes used in gene cloning in plants. From other companies he bought several thousand dollars worth of generally useful enzymes and re-packaged them with labels from his "new company". Thus armed, he flew south.

Kiren was frazzled and not anxious to be bothered.

"Dr. Moore? My name is Roger Isen and I am with Plantagene. Do you have a moment?"

"Oh, shit, not another salesman. You please go away! I am overworked and have no money to waste on damn cloning kits."

Brian turned white as Kiren's most evil stare sliced through him. He was about to run off but realized that he had to press on and get to the point fast. He stuttered on.

Pli- pli-pli please. Ah ah ah ah ah I have some free sa sa sa sa samples. Thousand dollars worth of enzymes. Free."

"Oh shit, the verbally handicapped. Give me a break. You don't look like the Ed McMahon of biotechnology."

"Pli pli pli please. Here's my card, and a list of enzymes I bra bra bra bra brought for you." He thrust the card and the full list of enzymes he had bought into her hand and then leapt back as if he might be shocked. Kiren grabbed the paper and then gazing over the list, looked back at him a bit softer this time.

"Jesus. Ah Mr. Roger, this is a long list, and we are currently buying many of these from my start up funds. You said free?"

"Yi yi yi yi yes. My company is just starting and we need to have a good lab like yours try these and be be be be be willing to tell others. I pra pra pra pra promise that our quality control is better than any other company out there. We'll focus just on the plant molecular biology market."

"I don't have to sign anything or call people?"

Brian crept forward and explained in detail each enzyme, its specifications and degree of purity. He promised to continue to supply her with these and others she might need. She was not being asked to do anything more than to be cited as a satisfied user in the company brochure. He asked that he be allowed to check in once or twice a week with her students to see if they had any complaints or problems with the enzymes.

"Well, I don't know how you got my name, ah, Roger, but this sounds too good to be true. Keep me supplied with a list like this and you can talk to my students any time you want to. Oh yes, thank you."

Brian left his complete collection of enzymes. Well, he thought, first contact with aliens is always expensive. Better fly back to Boston and get more.

In the following several weeks Brian made weekly visits with more supplies. Kiren would thank him and then turn him loose with her students. It was immediately clear that they were working on Gemini viruses, but he already knew that. Part of the problem was that all of Kiren's students were Asian and their English was marginal. Thus they were able to answer direct questions but offered little chit chat. He could hardly come straight out and ask them if they were working on dope viruses.

Brian related all of this to Raul who seemed amused at paying for Kiren's work and pressed Brian that since he had done such a good job so far that he should to continue for three more weeks before putting the project to bed.

Matt picked Ros up at her townhouse and they set off for the 50 minute drive across Washington D.C. to attend a party honoring the upcoming wedding of a psychiatrist friend. Matt dreaded the drive as he assumed that Ros would use the time to place him on a bar-b-que grill with Kiren's name on it. As it turned out. Matt's oldest sister had provided the sauce.

"Well, Matt, my little abhorrent teenager, guess who I had lunch with today."

"No, idea." Matt countered, suspecting it was not to his favor.

"Your sister Ramona. She was through on business for the day and since you were away, she thought it would be fun for us girls to trade stories."

"Oh, shit, you mean cut my liver out and cook it just like the wicked witch told the woodsman to do to Snow White."

"Exactly, except you are Snow Black."

"So what lies did dear Ramona lay on your already suspicious nature?"

"Well, nothing that I have not already put down in your case history."

"My what?"

"Your case history. I'm writing your case history. You don't think I would pass this up. Your life story could get me elected to the most prestigious academies of psychiatry."

"Great, so what did the dear girl tell you?"

"Well, first of all, we worked over your adolescence. She told me about growing up in the boondocks of Alaska and your spending all of your time being the ultimate baby Daniel Boone. Hunting and camping with your father, shooting moose and anything else that moved. Said you had been given your first gun when you were six."

"So what's wrong with that? It was just a .22."

"Oh, nothing! I suppose you have a bumper sticker saying "Stop child abuse–arm the babies". Besides it helps explain your behavior with women when things don't go your way. Shoot first and think later."

"I've never shot a woman— yet."

"I recall your threatening to shoot that Russian girl friend—"

"Drop it."

"Ramona told me that one summer you and your friends had a contest as to who could eat off the land the longest and you won. She told me what you ate. I almost lost my lunch."

"That's why I never like to lie on the beach with you. I look up and all I see is flying seagull sandwiches. Can't look a seagull in the face since. They taste like rotten fish. You have to soak them in salt water for a day and then boil them with willow leaves just to hide the taste. Saute' of seagull, seagull supreme, my favorite was —"

"Shut up. Now, according to her, you spent most of your time pestering your sisters unmercifully. How could you do that? You must have been a real little shit."

"Just Ramona's clouded memory. I was training them for real life. Ramona is a highly successful business woman making a lot more than I am and it's all because I taught her how to stick up for herself. If I had protected her and been a lovey-dovey brother she would probably be a divorced mother of five living on welfare. I should send her a bill. —Dear Sis didn't have anything good to say about her brother?"

"Oh, of course; even Count Dracula loved his pet canary."

"I thought he fed it to his cat."

"He did. She said that you were extremely close to your folks, your dad in particular, and you always did things designed to please them. She suspects that you are still trying to gain their applause. Poor little boy, forty something going on twelve. Do you want to know what I think?"

"I have a choice?"

"No. I think that you didn't have a lot of friends when you grew up because you lived a long ways from other families. You became very self sufficient and able to solve your problems on your own-- even if it meant eating seagulls for two weeks. In the bush winning is all important. To lose means getting lost, frozen or eaten by a bear. No gray areas. When I grew up in New York City, there were few things that were dangerous in that way. What we had to learn to survive was how to deal with people not bears. That means learning to deal with personal feelings and gray areas."

"So you became the consummate gray area creature. That's why I like dealing with bears. Easier to predict their behavior."

"Right, you grew up with a set of tools that was fine for the outback, but here in my environment, —my cultural misfit, you need softer, more pliable tools."

"And you can teach me?"

"Unlikely, you are too set in your ways. My guess is that science is a perfect refuge for you. Physicists-chemists-biologists, hard scientists don't have to develop the people skills to the level that we social scientists do. We established that the other day."

"I thought that we established that the term "social science" was the ultimate absurdity."

"Screw you! Just because you can't grow it on a petri dish doesn't mean that it can't be quantitated."

"Word is quantified. You don't even know the right word let alone how to do it. But back to my being too set in my ways. I agree I had an unusual upbringing and when I grew up, I shot and ate my way through the zoological kingdom. But now I'm almost a vegetarian. Can't stand to shoot a thing. Maybe I was a bit hard on my sisters, but we had to compete for our folk's attention. Now I am overly loving, attentive, and forgiving to women just to make up for my flawed youth."

"Well, she did say that your attitude toward women was your one, and I quote, O-N-E good point."

"She elaborated? Am curious what my sisters will put on my grave stone."

"Ramona said that for someone brought up in a 19th century environment you ended up with a 21st century attitude about women."

"Ah, go on."

"Her theory was that in your home your mother and father were complete equals– in how much money they made, how bright they were, and how much say they had about matters of day to day life as well as long range plans."

"Absolutely. I wouldn't have it any other way; would you?"

"I would not. But most American families are still male-dominated. She felt that you still haven't gotten married because you only like women who are as independent as you are – just like your mother and dad. How's that for a couch in absentia? You can split the fee between the two of us."

"Fat chance. Well, some truth, I suppose. I do feel sorry for bright women of my generation. When I was in college, most women were still being sold a bill of goods that included no sex before marriage and the idea that education was there so that they could provide polite chatter at dinner parties. Suddenly these same women are told that they have to go out and be just like men. Not surprising that the ones who have made the transition and are competing on an equal footing have a few sharp edges as a result."

Matt reached over and began kissing Rosalind on the neck as he drove and rubbed her legs as a means of distracting her and ending the conversation. Soon they arrived at the party, with Matt having put off any discussion of Kiren.

As they left the party and got into the car, Matt thought of something that had caught Ros's interest recently— the molecular biology of behavior. This was an area in which Rosalind was totally devoid of any grounding and was, Matt had discovered, willing to swallow nearly anything he fed her no matter how absurd it would seem to his molecular colleagues. Thus on his last lecture he had strayed a bit from the truth. The story had begun factually, a discussion of whether behavioral traits such as male homosexuality were in part genetic. There were recent publications in the most respected journals that suggested a genetic link, based on studies of identical twins. This study had raised many questions as to whether there could be genetic and thus molecular explanations for some broad human behaviors. Rosalind had found this highly fascinating, but at the same time vaguely threatening since if projected, it suggested that certain abnormal behaviors were not the result of being nursed on the mother's left nipple as contrasted to the right one, but rather had to do with tiny molecules that were present in the brain. If so, then some day in the future, it might be possible to take a pill or submit to genetic therapy to correct these abnormal traits– if one (or society?) felt that they were undesirable.

This discussion had been on the up and up. Toward the end, however, Matt had switched to discussion of the genetics of fruit fly behavior, and here he had —shall we say, projected some distance into the future. His musings however had clearly caught Rosalind's interest and to avoid discussions of Kiren, Matt brought the topic up again.

"Recall what I told you a few weeks ago about Drosophila – that is fruit fly– behavior? I recently saw some preprints of papers that will appear shortly which report some amazing findings. Some of it you will find most interesting as a woman with a basic distrust of men."

"O.K. sounds interesting, fill me in" Replied Rosalind clearly perking up.

"Well, as I told you last time, scientists who study Drosophila name the genes they discover by funny but descriptive tags such as "Rosy" for red eyes, "Droopy" for hairs on the back that bend over, and so on. Well the group that has been looking at the genetics of Drosophila behavior had discovered a new cluster of genes on the X and Y chromosomes. The test that they were applying involved marking a young male fruit fly and then watching until it selected a mate. The female was then marked and they measured the frequency at which the male either mated only with that female fruit fly or with other females. They then did the reverse, following the females."

Rosalind was clearly hooked, and Matt realized that he might be able to string this story out all the way home to keep Ros off the topic of Kiren. He just had to keep the story running.

"So this group has been doing this research for the last 2 years. Once they found what the normal range of switching to new mates was, they began to look at flies that contained mutations on the X and Y chromosomes. Recall that the females have two X and no Y chromosome while the male has one X and one Y. At first they just found marginal differences until a few months ago when they hit the jackpot."

"What they found was a gene that only occurs on the X chromosome. They call it "Fidelity". The females have two copies of Fidelity and the males only one. What they discovered was that if there was a mutation in the Fidelity gene on the single X chromosome of the male, then he would not bond with any one female but would go from one to the next. Same for the female – but here she had to have both Fidelity genes knocked out– one on each of her two X chromosomes and thus this was much less common."

Rosalind broke in: "Unbelievable, but what is the effect of females having two copies of Fidelity and males only one?"

"Very interesting," continued Matt. "First, for normal flies a female bonded with a single male at a 5 fold higher frequency than a male bonded with a single female. This suggested immediately that the double dose of Fidelity in the female was having a major effect. Now comes the earthshaking experiment."

"Yes -yes- yes? go on." Rosalind urged, as Matt fought to keep a straight face and not become too outrageous.

"They were able to breed male flies that had a double or quadruple dose of Fidelity. With the double copy– equal to the females, then the frequency of moving to a new female after meeting the first one was now much lower. With a quadruple dose they were even more monogamous than the normal females. What do you think about that?"

Rosalind was stunned as clearly Matt had pushed many of her buttons simultaneously, from her professional buttons to her "men are slime" button. Unfortunately they were still 10 minutes away and so Matt continued.

"Now that is the first of the two papers. In the second, they went back and noted that while the females usually have only one mate and at most 3, some of the males showed extreme variations often having a dozen or more mates. Upon tracking this, it was discovered that there is at least one more gene involved and they call it "Repressor of Fidelity". As you might guess, it resides on the Y chromosome. Most males contain an active "Repressor of Fidelity" gene. This gene can be turned on by a variety of factors. One factor is being housed in the presence of an excess of females."

One thing about Rosalind, Matt had to admit, she was extremely bright and quick to see the long range implications in scientific findings. The impact of the discovery of "Fidelity" and "Repressor of Fidelity" in fruit flies was immediately clear to Rosalind. She assumed that these same genes were present in human males, and she had little reason to doubt this given her personal experiences with men. If so, this suggested that a large portion of human male behavior was deeply ingrained in their genes – going back possibly 300 million years to some ancestor common to both flies and humans. Rosalind had little notion of how genes worked, apparently having passed out of what little molecular courses had been offered in medical school. Her attitude about all of the science courses was the simple equation P=MD (pass equals an MD degree). She had a nearly photographic memory however and had memorized a long list of drugs and what diseases they were used for. Thus she assumed that for nearly any medical problem there eventually would be a solution in the form of a pill. Rosalind pressed Matt as to how one might use drugs to inhibit "Repressor of Fidelity" or use genetic therapy to insert extra copies of Fidelity back into men. Matt was having extreme difficulty in keeping a serious expression as they parked on her driveway.

As Rosalind was bidding Matt good night, she mentioned that she was a member of a Psychiatrists study group that met once a week and that she would review the work on the Fidelity and Repressor of Fidelity genes the next time they met. On the drive back to his farm, to avoid thinking about what would happen if one of her study group knew some molecular biology, he turned his thoughts to Kiren and his worries over how much the Cartel knew. As it was, Matt and Kiren were unaware that Raul was watching them.

CHAPTER SEVEN

RUNNING OUT OF TIME

Kiren was not in a good mood. True, the money from Roland had started coming in, and that helped make it possible to buy much needed supplies. The problem for Kiren was that she loved to work in the lab herself, and the growing demands on her time was making it progressively more difficult to find time for her to do lab work. She phoned Matt. He had not been down in several weeks and she felt that he had done very little recently to help.

"How the Hell can I get this work done when there are so many other things I have to do?"

"Like what in specific?"

"Like things I am sure you don't know anything about —teaching and committees. Teaching, I understand is part of what I do. Also being on graduate student committees— that I look at as teaching on a more informal basis. What I hate and is taking up so much time is these intensely stupid dean's committees I am forced to be on. Being a woman, I'm asked to be on endless committees. Maybe I'll tell them I'm a transvestite! There is no quota for them."

"My problem is the project is getting to where I either need to put a great deal more time in the lab myself, or get some help. I could have one or two of my graduate students take some of the load but I don't want to put them in a compromising situation."

"I assume they are not aware of what you are up to?"

"Not really, they think that the coca virus is a new virus I isolated from potatoes in Idaho."

"Well, Kiren, here's my suggestion. Have one of your students do some of the RNA analysis and another one work up the DNA. The good thing about Asian students in my experience is that they don't question what you are doing like American students do."

"And what about the sequencing? I've got a lot of that to verify the new virus constructions I'm making. Sequencing as you know costs money and time."

"I know you consider Hopkins to be a bastion of old boy science, but my department has a large automated DNA sequencing facility. It was set up by funding from the Genome project. If you can get your DNAs to me in the right format I can run them through on my account and will happily send the bill to Roland."

"You can do that for me?"

"Roland made it clear I was to grease your wheels. The facility has rows of these automated machines. You just put the DNA in one end and out the other end comes the sequence written on a computer disk. You can download it from our site on the Internet."

"Thanks, that would take a lot of pressure off of me. If you can email the details of how I need to prep the DNA, I can start sending it any time."

"Better idea. You sound like you are in a crisis mode. Why don't Roland and I fly down next Saturday morning. Vitz can drive over. That will give us all a chance to go over the details of the ribozymes that Roland wanted to hear."

"You always insist on paying for dinner and the movie too?" Kiren joked.

"They always drag me off pleading that we bag the movie. See you Saturday morning if the weather is reasonable, bye." Matt hung up before Kiren could respond.

Matt had planned to slip away quietly in the Moose Gooser with Roland and then fly back on Sunday. To his horror, Ros announced that she had friends at Duke and she would accompany them on the trip. Matt protested that the project was secret but Rosalind said only that she expected to be introduced to Kiren and that she would then leave and meet Matt Sunday morning for the flight back. Trapped, Matt had little choice but to take her along. Further, there was the possibility that she would indeed find Kiren unattractive, or perhaps Kiren would be dressed in her Alice in Wonderland costume. Besides, he had long since learned to not underestimate the ability of one woman to find fault in another.

A keen reader of Matt's body language, Rosalind clued into Matt's nervousness as they approached the Raleigh/Durham airport and repeatedly asked him to again describe this "Kiren person" as she was referred to by Rosalind. Using her "1000 nerve endings for personal feelings" to her advantage, Rosalind picked and poked at Matt from every direction like a cat bats a mouse prior to crunching its head. Roland refused to say a word. The drive to Duke was far too short as Matt kept offering to drop her off at her friend's. No, Rosalind had arranged for the friend to meet them at Duke. Damn women.

The only positive thing about the meeting was its brevity. Kiren was dressed in tight black riding britches that made her seem particularly slim, with mock riding boots and a short sleeved white silk blouse. A red scarf that matched her hair was tied about her neck. She looked as if she was ready for a garden party with Prince

Charles. Rosalind shook her hand, ignored Vitz who stood imposingly to the side, looked at Matt and stated:

"I'll see you tomorrow, 11 AM. Back here! You and I are going to discuss what happened in your early childhood that stopped your psychological development at the third god-damned grade."

Kiren looked stunned, Roland chuckled and Vitz grinned as Rosalind strode off. Following a mumbled explanation from Matt as to who Rosalind was, Kiren told them that she had arranged a visit with a world's expert in genetic engineering at UNC in Chapel Hill.

As they were leaving the lab, Matt and Brian came face to face and both stared at each other as if they should know the other but were not certain why. Kiren made a quick introduction and then led them to her car. Matt seemed bothered. This guy somehow didn't seem like a salesman and why was he there on Saturday? But, who knows about these people. Further, the biotech companies are full of Ph.D. types selling their wares.

As they drove over in Kiren's Wagoneer, she described the man they were to visit.

"Hassan is one of the best examples of how the US has benefited from our strong training program in molecular biology. Some 30 years ago, he came here from Turkey with a medical education. He obtained a Ph.D. and did postdoctoral work at one of the top eastern universities. There, he invented many of the cloning approaches that are so routine now that our graduate students have no idea how hard this work was just 10 to 15 years ago."

Wending their way past graduate students who were working as hard on a sunny Saturday as they would have on any other day, they found chairs in Hassan's small office crammed with journals and 4 foot high piles of ungraded exams left over from some forgotten course he had taught. Vitz took on a more subdued attitude. Matt noticed this, and wondered whether in the past Vitz had gotten the bad end of a bar room brawl with a group of Turks, or whether the atmosphere of science with a fierce intensity made him realize that he was sitting in someone else's kitty liter box while their giant house cat considered his fate.

Kiren made the introductions and began by reviewing the project to date. She had previously brought Hassan up to speed on the Gemini viruses. He was one of the few scientists to whom they felt they could trust to not reveal the true objective of the project. He was so far removed from plant viruses that this would not put him in any danger. The discussion was pitched more for Roland than Matt, as Roland had insisted on being given a rough overview of what was going to be done and possible pitfalls that lay ahead.

"To begin with, we want to insert a ribozyme into our engineered Gemini virus. This will add a second punch to the virus. It's small, in fact the part of it that seeks out RNAs to cut up is only 16 bases."

"Guys, I am confusional and my neurons are in chocolate deprivation. How is your little virus going to make these ribozyme things?" Roland complained.

"Sorry, Roly Poly, there are a lot of points here outside your chocolate factory. Recall that the basic genetic information is stored in the Gemini virus DNA. If we make a piece of DNA that has the ribozyme's sequence of bases, and stick that chunk of DNA into our new Gemini virus we will have inserted our little bomb into our new virus. Got it?" Kiren explained.

"You've been lecturing undergrads haven't you." commented Hassan.

Kiren continued: "There are so many similarities in the DNA sequence of the coca and bean Gemini viruses that we know precisely where in the coca virus we can add new DNA. I figure we can add up to 100 bases of new DNA without making the DNA too big to fit into the virus shell."

"Recall it's not as simple as just adding one ribozyme sequence to make my bomb. Not at all. I need to split the ribozyme into its two parts: the part that does the cutting and the part that recognizes its target. Let's call that the targeting sequence. Now each and every one of the engineered Gemini viruses is going to get the half of the ribozyme that does the cutting. I will then make a mixture of millions of different possible targeting sequences, insert each into a different one of these Gemini viruses, and then let the plants select the combination that is the most harmful."

"Flippin amazing! And you expect to get this done before the next century?" askedVitz.

"Vitzie, in the world of molecular biology we are used to such numbers. In a single test tube I can have many millions of different targeting sequences. I can add that to a tube with millions of new Gemini virus DNAs and what do you know, in a day I will have a million different viruses, each with a ribozyme that will look for a different target."

Vitz made a "got-it" expression and Matt and Hassan rolled their eyes up indicating to Kiren that they were getting anxious to get to the heart of the matter.

"Tell Roland how you plan to get cocaine specific RNAs," urged Matt.

"As a start, we have begun to generate a set of RNA molecules specific for young leaf tissue where drug production is high. These RNAs should be highly enriched in genes for cocaine production."

She stood up and began outlining the methods on the blackboard. Hassan twitched his nose, and asked a number of questions. He approved of the overall approach, but added numerous detailed suggestions at each of the steps.

Hassan helped them examine the region of the Gemini virus DNA around the site into which the new information would be inserted. This region contained the place where the replication of the circles began as well as the genetic signals controlling the expression of the genetic material. The DNA would be cut open by specific proteins at these sites to allow the new information to be inserted.

A long discussion ensued between Kiren, Matt, and Hassan over the details of how the DNA would be cut open, how best to engineer the new segments to DNA to be inserted back in and finally how to arrange things so that each of the newly engineered viruses would have an "open portal" that would accept one of the ribozyme targeting sequences. Much of the discussion kept coming back to making short DNA molecules, and Roland finally broke in.

"And where are you going to get all of this new DNA?" Roland asked.

"You are going to pay for it, my friend." Matt replied, and continued: We can write down the genetic code we need and have my service laboratory synthesize it."

"That's within my operational envelope."

Matt asked Roland if he understood how they would go from DNA to viruses. Both Roland and Vitz shook their heads and Kiren explained.

"There were two key steps in the genetic engineering revolution. The first was the development of methods to stick different pieces of DNA together to create new combinations of genes that had never been tried out in nature. That work was done at the Stanford Biochemistry Department by Paul Berg and his colleagues, based on very important studies by two professors, Bob Lehman and Arthur Kornberg. The next step was learning how to put this test tube-engineered DNA back into cells. This was first done by Stan Cohen working with bacteria. A few years ago it was discovered that one could shoot DNA into cells with a gun. We now use a tiny "shotgun" that fires minute metal or plastic pellets with enough force to penetrate the plant cell wall. If the micro-pellets are coated with DNA, then the DNA is taken in and can diffuse to nearby cells." She continued:

"So we shoot our newly engineered DNA into the plant leaf, and once inside, this new DNA will begin the virus replication cycle of making copies of itself and new virus particles. Zappo—after a few weeks we will begin to see a virus lesion at the site where the DNA was shot in, and we can isolate new progeny Gemini virus particles from the leaf."

Hassan stood up and gazed at a photograph on his office wall of an old Turkish town from which he had emigrated. He sighed and looked at asked Kiren.

"I can help you with the genetic engineering but there is one thing I cannot advise you on. You are about to alter the life patterns of a lot of people. Not just the drug lords and the users— I could put all of them in a pot and boil them, but have you thought about the little people of Colombia? As I understand it, the peasants in the mountains of Colombia, Chile, Peru, all use coca leaves much as we use coffee or tea. It's part of their day to day life. They chew the leaves for a hit and something to take the chill out of the morning air. It just may be the oldest known medicinal drug. Coca use has been around for 4000 years and a part of their culture that long. I was told once that if the Germans had cut off all tea routes from India to England during the war that the British would have given up instantly. Would you give up coffee to help people in some other country solve a problem that is theirs and not yours? Here of course it's not as clear cut. The cocaine trade is doing a lot of harm in the countries where it is produced. I'm not willing to make a judgment, but you need to make sure that you are clear in your mind."

Matt sat back smiling to himself and Vitz had a large grin. Hassan had been able to voice concerns that neither of them had been able to get across and both knew that Kiren would not tell Hassan to "Fuck Off" or some other variation of "F-O" as she needed his help and respected him highly.

Kiren started to snap at Hassan then cut herself off, giving Matt a "say a word and you are dead" look and replied:

"OK, OK, I've heard such concerns from these fools before. You are correct– it may have an effect on the locals. I feel that the overall good will outweigh the bad. Furthermore, how do we know that one of the major reasons why the mountain peasants in those countries are still in the stone age isn't that they are doped out of their minds from birth to death. If we could get rid of this plant, it might start a renaissance in that area the likes of which has not happened since the Incas."

To put a break in things, Matt mentioned that he had an old acquaintance, Mike, in the next building who could give them a tour of the electron microscope facility. This was one of the most sophisticated of its kind in the world, and was operated by a virologist who was, it turned out, a fellow pilot.

The EM (electron microscope) laboratory was also busy, and to the extreme boredom of Kiren, a half hour was spent discussing airplanes.

"Hey blubber-brains, we came to see a ribozyme. I thought you guys were experts in looking at molecules not bullshitting about propellers."

Mike recoiled and retreated to find a sample of the ribozymes they were studying. While he was gone, Matt scolded Kiren for her "in your face" version of diplomacy, which in Matt's view, was an excuse for no diplomacy at all.

Although Matt had seen electron microscopes before, and had used several himself, he was, nonetheless, awed by the size of the instrument which filled up a 150 square foot room. This one cost nearly one million and was capable of magnifying molecules several million times as seen on the television screens placed around the room.

The ribozyme sample was retrieved and Mike placed it in the microscope. The ribozyme was the one that had been discovered in Colorado. It was exciting to see one of these small "creatures" as he called them. The ribozyme appeared much like a cigarette butt, a short rod several times longer than its width. This viewing required that the microscope be operated at the maximum magnification.

Another interesting sample they viewed was a collection of very short DNAs that had been created by a molecular technique called PCR, for "polymerase chain reaction". This provides a means of amplifying a segment of DNA millions of times to a level such that even tiny trace segments of DNA can be detected. Its application to the diagnosis of disease organisms, to forensic medicine, and other areas has transformed medical science.

After a few minutes of viewing these DNAs, Kiren turned on the lights and announced:

"Enough! I don't like machines, and I don't think it's fair to look at what you are working on."

Matt thought to himself: "She probably shut her eyes when she makes love– but given her fat Englishman, maybe she has reason to." Kiren continued:

"It's 4 o'clock and I've given you all the time I had allocated for this. My riding lesson is at 5:00. Matt, here doesn't know anything about horses, we established that the last time. Vitzie-poo, I'll bet you are not far behind. Roland said he wanted to get back, so give him your rental car and you two follow me in Vitz' car. Maybe with enough time you two could learn to appreciate horses. Seems to me we are done for now and Matt, you are going to have to stick around until tomorrow for that woman of yours."

"But Kiren I actually–"

"Enough. Off we go."

On the drive following Kiren, Matt and Vitz mused about Kiren.

"God, little miss "can't get a word in edgewise" bit me again. Damn, I like horses but she has decided I have never seen one, and that is that! I give up! I actually enjoy her, and appreciate the pressure she is under. I just wish we could unwind her crank a few turns," Matt joked.

"Not my kind of meow-meow. I like them soft and with a lot more padding. You could get mightily bruised bouncing up and down on her. Pretty sharp though."

Arriving at the horse facility, Kiren changed clothes and Vitz and Matt followed her around, enjoyed the sun and watching the riding. The outdoor dressage ring was a rectangle 60 meters long and 20 meters wide with letters placed along the side to denote transitions from one gait or move to the next. Kiren entered with Mr. Copper. Matt provided a running description for Vitz.

"Watch closely and you will see that she moves her leg slightly back on this side but not on the other when she transitions to the canter. Now there, see how she moves her weight back just a bit to make a transition back down to the trot—. Now weight forward and see the heel work the horse.– Now watch the horse's mouth. That's called "being on the bit", and his head is tipped to the vertical."

"You sure see a lot more than I can. Looks easy, just sit there and get bounced up and down a bit, and round and round she goes."

"Right, and you would last ten seconds before being tossed off. The reason it looks easy is that she is very good and has her balance so well in tune that she moves with the horse. Requires strong thighs."

"Yah, I saw that. Not a bit of cellulite on these women. But I would like to do an in depth inspection to see if there was any somewhere."

Kiren finished her lesson and brought Mr. Copper to Matt and Vitz.

"Matt. Hold him for a minute if you will. I need to take a quick shower in the dressing room and change. Francis and I have dinner plans. Mr. Copper here needs a bit more riding before I put him up, he's still a bit stiff. Hold him and I will see if Sandy can ride him a few more minutes. Thanks."

Matt and Vitz looked at each other. Vitz broke the silence. "You first."

Watching Kiren ride such a well trained and smooth horse had teased Matt nearly to the breaking point. It would have been like asking Stirling Moss to watch a friend play with a D type Jaguar and then refuse to let him have a go at it.

"OK, but just until Kiren's friend comes out."

Matt adjusted the stirrups and swung up on Mr. Copper. Once mounted, he began with a gentle posting trot to warm his legs up and then settled into a sitting trot. At this point a striking black-haired woman walked over to Vitz.

"Heh, is that Kiren's friend on Mr. Copper?"

"Yah, she said that the horse needed a bit more riding so Matt here is just helping out."

"But Kiren said you guys don't know anything about horses!"

"Right."

"But, he has a very good position and seat! Nobody can just get on a horse and do that!"

Kiren joined them, eyes wide.

"Oh no! He's never been on a horse before!"

Vitz grabbed the opportunity as Kiren and Sandy stood transfixed.

"Right. What you see here is the natural athlete, a one of a kind. This guy just sat back and analyzed every little thing that you were doing. It was just amazing for me to listen to how he picked up on every move you made. He just analyzed it and then got on and off he went. Just like baby Beethoven. As a child, Beethoven watched his father play the piano and then one day with not a single lesson, he sat down and played his first symphony."

Matt had focused so much attention on the riding that he failed to see Kiren and Sandy and was working on getting Mr. Copper into his favorite movement, a half pass down the centerline of the ring. Kiren was transfixed. Had she felt that Mr. Copper was being abused in any way she would have ripped him off HER horse, but as it was, Mr. Copper seemed to be willing to respond to Matt's gentle commands and aids. Vitz continued:

"Knew only one other natural athlete like Matt here in my day. This guy picked up golf in one afternoon and made a fortune playing for money before he was black listed on all the major country clubs. Mind over body that's all it is."

Matt had Mr. Copper's attention. As they rounded the turn of the ring, Matt settled into a forward sitting trot, and headed straight down the centerline. He used his left heel to ask Mr. Copper to keep shifting his left legs under himself. The result was that Mr. Copper headed straight ahead but at the same time moved laterally to the side so that just at the point when they had arrived at the end of the ring, they were also at the far right corner. Kiren exploded:

"I cant' believe what I am seeing. That was a nice half pass. This is impossible!"

"No mam, just a natural athlete at work mam." Vitz slurred, faking a Southern accent.

Matt looked up to see Kiren and blushing, rode over and quickly dismounted.

"Kiren, this is a splendid animal! Wonderful! I hope you didn't mind, I just—"

"Give me my horse, oh! This is so embarrassing!" Kiren snatched the reigns and strode off to the barn.

"Did we do something wrong Tonto?" Vitz joked.

"More than you could understand, masked man." Matt countered, turning to try to offer an explanation to Sandy but saw her rushing off after Kiren.

"What did you tell them?" Matt asked feeling that Vitz may have worsened a situation that was only partly his making.

"Just that you had never ridden a horse before but that you were a natural athlete."

"Oh great. Roland may have to find another pair of handlers for her, you understand."

Matt and Vitz caught an early dinner at a Carolina barbecue in Durham. Most of the dinner was spent explaining to Vitz that the world is full of viruses and that there was no way a plant virus could cause any disease in people, so he had nothing to worry about from the coca virus. True, Matt explained, people can get into real trouble if they contract some closely related animal virus like Rabies from dogs or the Hanta virus from mice, but plant viruses are so far evolved from animal viruses, that you could eat a pound and only get the burps. The genetic signals were just too far apart.

Vitz seemed happier and Matt retired to his motel room to contemplate which of the two women, Kiren or Rosalind, he would rather face. Not a pleasant choice.

The next morning, Kiren was quiet and more relaxed, refusing to comment on his riding and Matt had no interest in bringing it up. Indeed, Matt considered sending Francis a bottle of wine as thanks for apparently calming her down. Over coffee, they laid the schedule out and it was tighter than they wanted to think about. One problem was to get all of the work accomplished which they had outlined. This could be done in 2 months if she worked day and night and got some help from her students. It would take them to a point where they would have a mixture of engineered viruses, in fact tens of billions of different ones all mixed up in the test tubes. However, that brought Kiren to the second very large problem.

She explained:

"I can create viruses in the test tube for the next 50 years but that doesn't mean that the natural mechanism of virus spread will work for these engineered viruses. Recall that in nature these viruses are spread by White Flies that carry the virus in their saliva and inject the virus as they take liquid from the plant leaves. I am concerned that our engineered viruses will have lost their ability to be carried by the flies. Thus, once we have a large mix of viruses made, we have to screen out all of those that are not able to be transmitted by the flies – and this is going to have to be done in real coca plants." She continued:

"As I told you a month ago, I don't want to do this screening in North Carolina. You were supposed to look for a place to set up our final engineering and testing where the winter is so harsh that it will kill every single fly that might escape. You need to find us a cool hideaway and soon!"

Kiren and Matt turned as they heard a noise. Rosalind had walked in and was staring at Matt like a mother catching her teenage son together with a girl of greatly questioned reputation.

"Oh, don't let ME break up your hideaway plans."

"Ros, so good to see you, no, want some coffee? Kiren and I had just finished and she had given me my homework so to speak."

"I'll bet you like playing house."

This was ignored as Matt scooped up his papers and turned to leave. Rosalind was not done with the two of them. Staring at Kiren who was dressed for more riding Rosalind blurted:

"I guess unlike me who is a city lady, you two have a lot to talk about — since you both own horses."

"What?" Kiren yelled at Matt as he was dragging Ros out of the door. It would be a long trip home.

Not long after Matt left, Brian, alias Roger, made another visit to Kiren's lab with more enzymes. He mentioned that he needed to go over some details of several new ones, and Kiren asked him to sit in her office for a moment while she finished an experiment in the next room. Sitting alone, Brian noted the piles of books on the floor. Some were on plant biochemistry. Reading other scientist's books is not considered a violation of privacy and he thumbed through several. Noting yellow sticky paper marking a chapter in one, he turned to the marked page. Brian muttered:

"Oh, shit!"

He quickly scanned the chapter, and watching for Kiren, looked over several other books similarly marked. In each, the tagged pages had to do with biochemical studies of the production of the cocaine molecule in coca plants. Brian rearranged the books and fought a particularly bad case of the stutters while he took Kiren through the details of the enzymes he had for her.

Brian called Henry who relayed the information to Raul.

"Oh fuck my brains! Jesus H God! Damn that woman! I was hoping that she was just doing stuff, but not our stuff."

"So what now, Raul?"

"Well, just because she was reading about dope doesn't give us enough. Maybe she is teaching a class on plant pharmacology. This stinks like real shit but we only have the dirty toilet paper. Damn!"

"So what next, Raul, seems to me Brian has done all he can."

"Yah, right. Pay him off. I'm going to send my man Estaban up for a few weeks. He's a good watcher. He can poke around her lab at night and maybe bug her phone. Yah, bug her phone. That's it. If she is working on this project she must be talking about it with her connections. Make her connections and we have all we need. Maybe he can copy her hard drive."

"Oh, along that track Raul, Brian said that one Saturday two guys showed up and spent the day with her. One was the biggest blonde dude he had ever seen and looked real uncomfortable around the lab. Nasty looking guy. The other one also maybe in his late 40's, was clearly a scientist, but also hard looking. Brian said that there was something odd and out of place about these guys."

"Fuck if I know, this whole thing is not going like I want. We'll see what Estaban can get."

CHAPTER EIGHT

BETWEEN THE KANIKUKA AND THE TOKOSITNA

The ride from Duke to the airport was made in stone silence. As they were loading their gear into the Cessna, Matt made a valiant effort to break the ice. Walking up from behind, he grabbed Ros and gave her a big hug, asking how her evening had gone. Good try. It might have worked had Rosalind not had an MD and 4 years of residency working with the devious as well as some 25+ years of dealing with men. She pushed him away and began her planned attack.

"Give me again from the top exactly as you did before, your description of this "Kiren Person" and your feelings about her."

"Ah, well as I told you, she is about 5 foot 5, slightly built, short red hair, gray eyes– what else?"

"My feelings, you always ignore my feelings! You said she was an ugly duckling– you used those exact words. Further, you slime, you said that she was unattractive and spindly. She is one of the most striking women I have seen you drool over in years! She is very very very New York chic and you know it, Ass Hole. I assume you thought I wouldn't meet her."

"But Ros, sure, she was smartly dressed, but really I've never seen her that way before. All the other times she has been in her lab garb which is some shapeless coverall. I thought she looked far too harsh. Her hair makes her look like a boy."

"Where did the two of you sleep last night?"

"Really, Ros, you know very well I had a motel near Duke. She was with her boyfriend this morning."

In the air, Ros kept firing little verbal rockets, not particularly aimed in any direction. "All men are ass holes, I keep trying to ignore that primal fact of life but it keeps coming back in my face."

"Maybe it's related to the gene for fidelity, possibly a close genetic linkage." Matt gritted his teeth realizing that the fidelity gene topic was best let lie.

Another lull ensued while they were vectored around traffic in the Richmond area and given a new altitude. Matt wished for a convention of jets that might keep him so tied up that Rosalind would give up. No luck.

"Do you want to continue seeing me? Or am I just your bimbo d' jour with whom you engage in sport fucking?"

"Ros, you burn my ears. You know that I am very attached to you and that we are an item– you are for me, I am for you and all that stuff."

"And you just take all this lightly, you can lie through your teeth when you feel like it, if it allows you to bed me one more time?– Assholes the lot of you".

"Maybe I should put this on autopilot and lie down on the back seat and you can pretend it's a couch." No response.

"This Kiren Person, tell me more."

"What do you want to hear?"

"First, some bit of truth. How much time have you spent with her alone, and what are your long term intentions? Are the two of you going to go away somewhere, like that last woman Roland mated you with?"

"She was a dog's dog. She had hair growing out from under her fingernails. Flies blew their lunch at the sight of her. She was so ugly that the Environmental Protection Agency listed her as a serious pollutant."

"Right, and you bedded her anyway."

"Ros!" Matt was feeling uneasy on this topic since the lady in question hadn't been quite so unattractive, and whether or not he had bedded her was of no concern to Rosalind. He replied.

"Really Ros, you are being highly unreasonable, you know that I need to do these projects for Roland in trade for his support. Just trust me and be a big girl."

"You are avoiding the question. How long is this Kiren Person going to be flitting around in her tight britches stressing your undershorts?"

"Ros."

"Roland has promised this will be a very short project. I expect it will be all over in a couple of months at the most. I don't even know if I will see her again. It's possible I can handle all of the work by email. Besides, you saw that big blonde beast with her. He's her body guard. He has major designs on her and she goes all gushy when he's around. There's no way in hell I am going to fight him for her. He thinks that killing people is an art form that must be done as slowly as possible. He's the one you need to concentrate on. His background is one for your journal."

Matt began to describe Vitz' upbringing, escape from the KGB, and general demeanor. Rosalind had taken a good look at him and so was as stunned as most women were at the sight of Vitz, and the combination of this memory and Matt's description side tracked Rosalind from her analysis of Matt's early childhood. Finally entering the Washington D.C. airspace Matt had to attend to the flying and was able to avoid any further discussion of Kiren until they landed.

Matt drove Rosalind back to her townhouse and dropped her off with a promise that he would at least consider serious discussions about how he related to her— in return for Rosalind's not leaving him on the spot. Being a shrink, Rosalind firmly believed that everyone needed a therapy session at least once a week. By Matt's estimate, this would require that in the US alone, there would be more therapists than any other occupation and that the total number would come close to the population of California.

This was not the first tangle with Rosalind's jealousy or insistence on his being "honest" with her at a level beyond which most men are able to cope with. Possibly it was her highly verbal New York upbringing. Maybe it was the fact that she spent all day long dealing with seriously nutty people and this led her to see more in his actions than were there. He didn't know. As he drove back to his farm after dropping Rosalind off, he wondered if Kiren's sharp tongue might do less damage in the long run than Rosalind's continual analysis.

Later that evening with a shower and vintage wine to provide some respite from the previous few hours Matt sat watching out of the sun porch window and pondered the progress of this project, and Kiren in particular. First off, some kind of explanation or apology for the horse disaster was due her. Noting that it was late enough that Francis would have likely departed, he picked up the phone and called her at her townhouse. He was suddenly at a loss for words. Kiren didn't help matters.

"You! You are a class-A goon. Call to tease me?"

"Kiren, I am on my hands and knees. I kept trying to tell you that I like horses and you wouldn't listen. Really, I didn't mean to embarrass you. Vitz told me afterwards what he said and that was his doing. I was just entranced with Mr. Copper."

"You could have emailed or texted me that you had a horse– or something."

"Right, maybe Kobuck my horse could have friended Copper on his Facebook page. But really Mr. Copper has the smoothest rolling trot I have ever felt, really amazing!"

"You mean that?" She asked. Matt realized he had found a tender spot.

"Absolutely. I took a few English lessons a few years ago to help my Western riding. His response to my leg aids, wow, so sensitive!"

Matt and Kiren continued the mutual adoration of Mr. Copper for some time and then she asked about his horse.

"Oh, Kobuck is a 15-2 hand dunn quarter horse, from good reining lines. Very safe, lots of fun to ride. I trail ride, fox hunt, gave up reining shows when I kept being beat by 13 year old kids."

"Well, you are partially rehabilitated, but not until I see this Kobuck. For all I know it's a donkey and you don't know the difference. Good bye."

Matt finished a half bottle of wine, realizing that he had done a good bit of flying the past several days and was unlikely to be called into action immediately. He felt an attraction to Kiren, she gave him a buzz, but he suspected it was more her situation and state of vulnerability than anything else. Certainly her tongue could be patented as a lethal weapon, and might have been considered seriously in the days of star wars.

Matt had never married and was frequently at a loss to understand the group he considered to be "chromosomally challenged"– that is, lacking a Y chromosome. He had little interest in women who would consider taking his name or being content at being Mrs. Lynx. A woman needed, he felt, to be her own person, capable of making her own decisions and selecting her own hobbies. He felt little sorrow for wives who sat unhappily watching husbands play golf or watch football on TV. Why the hell, he thought, don't these women get up and go bungee jumping? Matt's first love had been a physics graduate student at Caltech who had a very sharp chiseled face, not unlike Kiren's, and had the strongest legs of any woman he had ever encountered. She spent weekends hiking in the Sierras, climbing in Yosemite, and had been known to walk male "mountain types" into mush. She was also an airframe and engine mechanic, and owned the most cobbled together, rattiest Cessna 180 he had ever seen. Since then in addition to Roland's projects he had gone off on expeditions to the Himalayas, South America, and one run to the Antarctic and these trips had interfered with holding on to long term relationships. Further, he found himself attracted to career women and insisted that their careers come first, the result of which had been several geographic rather than romantic splits.

The following afternoon, maps were spread out over the floor of the sun room, a lovely room that he had converted from a screened porch. Kiren's requirement for a site where the winter froze hard for a long period of time, and where the summer days would be as long as possible so that the plants would grow rapidly dictated two possible locations– the Yukon in Canada, or Alaska. Canada had to be excluded as creating serious troubles were they discovered. So if Alaska, then where? He called Roland and ran his thoughts past him.

"One option, and I hesitate to offer this, is my Dad's gold mine on the southern slopes of the Alaska range near Talkeetna. The advantage there is that the people know me, and there would be no suspicion if I were to tell them that I was doing some repair on the mine houses to keep them from falling apart. Further, the mine has a good southern exposure and the daylight in the summer is up 20 hours a day. Biggest advantage, I see, is the isolation and its attendant higher security."

"The disadvantage is that it's a long way to get there and the snow is not off the ground until later in May. Thus we will have to get started setting things up when the snow is still on the ground. Oh, yes, there are no roads. We'll have to fly the stuff in with a ski plane." Roland was more than happy to accept this offer.

Matt called Kiren, who was delighted and exclaimed "I'll call it the Alaska Virus!".

She had yet to visit Alaska and this seemed like a perk. Clearly she had little feeling for how cold it could get there even in May, or other minor things such as mosquitoes that had been known to carry off an entire wolf pack. She agreed that security was of prime importance, after the absolute requirement for not spreading the White Flies beyond one summer.

After some discussion as to how this might be accomplished, it was agreed that Vitz would be of great help in setting up the needed facilities, and Matt realized that if he didn't give Vitz something to do, that he might conscripted by some agency for a different task.

It was mid-March. If the Talkeetna site was not workable for some reason, a crash effort would have to be made to find another. Thus, it was imperative that Matt and Vitz make a quick trip to Talkeetna to inspect the mine.

Two days later, Vitz and Matt flew United Airlines to Chicago, and then to Anchorage, Matt's favorite routing —as it avoided the fog-bound Seattle-Tacoma airport. The 4 PM arrival also provided time for them to pick up a rental car and drive the 100 plus miles to Talkeetna.

Mid March in central Alaska is dramatic. With the full brunt of the snow remaining on the ground, there are clear, cold nights and the daylight has begun to return, so it is not all that different from the daylight periods in The States. The long blocks of sub-zero temperatures are gone, and daytime temperatures warm to 45 degrees. The road was paved and clear all the way. Matt carried on a tour-guide account of the build up of the area they were passing through.

"Before the 60's, there was no highway linking these little towns of Palmer, Willow, Talkeetna, Summit, Denali Park and so on – only the railroad. The rail line had been put in during WWII to link Anchorage and Fairbanks, and it ran up the Susitna Valley past Denali Park and on to Fairbanks. During the late 1950's the road was put in. In the old days, these little towns provided gateways for trappers to bring furs into town and to get their supplies. The railroad train would stop anywhere along the tracks to let people off and take on new passengers and their gear, so progress was tedious. In the winter, moose use the railroad tracks as paths since they are plowed and try as they can to avoid moose, the trains hit many, and moose meat fed an entire generation of school children in Anchorage."

"Talkeetna" Matt went on to say, "was where I grew up. It served several purposes. It was the farthest north town in the Susitna valley and provided the link to civilization for the trappers working the Talkeetna Mountains to the East. More importantly, there were a number of gold mines like father's in the lower elevations of the Alaska range. To get to these mines one had to cross the Susitna River from Talkeetna and traverse 20 to 50 miles of swamp– muskeg– and then climb to the mining areas. The mines were scattered here and there along the Alaska range. They were all hard rock operations. Most had been put in before the war and were just eking out a living for the operators. During the war, such mining was considered nonessential, and a lot were closed down, or the operators went off to war. After the war, the price of gold was down and the cost of re-opening the mines and replacing rusted equipment was too high for most. Some miners have continued working left over tailings and picking away, but it is not a thriving business."

"Of course" Matt continued, "as time went on, and the road was put through, it was easier for the trappers to drive to Anchorage. So Talkeetna, Willow, and the other places became even quieter. Talkeetna, however, has grown mostly due to its proximity to the south side of Mt. McKinley. For anyone who wishes to climb Mt. McKinley– and last year there were hundreds of such fools, the only practical approach is to begin at the Talkeetna airstrip, and have one of several flying services fly you, your gear, and buddies to the 7200 foot level of the Kahiltna Glacier. From there, there are a number of standard routes to the top. Flying climbers to and from the glaciers has become a major economic enterprise for Talkeetna."

They checked into the Sled Dog Motel in Talkeetna for the night, and the next morning walked over to the Talkeetna airfield where Matt spent an hour chatting with long time acquaintances. He had called ahead to arrange for one of the pilots to fly him and Vitz to the mine. He selected the pilot whom he felt was most likely to relate every word that Matt fed him to everyone in Talkeetna. Matt carefully rehearsed Vitz with the story that they were considering working on the old mine buildings the coming summer to put them into a state of repair that would make it possible to use them as overnight accommodations for hikers who might be flown in for a few days, or for hunters in the fall. There was also discussion about keeping them up or losing the structures entirely.

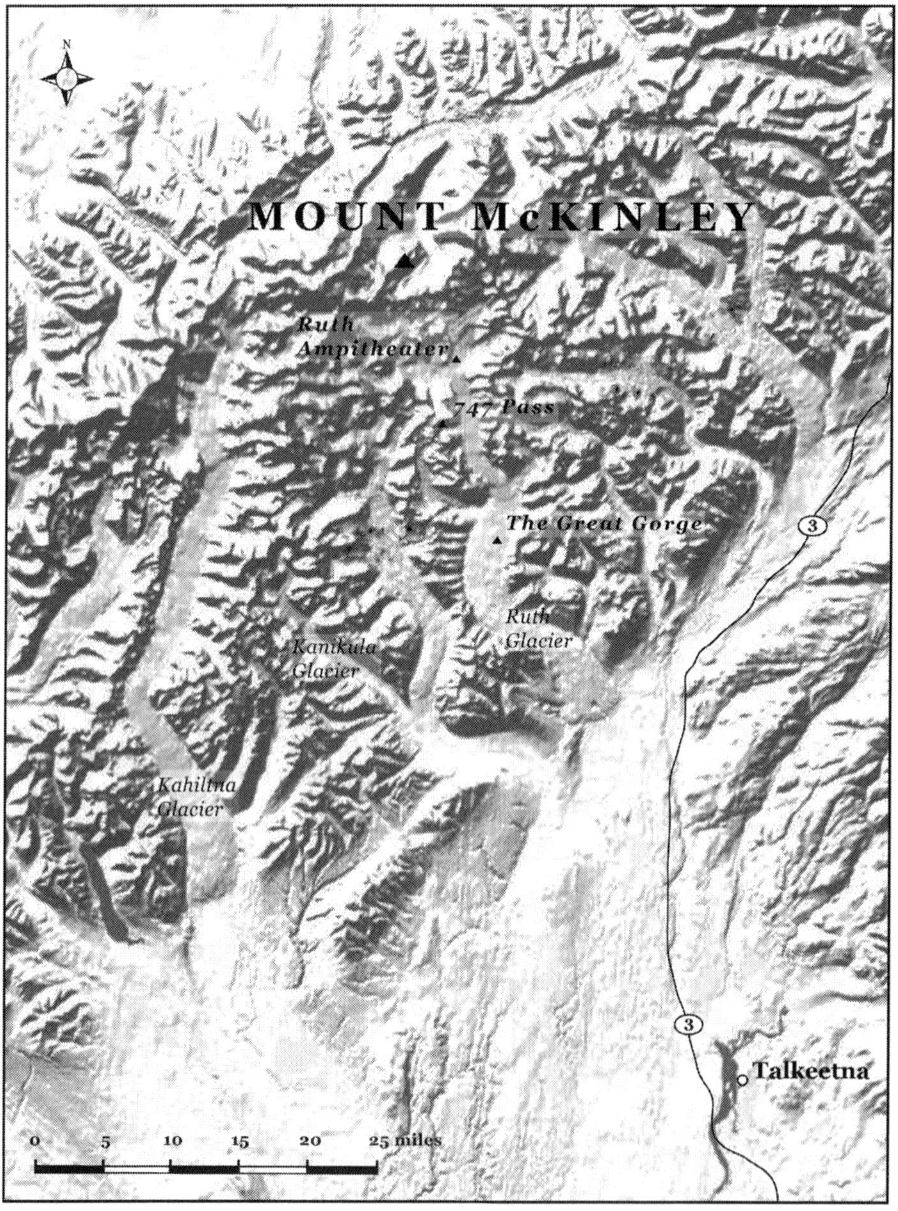

The Great Gorge

There are several flying services on the airfield, and during the summer, they compete vigorously with each other for the climbing trade, and for sightseeing flights. It did not take long to realize that one could put only a few climbers in a Cessna 185 on skis, since the huge amount of gear they bring along fills up most of the space. Further, the gear consists of sharp ice axes, skis with sharp tips, sharp ice crampons etc., etc. all of which rapidly trash the interior of the costly airplanes. Finally, one has to land on the glacier, and often this is chancy due to winds; later in the summer the snow is too soft for safe landings. It also involves considerable time unloading the climbers, and their gear, and making them feel that you (the pilot) care very much about their welfare and will be their link to the outside world. The fact is, that with the number of climbers flown in, the pilots seldom remember who is who. None of the pilots, however, relishes the job of pulling the seats out of a 185 and stacking bodies of frozen climbers in for a solemn flight back. Therefore, in a backwards way they do wish the climbers well, as they depart from the aircraft.

However, sightseeing trips from Talkeetna are much easier and they do not tax the piloting skills to the same level that landing climbers does. Further the insurance is much lower if you do not land on the glaciers and tourists will not push the air taxi operators to fly if the weather is bad. Further, they board the airplanes with only cameras, and are much easier on the aircraft. The worst that happens is the full service barf – known as power yawns. Finally, if they don't want to land on the glacier, they can use larger aircraft into which they can stuff more people.

Matt and Vitz climbed into the 185 equipped with wheel-skis. In the wheels mode, the airplane is supported by the tires, and is able to take off from a normal runway. In the air, the skis are lowered to be below the tires, allowing the 185 to land on the snow.

Since Uncle Sam would be picking up the tab for the flight, Matt suggested to Craig the pilot that they give Vitz the grand tour of the Ruth Amphitheater before heading to the mine. Matt knew that no matter how many times he made this flight himself, the feeling was always the same of awe and wonderment. Five hundred feet above the frozen muskeg, they crossed the Susitna and Squentna rivers and began the slow climb up to the beginning of the Ruth Glacier. Looking at the South Face of Mt. McKinley, they were reminded that this is the tallest mountain in the world. Not the highest– that belongs to Everest, but the tallest. If one measures the might of a mountain from where its straight-to-the-top rise begins, then Everest, K-2, and others in the Himalayas are small mountainlets that begin from a plateau of nearly 17,000 feet. McKinley begins its rise on the south side from only 1000 feet elevation, and thus can claim nearly 19,000 feet of sheer height. As one looks at the south face of this wall, there is an opening from which the Ruth Glacier spills. On either side of the glacier are rock walls, with sheer vertical faces thousands of feet high. As they entered this canyon, known as "The Great Gorge," the glacier was several miles wide, but as they ascended, the walls hanging with snow steadily came together.

Within The Great Gorge, it appeared that the rock walls would pinch the glacier off entirely, but suddenly they opened to reveal the Ruth Amphitheater. They were at The Gateway of the Amphitheater. The Gateway is guarded on the east by the Moose's Tooth, and on the west by The Rooster's Comb, Pittlock and 747 passes. The peak of McKinley lies to the northwest, and can also be reached from the south via an approach beginning on the great Kahiltna Glacier. The Ruth Amphitheater is several miles wide and its floor is relatively flat. At its end, rock walls rise uncontested to over 20,000 feet. Within the Amphitheater, is a rock and ice outcropping, and Craig flew over to show Vitz a tiny wooden cabin perched there. Don Sheldon, the most famous of the earlier generation of Mt. McKinley air guides, had ferried all of the wood there in his ski plane, and had constructed the cabin for reasons that only his ghost could explain.

Leaving the Amphitheater, they flew down the Ruth Glacier to its end, where the ice is black due to a layer of rocks and dirt forced over the moving glacial front. They then flew 15 miles to the west around the base of the Tokositna Mountains, past the black ice of the Tokositna Glacier, and then north up a small green valley to the beginning of the Kanikula Glacier where the mine was located. Craig buzzed the site several times before setting up for a carefully controlled descent. He had no idea how soft the snow would be, or how deep it was, and were he to plop the airplane down too hard, it might become buried to its wing tips or worse, do a tail-over-nose flip. Craig's expertise was, for Matt, a delight to watch as they skimmed the snow in the flat area just below the mine one time to fluff the snow up a bit, and then came around for another look— and finally on the third loop, a full landing to a stop. Craig swung the airplane so that it stopped, resting on the packed ski tracks it had just created.

The Kanikula valley is about five miles long. At its mouth it is several miles wide but narrows to a mile or less across when one reaches the glacier. From then on the glacier fills the valley as it rises upwards to where it begins high on the frontal slopes of Mt. McKinley. Below the glacier, the valley floor is flat, smoothed by a giant earth moving machine— the retreating glacier. The ridges on either side that create the valley are steep and covered by grasses and alder brush. The Kanikula River is a small stream by most standards and flows from the glacier down the middle of the valley. Eventually as the valley widens and the ridges come to and end, the river breaks up and part of it is channeled into ponds created by over-active beaver.

The glacier itself is one of the blackest glaciers on the entire McKinley mastiff. Black ice results from rocks and dirt falling down onto the ice from the mountain slopes on either side of the glacier. Here, for a series of geologic reasons much more rock than usual finds its way onto the ice creating a very black glacier. At the face of the glacier, a rush of milky water emerges from under the ice – the beginning of the Kanikula River. The river is strongest in the summer when the sun heats the black rocks and in turn helps melt the ice.

The mine was just inside the present expanded boundary of Denali park. When the mine had been put in, it was not and thus Matt's family had been allowed to retain ownership and use of the mine as long as it did not do any damage to the environment. It had been sited on the floor of the valley but tight against the ridge on the East. This steep ridge separates the Kanicula valley from the adjoining larger Ruth Glacier and its valley. The river at that point had changed its path so often that it had left behind a series of straight, dry gravel strips one of which Matt had improved just enough so that a skilled pilot in a tail wheel bush plane could land and take off. He had purposely not improved or lengthened it to an extent that would have allowed entrée to any nose wheel airplane or one piloted by weekend pilots from Anchorage.

Snow shoes on, Matt and Vitz tromped to the mine house and spent several hours discussing what would be needed to make the place habitable, and how they could create a greenhouse out of a large adjoining building that houses equipment. Matt shot lots of digi-photos to provide memory jogs and details for the plans to be be worked out later. He was surprised to find the door open and nearly torn off of its hinges. The interior near the door was in worse shambles than he had remembered.

The mine house was large and sturdy, having been constructed from half-round timbers sawn at the mill in Talkeetna and sledded to the mine in the winter. There were a number of rooms opening to a central eating and living area heated by an oil stove. The roof was still intact, having been repaired a number of times, the last of which added galvanized corrugated metal over a layer of tar paper.

Modern amenities were lacking. The hard rocky ground made septic systems impossible, and none of the former inhabitants, in particular Matt's father, had been interested in states-side plumbing. Thus, there were several outhouses placed here and there 100 to 200 feet from the main house. There was a crude shower, constructed by someone needing to vent his creative instincts. It consisted of a 50 gallon oil barrel with an oil heater under it. From the barrel emerged a pipe with a hand carved wooden shower head. There was no choice of water temperature, other than how long one heated the water.

They concluded that this would do quite well although a good deal of reconstruction was needed, including patching the roof, and the oil stoves required cleaning. The relevant model numbers on the stoves were recorded so that new burners and injectors could be ordered. In all, Matt was jubilant and Vitz seemed elated at anything that would get him out of North Carolina even if it took him away from The Hole. On the flight back, as Vitz was looking elsewhere, Matt cut Vitz' headset out of the 3-way intercom and suggested to Craig that since Vitz would be coming ahead of the others, and would be alone, that a few comments from Craig as to the high concentration of hungry polar bears in the area would be appropriate (the only polar bear within 1500 miles lived in the Anchorage Zoo, and was well fed). Vitz' headset cut back on, Matt leaned back in the right seat of the 185 to smile to himself, and add little comments about polar bears being invisible as soon as they move from the rocky areas back onto the snow fields.

Back in The States Matt spent a few days making out orders for lumber, stove parts, plastic sheeting, and several 50 gallon drums of oil to be delivered to Talkeetna. He had no trouble arranging for one of the aircraft mechanics who owned a large snow tractor to take the materials on a sled across the frozen rivers to the mine. This needed to be done before the river broke up and to be there when Vitz arrived mid-April.

Kiren had had her typical over-stressed week and was not receptive to Matt's long discussion over the telephone as to how beautiful the spring snows on McKinley were, but did lighten up a bit when he described Craig's description (for Vitz' benefit) of the ability of polar bears to undress a victim slowly boot-by -boot, shirt, and then pants without so much as drawing a spot of blood prior to chowing down on dinner. This odd behavior, Craig had explained, was due to their dislike of eating seal skin.

Kiren agreed that having a hundred coca plants moved to Alaska mid-May would fit her experimental schedule.

"How the Hell we are supposed to do this in secret is beyond me. If Roland ships them to Alaska, then everyone and their mother is going to know what we are up to. If he delivers them to me here, there is the problem of getting them past Canadian customs." Matt complained.

There were several other complications Matt had realized would come up. One was how to explain a several month disappearance to their respective laboratories. For Matt, this was more easily accomplished. He did little teaching, and none in the summer. Further, like many molecular biologists in medical schools, he traveled a great deal. He frequently packed up samples and spent a month or two in the laboratory of a colleague in France carrying out analyses that were more easily done there than back home. Matt's students and fellows were used to such disappearances and took care of the day to day problems when he was gone. Kiren, however, was still running her lab by herself and had not begun to delegate responsibilities to her students or technicians.

Thus some contact with them would be required. Kiren did not teach in the summer either, and would explain to her chairman and students that in return for the grant funds (her chairman was mildly curious over the non-traditional source of support), she was to spend the summer traveling and collecting plant samples for later analysis. Thus she would be calling back, but likely would not have any address where she could be reached. This ruse seemed to satisfy Kiren, but Matt wasn't sure how to deal with phone calls back to North Carolina in a way that would avoid their being traced even from satellite phones. He did not trust communication lines linked to outer space.

Kiren dropped the demand Matt had been fearing. There was a major A show mid-summer in Raleigh, and Kiren insisted that Mr. Copper had to be shown and she wanted to ride herself. Further she needed to be able to email back routinely to check on the care and progress of Mr. Copper. Matt gave the appearance of acquiescence while realizing that once Kiren was in Alaska he would be at the advantage in the negotiations.

Kiren felt it would be imperative she do some experimental work on site in Alaska, including a series of infections with the final engineered variations of the new virus. Matt added up what would be needed; it didn't seem that much. They would have a generator, a cold room would not be needed as the outside air temperature would be cool even in the summer, and there would be local snow fields for ice. Possibly a few gel electrophoresis boxes, power supplies, and a handful of small instruments would do. Fortunately she would package up her boxes of DNA primer fragments, not knowing how important they would become.

The following week for Matt was spent working hard in the lab himself testing samples for possible traces of a new Herpes virus. His own research area had to do with trying to identify new human viruses that might be responsible for common human diseases such as arthritis or muscular dystrophy. Kiren was on his mind a lot, and that bothered him. In spite of her way of dealing with men, and Matt in particular, he felt a certain closeness to her he knew he could never have with Rosalind, or for that matter, any woman who was not a scientist. It was as if the two of them were refugees from some great conflagration. It was a common language they shared which Rosalind didn't speak. Also, like it or not, he found her extremely sexy. But it took more than speaking French and a nice ass to make a love affair, Matt told himself.

Checking with Kiren on the progress of her work, it had come a long way. It would not be long until Kiren advanced to the final step in which she would place the targeting sequences back into the engineered DNA and shotgun these into plants. This would be a critical test since seeing severe lesions appear in some of the plants would be her first major biological test of her "killer virus" construction. Friends at the University of Bogota had sent several vials of White Fly eggs and she had grown up 20 milk bottles of these flies. This work would be done in Alaska and she was getting anxious for Matt to acquire the plants from Roland and move them to Alaska so that they would be ready for her in time. She and Matt both assumed that since there had been no indications of anyone trying to stop them, that Roland had squelched the rumors and they would have free sailing the rest of the way. This was not to be the case.

The news had been worrisome enough for Raul that he had dispatched his personal lieutenant, Estaban, to tail Kiren and find out one way or the other what she was doing. Raul strongly suspected that if she was engaged in work with coca plant viruses that she must be growing them somewhere and that Estaban could follow her to the site. Estaban knew the plants well. In addition, he was a skilled observer. He was born in Colombia of a merchant family, and learned English from a Pakistani house keeper hired to take care of the children. It was amusing that Estaban, a dark skinned South American with strong Inca blood, spoke fluent English but sounded as if he were one of Ghandi's followers. Estaban had fallen into bad company, and been involved as a driver for a Cartel soldier who machine gunned a judge. After that, he had little choice but to accept their employment. He also enjoyed the cat and mouse games they played with the Colombian authorities. The number of "jobs" he had undertaken for the Cartel had gotten so large that the Cartel had moved him to Cancun to allow his trail to cool. Further, his fluent, albeit odd, English was useful since he was able to pass himself off as any of a number of nationalities other than South American.

Estaban's first two weeks watching Kiren defined boredom. Her time table was predictable, as she rose early, ran for a half an hour, went to the lab, and after dinner, back to the lab. Three evenings a week and Saturday midday she drove to the stable to ride. Saturday evenings appeared reserved for the same well dressed man and Estaban assumed that it was not necessary to trail the two of them, as it was unlikely that she would take him picking coca leaves. However one afternoon Kiren disappeared and only returned to her townhouse late. He had no idea where she had been.

Estaban stepped up his surveillance. He broke into the departmental greenhouse and spent the night, flashlight in hand, looking for coca plants. None were found. He next took a bigger chance and broke into her labs at night and searched the cold rooms, her refrigerator, and freezers for anything labeled coca or cocaine virus or the like. Nothing here either so he copied all the files on the students computers onto a portable USB drive. Looking at the files later most were in Chinese characters or related to communication with the US immigration lawyers helping with H1 visa applications.

A few days later Kiren again disappeared in her Wagoneer midday returning only late at night. This bothered Estaban as he suspected that she might have some hidden laboratory at another location.

Estaban had too much to drink and was feeling unwisely bold. He slipped into her townhouse that night as Kiren slept to plant a phone bug to monitor her calls from her Bell telephone line and a WiFi transmitter to monitor her emails from her computer. As he finished installing the phone bug, it triggered the phone to ring, which startled him causing him to drop his flashlight– which on hitting the floor, turned on. He bolted through the door feeling that it was better to be gone, than to risk being seen, and he left the area for the rest of the night.

Kiren was frightened and after a visit by the police, she called Matt whom she had begun to rely on more and more, for moral support. Matt quizzed her in detail. Kiren had previously mentioned that someone broke into the departmental greenhouse, but that had not led Kiren or Matt to link it directly to her. She went on to say that in addition, her graduate students had complained that one morning it seemed as if someone had ransacked their freezers and notebooks.

Matt told Kiren that they would have to assume she was being watched, and that she should take great care to be sure that she was not being followed when she left the area.

Kiren's trips of the past week were to Southern Pines where Mr. Copper was being schooled by a visiting dressage master from Vienna. As the roads are mostly two lanes, it was a simple matter to pull over at a gas station now and then, and to watch who comes by, or note anyone refusing to pass. Half way to Southern Pines and three pull overs, it was clear that a blue sedan with a stocky Mexican-looking man was either following her or was afraid of passing a Jeep Wagoneer. Fearing what might happen if she was forced over along the roads which ran through open country, she turned around and returned to Duke. Shaken, she called Matt and related the episode. Matt was concerned, but felt she might have been imagining things, and suggested the next day she repeat the experiment.

Kiren did as told, and in almost an exact replay, the same stocky man followed her. Whether he realized he was being watched himself, or he assumed she was in need of stopping at a lot at gas station rest rooms, was unclear. Again, half way to Southern Pines and before the unpopulated stretch, she turned around and drove back to the lab.

Fearing for Kiren's safety, Matt told her to stay overnight with Francis, and he would see her the next morning. Kiren did so using an excuse of broken water pipes.

The next morning, Matt flew The Moose Gooser straight to RDU airport, a now routine 2 hour flight. After calming her a bit, and out of her sight, he checked his Army issue 45 auto, a Remington. The two of them got into Kiren's Wagoneer and took her usual route toward Southern Pines. It did not take long to pick up a blue sedan and its dark-skinned driver.

Matt suggested they continue until he had formulated a plan. Several circular courses verified the blue car was attached to them like a nun to a crucifix. Matt smiled to himself and directed Kiren to Ft. Bragg. Nearing The Hole, he told Kiren to park in front, that the two of them would go in the front door, but as soon as she was inside, she was to duck into the Woman's room near the door and to wait until she heard a ruckus break out, then count to 100, and dash to the car.

They slowed to allow their tail to get close, then parked the Wagoneer, and strolled inside. Once inside, Kiren ducked into the women's john.

Estaban strode in, assuming this was just one more bar peopled by typical American soldiers.

Matt came up quickly behind him and yelled:

"This guy told me that he worked for Al qaeda. Says he loved to shoot Green Berets, since he always killed 2 with a single bullet. Says Green Berets were always paired-up screwing each other."

Matt pulled Kiren along as they exited, stuffed her into the Wagoneer and sped off. Eventually, Estaban unconscious, sporting bruises head to toe was deposited outside after one of The Hole's owners threatened to call the MPs unless the crowd stopped pounding him. Driving away, Matt and Kiren discussed what this meant.

"Matt, this scared the hell out of me. But it also makes me mad. I am even more determined to continue, but I don't want you or anyone I'm close to getting hurt on my account."

"Don't worry, Roland has an insurance policy on my head. Whoever that character was, he was hired to follow you. What this means to me is some people, and from his looks I would guess someone in the South American drug business, got wind of what you were up to, but they don't have any evidence either. If they did, you would certainly have heard from them in a much more in-your-face way by now. Hopefully that guy won't be tailing you for a while."

"So, what do we do?"

"What we do is rid your lab of anything that has the words cocaine, or coca attached to it. I'll get Roland to secure an encoded satellite phone from your lab to mine and we can talk that way. We need to step up the time table for moving things to Alaska. Roland says the coca plants are ready to be dug up and shipped. I'll see if I can get them pronto and fly to Alaska. It's time we put Vitz to work as a farmer anyhow. As soon as I get back it will take me a few weeks to arrange things. After that we can get the hell out of town. Once we are there, only the polar bears will know what we are doing. So, can you hold on for three, four weeks at the most? I want to hear from you each and every day to be sure you are OK. "

"Jesus that's not much time, but being shadowed by Odd Job is no fun either. I may live in the lab but I should be ready."

Matt drove on and certain they were not being followed, turned toward Southern Pines, knowing Kiren was anxious to see Mr. Copper. He kept thinking of various schemes for getting the coca plants into Alaska with the least chance of getting caught.

Vitz had been in Alaska for several weeks. He had moved to the mine at Kanikula since soon there would be a full month during which it would be difficult to get there. That was when the snow at the mine becomes too soft to land ski planes, and the river ice is too thin to cross with a snow machine –and too icy for boats. Not until enough snow is gone would Craig be able to land a wheel plane equipped with large balloon tundra tires. They couldn't wait that late to get the renovations started.

Late April and early May in Anchorage is a mix of flowers, and a great deal of mud. Mud, mud, mud– everywhere. The melting snows create pools of water, and the saturated ground turns to mud. Although some parts of Anchorage had taken on a semi-cultivated appearance, the majority of the city still had the frontier appearance in which there was nothing out of the ordinary about seeing a $500,000 house whose landscaping consists of 2 tractor trailers parked in the front yard and several rusted air boats beside them. At the mine, the break up had yet to arrive, and although the daytime temperatures, warmed by the long hours of sun, were reaching into the 50s, the nights were well below freezing, and the possibility of an early May blizzard was real.

Craig had picked up Vitz in Anchorage and they drove to Talkeetna. Several flights were required to get all the gear to the mine. On the last flight, Craig took Vitz along with a major haul of Jim Beam whiskey. Vitz had perused the Anchorage bars and environs, and noted that one major plus for Anchorage over North Carolina, was the nearly 10:1 ratio of liquor stores to churches– a ratio that Vitz felt was a very accurate descriptor of the quality of life. Rural North Carolina, on the other hand, had a ratio that approached zero, and for Vitz, this described his feeling about rural North Carolina.

After Craig departed Talkeetna with Vitz and this cargo of Beam, he edged the discussion around to polar bears, asking if he had taken sufficient armament. Yes indeed, Vitz had his .243 semiautomatic. Craig rolled his eyes.

"Better file the front sight off before you encounter a bear."

Why is that? Vitz asked.

"Cause it won't hurt as much when he shoves it up your ass!" Was the reply.

For Alaskans such as Matt and Craig, guns are simply tools of life— different guns for different needs. If one was ambling about looking for rabbits or spruce hens for dinner– an extremely tasty and stupid bird, then a .22 pistol is ideal and provides more sport than a shotgun. If on the other hand, one is hunting for medium game such as caribou, Dall sheep, or mountain goats, then a high velocity caliber such as a .270 or .300 in a magnum such as the Weatherby rifle equipped with a 10 power scope will bring down game over distances up to 300 yards and often farther. If however, one is concerned over protection from large bears, or if one is hunting them, a different gun is called for. Stopping a large bear requires a much larger punch– at least a .300 Weatherby, and preferably something in a .375 magnum.

Remembering why he had begun the line of discussion, he reminded Vitz that it would be a number of weeks before the polar bears come out of hibernation. It was when the snow patches are scattered about with dirt in between, that he would have to start watching.

Craig left Vitz, the .243, a pair of snowshoes, boxes of Beam, and flew back, reminding Vitz that the month during which it would be difficult get in was just weeks away. Vitz had been given a King KX99 hand held aircraft radio and Craig promised that he would fly over now and then, and all Vitz had to do was contact him on the frequency of 122.95, or if there was an emergency, 122.6. Vitz had a satellite phone as well which he used to call Matt.

As Craig departed, Vitz felt very much alone, surrounded by the pile of equipment left by the snow cat, and the ice cold mine buildings. He had survived for weeks by himself in South American jungles and there was no reason that he would have any problems here. If he, Vitz, had eluded fer d'lance snakes, poisonous bugs, and an occasional jaguar, why worry about a mere polar bear? His problem of the day was to shovel out the mine house of all of the debris, get the oil barrels in, and the stoves rebuilt. The next several days were not that bad. It remained below freezing most of the time, a bit cooler than usual for that time of the year, and Vitz was able to spend the time getting the oil stoves running, clearing out the equipment shed, and beginning to build long wooden boxes for the plants.

Three days later, the break-up hit in full force. At this time of the year the sun is up for nearly 12 hours and the temperature rise into the 50s. This triggered a melt of the 6 feet of snow that had accumulated on the roof of the mine buildings. Its mass kept the melting water from running off the roof as rain water would. Instead, the ice water had no other route of escape than to drain down through cracks, and into the building.

Vitz had lived through hurricanes in Belize, but this time, the rain defined ice cold. There was no way to get away from it, and finally Vitz fled the buildings, a bottle of Beam in hand, and sat staring at the torrent of water. He realized he might have to accept an endless cold shower. As the sun dropped behind The Mountain (Mt. McKinley is known by the locals simply as "The Mountain"), he re-entered.

Everything was wet: his clothes, his sleeping bag, everything. The oil stove was popping and sizzling, as the rain from the roof fell onto the hot surface. He had a water-proof jacket and began to imagine living in it for the next month. He wondered if this was why Matt had included a tent in the roster of equipment. He pitched the tent with its opening close to the oil stove, and did his best to dry out the soggy sleeping bag before retreating into the tent for the night. The following morning, he decided that removing the snow from the roof would stop the internal rain shower, but the roof was so steep, and covered by very slick corrugated metal, that it was impossible to get up onto it. Finally a make-shift scoop on a pole was fashioned, and slowly the snow was pulled from the roof. Each scoop he pulled off came straight at him and though many were dodged, those that were not resulted in his remaining wet and cold all day. Finally, by the end of the day most of the snow had been pulled down and the rain fall inside the main house had diminished to a trickle. That night he again slept in the tent and the following day the equipment building was cleared of snow.

Feeling good about his accomplishments, and the warm sun urging him to be out, Vitz tromped a path to a large beaver pond down the valley from the mine. The pond was still frozen, and the ice appeared to be several feet thick along the shore. Vitz walked several hundred feet out onto the pond before suddenly plunging downwards as if a man being hanged. His fall was stopped by a solid footing of ice so that he found himself standing in water up to his waist. Above the water, was a two foot thick layer of snow, so that his head and arms were all that were in the air. He had discovered overflow.

When a lake or pond freezes in the winter, the ice forms a barrier to any water that later might flow out onto it from creeks or melting snow in the spring. This water will build up on top of the ice, lifting the overlaying snow up to generate a sandwich of snow, water, and then below it, solid ice covering the lake. This water is called overflow and can be several feet deep in the spring. Overflow is kept from freezing by the insulating effect of the snow.

As Vitz struggled, he only succeeded in breaking through the crusted snow and plunged again and again into the overflow. He realized that if he was not able to get back to the shore before the sun went down, he would freeze, or die of hypothermia. Jumping as high as he could, and out away from the hole he had created, he managed to flop prone onto the snow and spread his weight out. This time he stayed on the top of the snow. Doing something that resembled a breast stroke, Vitz slowly moved over the surface of the snow back to shore, then ran soaking wet back to the mine house.

He sat by the oil stove shivering, feeling very much alone and wishing for an immediate re-assignment to the FARC infested jungles of Columbia.

The following days brought more warm weather, and slowly spots of bare ground were beginning to appear. Craig flew by once every several days and Vitz was cheered by their brief chats on the radio. Craig breached the subject of polar bears one afternoon during his fly-by.

"I say, Vitz", Craig radioed, "recall the polar bears? They hibernate most of the winter— start coming out when the ground is half bare and half covered by snow— better start keeping an eye out. When they are just out, they are mighty hungry. Also remember they disappear when they move onto the snow." Craig chuckled and signed off.

Vitz began carrying the .243 with him continually, and searched the snow for any evidence of bear tracks. None were found, but this gave him little reason to feel safer.

A week later, Craig flew by sporting tundra tires on a souped-up 180 horse power Piper Super Cub and buzzed several times looking over a patch of bare ground below the mine house to see if it might be long enough to land. On the radio he asked Vitz if it was firm, and got a positive reply. Craig landed, and they chatted a bit before he flew out. Vitz offered to pay him to pick up his mail at Talkeetna.

Craig returned the next day in the Super Cub with Vitz' mail, and in the back seat were his 'bear paws' created by his son from an old bear rug the dogs had torn apart. The rear paws had been glued to the bottom of a pair of tennis shoes and the front paws to a pair of gloves. The problem was how to utilize this to the best effect. After handing over the mail, Craig asked Vitz to hike to the top of the hill above the mine and to photograph him as he took off. Climbing, Vitz would face away from Craig for at least 15 minutes. This gave time for Craig to create a trail of bear tracks that ambled back and forth across the snow. Smiling to himself, he lifted the Cub off as Vitz photographed his departure.

It wasn't until the next morning that Vitz discovered the evidence of polar bear incursions. The tracks were enormous and fresh. It was difficult to determine where they had come from and in particular, where they had gone. Vitz retreated to the mine house and from then on, spent a great deal of each day watching the snow fields, and constructing elaborate tin can alarms rigged together with string. Often as not, the wind or marmots who were beginning to appear around the mine triggered the alarm, which brought Vitz to his feet, rifle in hand, looking this way and that.

Back in North Carolina Matt and Kiren were working frantically to finish and move the plants to the mine.

CHAPTER NINE
SMUGGLING COCA PLANTS INTO ALASKA

Matt phoned Roland to ask about the plants.

"Matt, we have a secured coca field in Peru that will provision you with a hundred and fifty small plants. All switch covers are off. You push the big red button and they will be dug up, potted, and put on a military plane. Where do you want them delivered?"

"That, Roland, is the thousand dollar question. The most convenient place would be Elmendorf Air Force base in Anchorage, but there are too many eyes up there, and once my face was linked to a bunch of dope plants, we might as well take an ad out in the local paper for people to work on dope viruses and give your phone number. Equally worse would be Raleigh/Durham airport since that might link them to Kiren if someone saw what was going on. I think the best place is your backyard."

"I'm rationally challenged."

"Well of sorts. Have the plane fly into Andrews Air Force base. They can pull into a secured hangar and load the plants into a van. If they have a radio in the car I can give them directions where to meet me. There are a number of private airfields nearby in Virginia I can use. Does that sound reasonable?"

Matt asked Roland to give him several days to make arrangements for members of his lab to care for his house and pets for 10 days while he ferried the plants to Alaska. Rosalind was nearly hysterical over Matt's concern for Kiren's safety and was calmed only by having Kiren herself explain to Ros that she, Kiren, was not going anywhere with Matt– in the immediate future. This cost Matt many credits with Kiren. Although Kiren may have only 100 nerve endings for personal feelings (to Rosalind's 1000), she was nonetheless a woman, and sensed that Rosalind was not pleased over Matt's involvement with her and understood that this could, in the future, be used to her advantage. Rosalind had pushed Matt close to the breaking point as to where he would be. Matt would not tell – for Rosalind's own good, since he had learned before that if you are going to disappear – leave as few trails as possible.

Rosalind's birthday fell on the day before he was to leave and Matt had arranged for them to spend the evening together. Matt was still being "rehabilitated" in Rosalind's terminology for the Drosophila genetics scam. She had related his Fidelity gene story to a friend whose husband was a biochemist and several weeks earlier she stormed into Matt's house furious. Indeed Matt felt some remorse but refused to admit that it was not funny. Rehabilitation involved two weeks during which he was made to think that she was out of his life for good, followed by his depositing a series of expensive baubles at her doorstep. Doing this, he felt like a male penguin leaving shiny rocks for the female. The evening was to be spent cooking dinner together and sampling several fine wines.

Ros arrived wearing all black. As soon as she sat down, Matt's 22 pound neutered Maine Coon tomcat "Loqui" headed for her lap. Loqui was the Norse god of chaos and the cat was aptly named as his long white fur created a cloud that surrounded him. Matt proclaimed Loqui to be a "self-propelled pillow". Ros was not fond of cats and could see no use for something whose sole purpose was to describe three points on a triangle: the food bowl, the litter box, and the spot d' jour for sleeping. Why not just pour the cat food directly into the litter box and dispense with the cat?

Ros yelled "no" as Loqui landed in her lap.

"Get this creature off of me! Oh god, look at my dress!" Smiling and stroking Loqui, Matt moved the self-propelled pillow to a window ledge.

"Ros, you may not know it, but Loqui is an honorary Lynx, and in the wild Arctic, lynx stalk and eat little bunnies like you. Its just in his blood – don't blame him." He took a more serious tact before she could snap at him.

"I know you don't like my going away on these little episodes, and that you are unhappy about my not being able to communicate with you. But this trip is short, a week, and later it won't be more than a couple of months, possibly six weeks. I'll call if I can, and when I get this project of Roland's out of my hair, I will consider resigning from his employ."

"Your body language is not signaling openness. Quit shuffling your feet and look at me! Now tell me exactly who is going to be there and where you will be. Are you planning to sleep with this Kiren Person?"

Matt hated this body language attack since there was no defending himself in the court of Ros.

"Tacky, tacky, Ros, I never said that Kiren would be along, it's possible she will not or that she will be moved elsewhere. I told you before I can't reveal details."

"I have a long case load of paranoid schizos who really believe that they work for the CIA and time to time they have to go away.

Some really think they are off to the moon or Venus. Most opt for some nasty little Central American country. How do I know that you are going anywhere? Maybe you are just more clever than my typical screwball of the day."

"You caught me, but seriously, you've met Roland. Is he a figment?"

"No, even you couldn't dream up a chubby choclaholic with buggy eyes and a leer. Back to Kiren. Is this Vitz creature going? What about her boyfriend, what does he think about all of this? I didn't think that women were allowed on these secret projects."

"They aren't. She'll be towed behind our submarine in a dingy."

"Ah Ha! So she will be there."

"Jesus, Ros I was just joking."

"Then quit shuffling your feet and joking. Jokes are just your boy-child defense mechanism. Look straight in my eyes and tell me what you are up to."

"I told you I can't do that, and the more you push the less I am going to say. It's for you own welfare."

"Screw my welfare, you lie. In fact, you are a man, you lie all the time. It's clear that you and this Kiren Person are going somewhere alone and for all I know it may have nothing to do with Roland."

"Well all right, here's the story. It's a matter of great concern to our national pride, and involves the underworld. It also has to do with genetic engineering and that is why Kiren and I are involved. You see, several years ago, world class wrestling on Saturday morning TV began to be dominated by huge creatures twice the size of other wrestlers and they were four times as strong. They all came from Siberia. Well, about 6 months ago the officials began to require that the wrestlers be tested for HIV virus since they often bite each other. Well, one of the "Siberian" types tested positive. But not for HIV, rather for SIV which is the monkey version of HIV. That made Roland suspicious that the Russians were experimenting with transgenic animals. In this case they may have moved the genes for hairless skin and light skin color into Gorillas, and –"

"Oh, God Damn you, give me a straight story or nothing at all!"

Thus went the following two hours while Matt cooked and they ate dinner. Rosalind's patience was coming to an end and Matt was just hoping to get through dinner. Finally she blurted out:

"I still haven't been able to feel what's inside you, my love. I just want to know what you plan vis a vis you and me when you return. Why don't we just write out a promise here and now that this is the last project and you will never speak to this Kiren Person after you get back. What about getting married? The clock of my child bearing years is going to clang midnight soon. Don't you want to have a little Matt Jr.?"

Matt could clearly see where Ros was headed. Deciding that desert had better wait, he smiled and responded:

"OK, OK. But first a little game. It's called where or where are my birthday presents? The first clue is close at hand."

"What do you mean?"

"Today is your birthday, right? I hid a few things here and there in the house. Your job, if you want your presents, is to find the clues. Each present will have a clue leading to the next."

This was, Matt realized, the only way to divert Ros's questioning and he was pleased with himself that he had had the foresight to set up this little game.

The first clue was under Ros's plate and led to a cabinet that contained a wrapped box with a set of earrings. The second clue took longer and more wine to figure out. It led to the hot tub and a plastic bag at the bottom containing a bottle of perfume. From there, the search moved upstairs and turned up a hat she had admired one Saturday when they were shopping. She was stumped over the last clue.

"To find your final present, you must use a mirror to view your most private view."

Rosalind finally did as instructed and went to the bedroom, finding a hand held mirror. She then sat on the bed and shook her head.

"I don't get this, the clue says it's on my privates."

Anxious to find what Matt said was her major present, Ros began removing her clothing and finally with only bra and panties remaining, she turned to Matt.

"Turn your head now, I can't believe that I'll find anything."

She turned the mirror to view her bottom and in black letters were two words which Matt had painted in ink in reverse on the seat of the toilet she used when she visited. The words read: "under covers".

Giggling, Ros dove for the bed, threw the covers away, and found a wrapped box. Ignoring the fact that she was nearly naked, the wrapping was quickly dispatched to reveal an elegant turquoise bracelet Matt found in Santa Fe. Ros turned around and pulled Matt to her, kissed him and laughed. She realized that this game had been carefully orchestrated for her delight and his, but at this moment wearing only the bracelet, she looked forward to the rest of the game.

Ros pulled Matt's clothes off and poured the small remaining amount of wine on his back as an ointment while sitting naked on top of him and administered a back rub. He was eventually allowed to rotate around and deliver his final birthday present which she had been given numerous times before but always seemed to delight in, anew.

As Ros lay relaxed on the bed she asked: "Matt, if I agree to marry you will you tell me how you got that scar on your chin?"

"Ah, this already sounds like a trick question. But I told you, I fell asleep during a therapy session with my shrink and tumbled forward onto her bust of Sigmund Freud playing a violin. Impaled on the brass bow." He was smothered with a pillow.

The next morning Matt stripped the airplane interior of everything except the pilot's seat, and removed the rudder pedals and steering wheel on the right so that the airplane could be filled with as many plants as possible, while not risking the possibility that if the load shifted, it would jam the controls, sending Matt and the cargo into some unwanted aerobatics. A 185 emptied of its extra seats, and minus gas, will take off with 1300 pounds of weight, and pushing it, Matt figured 1500, in particular in the colder Alaskan air. He subtracted the weight of 80 gallons of fuel (6 pounds per gallon amounts to 480 pounds). This left almost 900 pounds he could carry. He constructed a wooden deck of 1/4 inch plywood so that two levels of plants would fit inside. Matt had done one more thing and that was to cover over his aircraft identification numbers with duct tape so that if they were spotted transferring the plants into his airplane, he could not be easily traced. Contacting Roland, he confirmed that as planned, the military airplane had arrived late the previous night, and that the plants had been transferred to an unmarked van ready to roll at his call. Roland gave Matt the frequency for the radio and his blessings.

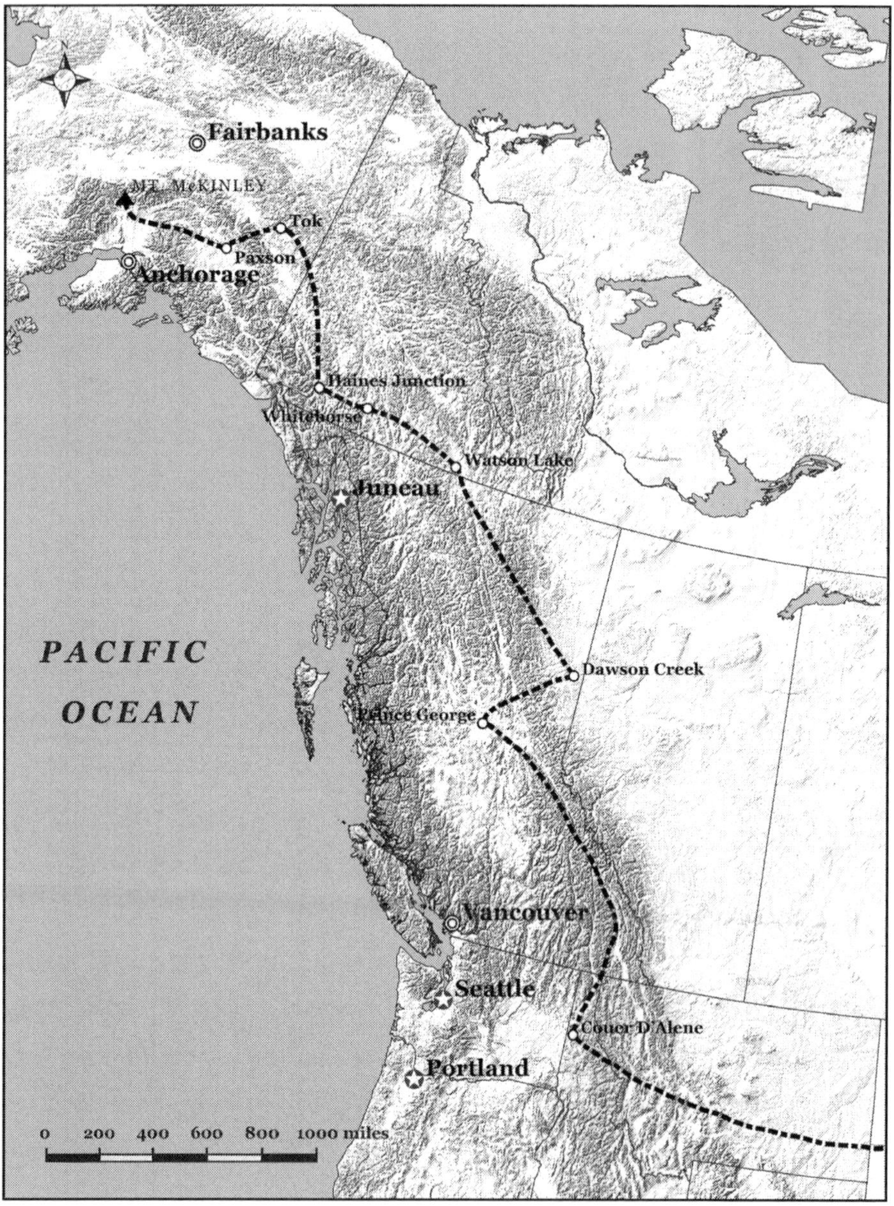

Matt took off from the private strip where he kept the Moose Gooser and flew a short distance at low elevation under the local radar coverage to a private strip near the Airy House in Virginia. In the air he contacted the soldier driving the van and gave him instructions to the Airy House strip. Transfer took less than a half an hour and he was just able to accommodate the 150 plants plus a box of bottles containing the White Flies Kiren had grown. Weighing everything, it came in a good bit under his allowed gross weight.

His plan was to fly high, straight, and on an IFR (instrument flight rules) flight plan from North Carolina to somewhere near Spokane in eastern Washington. His fuel stops would be at airports where he could pull up to a pump and fill The Moose Gooser himself. This would require two long days. The first day took him to Madison, Wisconsin where he stayed with a biochemist friend. The second day was a delight, being clear and VFR (visual flight rules) all the way, even though he remained on an instrument plan. On an IFR plan, the air controllers with radar coverage have some responsibility to watch out for other airplanes around you, making the flight more relaxed.

As he crossed the Dakotas, and into Montana, the flat land, although similar in every direction, was, nonetheless filled with enough discontinuities to make the time pass at a decent pace. As he continued through Montana, and approached the northern end of the Rockies, there were standing clouds over the peaks, and he flew more and more by instruments. Even at 14,000 feet, he was bounced about by the turbulence resulting from the easterly air flow hitting the Rocky Mountain wall which deflected the air upwards much as an even flowing stream forms rolling waves as it impacts a low rock shelf. Matt realized that if the weather got worse, he might be forced to fly on to Spokane as filed, and wait out the weather. Fortunately, the weather behaved, and once past the mountains in the Yellowstone area, the clouds broke up, and he was able to see into Idaho. Over Lake Coeur d'Alene, Idaho, he canceled IFR and dropped down, VFR, into Kellogg– a small town that had once been ravaged by lead and silver mining. Now that the mines were closed, and the air had been rid of pollution, it was a sleepy town in a valley that was recovering its original beauty. By the mid 1960's, the sulfuric acid in the air had actually stripped the trees around the town of foliage, and Matt suspected, killed many of the inhabitants prematurely of cancer, and other pollution-related diseases.

The Moose Gooser was tied down and the windows covered with silvered plastic sheeting used by aircraft owners to reflect the sunlight out of the interior. It also served to bar any prying eyes wondering about the nature of his cargo. He found a small motel nearby, and after dinner, studied the Canadian and US air charts.

Matt knew that Canadian customs was extremely thorough and that there was no way in hell he could talk his way through. It was also clear that assuming he slipped across the border unnoticed, were he to file Canadian IFR, they would realize that he had not cleared customs. Thus he would have to cross over VFR, and remain low, and VFR the whole way.

He had taken along a copy of the used aircraft bible, Trade-A-Plane, and perused the ads until he found exactly what he wanted. It was an add for a 185 in Quebec that needed a new engine before being airworthy. He called and chatted with the owner and casually asked the Canadian registration I.D. letters. It was CADBD and thus were a 185 to appear in British Columbia with CADBD on its side, no particular notice would be made. Further if some zealous flight service person entered the letters into the computer, there would be no chance of finding two 185s with the same ID letters flying at the same time. Matt had purposely kept the letters on The Moose Gooser as small as possible and thus it would not be difficult to cover over them with larger letters.

The next morning he arose before day break, called aircraft weather in Spokane using a fake identification number, and getting a report of clear weather throughout the area, departed Kellogg just as light broke. Flying within 500 feet of the ground, he flew straight north toward the Canadian border. Within 50 miles, Matt found a dirt road with no power lines on either side that was straight for a half mile. He landed, and with red and white tape and his Leatherman Model One in hand quickly covered over his US N numbers, and added the new Canadian letters. He lifted off in what seemed a long time, but in reality was only 5 minutes. He was not exactly sure when he passed over the border, but continued low for another 100 miles, weaving in and out of small valleys, and skimming over the tops of the hills. When he was far enough into Canada so that his proximity to the border would not be questioned, he flew higher, and in a line that was designed to take him towards his first major target of Prince George, British Columbia. While he still carried his old paper sectional charts, he had transitioned along with most pilots to using an Apple iPad and software such as Foreflight that provided real time positioning including altitude, heading and ground track along with real time radar for weather. This was backed up with an older Garmin aviation grade GPS. This gave him the feeling of having a "glass cockpit" while still relying on the mechanical gauges which he had grown up with.

In many ways, Matt would have preferred to fly up the coast from Vancouver to Prince Rupert, and then into Alaska via Sitka, Juneau, and on. However, it would have forced him to fly along the coast, and that route is monitored. Further, the chance of hitting rain and having to either go IFR, or ground himself along the Canadian coast were risks he did not want to take. The routing he chose along the Alaskan highway goes through the interior, causing him to spend a good deal more time in Canada, but he could fly anywhere along a broad path in British Columbia and the Yukon Territory. Further, the weather in the interior in early summer is dry most of the time.

The first leg took him toward Prince George, British Columbia at the beginning of the Alaskan highway. Matt flew mostly westward until he reached the Fraser River valley and then followed it north to Prince George. The Fraser River valley is a northern variation of the Grand Canyon, but with heavily forested walls. Possibly the most spectacular scenery in Canada, he flew within it and close to one canyon wall. Matt forgot the reason for the journey and the problems they faced, and delighted in the view, and fact that he was, –trite as it seemed–, just a large hawk, able to fly up and down, left and right, to feel the updrafts and down drafts, and to respond to them. He flew slow Roller Coaster in which he allowed the 185 to climb, then slowly fall off to one side or the other, dip, regain the climb, and continue first to one side and then to the other. Matt flew this way for nearly a half hour before deciding exactly how he would handle buying gas in Prince George.

A plan was formulated based on his fluency in French and his presumption that an arrogant French-speaking Quebecois would get little help in British Columbia. He landed at the airport, calling in only at the last minute, speaking first French, and then with his best French accent, announcing that he was downwind for Prince George. He taxied to the ramp and directly to the gas pump. He felt a bit sorry for the young fellow who came out and was subjected to his barrage of French. The fellow reacted in exactly the way Matt had expected, and as Matt climbed up on the wing to fuel The Moose Gooser (now CADBD), the fellow stood back until it was fueled, the oil was checked, and a handful of Canadian bills given to him for the gas. The whole process took little time, and once Matt had completed his pit stop, and bought several machine sandwiches, he departed Prince George.

From there, he could fly along the Alaskan highway, following it to Dawson Creek, Ft. St. John, Watson Lake, Whitehorse, Haines Junction, and finally the Alaska/Canadian border. Figuring his fuel, he felt that it might be possible to get all the way through Canada on just one more stop, if he were to refuel along the highway just south of Whitehorse. Nearing the town of Teslin in the Yukon, he landed and again took on the French accent. This time the effect was so much that he was nearly refused gas.

As he flew north he passed the 14,000 to 18,000 peaks to his left that form the barrier between the Yukon and the coast of Alaska. He thought back to Kiren and the project. It troubled him that just two people, Kiren and himself had been set loose on a project that could, if it were successful, significantly alter the lives of thousands —or if one counted the peasants of South America— millions of people. Kiren was so single-minded about eradicating cocaine, and for good personal reasons, that she was refractory to any discussion of moral ethics or greater wisdom. Indeed some of the best arguments for being wary of the US government had come from Vitz. The minute any inkling of such questions arose, Roland would cut the conversation off by stating categorically that this project was kissed by the highest of the high. Certainly there had been secret projects in the past such as the Manhattan project that produced the atom bomb. But that had been orchestrated by the President himself, and it was the President who decided whether or not the bomb was to be dropped. In this case, since only plant and not human lives were at stake, it seemed that the decision was to be made at a much lower level and with a lot less discussion. That bothered Matt.

From Teslin, Matt flew along the highway but nearing Whitehorse, he turned to the west to avoid having to talk to any air controllers and to give his identification number. He preferred that they think CADBD had stopped far short of the border. Several hours later, his Garmin GPS and iPad both showed that the Canadian/Alaskan border was 50 miles ahead. Now where to change back to US N numbers? He had to refuel in Tok which is 100 miles into Alaska, and thus flew low along the Alaskan highway until he noted a segment 10 miles long with no traffic. He made a quick 180 degree turn, flew 5 miles and landed. The make-shift letters were pulled off along with the duct tape and the 185, now as N186MG again, took off.

The final concern was to cross the border some distance from the highway and as low as possible to avoid being picked up by either country's radar. The appropriate procedure would be to announce his intention to cross and then to present himself to the customs people at Northway. Matt's idea was to slip past and refuel at Tok, making no mention of his recent presence in Canada. Just another Cessna 185 stopping for fuel should raise no curiosity as the 185 is a uniquely Northern bush plane, unlikely to be flown up the highway by the normal summer crowd of stateside air tourists who fly effete nose-wheeled Cessnas, Pipers, or god forbid, a Cirrus or Mooney.

Matt flew south and entered Alaska in the large uninhabited Tetlin Indian reservation, picked up the Little Tok River, and then flew it north to Tok. All of this required more fuel than he had figured on, and he was nervous by the time Tok came into sight.

Refueled in Tok, he considered his options. He was exhausted from the flying, and considered staying there but also wanted to move farther from the border as soon as possible with his cargo. Paxson and Summit Lake were 100 miles south along the Richardson highway and that would take less than an hour and would place him far from the border. There was a strip there and an old roadhouse where he could stay –or at least roll his sleeping bag out under The Moose Gooser's friendly wing.

As it was, there was room for him and The Moose Gooser was tied up and the windows blanked safely for the night. The next morning, Matt slept in and then enjoyed one of his greatest pleasures in life– Alaskan sourdough pancakes. These tart-tasting pancakes are thin and light, allowing him to eat a dozen before he was full.

Over breakfast, chatting with lodge guests at the adjacent table, Matt mentioned that he was a molecular biologist, associated with basic studies of viruses and cancer. One of the lodge guests commented:

"Several members of my family died of colon cancer at very young age. The slow progress toward a cure for cancer really frustrates me. HIV/AIDS seems to have been cured, so why not cancer?

Matt ordered another round of pancakes and explained the politics and finances of the respective wars on HIV/AIDS and cancer.

"HIV/AIDS is a terrible disease, and hits relatively young people who have yet to face their mortality. It first appeared in the US in a group of people who were highly educated and already organized. These were the gay men of New York and San Francisco. Once it was clear that AIDS was the result of the HIV virus, then largely due to the initial efforts of the gay activist groups, there was a highly organized pressure put on the Congress and Senate to devote a great deal of money to studies of HIV and AIDS. Thus funding for HIV and AIDS increased dramatically. As I see it, although we don't have a vaccine yet we do have the multiple drug treatments that keep the virus repressed and have given people infected with the virus greatly extended lives."

"Fine-fine-fine, but I asked about cancer." The guest asked.

"First of all, HIV/AIDS is a single virus and a single disease. Knock out the virus, and knock out or knock down the disease. Cancer is a spectrum of many many different diseases, and only a few are caused by viruses. So some versions of cancer will be taken off the board faster than others. But back to AIDS, the down side of all the in-pouring of money for HIV/AIDS is that it has come at the expense of research on cancer and other basic medical problems. The Congress did give some new money for HIV and AIDS but in my view a lot came from money that would have been used to increase our efforts on curing cancer. The Congress is going to devote only a certain amount of money for basic research. Recently with budget cuts across the board, this whole effort has been placed in a great crisis. Thus to some degree, every dollar devoted to research on Alzheimer's disease or any other disease takes money from cancer, and vice versa."

Matt continued. "You see, the problem is that when the activists for the disease-of-the-day scream, the NIH takes money from one kitty and shifts it to another. This is horribly disruptive to laboratories who have devoted years and years to basic studies that may have a major payoff just down the road. They cannot shift their efforts here and there. We are not shoe salesmen. Also it means that the squeaky disease gets the attention. Further, the funding has been trimmed as tight as possible. Now with this glee for balancing the budget, one senator in power could destroy what all of us have dedicated our lives to working on."

Matt continued: "You have been reading about the tests for the human colon cancer gene. That story is one of the best arguments for the importance of doing basic research. Two research teams, one in North Carolina and the other up East, had been examining the genes in yeast and bacterial cells responsible for the repair of certain kinds of damage to DNA. They had worked on this for years. Then, they realized that these genes might be very similar to parallel human genes. If so, they reasoned, then they might be able to use the yeast and bacterial genes as guideposts to identify the human genes. Working day and night they accomplished this, and what do you know— when these genes are defective in people, the afflicted people have a high incidence of certain cancers, in particular colon cancer. These are some of the most common cancers. Recently it has been possible to design a simple laboratory test to determine if someone is carrying this defective gene."

"So what can the average concerned citizen do?" Asked the guest's wife.

"I would love to see action groups formed by all the people in a city whose friends or relatives have cancer. They should get a copy of the Federal budget and make specific demands for cuts, in particular ones close to home— to make more money available for cancer research. Perhaps the runway extension for the local podunk airport which is going to cost 10 million dollars now seems less important that having 10 million more dollars more for prostate cancer research. You are the tax payers and it is your money. Do you want an cancer-free life for your children, or two more stealth bombers?"

"So you are saying that we need to divert money from defense?" asked the waitress who has just joined in listening.

"In fact, yes! We are in a war and our young people are dying of cancer. In our parent's generation it was wars with guns and bombs. Unfortunately the Congress is still spending our tax dollars to buy bombs and bombers when the real war needs to be fought in the research laboratories. It's even worse than that, since in the face of the Pearl Harbor of our generation— the cancer epidemic, congress has shrugged its shoulders and turned its back on those who are only hope for an eventual victory."

"The NIH, what is that again?" asked one of the guests,

"National Institutes of Health—where the funds come from to pay for the research to cure all of these diseases. You have hit the problem on the head. Not that many people understand the role of the NIH. Our first priority really should be making it such a common household term that kids in second grade would be writing letters to the NIH. Then we might finally see the kind of stable research support we need." Matt realized it was time to move the conversation to lighter topics and also realized that if he downed any more pancakes that his airplane might not clear the trees at the end of the strip.

Matt left the Paxson roadhouse and flew west along the Denali highway. This gravel road winds for 150 miles between the Richardson and Parks highways without a single gas station or phone after the first 30 miles. He flew over the Tangle Lakes, clear, deep, cold, rich with fish. Even for an Alaskan who had seen the region before, the scenery evokes a reverence that caused him to turn the radio off and place his headphones on the seat beside him. He flew to the right side of the broad valley to get a closer look at the mountains splashed with yellows, reds, and deep blacks, colors created by mixtures of minerals that lay within. The floor of the valley was high enough so that at that latitude, there were fewer trees, with mostly open grasses and brush. Clear braided streams laced the valley and Matt finally gave up circling moose for fear of running out of gas before he arrived at the mine. Half way along, he spotted a dozen bicyclists and made a low pass over them for fun. Must be Alaskans he thought, no other nuts would brave the dust and gravel for that distance. Not long after that he reached the Parks highway and turned south toward Talkeetna. Home would be in sight.

As he turned south along the highway, Matt felt the presence of The Mountain, 100 miles away. He could not see it as lower mountains blanked it from view even though the peaks were free of clouds. Matt had taken on enough fuel to allow him to reach the mine. He was not anxious to land at Talkeetna until he was rid of his cargo, since there would be too many friends who would open up his 185 to see what he was carrying. How he would explain his way out of an airplane load of potted plants, he didn't even want to consider. They would think that he had gone totally fruity, or had spent far too much time in – as they called it–the Effete East.

The flight to the northern end of the Susitna valley took him past Devil's Canyon of the Susitna. This 20 mile long canyon is so narrow and deep that it forges the Susitna River into one of the most fierce, impassable, wild water runs in North America. The water has been given a class 6 rating by boaters and it has been run only a very few times.

Nearing Talkeetna, Matt skirted to the west and flew by instinct toward the Kanikula. The Mountain was not out– as locals say. Its top was covered by clouds beginning at the 13,000 foot level, clouds that cap it a large fraction of the time.

Approaching the mine, Matt wished that he had fitted The Moose Gooser with larger tires. He had not had time before leaving to remove the smaller, high pressure tires that he used for landing on smooth stateside paved runways and install larger soft tires he preferred for the rough Alaskan strips. The larger tires reduce airspeed and are seldom used outside of Alaska. However, he would have to do with what he had, and at least the low fuel load would lessen the ground roll. "Damn", he thought, "I hate these skinny tires."

His strip at the mine had been cleared of the largest rocks but he had not landed there himself in several years. It was less than

1000 feet long and there always had been a few soggy spots but with the tundra tires these spots had not been a problem. He buzzed the mine several times to catch Vitz' attention and raised him on the KX99. Matt had a message relayed via Craig that company might be arriving, but without details.

The Moose Gooser was set up on a long, slow final with full flaps and 13 inches of manifold pressure. Clearing the brush at the start of the runway, he lowered it onto the gravel as carefully as possible using enough power to limit the descent and impact on the tires. The airplane was carrying a heavy load and the small tires began to dig into the loose gravel. Suddenly he ran into one of the soggy spots and the left tire dug in abruptly. This caused the Cessna to cartwheel about the tire, a classic ground loop. The result was that the left wing tip became a pivot point. The Moose Gooser spun about to a stop. The interior was a mass of pots, plants, dirt, and bottles of White Flies, and the wing tip was splayed open.

Matt unstrapped himself and stumbled out to stare at his first major accident in a long time.

Vitz ran over, ecstatic to see a human being, having been sleepless for nearly a week following Craig's visit with the bear paws. Indeed Vitz was nearing physical and mental exhaustion from tending his tin can alarm system and watching first one snow patch and then another for signs of the polar bears.

Vitz blurted out: "Polar bears, they are all over! Came out a week ago! Giant tracks right close to the cabin! Jesus —no sleep in a week. Am I glad to see you!"

Matt was too upset to recall who had started the polar bear hoax, and pushed him away.

"Are you fucking out of your mind, there are no polar bears around here, there isn't one in a thousand miles. They live on the

Arctic coast and on the ice flows. This is the mountains you idiot. Prints, what do you mean bear prints?"

Remembering Craig's bear paws on the shoes and gloves, he continued:

"I suppose the prints appeared just after Craig was here, right?"

Vitz put two and two together. He strode over to Matt, and whacked him unconscious with one single roundhouse blow.

It took Matt some time to regain consciousness and he staggered up to see Vitz sitting on a rock glowering at him through a half emptied bottle of Jim Beam. He knew that he had just reaped the rewards of his earlier humor, and also that it may have had a stronger effect on Vitz being there alone, than he had considered when he initiated it.

Matt mumbled: "Sorry, I guess our humor might have been a bit mean. No harm meant. Say, can you help me turn the 185 around?"

The remainder of the day was spent in silence filling the pots with spilled potting soil, transporting the plants to the greenhouse, and finally cleaning out the interior of The Moose Gooser. Fortunately the 20 bottles of White Flies had not come open, for had that happened, the project would have suffered a major set back. It was clear, and Matt chose to sleep outside in his sleeping bag, not so much that he minded Vitz' snoring, but he was still concerned over another bashing as Vitz had continued to mumble things under his breath all afternoon.

The next morning, Vitz was put to work arranging the plants in the greenhouse while Matt set about repairing the wing tip. He straightened it the best he could and covered the open hole at the end of the wing with duct tape, his remedy for most ails. All he had to do was to get to Talkeetna where the mechanic could repair the wing tip, replace the plastic end piece and make sure things were straight.

That afternoon Vitz and Matt finally were able to talk in a marginally relaxed mode.

"Friggin north pole. Just after I got here nearly got washed out by the water coming through the roof. Then I walked up to that pond and fell through the ice, but only part way. Got out– but shit, I am telling you, I have never seen a bobby trap as bad as that."

"Wow, you walked out on the ice at this time of the year! Jesus, Vitz, there's always overflow on that pond! Damn, big guy, I guess in the hurry we didn't give you any kind of tourist guide on staying alive around here. Sorry about that."

"Any more friggin things you haven't told me about?"

"I'll think about it. Here's the plan. The 185 should make it out and I'll leave in Talkeetna for repairs. I had planned to return by commercial carrier anyhow. Kiren and I will be back in a couple of weeks and bring the lab equipment with us. You need to get the plants planted and the generator operating before we return. I'll get Craig to continue bringing supplies only if you promise not to pop him. Agreed?"

"Only if he brings more Jim Beam whiskey. About out."

In the morning, Matt measured the gas in The Moose Gooser, calculated exactly how much would be required for one trip to Talkeetna and 10 minutes extra– given the generally down hill run, and drained all but that from the tanks. This would lighten the airplane allowing him to lift off before getting to the soggy spot again. He would then fly at a low speed to lessen the stress on the duct tape.

As Matt was preparing to take off, he saw a movement on the hillside above the mine and walked up to investigate. Mounting the top of the rise, immediately above the mine, he came face to face with a large sow grizzly bear and two very young cubs, clearly just out of the den after being born that spring. Matt and the bears were equally startled, and as Matt ran down the hill, the bears crossed one of the larger snow patches near the mine and disappeared into a rocky canyon.

Given the thousands of man hours spent in the bush each year by hunters, locals, and natives in Alaska, there are relatively few incidents of bear mauling. Most of the time these events involve grizzlies which weigh 500 to 800 pounds as adults, and are known across the north for their poor eye sight and ill temper. Black bears are much smaller, and although they are more plentiful, they are usually timid. Nonetheless bear attacks do occur, and in certain areas such as the localities around Mt. McKinley, bear incidents are not uncommon. The danger also varies with the season and the situation. A number of years ago, Matt recalled, an unusually early breakup in the interior woke the bears before the usual food– plants and small animals, were ready for them. The result was that several black bears wandered into downtown Fairbanks and one ate a woman in her garden. A few years later a marathon was being run in the early spring in the Aleutians and the last runner– a straggler– was snatched and eaten by a large brown bear. The following year the race times were considerably faster.

The greatest danger involves females with cubs. Since the sow keeps her cubs for two years, an encounter between a human and a sow with two two- year old cubs, pits nearly a ton of bear moving in 3 directions against 1/10th as much human flesh. Since bear encounters are normally at close range, many Alaskan guides prefer large bore rifles with no scope sights (scopes interfere with shooting at close range) for protection. Matt's favorite was a 5 shot pump 10 gauge shotgun loaded with buckshot. He felt that at close range –meaning less than 25 feet, that this would deliver the greatest stopping power. You just had to wait to let the bear get close. He had never had to try out his theory. By these standards,

Matt felt that Vitz' .243 was of value only in terminating yourself after being mauled.

Out of breath, Matt stopped to contemplate his situation. The sow was very likely the bear that had made a mess of the mine house and might well decide to come back and reclaim it for her summer lodging. The bears were gone for the moment, and no degree of searching on foot would likely turn them up. He could find them in the 185 but that would use precious gas. If, on the one hand, he were to try to tell Vitz about them, he would immediately be decked. If he did not, Vitz might wake up some morning with two little baby bears in his bed.

Deciding that Vitz was a big boy, he said in a casual way as he was strapping himself into The Moose Gooser:

"Keep the .243 handy, you never know what may come around."

To which he was greeted with: "Screw you and every marmot on the mountain!"

With 20 degrees of flaps, he ran the engine up, allowed the 185 to gain speed and lifted off with a good 150 feet before the soggy spot. As he turned The Moose Gooser over to the mechanic at Talkeetna, he spotted Craig and cautioned him to treat Vitz very gingerly and what ever he did, not to mention bears, even if he was to spot the sow and 2 cubs. Matt flew out on an all-nighter to Chicago and then to Baltimore.

It wasn't more than two hours after Matt had departed, that Vitz happened to stroll over to the large snow patch for ice and found the bear tracks. He couldn't believe that even after decking Matt, that the SOB would have had the balls to continue the joke. His epithets to Matt could have been heard all the way to the top of The Mountain. It never dawned on him that there were two sets of small tracks near the large ones. Vitz dismantled the tin can alarms in disgust.

CHAPTER TEN

ESCAPING NORTH CAROLINA

The usual panic set in with endless lists. One of Matt's students would live in the house and care for the animals. His senior research associate would be in charge of the lab. Hoping there would be some free time, he downloaded nearly a hundred research reports on viruses to his Mac laptop and brought a good supply of his favorite notebooks for jotting down ideas. Roland had arranged a mail drop that would route mail sent to Kiren or Matt's labs to Roland and then secretly to a box in Talkeetna. Email would come over the secure satellite phone line. Rosalind continued to be a major worry.

Matt was finding her 1000 nerve endings for personal feelings to be 1000 points of abrasion. She simply would not give up trying to find out where he was going and what he was to do with Kiren. Matt felt as if his head was full of ants and Rosalind was a giant woodpecker. He hated to lie to her but feared for her safety. She knew of the family homestead in Talkeetna, and if she was to guess that they were in Alaska, Rosalind was exactly the kind of person who would call up Kiren's laboratory and tell them that Matt and Kiren had run off to Talkeetna and that she, Rosalind, was going up to bring the rascals back.

They had devised a false trail that would keep everyone looking elsewhere. It went as follows: Kiren was working for the Feds for the summer on a Navy ship engaged in classified research on some Pacific islands where the H-bomb tests had been conducted after World War II. The story went that after the tests, virus-like plant diseases had begun to appear with increasing severity and that there was worry over mutant viruses. She would isolate unusual viruses for further analysis in The States; this was in return for some research funding. The fact that they would be on a ship would keep Rosalind from poking around Talkeetna, and make it more difficult to contact them. The notion of secret research was in line with Matt's previous endeavors. The H-bomb islands are restricted so anyone trying to trace Kiren or Matt would expect to run into a wall of denial. Roland's mail drop would have a Navy address to add more credibility.

Kiren's priorities were 1-2-3; first, Mr. Copper, second the lab, and a distant third, Francis. Francis was a big boy. Her lab people were organized into chores and Kiren told them that it might be as short as one month, but likely two. The major question was how she would get back to show Mr. Copper, or if she missed one of the major shows, who would ride in her place.

Matt called Kiren on the secured satellite phone and urged her to wrap things up ASAP, and get ready to move operations to Alaska. Matt was very concerned for her safety.

"Email a list of the lab equipment and supplies you will need: agarose, stains for RNA and DNA, and chemicals for the electrophoresis and enzyme work. I will pick it up from my sources, and air ship it to Anchorage. You need to pack two or three suitcases

—your clothes, lab notebooks and anything else you'll need. In addition, any restriction enzymes, proteins, and your DNA, RNA, and virus samples should be packed on wet ice in Styrofoam boxes."

Matt continued: "I assume you are being watched, at least we have to go on that. I'll give you four days to get ready and then call you with instructions. I've been working on the best way to slip you into Alaska with no trail of airlines tickets and watching eyes."

Kiren asked about Vitz. "Old bear bate is just fine." Matt commented. "I just hope that when we get there he hasn't joined the big food chain in the sky."

Kiren didn't understand and signed off.

Three days later Matt called, and relayed instructions.

"Be ready early in the morning the day after tomorrow. Dress in very quiet clothing and wear a hat please. I made reservations in your name from Raleigh, on American to Dulles, with connections on Air France to Guam. You will check your luggage and the Styrofoam boxes through as if you were going the whole way. Be sure to bring your passport."

Kiren objected, but was interrupted.

"Just wait. When the airlines announce boarding for First Class, go through the door and look for a black man just inside the door. His name is Billy. Tell him you are Kiren, and he will take you down the stairs to another plane that will be waiting for you. I'll be there. We will fly to Seattle, and pick up your bags – I will have intercepted your bags at Dulles and re-tagged them for Seattle using a friend's name. She lives in Seattle and looks like you. We will fly Alaska Airlines to Anchorage. I've arranged the timing so that by the time anyone watching realizes they have lost track of you, you will be on the ground in Anchorage."

Two days later, Kiren took a cab loaded with her bags to the RDU airport and took the 43 minute American flight to Dulles. At

Dulles, she checked through customs and went to the Air France lounge.

Sitting in the lounge, she mused that of all of the people waiting for the flight to the South Pacific, she was the only one wearing hiking shoes from L.L. Bean, and carrying a warm Gortex jacket.

When the flight was called, Kiren had nearly fallen asleep and after handing her ticket to the stewardess, almost walked onto the jet, but a black man took hold of her arm and asked if she was Kiren. She said yes and he told her that he was Billy and to follow him. She nodded.

They exited by a stairway, climbed down onto the tarmac below the 747, and walked 100 yards to a small single engine airplane beside which Matt was standing. The airplane looked like a polished white egg.

Kiren looked at the airplane and attacked, cutting into Matt with her most deadly focused stare from her giant gray eyes. She thought: "Its time to play games, macho-man."

"We are not going in this!" She said.

"Sure are, it's a Questar Venture. Beautiful isn't it! I borrowed it from a friend who has been using it as an advertising platform for his new generation of avionics."

"You don't expect me to fly in that!"

"Now Kiren, this is an extremely safe airplane. It's also extraordinarily fast. We will be able to fly from here to Seattle in three legs and at a speed pushing 300 knots. Hop in."

"Kiss off! I refuse to put my life in your hands."

"Kiren, please, it's safe."

"Safe, well let's just do some science here. How many landings are you planning to make?"

"Three."

"Fine, and averaged over your past two landings what is your percentage of crashes per landing?"

Matt regretted relating the details of his recent mishap in the Moose Gooser.

"Well, what is it?"

"Ah, fifty percent, but—"

"Right, you must have taken some statistics along the way, three landings required on this little jaunt, and a 50/50 chance of crashing each time, given your recent record. So you tell me what the probability is that we will get through this without a crash based on these scientific calculations."

"Now really Kiren, I've made thousands of landings."

"Number, Mr. Scientist. I want a number."

"Ah, lets see, point five times point five times point five, I would guess twelve and a half percent."

"Right! You stand here telling me that this is very safe and then in the same breath explain that I have only a one in eight chance of getting through it alive."

"I didn't kill myself at Talkeetna, now did I? Really, what can I do to convince you that this is safe?"

"Well I hate to be out of control. Particularly when someone like you is in control. The only solution is that I need to be in control. Yes, that's it. I will fly!"

"Give me a break! You've never flown before and you want to fly this!"

"Oh, you can take off and land, I'll let you do that, just once we are up there I will handle the controls. Can't be that hard, men do it all the time —so women should be able to pick it up in a flash."

Matt thought to himself: "If I could cold cock her and she wakes up in Seattle, it really won't be kidnapping. Oh well, what harm can it do to let her hold the control stick?

The front seats were arranged side-by-side with control sticks mounted on each side instead of wheels. Matt was waiting for instructions from Dulles ground control and described the airplane to Kiren.

"Questar Ventures were made in Waukegan Illinois as a kit. The kit is furnished with the basic body, and the builder must install the engine and put the major components together. Questar Ventures hold many cross country speed records for a single engine aircraft of its class. As you can see the wings are stubby and thin, designed for raw speed. The landing gear is substantial, and wheels retract after takeoff. This Venture is equipped with a specially designed 350 hp twin turbocharged engine. Ventures will cruise at 330 miles per hour, not far off of the average speed of many business jets. This one is also pressurized so it can fly at 24,000 feet, above most weather. It recently made a hop from Palm Springs California to Chicago in 5 hours flat with no stops."

"If you are interested, here's the flight plan. We will make it in three legs with two fuel stops. The first two legs will be 900 miles long and take roughly 3 hours each and the last leg will be 600 miles, giving us some reserve fuel in case Seattle is fogged in. Stretching it, we have a range of 1450 miles between fueling so could make it with one stop, but that would give us little reserve."

"So take off. I'll tell you when I want to fly."

In the air, the Venture climbed at 2500 feet per minute to 12,000 feet where Matt leveled out. Just as he was about to relax Kiren said loudly:

"Feeling loss of control here. Time to fly. I've been watching you and it can't be that hard. I'm a natural learner. That lever there is the gas pedal and this stick thing on my right is like a steering wheel. What do these foot rests do?" Kiren asked, jamming one foot against the right pedal which shoved the nose hard to the right.

"Oh, I see it turns things, but if the foot rests turn the plane, why do we have this stick?"

"Oh, god, deliver me please. Kiren, the airplane must fly in three axes, not like a car which only moves on two. The pedals move the rudder behind us turning the airplane left or right. The stick makes the airplane go up or down— if you pull the stick back or push it forward. Or if you pull it to the left or right, it rotates the airplane about its length."

"Cute. How does it do that?"

"Up and down is done by the elevator on the tail and rolling the airplane about its axis is done by the ailerons on the wings."

"OK, now I understand all about flying. Here let me hold the stick."

Matt pointed out which instruments she needed to watch to be sure that they kept their altitude and compass heading. Kiren tipped the Venture this way and that, up and down and finally at Matt's pleading settled down to her version of flying in a straight heading.

"This is easy. I can see why you like flying. It's really easy as pie but people think it's hard and thus you can fool them into thinking that you are special. You just go to sleep and I'll tell you when we get there."

"We can engage the autopilot now, Kiren."

"No! not fair!"

Kiren was sitting in the right seat so had to look to her left rather than straight on to see the instruments. Nonetheless she kept them on the correct heading and altitude. Once Matt began to relax, Kiren began exerting a see-sawing pressure on the rudder pedals first to one side and then the other which was coordinated with a slight back and forth movement of the stick. If this is done in a subtle way, the person flying the airplane will feel little distress. For the passenger, however this is equivalent to a sailboat wallowing in the waves nearly out of control and can lead to nausea for even the most hardened pilot. After fifteen minutes Matt started to feel queasy.

"Ah, Kiren, let me have the controls a bit. You've done a great job."

Slapping his hand off the controls she replied:

"No! If I'm doing a great job then I will fly it all the way to Minnesota. You can land there."

Matt gritted his teeth and stared at the GPS navigational unit hoping that somehow St. Cloud was closer than he suspected it was. Over the next hour and a half, Matt's life was miserable. Kiren would somehow manage to figure out how to keep the airplane straight ahead so that his stomach would partially recover and then she would go back to her gentle wallowing. Every time Matt asked to take over or suggested that they use the autopilot, she would remind him of their bargain. Finally as he was about to lose his breakfast, St. Cloud approach cleared them for a slow descent and he took over the flying.

As soon as they landed Matt excused himself, jogged to the FBO office and bought a bottle of air sick pills and stretched out for a few minutes on the couch to clear his inner ears. Kiren found him there and began teasing him.

"Oh, poor Mattie, are you OK? You should be happy, by your calculations, our chance of not crashing has now gone from only twelve percent up to twenty five percent, reasonable odds I would say. You look ill."

"No no, I'll be fine, it's just that the wallowing back there got to my stomach. Will take just a minute, I'll be fine."

"Oh, poor you, your tummy is upset. I found something to read in the airplane. Guess what it is!"

"No idea."

"A book on how to fly the airplane and in the back are some fun things you can do. One is called an aileron roll. It describes how you do it."

"Give me a break. That's an acrobatic maneuver."

"Looks easy to me."

Matt wondered if he would survive the next leg. After taking off, he felt better and climbed to 12,000 feet. Kiren had stretched back and was reading the airplane manual with interest. Just as Matt leveled out she reached over and pulled the throttle back.

"What are you doing?" Matt blurted out.

"The book says that we need to slow to 170 knots to do the roll. Now according to the book you put the nose down 20 degrees and then up 20 degrees and then just roll it over. You go first. Then I will do it!"

"Kiren do you know what you are asking me to do?"

"You're scared?" She taunted him.

"I am not scared and I have done aileron rolls many times before. It's just that this is acrobatics, not normal flying. Legally we should have parachutes on to do it."

"Book says this is a 1-G maneuver. That doesn't sound bad." She countered.

"No, if done well, you just bring the nose up a bit, and roll the airplane slowly over until it is upside down and then back. But it takes a lot of skill coordinating the controls. It's not something that someone who has been flying for two hours is supposed to do. Sure, a Boeing 707 was rolled once this way. I've done it in my 185."

"Then it's settled, You first –then me." Kiren giggled.

"And what after that? Fly straight up to the sun?"

"No, after that you can fly all the way to Seattle. I'll have gotten bored with flying."

The temptation was too strong. One simple aileron roll, Kiren would wet her pants, would have no interest in trying it —and the airplane would be his again.

"OK, agreed. I do one. If you think you can, then you try. But you don't have to. After that, no negotiations, its all mine all the way to Seattle."

It had been a year or more since Matt had tried one of these rolls. Done well, a glass of water can be placed on the dash of the airplane and it will be there without a ripple at the end. Matt made sure that there were no loose objects inside, dropped the nose to pick up a bit of speed, pulled the nose up to 20 degrees above the horizon and pulled the stick to the left causing the left wing to drop rolling the airplane. As the Questar reached the upside down point, Matt lost track of the horizon and horsed it back around adding a bundle of power to pull the airplane through the rest of the maneuver. Level, he looked at Kiren. She had a scowl on her face.

"You forced it around. Very very sloppy. Here take your hands off the stick."

Kiren dropped the nose and pulled it up, but rather than snatching the stick to the left, she brought it over smoothly and reaching a 60 bank, added just a touch of power. The airplane responded with a smooth roll over to the inverted position where she added a small amount of forward pressure on the stick to keep the nose at the horizontal and then made a smooth roll back to the horizontal, pulling the power back as they rolled upright. Smiling at Matt she said:

"See, I do good rolls, you do bad rolls. Here, you've got the controls."

Matt was stunned, then blurted out: "What did you say?"

"I said, —here you've got the controls."

"Only someone who has been working with a flying instructor would know the lingo— you said you have never flown."

"No I didn't, you did. Just like I said that you had never ridden a horse!" Kiren laughed.

"Oh, Jesus, so that's what all this has been about. How long have you had a license?"

"I don't. You see, Ralph was always wanting me to go along on his trips in the Cessna 152. He took off and landed and I flew it in the air. Perfect arrangement. Later when Dad traded the 152 in for the Decathalon, Ralph and Dad would go out and do acrobatics. Ralph promised Dad he wouldn't practice them with me along, but he never said that I couldn't do them. I loved the Decathalon. It had an inverted oil system so I could fly around all day long upside down."

"God, I guess I had it coming. And all that wallowing, that was for me?"

"Of course, good practice in stick and rudder coordination, particularly from the right seat wouldn't you say?"

"Oh yah, so why didn't you get a ticket?"

"Maybe some day, I was going to and then Ralph was killed in the crash. It's been hard to think about flying since then. But really, I still can't land well and I do respect your flying skills."

"I guess we are even."

"Absolutely not." Kiren kissed his cheek.

A few minutes later Kiren asked. "That scar on your chin. Interesting. How did you come by it?"

"Was hit by a poison arrow in Brazil. This is the entry hole. Came out my ear."

"Bullshit. Correct answer please."

"Playboy bunny and I were sword fighting in the raw and —"

"I give up."

They flew on to Great Falls Montana where they refueled and made the third leg to Seattle, stopping not far off the time allotted for the trip. The Venture was handed over to its owner who would fly it back to Washington D.C. It was late and a young fellow at the FBO drove them to a motel for the night.

The next morning Kiren checked in under Matt's friend's name and they boarded the flight to Anchorage. As the flight approached Anchorage, they passed over Prince William Sound where Matt first heard of Kiren months earlier. Within 50 miles of Anchorage, they descended into Turnagain arm, flying below the peaks on either side. For all on board the view was breathtaking.

Following Matt's departure, Vitz had a spectacular week. Freed of the concern over polar bears, he had demolished his bear alarms and thrown the .243 rifle in a pile of gear next to his sleeping bag.

He spent the week hiking in the foothills above the mine armed with a new digital Nikon. The weather was warm, in the 60's mid-day, and the views of the glaciers from the tops of the hills was spectacular. Although he hesitated to stay overnight, had he taken several days, he could have hiked around to the Kahiltna Glacier and worked his way up toward the staging areas where the climbs begin. His animal encounters generally involved curious marmots, a large, red, ground squirrel that lives in the rocks. When he was training in the California mountains prior to Desert Storm, he had a Korean comrade who loved watching marmots but in error kept calling them Mormons.

After a week of hikes, sunshine, and watching Mormons build their houses, Vitz was beginning to think that the summer might be very nice if Kiren and Matt never did show up. It was at the end of such a day that he ambled back to the mine just before dinner.

Walking uphill to the mine house, he noticed that the front door was open. He suspected that Craig may have snuck in and didn't feel the surge of adrenaline until almost inside. At that point he saw that the door was not open, rather it had been demolished and lay in pieces about the opening. He took on his "attack with surprise" approach by bolting through the opening, hunting knife in hand, and half crouched, looked this way and that.

What he saw was an enormous mass of brown fur. The sow grizzly lay on her side nursing two cubs who were firmly attached to her nipples. She had heard his footsteps and was turning toward him as he entered the door.

Vitz' brain required several seconds to reset itself from the "attack them at all costs" to the "them is not people, them is lots of big bears and get the fuck out of here" mode. In these few seconds, the sow raised herself and made a guttural snort. It was only because the two cubs hung on tightly to her nipples that she was stopped from covering the few feet to the door and removing Vitz' head with a swipe of her paw. In such situations at close encounter, and with two cubs in immediate proximity, humans seldom escape alive.

The two cubs' attachment provided him with just enough time to turn, dash around the side of the mine house, and then looking left and right for a route of escape, to run to the greenhouse building. He barred the door with a 50 gallon oil drum. The sow had missed seeing how he departed and stood in the door bellowing, not wanting to be too far from her two young cubs who were squalling over the loss of their food.

Vitz shook for several hours before gaining some confidence that he would not be torn apart and eaten within the hour. He climbed to the second story window that looked out over the mine and watched. Once every half an hour the sow would stick her head out of the front door, look this way and that, and then disappear. This game went on until the sun had dipped far enough behind The Mountain so that it began to cool down, and take on an even deeper silence. The sow appeared to have decided that the threat was gone. Vitz, tired, curled up in his jacket on a ledge on the second floor, and slept until early the following morning.

The next morning, he again took up his vigilance. He could hear the bears inside the mine house, as the cubs would occasionally engage in growling games which would be silenced by snorts from their mother. Vitz considered, and reconsidered his limited options and realized that there were in essence only two. He could sneak off, trying to walk out to Talkeetna, but he had little innate sense of what direction that was. Further, once he left the higher ground, he would have to cross a number of large braided glacier streams which Craig and Matt had both cautioned him about with great seriousness. These streams rage rapidly from the glaciers, and the water is a chalky white-gray color. It is so dense with ground rock, that one cannot see more than a few inches into it, and there is no way to tell by looking, the depth of the water. The water flows with great speed frequently carrying large boulders that have fallen away from the melting glacier. These boulders can crush a man's leg if he tries to wade across. Further, the lowlands between the Susitna River and the beginning of the hills consist of swamps, muskeg lakes, and nearly impassable fields of 3 foot high grass clumps.

Another problem was the bugs. The mine area was relatively dry so that the insect population was tolerable in the summer. The swamps between the mine and Talkeetna however were a different matter. There the air itself was, Matt figured, nearly 30% protein by mass, due to the millions of mosquitoes per cubic foot. Indeed it was impossible to slam a book shut without killing at least a hundred in the process. His record was 515 using a World Book. Bug tales from the interior of Alaska were countless. Domestic dogs frequently died as the result of thousands of bites per day. There were areas where being outside meant wearing mosquito nets or going totally mad. Those of course were just the mosquitoes. What Matt hated were smaller more carnivorous gnats called “no see ‘ums”. These little beasts were at least as plentiful and left unpleasant welts. His theory was they would fly at you, mouth open, take a bite and then lay their eggs in the hole.

Vitz’ other option was to wait and watch, hoping that the mother bear and the two cubs would depart at least long enough for him to enter the cabin and retrieve the .243, hand held radio, and snag some food.

For two days, this wait and watch game went on with the sow remaining in the mine house with the cubs. On the third day, the sow departed without the cubs and was gone for several hours and this was repeated the next day. By now Vitz was very hungry. Water was no problem since he had arranged a water line from a stream nearby to water the plants. He was beginning to consider eating them.

Vitz watched the sow move up the hill above the mine and disappear over the top. He figured that even at her top speed moving down the hill, it would take her at least 3 minutes to return to the mine house once the cubs began to squeal. This seemed enough time to enter the mine house, snag the gun and retreat to the greenhouse. Leaving the door ajar, he made his way to the mine house and looked in. The two cubs were a good 100 pounds each, and both were equipped with sizable teeth and claws. They had taken up residence on all that remained of his sleeping bag and as he peered at them, he saw that his .243 and the radio were somewhere under them.

Realizing that retrieving his gear was hopeless, he tiptoed 15 feet inside to where he could grab a loaf of bread and a couple of cans of beans lying on the kitchen counter. He retreated to the greenhouse building, not wanting to be caught out in the open by the sow.

Thus went the remainder of the week. Mama bear spent most of the time with the cubs in the mine house, and left every day for several hours to forage for food. The cubs had apparently been given instructions not to leave as they stayed put. Vitz was able to slip in for a minute here and there, but several times roused the cubs who bawled loudly sending him back to the security of the greenhouse.

Several times Craig flew over, but Vitz was unable to come out as mother bear was with the cubs. Finally, at the end of what had become the longest week of his life, Craig's fly by coincided with the absence of the sow. He ran out and waved, jumped up and down, and finally fell flat on the ground. It was the latter that prompted Craig to land and see how he was doing.

In a burst of mostly incomprehensible babble, Vitz related the events of the week. Craig was immediately concerned for the safety of the Super Cub since if the sow was to return, she might turn her attention to his $100,000 airplane, and Craig was not armed. Following a series of questions, he gave Vitz the following instructions:

"Only one way to get rid of her, other than shooting her– no one around here would do that. I'm going to get out of here for a couple of hours – protect the Super Cub. You go back into the greenhouse and take the mufflers off of the gas powered electrical generator. Move the generator as close to one of the windows as possible. After Mama has returned, start the generator. It will be so loud, like a herd of Hells Angels on Hogs, I guarantee she will depart. I'll be back over and when I see her out in the open, I'll herd her a bit to move her along. I'll land and pick you up. Matt, by the way, needs you back in Anchorage tomorrow anyhow."

Vitz didn't like this plan for two reasons. First, he would have strongly preferred to fly away from the grizzly and her cubs rather than being left behind. Second, he had been tripping over the god-damned generator all week, and had never thought of using it.

The plan worked like clockwork. Two hours later, Craig slowed the Super Cub to a leisurely 55 mph with half flaps and flew lazy circles between the mine and the retreating trio keeping at least 50 feet above the terrain. Craig landed, and they constructed a new door. They flew out, and Vitz enjoyed the first real dinner, shower, and a good night's sleep in a full week.

At the baggage carousel, as they were waiting to collect their bags and equipment, Vitz strode into view. Kiren ran to him giving him a big hug and allowed him to carry her back to Matt.

"Matt, tell Vitz what a natural athlete I am. Why I was able to fly the airplane even though to quote Matt, "I had never flown before". Poor macho pilot got all air sick and lost his lunch in the boy's room. It was awful, Vitz, I nearly had to fly all the way myself."

Matt was trying to ignore her while Vitz stood listening with a grin.

"Do you know how I fixed his stomach?" She asked as Vitz shook his head.

"I flew the airplane upside down until all the bad energy fell out and from then on everything was just fine."

Vitz shook his head. "Heh guy, what is the little one here going on about?"

"The little one is trying to tell you that I flew Matt's fancy airplane and that by corkscrewing it long enough I managed to make him sick and then for icing on the cake – in revenge for the two of you jerking me around about Matt being a natural athlete– you jerks, I did the smoothest aileron roll Matt here has ever seen. That's what the little one is telling you." Kiren related in a mix of smirk and sneer.

"Its called revenge, Vitz, something you should understand particularly since you had something of a hand in it."

It was evening by the time the bags and boxes were collected and Matt wanted to drive to Talkeetna. He drove and Kiren and Vitz sat in the back. Kiren whispered, laughed and made gagging sounds depicting Matt's imagined barfing. Out of the Anchorage traffic and heading up the Matanuska valley, Kiren finally quieted down and Vitz related every detail of "the week of bear hell" as he called it. At each appropriate place, Kiren interjected some comment such as:

"You poor baby,– you could have been eaten, –it must have been awful."

Matt had to turn the rear view mirror away to avoid being caught with a smirk.

Finally passing Palmer, the "week of bear hell" story was getting old, and for some reason, Matt felt the urge to push Vitz' and Kiren's buttons again. He began to relate the stories of the great earthquake of 1964.

"The good Friday earthquake has recently been uprated to a 9.2 quake, the largest yet recorded in North America, and second only to the one in Chile. Its epicenter was in Prince William sound. The tidal waves destroyed the downtown areas of Valdez and Kodiak and damaged a lot of Anchorage. I have been through quite a few quakes in Alaska. When you are close to the epicenter, you can hear the quake coming. This is very common here in Alaska. There are a number of explanations.

One is that the sonic wave – the noise, outruns the compression wave-- the movement of the ground. Another is that the crack front which is involved in fragmenting the rock so that it can shift, moves through before the major ground movement. What ever the reason, we frequently hear them coming and the ones I have experienced sounded exactly like a freight train was coming right through my house."

This discussion had its intended effect of sobering Kiren and Vitz and making them appropriately humbled over Alaska's enormous natural forces. The imagery of the earthquake rumbling like a freight train as it swelled up from the ground below was particularly frightening to Kiren, who had yet to experience an earthquake.

That night they checked into the Sled Dog motel, and after a dinner of meat loaf and potatoes served at the bar, Matt excused himself for bed. Vitz and Kiren made a point of letting him know that they were planning to stay up and finish off a bottle of Jim Beam before they retired. Kiren couldn't believe that it was 11:30 at night and still light out. Finally at 1:30 AM the bartender closed the bar, and Vitz and Kiren trundled off to their respective rooms. Vitz was impaired from his contribution to the "demise of Mr. Beam" and Kiren was feeling the cumulative effects of a long day of flying and Mr. Beam's blessings.

At 2:30 AM the sun was playing with its imminent appearance but it was still dusk. The trailing edge of a cold front was passing, and it was drizzling. The temperature had fallen into the low 50's. Matt, Kiren, and Vitz had sequential rooms along the long motel hallway. Suddenly, Kiren was awakened by her room shaking, and as she sat upright, she heard a rumbling that grew and grew. It was an almost a perfect replay of what Matt had described. She screamed "earthquake!", ran from the room, pounded for a moment on Matt and Vitz' doors, and then ran down the hall in her night gown and out into the rain.

Matt got up immediately and stood at his window looking out. Shaking the sleep from his head, he watched as Vitz too, stumbled outside wearing only his boxer shorts.

The two of them standing scantily clothed in the drizzle were now the object of attention of numerous motel clients looking out of their windows as the rumbling grew to a roar. At this moment, the conductor of the Alaska Railroad train seeing two nearly naked people standing by the tracks at 2:30 AM, blew his horn loudly as the train passed feet from the motel.

Matt shook his head realizing that the next morning it would be him against the two of them in a face-off over their fried eggs–although in his mind, they would have the eggs in their faces.

Kiren slept until nearly noon and joined Vitz and Matt for lunch. The Moose Gooser had a new wing tip. After looking around Talkeetna and visiting several of the flying services to chat with climbers excited over their upcoming adventures, they loaded their gear in for the first of several flights needed to ferry their equipment to the mine. Even Matt was astounded at the mess the bears had made. Although the interior had not been wrecked, it needed a major hosing. Much work lay ahead and unknown to them, Raul was getting very nervous and determined to find Kiren.

CHAPTER ELEVEN
SCIENCE AT THE KANIKULA

It took a number of days to get the "laboratory" set up to Kiren's specifications. She rearranged the pots of plants in the greenhouse and commandeered the small electric refrigerator Vitz had taken over for storing beer and steaks. It was, she explained, off limits to food and would be used for her virus extracts and enzymes. He could put his beer and steaks in the snow patch up the hill. Although Vitz complained that the animals would get the steaks, and this was true, once she had "contaminated" it with her virus, he ceased to whine. The electrophoresis units and power supplies were put together and Kiren neatly arranged a bench so that it looked surprisingly like one would find in any molecular biology laboratory, replete with pipetting devices, timers, and an electric water bath heated to 37 degrees centigrade. The closer she was to having things arranged to her liking, the less she fussed. The final test was an electrophoresis experiment with plasmid DNAs. Indeed Kiren was able to stain and visualize the DNA using a hand held ultraviolet light. At this point she was finally able to relax and shifted her worries to other topics. Top on the list was Mr. Copper.

As soon as she mentioned Mr. Copper, Matt disappeared and returned with a hand held radio. He explained that Roland had managed to set up a satellite phone link to a secured Air Force communications satellite and that they would be able to patch into the phone system with no worry of anyone being able to trace their whereabouts. Skype was too insecure. Getting the phone link established took a few minutes but when it was done he handed the phone to Kiren. In a short time Kiren was engrossed in relaying details of special care for Mr. Copper and asking about each day's training session.

The next morning was unusually crisp and clear. The Mountain was out and they all had taken a short wake-up hike to get a good view of the peaks along the Alaska range. The range begins with the McKinley mastiff and continues as a chain of volcanoes that extend for over a thousand miles forming the Alaska Peninsula. They could see Mt. Spurr, an active volcano across from Anchorage. Several years before it had rudely spit a blast of volcanic ash into the face of the Alaskans, soiling the windshields of expensive BMWs and disrupting air traffic. A few hundred miles further south was Katmai and "The Land of Ten Thousand Smokes", moon-like with its lifeless terrain created by one of the largest volcanic eruptions in recorded history. The fact that this had occurred in our century reminded them of the young violent nature of this land. After walking back, Matt cooked sourdough pancakes and the three sat around the large wooden table in the kitchen. Kiren was wearing her favored gear at the mine: her floppy hat, jeans, and a multicolored sweater. Vitz alternated between hiking shorts and jeans and always had his green wool cap nearby. Matt was seldom seen in anything other than jeans and a dark green shirt. Kiren had her pad of paper which meant that she was in the mood to discuss science.

Vitz still had trouble following the logic of using a cosmic number of different targeting segments. Kiren tried another explanation.

"We started with a very very large collection of possible targeting segments and have put them into the engineered virus. Many of these will be impotent or functionless, but some will target the ribozyme to an RNA that will be critical for cocaine production or leaf development. It is those we will be searching for. That work is done, and we are assuming the newly engineered Gemini viruses are reproducing themselves in the plants in which they were injected with the DNA gun. The next selection step is up to the White Flies, and I assume it is now progressing. To test this, in a side room of the greenhouse I put some plants that had the engineered DNA injected side-by-side with uninfected plants, and let a lot of flies loose. I am hoping that we will soon see lesions in the plants due to the flies bringing the virus to them."

Vitz screwed up his nose and asked. "Remind me why you didn't just shoot the virus straight into the uninfected plants, or isolate virus from the plants you gunned the DNA into. All of this seems too complicated."

"Roger, Vitz, but recall I am concerned that we might select some virus that cannot be carried by the flies in real life. If it required a laboratory gun to get it into the plant, it sure wouldn't get very far in South America would it?"

"We are applying two different selections in this last stage. First, we are asking the flies to decide which virus can be carried. Of course we are giving them many and only those that survive in their guts and saliva can go to the next step. Next, we are letting the plants select those viruses that grow rapidly and create damaging lesions. The end point involves looking at the plants infected by the flies for the appearance of serious lesions. These might be holes in the leaves, bright yellow areas or dwarfed leaves. It's the same way I select the most virulent virus strains that infect bean plants."

Matt sat back listening and admiring Kiren's nose and slim but strong arms. "Damn", he thought, "different circumstances and I might–."

"Once we have plants that show clear lesions, we will pick the leaves and make crude virus preparations. Back in The States with these we can infect plants over the winter and start preparing large amounts of the virus to be spread throughout the South American coca fields. Roland will find someone to do this work– not me. Frankly, it can be done by anyone with a green thumb and a high school education. I've spoken to him and he has assured me that he has some secure sites and hands to do the work. So, my friends, with any luck we will be able to hand all of this over to the next crew soon and get back to what ever we do for a living."

Vitz seldom missed a day when he would ask Matt about the grizzly and her cubs. Had Matt seen they them yet? How likely was it that she would return? What did they eat in the summer? Indeed Matt kept the bears in the back of his mind and each time he took off in the Moose Gooser he flew spirals about the mine looking for them. None were seen but frequently they spotted mountain sheep at the higher elevations, and wolves were often seen in small packs moving through areas where moose might be, in particular cows with calves. One occasion as they were flying along a steep mountain ridge at 4000 feet elevation, Matt noticed that a herd of mountain sheep were moving up the mountain with haste. As they circled around for another look, Kiren spotted a pack of 15 wolves working their way up the mountain from below. Matt buzzed the wolves to distract them long enough to give the sheep an extra margin.

While Matt was changing oil in the Moose Gooser after the flight, Kiren suggested to Vitz that the two of them might like to take a walk down the valley to the cluster of beaver ponds. The sun was warm and Vitz, already clad in his favorite hiking shorts felt that this was a great idea. Besides, Kiren seemed unusually relaxed and was looking rather yummy he thought to himself. Strolling along the stream bank, Kiren picked up the conversation.

"So Vitz, here you are, 45 or 50, seem in good health, you've traveled to bizarre places and are educated. All in the plus column in my book. A few negatives, like you may have killed more people than were graduated in your college class. But no one is perfect. Why haven't you gotten married and done the family thing? You'd make a great president of the local PTA. If some fat mother with an unruly kid gets out of line at a meeting you could rip her throat out and flog her kid with it.

"Well, who says I don't have a family and maybe I am the president of the whole PTA of the whole USA"

"Right and Mother Theresa carried an Uzi to confession. You don't have a family do you?"

"Kiren, I have lives layered over lives. In the life you see me in now, I do not. Can't focus every moment of my time worrying about you and Matt here and worry about my 6 kids in Detroit can I?"

"I give up, no straight answers on this path, let's try another approach. Have you been in love? What kind of women do you like? Are you attracted to women who resemble your mother?"

"Kiren, I thought you wanted to go look for a beaver, not find out why I like beavers. Love, love, love. Makes my stomach turn."

They walked along for some time not talking, Kiren waiting for a response. Finally, Vitz either gave up or had sorted his response.

"Love, of course, we all go through it when we are 15, sometimes it lasts for years after that. I had my high school loves, and in college actually proposed a couple of times. If that was love, it was painful, one sided and driven by small hormone molecules you know more about than I do." He waited for a while and then continued.

"South America, Middle East, Asia, pay your money and boink it if it looks cute."

Kiren gagged.

"But you know, some of them could speakie a bit of English. So after I had paid my money we talked – you know to help her practice a bit – sort of the humanitarian thing to do."

Kiren kicked a stone, mumbling that men were all alike. She asked sneering: "And what did you talk about?"

"Them, their lives, what they wanted. You know, some of them were really bright and had good schooling. A different eye slant or color but the same damn discussions about the same damn things I had spent hours and hours talking about in college with them rich USA girls. And those discussions had the same effect on me it had had before. I fell in love with one. At least love by my standards."

"So what happened, Did you bring her back? Did you have kids? Tell me?" Kiren exploded with curiosity.

"She's fine. Lives in Hong Kong. I wanted to bring her to the US but it wouldn't have been fair with my being gone in the Delta Force all the time. I've seen how unhappy foreign wives can be living alone near some Army base."

"So how did she get to Hong Kong? Do you see her?"

"When I can– I moved her and her family to Hong Kong and got them started in a small business. They're fine. She married." Vitz seemed sad.

"She has kids?"

"Yeh, oldest one has blue eyes. Hey! Look over there at the beavers, they're building a new damn."

On the walk back Vitz had lightened up and Kiren returned to her questioning.

"So you just have the one kid." "I never said that."

"So how many?"

"No idea. A lot of women take one look at me in the supermarket and just plead for me to add my superior genes to their rundown, depleted genetic stock. Hard work you know, but my destiny."

Kiren gave up realizing that Vitz had opened up more than she expected and for now the door would be barred by macho-talk.

Raul called Henry, not being certain what Kiren's disappearance meant.

"Henry, I'm not sure what the fuck to think. After I figured out who was boasting about doomsday viruses around Washington D.C. your stuttering Brian went out and poked around. You know what he found. So then I sent Estaban to see what he could find out."

"Yah, but you never told me how that came out."

"Shit if I know, he didn't find anything more than Brian, and frankly screwed things up by almost getting caught in her apartment at night."

"Dumb. Did you cut his nuts off?"

"Didn't have to, he got so trashed in a bar I had to have my plane sent out to fetch him."

"So why are you calling me now?"

"Well, after Estaban got his butt whupped, I hired a detective agency to keep track of her. Nothing odd for a while and then one week ago she just fucking disappeared. No god damn idea where she is."

"How did this happen?"

"Just fuck'n flew off. She had taken a number of trips here and there, scientific meetings I guess, we have all of the airlines logs on her. So the detective wasn't surprised to see her fly to Washington D.C. His contact in D.C. saw her get on a flight to Guam with a stop in Hawaii. His contacts at those places never saw her."

"Jesus, so what does this mean? What would she be doing in Guam?"

"Hell, I don't understand women, in particular this one. Maybe she is off on some vacation, maybe she is doing some conference, I can't make sense of it. Get Brian to call me. He's the only one who can make sense of this bull shit."

"Sure, but Brian thinks we are done with him. Hope we can twist him for a few more efforts."

A day later Brian hesitantly called Raul in Cancun. "Raul, I thought I was done ru ru ru running around after sharp tongued, female scientists. You ought to meet her."

"Can't. Brian, we are fucking nowhere. She just fell off the edge of the world. I'd deliver the Pope's balls on a platter if you could clear this up for me. I just want to get back to a quiet life here in Cancun."

"Life of what?— oh shi shi shi shit, sorry, I don't want to know. Bu bu bu but seems it should be be be be simple to find out where she is. Was she planning some trip?"

"We don't have any way to find out. Our detective called her department and got some vague answer that she was gone and would be back in a while. You talk to scientists. Make some calls, go down if you have to. See what you can find out. Maybe it's simple and we can forget this fucking virus shit!"

"Sure, whi whi whi why not, I'll let you know." Brian signed off and threw a glass against the wall of his townhouse. He was beginning to realize that he had gotten involved in something from which it might be very hard to extract himself.

The next day Brian spent numerous hours on the phone trying different angles before hitting the right person. Calling the lab and asking for her, he got the same vague response from one of Kiren's Asian students that Raul's detective had gotten. Brian then tried another tact. Guessing that a major offer of more enzymes might break loose information he called Kiren's technician.

"Lisa, Ra Ra Ra Roger Isen here again from Plantagene. Wi Wi Wi, We would like to offer you a year's free supply of any enzyme in our ca ca ca ca catalog, bu bu bu bu but I need to have her call us and O.K. our using her name in an advertisement in Science."

"Oh, Roger, I'm sure she will say yes. But she is on a ship in the Pacific. She will be gone for a month or two. We can take messages. She said that she can relay messages through us."

"I see, may I ask wha wha wha what she is doing? Might this be something she would talk abu abu abu about to our company brass."

"Well, I'm not supposed to say, but she is working on a secret project for the Navy. Something to do with odd viruses that are cropping up on the islands where the H bombs were tested. So, I don't know if that would be of interest to them or not."

"Ah. So there's no phone there?"

"No, she is on a small ship and she won't be back on land for a while. But if you can send me an email with the details I will forward it and also read it to her when she calls. She checks in with us by satellite phone from the ship every few days."

"Fine, thank you Lisa, I'll call in a few days."

Brian relayed the discussion to Raul who was greatly relieved to hear the news.

"Well, I owe you one on this, Brian. Frankly there's no place I would rather see this fucking lady than on a boat in the middle of the ocean. There's no damn way she can cause us trouble there."

"Yah, think so. My gu gu gu guess, Raul, is that she was hard up for research dollars and was trying every crazy idea in her head. Sounds like one hit and she is now off working for the Navy on one of their odd ball projects. Too ba ba ba bad in a way, that reporter lady I told you about has be be be been calling me once a week to see if I have heard anything more. She's convinced there's a story in this that will make her a Pulitzer prize. Pretty lady."

"Well fuck her all you want, guy, but you give Kiren's name to her and somebody will be rearranging your brains with a block of dry ice."

"No worry." Brian shuddered, then mused that indeed a twenty five pound block of dry ice was the perfect murder weapon. Heavy and dense it could cave a man's head in, but a hour later it would have vaporized and added its molecules to a few tens of trillions of others in the local atmosphere. Raul had made his point.

It had been several weeks since they arrived at the mine and Matt had yet to find time alone to call to Ros. He wondered if they would ever connect on the same wavelength and he was enjoying the freedom from her tongue. Guilt spurred the call. Ros was not in the best mood and was concerned over when Matt would return and what he was doing with Kiren. Matt in return was unable to say much about what was going on and was careful not to let go of the Guam ruse. The net effect was Ros getting pissed and cutting off the conversation.

Matt stomped out and climbed the hill above the mine. He could see peaks near Anchorage in the distance and Ros seemed far away. Kiren walked up from behind. She had heard bits and pieces of the phone call and had noted Matt's distressed look as he left.

"That was Ros?"

"Yah, God, I give up."

"She sounds like a boyfriend I had when I was a postdoc at The Rockefeller. He was a social scientist type. Well, this guy, Brad was his name, was very sensitive, he doted over me. He was bright for someone who worries all day long over how to quantify the number of times children pick their noses. The basic problem was we just lived in different worlds. Maybe if we had had kids to share, but as it was, I didn't give a damn about his stuff and he was clueless as to what DNA does."

"So what happened to Brad?"

"I introduced him to my roommate. She had a Ph.D. in statistics and created computer programs to calculate how many rat parts could be in each can of canned beans and still pass the USDA requirements. It turns out that if he company is scrupulous about keeping dead rat parts and droppings out of the canned food, the USDA would allow them to put an entire rat in the 955,432rd can. Or you could spread it out so that —"

"To the point, please."

"Right, well Brad fell in love with the rat girl and they made rat babies. I guess he is studying how the kids pick their noses and she is calculating how much can be canned."

"Sounds like a marriage made in Newark. But you seem to get along with Francis, the Brit."

"Oh, he's O.K., he understands my science to some extent and that's a major plus. My problem with him is that his idea of outdoor sports is putting a sports jacket on and wandering about the yard with a martini in one hand and a copy of the New York Times in the other. Horse shit makes him break out in hives."

Kiren continued: "Scientists have a hard time finding appropriate mates. We are driven and have compulsive personality profiles. No scientist of merit I know is able to leave their work at the lab. If the experiments are going slowly you think about it morning to night. If the experiments are going great, then you can't get them off your mind and are excited thinking about the next ones. This kind of life makes it hard to find a suitable mate unless that person is also a scientist."

"Right on. If I list my friends who are scientists and who seem to have good marriages, they fall into two groups. In one group both are scientists and they live their lives around the lab. In several cases they actually have combined their labs and share equipment, grants and write papers together. That may sound a bit much, but it's no different from a couple running a motel together. Those marriages seem awfully intense to me and if the science gets slow or they run into grant troubles, there is nothing in their lives to buffer them. If they have kids, that helps. The others are ones in which one is a scientist and the other does normal kinds of things and – this is the important thing, they share kids or some major hobby together."

"So why are you hanging onto this shrink? She's not the type I'd expect to see you with."

Before Matt could answer, Kiren pulled her face very close to Matt and beamed her giant gray eyes directly into his.

"So between Ros and me, who is more attractive?"

Matt squirmed, unable to avoid her eyes. "Ah, you are, no question."

"Fine, and who understands science more?"

"You do, no question."

"And who is a better horsewoman?"

"She hates horses."

"Just collecting data." Kiren reached up and lightly traced her finger tips across his face, then turned and walked back to the mine.

Matt's stomach was knotted the rest of the day. Whether it had been the row with Ros or more likely the intimate brush with Kiren he was not certain.

After lunch Kiren picked up Vitz' .243 rifle. Vitz was reluctant to let her touch it but that mattered little to Kiren. She found his stash of ammunition, set up a row of tin cans 100 yards down Matt's runway and in a prone position began firing. Noting that the rifle was shooting high and to the left, she adjusted the sights until she was able to hit the cans every time. She was obviously more skilled with it than Vitz whose theory had always been one of firepower rather than single bullet accuracy. Ralph had been a collegiate match rifle shooter and Kiren had tagged along many times. She liked the .243, it was not heavy and the recoil was hardly notable. She began carrying it everywhere, in particular on hikes.

Vitz was extremely unhappy over the loss of "his rifle". Whether it represented his phallic symbol, or more likely, security vis a vis the bears, he would not say. Every time he tried to get it back Kiren would tease him about his being afraid of baby bears and he would huff off. Kiren had found a Vitz button she could push at will.

The following weeks were particularly pleasant for Matt. He found Kiren's ability to tease Vitz amusing, and they had begun to enjoy each other and chat in a relaxed way about science, and common likes and dislikes. They teamed up to razz Vitz over topics ranging from religion (Jesus had been trained as a Buddhist at a young age) to politics (Harrison Ford should run for president) to gun control (if all children were armed, then there would be no child abuse). The science seemed to be progressing well and Kiren had seen no indication for concern. The increasing free time had allowed Matt to make a major dent in his pile of papers and he had filled two brown notebooks with thoughts and summaries. The calls to his lab to check on results left him withdrawn for an hour or so until he had digested the information and formulated new experiments.

The one thing that bothered Matt was, frankly, Kiren herself. Some days she would seem to purposely ignore him and other days she was in his face all day with her giant gray eyes. There were times when he had strong desire to drag her off to the bedroom – and then she would spend the day giving Vitz a back rub and purposely snub him. "Jesus" he told himself, "I am a grown man not a schoolboy", and did his best to ignore her behavior.

Several days later while Matt and Vitz hiked up to the Kanikula Glacier Kiren surveyed the plants in the side room where she had put some together with the White Flies. Although she put on a positive face for Matt and Vitz, she was worried why she had yet to find lesions on the leaves which should have been infected by the flies. Certainly the flies were as thick as fog in San Francisco and should have been doing their job of transferring the Gemini virus. She had been able to do this many times in North Carolina using the strain of Gemini virus that infects her laboratory plants.

Kiren reviewed the time schedule again. She was agonizing over this when Matt and Vitz walked up behind her and caught her off guard. Matt realized from her expression that she was worried and pushed to the point.

"What's wrong? I've seen that look on my colleagues once too often. What's up?"

Kiren explained that by now she should be seeing lesions on the leaves. This was particularly so, she said, since the plants were being incubated in a high humidity environment with temperatures from the sun warming the room to 85 degrees for at least 18 hours each day.

"Wish we had an electron microscope in this laughable laboratory. I could have a technician section the plant leaves from the sites where the DNA was shot in with the DNA gun to verify that new virus particles are being produced. If we could see some virus particles, it sure would make me feel better. At least we would have gotten past step one in the pathway."

Matt shrugged his shoulders and replied: "We could send some samples to Mike in Chapel Hill. Don't see why he wouldn't be willing to help."

She exclaimed. "We could cut a few plugs from the plants near the sites of DNA injection. The virus is hardy; it will stand shipping for a day or two."

Later that day, Matt flew The Moose Gooser to Anchorage International Airport and Federal Expressed a handful of 1/4 inch plugs cut from several leaves. A promise of some float plane flying was more than enough to elicit a promise of help. The plugs were fixed with formaldehyde and small chunks were mixed with a liquid plastic resin which infiltrated the plant tissue. It was then heated to harden the resin. The resulting solid plastic block contained the plant chunks embedded much like a fly is embedded in amber. These were then placed in an instrument that uses diamond knives to cut very thin slices, like micro-potato chips that contain the cells and tissue. The slices are so thin that the electron beam in the microscope can penetrate them and create an image of the cells and their contents.

While they were awaiting word from North Carolina, Matt and Vitz took an extended walk to the stream down the valley. The stream was ripe with Grayling, 20 inch long trout that will take a variety of lures and fight vigorously. They are extremely tasty. Returning, fish in hand, they were surprised upon coming into view of the mine. Kiren was pacing back and forth in a curious pattern. As they got nearer they spotted stakes in the ground each with a tin can over the top. She seemed to be dancing around and around in a complex pattern within an invisible circle formed by the stakes. Matt and Vitz sat down a comfortable distance away and observed. Occasionally she would stop and make notes on a writing pad and then go back to repeat the pattern. Matt broke the code.

"Well, damn, Vitz, she's doing a dressage test! See, each of the cans has a letter on it and they form a rectangular area within which she is trotting, cantering, walking, hopping up and down while going side ways or nowhere at all."

"Yup, our nutty buddy has brought horse culture to the Arctic."

Kiren was wearing short shorts. Vitz turned to Matt.

"Damn nice set of legs there. You know, I've seen her stare at you like Roland gazes at a chocolate pie. I think she's really hot for you. Give me the word and I'll go camping for a couple of days. Boink her all you want, I'll never tell."

Matt blushed slightly and laughed. "God, no-no. Remember, this is professional. Can't mix business and pleasure. Not that those legs don't get to me. Sometimes I think life sure would have been easier if I had fallen harder when I slipped off of the seat of my bike as a boy.

They waited until Kiren had finished and had taken her tin cans down. Thus a pattern was set. Vitz and Matt would announce that they were going fishing and were very careful not to be seen until Kiren had finished her dressage lesson for the day. She did seem to be getting better at this as time went on.

The thin sectioning done, they called Mike. A chat confirmed what she had hoped to hear —which was that nearly all of the samples showed evidence of the production of Gemini virus particles near the sites where the DNA had been shot in with the DNA gun. Kiren turned to Matt.

"Wow! Am I delighted that new virus are being made! I expected it, and there is no way that these viruses could have come from any other source than the engineered DNA. But am I pleased to have it confirmed! So we are making virus from our engineered DNA. Great! Now what I'm still concerned about is why we are not seeing any lesions growing outwards from the sites where the DNA was shot in, or lesions on the plants infected by the flies."

Matt replied: "Let's get the paper pad out again and look at your flow diagram. You suggested EM to check the first step, and that turned out to work well, possibly we can find some other way to check on the next stage."

The news was not good. The call to Raul from The Colombian verged on hysteria. Earlier Raul had explained Brian's discovery of his mystery virologist playing in the South Pacific collecting exotic viruses, concluding that the doomsday virus rumor could be put to rest. The hysteria resulted from the discovery that a group of American military personnel had raided a coca field in Peru but rather than burning the plants or spreading a defoliant, they had carefully dug up young plants and potted them, flying off in helicopters. The plants had been subsequently flown to the

US, but their trail had been lost after that. The Colombian had put two and two together and was convinced that the shipment of plants by the US military was directly linked to the doomsday virus project.

"My friend, I understand your concern. Worries me too. But we need to find out where these plants went. They could be in an exhibit at the Smithsonian. The other end of this puzzle is our virologist. If she is really in the South Pacific looking for A-bomb viruses, whatever is going on with the coca plants, it doesn't have any connection with her." Raul was trying to calm The Colombian who seemed to be blaming him for the whole business.

"Raul. I need assurances or people are going to be unhappy. You wanted to "be on top of this one". Then be on top and make us happy. What you plan?"

"Ah, well, I'll do everything I can to find out where this fuck'n woman is, and see about the plants. Keep you informed." Raul tried to sound calm all the while knotting the phone cord to tightly that it broke, cutting the connection. He then flung the phone through a window and stormed out. In his heart he knew that there must be a connection between Kiren and the very unusual shipment of coca plants.

Later that night he made a series of phone calls. Estaban was in Mexico and was to fly to New York City. There they would meet Henry and Brian. The objective of the meeting was to discuss options and see what could be done to trace Kiren and to find out where the plants were. Stage by stage Brian was being drawn in, and the guise of being just an information gatherer was frequently forgotten.

They met at a restaurant in one of the most expensive New York city hotels. Henry had sent Brian an airline ticket, and tickets to the best shows in town for the weekend. Brian brought a friend who was off shopping when they met. Raul and Henry were dressed in extremely fine suits making Brian feel a bit shabby. If Estaban had not been with them, one might have guessed that he was asking for research funding from a pair of New York City bankers. Estaban although dressed well, had an air of being out of place with his eyes flashing this way and that.

"So, Raul, anything exciting in Cancun recently?" Henry asked while pouring a round of wine.

"Fuck'n bad week. Two damn Mexicans tried to cross the moat that surrounds my compound. Apparently didn't read the signs and slipped past the high voltage wire. Hijeputa! (the Spanish/ Colombian version of "son of a bitch!")–Fucking thieves."

"They stole something?" Brian asked.

"Never got past the inner wall of the moat. Proved how good the moat is. The outside wall is 12 feet high with a high voltage line on the top and the inner face of the cement is smooth. The moat is 20 feet across with water and plants in the bottom. Authorities were really pissed and were threatening to make me clean it up. Had to use throw hooks to drag the buggers out."

"Your snakes?" Estaban asked shuddering.

Raul smirked at Estaban knowing how insanely afraid of snakes he was. Hooking his hand and making a snake mouth with his thumb and forefinger he reached over and pecked at Estaban's arm. Even knowing that this was just a joke, Estaban recoiled.

"Estaban, afraid of my little Fer de Lances? Fuck'n great way to die, real quick. They have a venom that is a mix of Rattlesnake venom, a neurotoxin like that in Cobra venom, and strong hemolytic that blows up your blood cells. Causes you to bleed to death from organ loss. Lots of tissue damage. Often they amputate. But if you get the full jolt you die in minutes."

"Jesus Raul, you weren't kidding when we were there a few months ago. You really keep that moat full of Fer de Lances." Henry responded.

"Collected them myself. Over 200 hundred. Maybe the best collection in the world. If you are quick, you can avoid one or two, not more. When I hired a whole pack of guards to watch the place they stole everything. Now I just have one gate and the moat. Never lose a thing and the Ferrari's are a lot safer."

Brian looked rather ill and turned the conversation back to why they were there in the first place. Turning to Henry he asked.

"Henry, I greatly ap ap ap appreciate the tickets and all, and it's a pleasure to meet your friends, but this makes me a bi bi bi bit uneasy. I thought I got all the information you needed." Raul replied:

"Yah, yah. We appreciated that. I'm certain this little lady is off in the South Pacific dreaming about sea horses, but something came up that made our friends very nervous."

"So what was this?" Brian asked.

"Well, about a month ago a bunch of American military types in gray helicopters dropped into a local coca field in Peru and then spent the day digging plants up and potting them as if they were Easter lilies. They were put on a transport that was tracked to Andrews Air Force base outside of Washington D.C – but the plants have disappeared. Our friends are worried that there is a connection between this and the doomsday virus."

"Could be be be be. The time table I sketched out the first time we talked indicated that experiments would have to move to using real co co co co coca plants. This would be be be be just about on schedule." Brian commented, seeming to be pleased with himself.

"Hijeputa!"

There was an explosion when the wine glass that Raul was holding shattered inward as he clenched it with a steel grip. Several glass fragments penetrated his hand and cursing, he extended his hand to Henry who tipped his bifocals and used a pen knife to remove them. The hand was wrapped in a cloth from the table and Raul glowering, picked up the discussion.

"Don't fucking want to believe this! Here's what we need. First we need to know exactly where this woman is and what the fuck she is doing. Second we need to know where those plants are. We need every bit of help we can get. I need each of you to think of every crazy damn way we can track her and the plants down. But before trying anything it has to be cleared with me. Is that clear? OK, OK, so ideas. I need ideas here."

Henry shook his head and turned to Brian. "Brian, can you go back to Duke and push them harder?" Raul broke in.

"We have only one chance here. If she is up to something, we can't just try this and that. It has to work the first time. Otherwise it will just drive her deeper underground. Maybe Henry can use his contacts to find out how many Navy research ships there are in the South Pacific and where they are. Brian. What about that reporter girl friend of yours?"

"Oh, her, she has been bu bu bu bugging the hell out of me — is still convinced that there is a Pu Pu Pu Pulitzer prize in this for her. But she seems to know less than we do."

"Fine, but let me make it clear. If this virus project is real, then your reporter is going to get her damn prize. That's for sure."

"Why not just kill these guys?" Estaban asked.

Brian looked very unhappy and Raul turned to Estaban.

"Hijeputa! You crap-head! No one gets killed! Maybe I'm the only one here who sees the long range picture, so let me spell it out in simple terms you can follow."

"This could be a lot bigger than just one little bunch of scientists making a virus. If this virus works, it will end everything to do with coca. Now, you kill the first wave of scientists and what happens my small brained one? They just get more scientists and now do this project under such security and so far underground that no one will know what is going on until it is too late. We can't let that happen. There is only one way to stop this thing. That is to get hard evidence and give it to this reporter lady. She splashes the story across the newspapers and I promise you that our friends down south can mount such a campaign of righteous screaming no one would touch it."

Estaban and Henry nodded vigorously as if this was the first time they understood Raul's line of thinking.

"Brian, all we need you to do right now is to keep your reporter pumped up over the story. Make her feel you think something is happening. Tell her the details of the coca plant shipment. I'll give you the exact dates and the ID number of the airplane that brought the plants in. Maybe she can track them better than we can. Couldn't hurt. Henry here is going to pull in some favors with his friends at the Navy. I have a card up my sleeve but I don't want to play it unless we are certain that this Kiren is working on the project. It's a one-time card. That's about all for now. Any ideas, let me know."

The conversation was moved to lighter topics and the dinner finished. Noting that Brian had finished his desert, Raul turned to him.

"Brian, the rest of us have a couple of details we need to work out. Go back to your girlfriend and let the three of us fight over the dinner bill. Have a great weekend on us. The hotel tab is on my card. Keep in touch. Call that reporter as soon as you get back."

Brian shook their hands and departed. Raul turned to Henry and Estaban.

"The Colombian is scared to death of viruses. I've been told that once he learned that AIDS is caused by a virus you get through sex, he hasn't had pussy in 5 years. Old Howard Hughes wasn't as freaky as he is. Problem here is that he's nuts on the topic and frankly has every right to be if this rumor is true. His approach is just make it OK– kill a bunch of people. I spent an hour on the phone with him trying to explain why the only way to stop it was a lot of publicity, but I still don't know how far I got. But he agreed on one thing and that is I am in charge of this thing. Is that clear Estaban?"

"Si, senior Raul." Estaban was taunting Raul just a bit. Raul pecked at Estaban's hand with his snake mouth getting the response he wanted. They adjourned agreeing that the next order of business was to get a better trace on Kiren.

Kiren, Matt, and Vitz convened their discussion the following morning over a large stack of sourdough pancakes. Matt was cutting and eating with the tool on his Leatherman Model One he called the "fork-o-knife". It looked to have been forged from a flat piece of steel, had four prongs, but lacked the curve of a normal fork. The outer prongs were sharpened to provide a cutting edge. Vitz and Kiren continually taunted him about it, which was why he was using it that morning. The ravens had discovered Matt was back and although they belonged to a different tribe from the clan in Prince William Sound, they were just as vocal and fond of pancakes. Kiren was very attached to them and claimed to be able to identify different ravens and tell male from female. She had named them after Rock stars. There was Madonna, Pat Benatar, and David Bowie. Younger ones were given names of her graduate students and thus had a particularly Asian flavor.

Kiren diagrammed the life cycle of the Gemini virus and the engineered variants and underlined the steps where the engineering had been fruitful. Progeny viruses were growing where they shot the DNA into the plant leaves. Why then, were they not seeing lesions in the leaves caused by White Flies carrying the new viruses over to the uninfected plants? Kiren outlined several possibilities.

"There are a number of steps where we might run into trouble. What worries me most is the possibility that few if any of the engineered viruses are being picked up by the White Flies. We really need to know if they are being carried by the flies. If not, then the project may be dead in the water since I have little idea what the determinants are that make the White Fly a good vector for transmitting the virus. Maybe we made too many changes."

Matt nodded: "So what you want to know is whether or not the flies are carrying the virus particles. We sure can't ask Mike to do electron microscopy of fly spit–he could never find a virus among all the slime."

Kiren twisted her nose and continued. "That's the central question right now guys —why aren't we seeing any lesions on the new plants? We need some way to amplify the virus and determine if any virus are being carried by the flies."

Vitz had nearly nodded off, and had the appearance of not paying much attention as he sat rigid holding a string attached to a stick that was propping up a wood box. Under the box was a pancake. His intent seemed to be to drop the box over a raven; for what reason was not apparent.

Vitz broke into the conversation. "If you need to amplify the virus, then how about that PCB test that we heard about in North Carolina, would that work?"

At this point, two things happened simultaneously. Kiren yelled "No!" and Vitz pulled the string. The box dropped around

Madonna, the raven. There was an awful thrashing inside the box as Vitz dove onto the box and thrust both hands under it to capture Madonna.

Seconds later, one hand emerged with a large black beak clamped around Vitz' thumb. Kiren pounced on the pair of them and pried the beak apart long enough to extract the hand. Copious spurts of blood were followed by howls from Vitz. Madonna took this opportunity to snatch a fresh pancake from Vitz' plate as she disappeared out the door on foot, unable to fly with such a large prize. Matt had watched Vitz construct his box trap fully aware of what he had in mind. He was also knew the power of an adult Alaskan raven– which stands knee high to a man.

Calm was finally restored as the hand was soaked in a glass of Jim Beam, and Kiren listed several things that would happen to either Matt or Vitz if they were to harm any of her pets. Matt had no interest in offending the ravens, and Vitz had gained a much greater respect for them. Finally Matt brought the conversation back to where it had been prior to Vitz' bloodletting.

"Before his episode of playing trapper, Vitz made a comment that may have some real value. If I can translate PCB for PCR, then possibly the PCR technique might have the power we need to amplify the Gemini virus sequences enough to determine if the virus is being carried by the flies. It is an enormously powerful method. Normally we would need a sophisticated machine to do it, but in a rough way, we might make do here. I brought along my stash of enzymes and may have what we need."

"So how would this work?" Vitz asked. Kiren glowered at Vitz and described the process:

"Recall nuclear fission. In that kind of chain reaction– one nucleus splits and gives rise to two —each of which hits another atom —splitting those and giving rise to 4, and so on. Not long, you have split millions. In the DNA world, a method called polymerase chain reaction was worked out using this same principle." Matt took over, smiling at Vitz holding his thumb in the glass of whiskey.

In our case the amplification is done by DNA polymerase enzymes that are stable to heating, and each round of amplification involves a precise series of steps in which the DNA in the mixture is heated to 203 degrees to separate all the strands, then lowered to 160 degrees to allow short bracketing segments to bind and then to 130 degrees to allow the polymerase molecules to work."

"What are bracketing segments?" Vitz asked.

"Well, we call them primers, but you can think of them as being short pieces of DNA that are added to direct the polymerase enzyme to amplify only the segment of DNA you are doing PCR on that lies between the two bracketing segments."

Kiren rolled her head up at the ceiling. "You might even be able to explain DNA to my mother."

Matt smiled and continued. "Normally 30 cycles of heating and polymerizing is carried out. With this many copies of the DNA, one can detect it by simple physical methods. The method that is used most frequently is gel electrophoresis.

Vitz had heard this term but asked Matt to explain gel electrophoresis.

"Simple actually," commented Matt. "DNA is a highly charged molecule. Much like a very long noodle that has electric charges strung all along its length. If one places a sample of the DNA in a slab of agarose, which is like jello, and then applies a strong electric field along the length of the jello slab, the DNA will move along the slab from one end to the other, driven by the electric field. The key is that the smaller the piece of DNA, the faster it moves. This method provides a very powerful way to separate DNA molecules by size. In this case, the DNA that we have amplified between the two primers will be of a known size and we can use gel electrophoresis to determine if a large amount of DNA of this particular size has been created. If the original sample lacks the sequences we are searching for, then the primers will have nothing to bind to and nothing will be amplified."

"Based on Vitz' brilliant suggestion, here's how I would do things. My guess is that in the DNAs we brought along, you have the appropriate primers we need to amplify a DNA segment that would be present in all of the Gemini viruses. We will capture single White Flies and grind them up and isolate all the small virus-sized DNA. That will be our starting material which we will test by PCR for the presence of Gemini virus DNA segments."

Kiren shook her head, understanding what Matt had in mind but they had not included a PCR cycling machine in the equipment she had shipped from her lab.

An inspection of their inventory revealed that Matt had included more than enough of the DNA polymerase enzyme. Fortunately Kiren had packed a box of primers that had been synthesized for her DNA sequencing work. The PCR machine would be another matter. Matt had several at Hopkins. The machines are the size of an old style typewriter. One could be shipped from Matt's lab, but that would take time, and Matt had concerns that the appearance of such a machine in Talkeetna might provide a trace to their whereabouts. Thus he felt that it might be worth a makeshift try first. The machine heats the sample to 203 degrees, then cools it to 13 degrees and finally raises the temperature to 160 degrees. Each step takes two minutes– over and over 30 times.

Heating the sample to 203 degrees could be accomplished by placing the tubes in water that has almost reached the boiling point. The bottom temperature of 130 degrees was easily obtained since they had brought along a common laboratory water bath that will hold this temperature. The intermediate temperature of 160 degrees centigrade however was more of a problem, as the electric heating bath they had would not go this high.

A perusal of the mine and greenhouse buildings raised nothing of value until Matt happened to take a look at the home made shower that had been relegated to a back corner. What it offered was a means of heating a very large quantity of water, nearly 50 gallons, with a small oil burning heater. Matt realized that although it might take some time to play with the heater so that the water reached 160 degrees centigrade that the large mass of the water would then remain relatively stable for some time. Vitz offered the perfect robot in Matt's mind, and after all, he had suggested it, of sorts.

The next morning a test of the "Kanikula PCR" system was begun using Gemini virus particles diluted to varying amounts. The PCR reaction mixtures were made in small test tubes and after nearly 4 hours of playing with the oil heater, the 160 degree temperature was achieved. Next to the shower they set up a small gas camping stove to boil the water water and beside that was the 130 degree laboratory water bath. Using a stop watch, Vitz was run through the drill of placing the sample in the boiling water for 2 minutes, then into the 130 degree bath for 2 minutes, and finally into 50 gallon oil barrel for 2 minutes– and around and around for 30 cycles. All this required 3 tedious hours, and by the end of the test Vitz was getting tired and ill tempered. Kiren and Matt did all that could be done to keep his spirits up other than offering Jim Beam.

Following the last round, a portion of the sample was placed in the slab of agarose and the electrophoresis carried out for 2 hours. By this time it was late at night but all three were very anxious to see if the test had worked. They stained the DNA and saw a bright staining band of DNA exactly at the position they expected. Delighted, Matt and Kiren realized that the next several days would involve a lot of tedium for all three if they were to apply the Kanikula PCR method for real.

Early the next morning, 50 flies were captured in the greenhouse and each was ground up and the DNA purified. Next, the PCR enzymes and primers were added. Matt took the first shift of moving tubes followed by Vitz and finally Kiren. It was late in the afternoon before the 30th round was completed. Matt and Vitz cooked dinner as Kiren numbered the tubes and started the electrophoresis.

Over dinner of freshly caught grayling they worried over how the experiment would work out. Following a half hour of staining the DNA in the gel, they looked at the slabs of agarose containing samples from the 50 flies. Of the 50 samples, 10 showed very strong bands that matched the expected position in the test.

"Wow!" exclaimed Kiren. "I'm delighted! A good fraction of our flies are carrying the Gemini virus plant to plant. We really have gotten past the next major hurdle."

She turned to Matt. "O.K., O.K. O.K., so the flies are carrying our new virus. Why aren't we seeing lesions on leaves of the plants that the flies should have infected?"

Kiren tipped the brow of her hat so that it covered her eyes and leaned back on her chair.

"I see no reason why we can't use PCR to check on what's happening in the plants following their infection. I can take some parts of plants that should have been infected, grind them up and do PCR — and see what we find."

They wrote out a procedure that involved washing the leaves to see if the engineered virus were at least being left on their surface by the flies. Next, slices of leaves were taken both at the sites where the DNA had been shot in and distant to it. Slices of stems, and roots were also cut. Kiren had seen very tiny spots on the plants that were supposed to be infected by the flies and samples were taken from these areas. The remainder of the day was spent working out the protocols and making the extracts. Kiren did most of this, not trusting Vitz at all, and Matt only marginally. Little did she know how close on her heels Raul and his group were.

CHAPTER TWELVE
TRACKED DOWN

Henry called Raul at the Cancun compound. The news was not encouraging.

"Raul, don't know what to think. Called in heavy favors– one time shots. Lot of poking around done on our behalf. To any one's knowledge, there is no US Navy ship the Bikini Atolls area. Tossed Kiren's name out saying we knew she was working for the Navy. Her name came up attached to a mail drop. Person handling that was in one of the other agencies, a secret obscure bunch. Had no way of getting at them. Doesn't sound good does it?"

"Oh damn that little bitch! Hijeputa! Does she have any idea what she is playing with? Jesus H Christ! Damn it! "

"Sounds like if you have finally joined the doomsday virus wagon."

"Shit, if I know, but it looks as if it may really be happening."

"We still don't know what happened to the plants, or if she and the plants are linked. Are you going to tell The Colombian?"

"Oh, fuck no, you just told me you still don't know where she is. Right? That's no more than we knew before, right? I recall you were planning to fly to L.A. next week. Stop down here. Let's think some more before making the "idiot of Bogota" even more paranoid."

A week later Raul, Estaban, and Henry sat on lawn chairs in Raul's compound looking down at the beach and the quietly breaking waves. Raul was sniffing coke which he frequently did at this time of the evening or when he was under stress. He started the conversation.

"Lets put all our ideas out on the table. We'll go around. Anything at all. Henry– you first."

"OK, still think the key to finding Kiren lies with Brian. He knows what lure she might bite. Asked him to keep working on the reporter. Been doing that– think we need to push him more."

"I'd go with that. Right, what ever she is up to, she is still a scientist driven by the same things that drive Brian. Tell Brian if he can find her and help us get evidence of this virus project I will guarantee him one hundred thousand in cash in a Swiss account."

"Woh! Mean that?" Henry looked surprised, realizing this sum that would not hurt Raul but was significant even so.

"Absolutely! And no fucking him over. I'll transfer it to a third party account if that would make him feel better. More ideas, Henry?"

"Not much, Brian and I could cook up some evidence and feed it to the reporter. Might make the tabloids."

Raul shook his head. "No, no. We don't know much about this virus shit and the first expert who looked into what you wrote would blow it. We need to flush her out." Estaban turned to Raul.

"Hit her family! Find where they live. Hurt them real bad, they be in hospital. When she come to see them —zap zap zap. " Estaban smiled at Raul and Henry as if being very proud of a clever plan.

Before Estaban could react, the barrel of Raul's H&K .380 double action semiautomatic had been jammed up his nose while his head was held by his hair. Raul slowly with his voice quivering, spoke to Estaban.

"You dirty stupid little Indian shit. All you know is killing. I told you no one gets killed. We need evidence. That's the only way to stop this thing. You kill them, you drive them underground!"

Twisting the barrel further into Estaban's flared nostril, Raul continued.

"If there is killing to be done, I say when. If you so much as get near her family, I will tie you up, and slowly lower you head first into a nest of freshly hatched Fer de Lances. I'm told it goes a lot slower that way."

Estaban was dropped back into his chair and he sat glowering at Raul who used Estaban's Mexican silk shirt to wipe his nose debris off of the H&K's barrel. Henry looked ill and somewhat surprised at the intensity of Raul's response but was pleased as he had continually urged the cartel members to avoid killing civilians at all costs– in particular in the US. Henry tried to lighten things by bringing the conversation back to Raul.

"So Raul, it's your turn. What do you offer here other than a large sum of cash? Assume the offer is open to me – if I get the evidence?"

"Sure. Even to Estaban – as long as you play by my rules. We know she is getting mail. I thought I would write her a letter, and ask her very nicely to stop. I can send it to her department;, you said they were forwarding her mail." Raul smirked at the two of them.

"You call me a stupid Indian shit. You more stupid." Estaban taunted Raul but kept his hand where he could push the H&K away. Henry shook his head.

"As a lawyer I'd say there is more to it than that. A threat? Offer her a million dollars in unmarked bills? What's the carrot?"

"Her stupid brother. I knew him well. He's the Friggin carrot."

"I thought you said he was dead?"

"I did. But she made a number of trips to the area where his plane disappeared. She never found the wreckage or a body. So, I write her. Tell her we know she is making this virus. Tell her we have strong reasons to believe her brother is alive in the jungles. I'll cook up the details—head injury, gave up smuggling— got religious, something likely. I can give her a few details about him that only some one who him knew well would know. I'll offer to help find him in return for her quitting and telling our reporter about the virus stuff."

Henry turned his head to and fro and Estaban sat quietly with his eyes narrowed trying to think. Henry responded:

"Huh, clever. I guess you knew him well enough to be able to drop in some tantalizing details. Think this would be enough to get her to stop?"

"From what my contacts at the University in Bogota told me, the reason she is working on this stupid virus is to put our asses out of business in revenge for her brother's death. If we bring him back to life, why wouldn't she quit?"

"OK, so now I understand how you knew who it was, but what happens when you can't produce him?"

"Hell, I can keep her stupid ass tromping the jungles for the next ten years. I can create leads faster than she can run them down. Besides once she has turned her project over to the reporter, so what if she finds out that we were just jerking her chain? It's all over and no one is killed, right Estaban?"

Estaban jumped as Raul pecked at his nose with his snake mouth. Henry was anxious not to miss his airplane to L.A. and summarized things.

"So, on my ledger, we offer Brian a small fortune to figure out where she is— keep the fake story as a last resort— you bait a hook with her dead brother."

As they left, Raul put his hand around Estaban's shoulder and led him over to the moat to point out a new nest of baby snakes then laughed loudly as Estaban nearly collapsed. Later that night Raul sat alone at the outdoor table, sniffed a great deal of cocaine and drafted his letter to Kiren. He seemed somber and made numerous drafts, frequently downing straight tequilas.

At the mine the morning arrived warm and sunny. Kiren, Matt, and Vitz decided to take a quick trip to the stream to catch breakfast trout before attending to a long day. On the way, Vitz broached the subject of ethics once again.

Vitz had a deep distrust for the "higher moral wisdom" of governments based in part on his youth under socialism. He felt that single individuals follow moral codes that differ amazingly little from one country or religion to another. Murder, robbery, adultery are "sins" irrespective of culture, and many vehicles have been created to convince society members that indulging in them is wrong. However collections of people, Vitz felt, frequently fail to follow the simple moral standards of the one. Thus the sum of the individuals is less than the sum of the parts. In a communal action, he explained, it was possible to hand the moral confrontation from one person to the next along an endless chain.

For many individuals in America it was obvious that there was something morally wrong with our actions in Viet Nam. Why then didn't the government see this? Vitz' answer was that the major job of government employees and in particular military staff is in passing the buck and protecting your ass.

It was from this standpoint that Vitz had tried several times to push Kiren to consider the larger ramifications of her project. Walking, fishing rods in hand, and with Kiren carrying the .243, Vitz dove in again.

"Do you realize what the two of you are doing? In a way it's the first use of a weapon that is as new and untried as the A-bomb was in 1945."

Kiren began to speed up but Matt held her hand tightly as a signal to slow down and listen to what Vitz might have to say.

"Each of the sciences has produced weapons for war. Gun powder was the gift of chemistry. Physics gave us the Atom bomb. That took thousands of physicists and engineers working in secret to produce the first one, and even now making one is beyond all but a few highly technological countries."

"The A bomb was created for the best of moral reasons, stopping the big war. It seems to me that your genetic engineering represents a major step in using molecular biology to create weapons. Yes, yes, I agree that the goal of this project is just. Frankly I don't care one way or the other about coke, and I'm looking forward to spreading your little viruses in the jungle. But there are two things that worry me in the larger sense. First, the precedent of what the two of you are doing and second, that it will be done by only two people, and not much of a laboratory, given what I have seen."

Kiren and Matt were speechless. Vitz had revealed a depth of understanding they had only recently begun to suspect was there.

As they continued to walk, Matt decided to work away at Vitz' worries bit by bit.

"That's the stuff that hand held signs at rallies are made of, Vitz. You have a real point, but let me see if I can assuage your fears a bit. First, genetic engineering has been changing our lives quietly for some time. Fruit trees are sprayed with bacteria that lower the freezing temperature of the fruit just enough to protect them from frost. No major complaints there. Tomatoes have been genetically engineered so that they ripen but remain firm for shipping, allowing us to buy much tastier veggies. No complaints from the BLT crowd! The new Hepatitis B vaccine is a product of genetic engineering as are a number of vaccines we use to protect our furry pet friends. No complaints from the pussy lovers. For me, it's all a matter of degree. Engineering a virus to kill people in ways that natural viruses do not is unthinkable. What we are doing, I admit makes me a bit nervous but I put it in the 'acceptable risk' category."

"We go from heaven to hell in acceptable little steps," replied Vitz.

"What's your specific objection about this project, Vitz?" snipped Kiren.

"Roland is a middle level Fed. Them guys make me nervous. They are just half way up the food chain. Coca leaves are part of the centuries-old culture in the Andes. The peasants chew the leaves when they work at high elevation in the belief that it gives them added strength. True or not, I don't know. But who are we to say that just because our advanced culture can't learn how it handles its own stress that another culture has to suffer for it?"

"You think that eradicating the coca plant would hurt the peasants in South America?" Kiren asked Matt, not wanting to hand Vitz a point.

"Well he has a real point. You should know, you've been there." Matt replied.

By this time they had reached the stream and Kiren ended the discussion by announcing that they couldn't talk– it would scare the fish. Kiren however had to have the last word and waved the .243 at them:

"As far as I am concerned, I'm doing the right thing and you two can stick with me or screw you. I owe it to Ralph."

She picked up her fishing rod and crossed the stream to the far side carrying the .243. Matt and Vitz looked at each other, shrugged their shoulders and began casting from their side. After 20 minutes, all three had worked their way 50 yards up the stream. A deep pool separated Kiren on one side from Matt and Vitz who were directly across on the other side.

Vitz was carrying the lure box and Matt began rummaging in it for a smaller lure. At that moment both he and Vitz looked up. Kiren stood facing them .243 shouldered in a ready to fire position and with the sights aimed directly at them– in particular it seemed, at Vitz. Her expression was one Matt had never seen before: a cold intensity that cut right through them.

Vitz froze, then began quietly pleading. "Kiren, please, no, no, we will go along with anything. I was just trying to see how much it meant to you. Please Kiren, you don't need to do this. We're your big brothers—Kirrr'–"

Matt broke in: "Shut up and don't move!"

The muzzle blast stung their faces. Vitz dove head first into the ice cold water while Matt spun around to catch the glimpse of a mass of brown fur retreating into the alder on the stream bank.

When he got to Kiren, and took the .243, she was shaking head to toe. She put both arms around Matt, holding him tightly.

"I looked up! Saw the bear behind you! It was on a line directly between your head and Vitz'. I wasn't going to shoot, but it started to raise up as if it was going to charge– like you had told me about. I shot just over its head!"

"You saved our butts, but Vitz thought you were gunning for him. By the way where is he?"

Vitz, assuming that Kiren had missed but would not miss a second time had swum under water to the far end of the pool where he was peeking out of the water at them, his green wool cap dripping water over his eyes.

"Should I drop a few shots around our blonde bud?"

"Jesus Christ, no, Kiren; by the way, you get to do his laundry tonight."

Vitz finally returned at Matt's calling.

The three returned to the mine and Kiren, being in an elated mood cooked the trout for lunch and recounted over and over how close it had been and mimicked Vitz' pleading for her not to shoot. Vitz countered:

"Look, being shot to death by the FARC in Columbia is all in a day's work, but I have no intention of being gunned down by a smart assed little red head. My buds back at Ft. Bragg would create a tombstone with an epithet that would ensure my perpetual disgrace. Besides I saw the two of you hugging and kissing back there and thought you guys wanted me out of the way so you could boink each other."

"What? And what's boinking?" Kiren was caught off guard and then recalled her holding Matt after the bear had run off.

Matt winced and replied. "Never mind."

Vitz lightened up and announced that he would make desert. Several weeks earlier, he and Matt had flown to Talkeetna to get the mail, and being a warm Saturday, they had walked around town. Passing a house with a yard sale in progress, Vitz had urged Matt to go on while he "shopped". He arrived back at the airplane with a bag but would not reveal its contents. In the ensuing week, he had disappeared now and then with a needle and thread but never explained what was up.

Kiren asked: "So what's for desert, Vitz? Your undies covered in chocolate do-do?" But Vitz quietly announced that it was specially for her. Disappearing, he returned with a large metal tray covered with tinfoil and placed it in front of Kiren. Kiren opened it and screamed.

"Oh God no! You shot and cooked the Bad Easter Rabbit!"

Lying on the platter was the most unusual creature Matt had ever seen. It had been constructed from two or three children's stuffed animals which– it turned out, Vitz had collected at the yard sale. The body had come from a white rabbit, and the head from a raccoon or possibly a lesser panda which resembles a raccoon. The creature had a tail which was sort of raccoon like. Lying on its back on the tray feet in the air, a large glob of red catsup had been placed on its chest and there was a note taped to one paw reading:

"Kiren shot me thinking I was a big bad bear."

"You shot it, Kiren, now the Bad Easter Rabbit will never steal Easter Eggs from the rich kids and its all your fault!"

Kiren fled out the door clutching the "rabbit" while Vitz and Matt let out screams of laughter. Matt turned to Vitz:

"You know she just might come back with the .243 and finish the job. That Bad Easter Rabbit seemed pretty real to her."

It was nearly an hour later when Kiren reappeared still holding Vitz' creation wrapped in a towel.

"I removed the bullet and he may live, but we can't talk loudly for the rest of the day and I am going to have to keep watch on him. Now we have work to do."

With the Bad Easter Rabbit watching over them, the "Big Experiment" was carried out. There were fewer samples this time, 25 in all, but it was again late before the gel electrophoresis was run.

The results revealed a pattern of virus DNA tracks that left Kiren and Matt pacing the floor. There was new virus DNA in the tiny lesions on the leaves infected by the flies. However when they looked at the rest of the leaf, it was clear that the virus had spread very poorly from the site of the infection. Looking at the pattern of virus spread in plants infected with the DNA gun using the non-engineered Gemini virus from South America, they saw the same slow, poor pattern of virus spread outwards from the site of infection. It had been a long and event filled day, and they decided to sleep on it and think again in the morning.

At breakfast they went over and over the changes Kiren had introduced into the Gemini virus. The new engineered DNA was replicating at a much higher rate near the sites of infection than the old virus– and that was good. But like the old virus, it seemed to be spreading throughout the leaf at a very slow rate. If it did not spread, it could not damage the leaf or shut down cocaine production.

As they were taking a break, Kiren indulged herself in her favorite past time of tossing breakfast scraps to the Ravens. Matt asked Kiren to remind him again what the virus components were that controlled virus spread. Kiren reminded him that the B circle contains several genes required for the movement of the virus through the plant. Matt asked Kiren what would be the result of these genes being poorly expressed.

"Well, obvious," she said. "The virus wouldn't spread much." She then paused. "Just like what we are seeing in the plants with both the engineered virus and the old virus, isn't it!"

Using her Mac laptop, they called up the sequences of the B circle in the region that had been changed to enhance its expression. Everything seemed fine.

Matt suggested they take a few minutes and look at the DNA sequence at the far ends of the genes for the A and B circles. He reminded her that correct signals are needed at both ends of a gene– at the start, to induce the cellular machinery to make the RNA from the gene, and then at the end of the RNA to cause the RNA molecule to be transported out of the nucleus of the cell to where the proteins are synthesized. If these ending sequences are not there, then even if the RNA is made in abundance – by having very strong start signals, the RNA becomes degraded and most is lost.

A search of the A and B chromosomes revealed a major difference. Kiren stormed out of the mine house cursing. Matt explained to Vitz that a perusal of the sequences of the A and B chromosomes had revealed that while the A circle had very good ending signals for the RNA, the B circle did not. They should have thought of checking this months ago. This would explain everything. The A circle was doing very well in its newly engineered form, and its genetic information was being made and processed at high levels. The B circle however was reproducing itself, but its genetic information was not being processed well into proteins. That would explain why the original virus and the engineered ones were not moving through the plant, since the genetic information of the B circle was needed for that process.

Kiren was gone most of the day. As dinner time approached, Matt prepared a canned ham that he had been saving and set out a bottle of his best red wine. They were quiet as they waited for her return. By 9 PM Kiren had yet to appear and Matt begun to wish that he had followed her. It was still light outside and they decided to fire up The Moose Gooser to look for her. They were hardly in the air before Vitz spotted Kiren sitting on the hilltop above the mine. Matt rolled back around and as the two of they were getting out, Kiren walked over.

"Short flight."

"Yah, just wanted to check the mags."

Dinner and wine finished, Kiren seemed to lighten up. She thanked them for the dinner and turned the discussion back to science.

"With luck we can still pull this thing off— but only if I can get help from my lab and your DNA synthesis facility. We need to synthesize a short segment that will replace the poor signals at the end of the B chromosome. If your lab can make the DNA and send it to my technician, I can give her the instructions by satellite phone to do the cutting and patching. She can get it done a lot faster and then send it to us to put into the plants with the good A DNA. We have most of our plants left. We'll be set back 3 weeks, but with luck we can make it before the summer ends."

"Let's do it! I can get the DNA made in a day's turn around and flown to Raleigh," responded Matt with renewed delight.

"Fine, but there's something else I have been thinking about." she replied.

"Vitz, I'm not indifferent to what happens to the indigies in South America. I really hadn't taken time to consider such things. My only goal has been to punish those responsible for Ralph's death— but I understand your concern." She stopped for a moment then continued.

"Even in its worst possible form, no virus would totally wipe out a plant species. At the rates these viruses spread, plants that are resistant to the viruses will develop naturally to rescue the species. It's very different from worrying over the demise of tigers. There are only a few thousand tigers left and if they were to face some new threat, the very last breeding pair might be lost. There are millions of individuals plants of all species. There will always be a few resistant members around to save the species. For plants, viruses may stunt and cripple a crop to the extent that in an agricultural sense, they may disappear from the economic world, but in a number of years they will be back. I promise you."

Vitz tipped his head side to side as if to indicate that he understood but still was not totally convinced.

The postmark did not alert Kiren as she frequently received correspondence from friends in Bogota. She waited until there was a free moment and sprawled on a large boulder near the door of the greenhouse expecting to hear about the latest details of their work, and personal items from others there. Kiren stood bolt upright as she read each sentence twice before moving to the next. At one point she put the letter down on the boulder and stared at it from a distance for minutes before picking it up and continuing. The letter was simple and to the point.

Dear Kiren.

My name is Raul. I was a close friend of your brother. We worked and flew together. He loved to tell about your flying upside down in the Decathalon over Cornell one spring Saturday morning. I am writing you for two reasons. I am very very worried about your safety. We know you are working on a virus to kill coca plants. You talked about that with your friends at the University in Colombia last year, and you have support from the US government. We know that you got a shipment of coca plants from Peru. This is a very terrible thing. You have hiked in the Alta Plana, you have seen the peasants, you know how important this life-giving plant is to them. You must not do this. I warn you, there are many people who will do anything to stop you. It could hurt you and others around you. Understand me. You will be stopped if you continue.

Ralph and I were in jail together. Before we got out he asked me to look after you if anything happened to him. I gave him my most solemn promise and take it to heart. I have helped you out before. Remember the incident in the hills in Colombia when you almost got caught in a police raid? Didn't it seem odd that you were the only one pulled to safety? I helped you. I want to help you again, but you must stop this work.

When Ralph disappeared in the mountains we looked for him. I know that you went to the area and found nothing. I assumed he flew straight into a rock wall and was buried under a landslide created by the crash. So, I believed Ralph was dead.

Two years ago one of our friends in the jungles on the Eastern side of the Andes told us of an American pilot who had crashed in an area habited only by primitive Indians. He was hurt but alive and living with the Indians. I doubted it was Ralph but the time this person was said to have gone down was close to when Ralph disappeared. No one else had been reported missing around then. When I had time, I have gone to the area where he was reported to be. I was there six months ago. The day before I had to leave I found an Indian who spoke Spanish. Fellow claimed to know where this Gringo was. Said his name was Ralph. Told me this Gringo had been sick for a long time but was fine now and he had married into the tribe. Teaching them modern stuff. I had to leave but could find the Indian again.

I know if we went back there with an air boat and goods for trading we could find him. It would cost money but we would find him. I can't promise it is your brother, but I know in my heart it is.

I will help find Ralph for you or tell you where to go, but you must quit this project. All I ask is that you give us a recording about what you are doing and talk to an American reporter. We will put you in touch with her. I know you can phone from where you are. I set up a telephone answering machine in Los Angeles. Call and leave a recording about what you are doing. The number is below. Then come back home. The reporter will call you. I will contact you about how to find Ralph.

Remember there are many of us who make our living from the coca plant and whose families depend on us.

Raul

Kiren left the letter on the boulder and climbed the ridge behind the mine. She just kept climbing and climbing as if to exhaust herself to a point where she couldn't think of anything at all. Finally an hour and a half later, she reached the crest of the ridge gasping and lay crying for another hour.

Matt and Vitz had been chatting over beers and happened to see paper flying about in the breeze. Walking out, they ran here and there picking up several sheets of writing paper. It was Vitz who began reading and exclaimed:

"Holly shit! Listen to this– get the other pages! Where the fuck did this come from?"

Matt and Vitz put the letter back together and Vitz read it out loud. They realized she was not to be seen.

"Matt, when did you see her last?"

"A couple of hours ago. I got back from Talkeetna with the mail and gave her the packet Roland had forwarded. Haven't seen her since. Get in the airplane lets see if we can find her."

"Wait! Think like a woman. If a woman wants to run away forever, she runs down hill. If a woman wants to hide away and think, she runs up hill. We only have two choices here, up or down, I say she went up. Want to join me or are you going to fly around in your noise maker, and let her know you are coming so she can play hide and seek?"

Matt looked at Vitz and nodded as to indicate touché. They spread apart 50 yards as they climbed the ridge. It was an hour later when they crested the top and found Kiren lying face up in the sun staring at the majestic peaks in the distance. They sat down beside her and waited.

"You guys know?"

"The letter was flying in the wind. We collected it and, yes, we read it. A real one-two punch. Do you believe it?" Matt replied.

"You mean about their knowing, or my brother?"

"Oh, we knew they knew something was up. That's no big surprise other than how much they know. No, I mean about your brother, do you believe it?"

"Oh, god, Matt, I don't know. He has been gone for over four years. For a couple of years I went to look for him. I really didn't expect to find him alive, I just wanted closure knowing where he crashed and to be able to bring something back to bury. After the first few months, we all gave up thinking he might have survived. Now this. It sounds crazy enough to be true."

"Are you going to pay their price?" Vitz asked.

"I can't make that decision now. Not now. I'd give my life to get him back. But I still believe they are the ones responsible for his death. Vitz, what do you think? You were trained to live in the jungles, could he have survived?"

"Kiren, this sounds like they are stringing you along. They seem to know a lot about you and what might cause you to quit. Matt knows more about airplane crashes. Seems to me that once he recovered he could have offered them enough money to buy his way out."

"Matt?"

"Oh, people have survived crashes of all kinds. He was trying to cross the Andes, and we know he lost an engine. If he cleared the peaks running on a single engine, he might have gotten out over the jungles and then lost the other one, either because he ran out of gas or more likely having pushed the remaining engine too hard. Crashing a twin engine airplane into dense trees is usually lethal, but he was an experienced pilot and might have landed in a shallow river, who knows– sure anything is possible. I don't see why it has taken so long to get word of him out to the rest of the world."

Vitz shook his head. " Time goes slow in the jungle. A week takes a year. I can see him settling in, no idea of which way is out and they might cook him if he tried. He could be special in the village. Besides, the young girls are really voluptuous."

"Oh fuck you he's not like you and Matt. So do you believe this or not?" Kiren snapped.

"Kiren, I don't want to say yes or no. I'd guess these guys are jerking you around. If I say no, and we continue with your project then you are going to hold it over my head that we are not looking for your brother. If I say yes, then I'll get burned for destroying your virus project."

"Ditto" Vitz responded.

"Assuming he is alive in the jungle, could Roland find him for me?"

"No, no way! The area where he could be is probably half the size of Texas since we have no idea how much fuel his King Air was carrying. The Indians out there are xenophobic. If they don't want to be seen, then we could send in the whole US Army and they wouldn't find a soul. If Ralph is alive, the only way to find him is through this Indian the letter described." Matt stared out at the scenery below and continued.

"Kiren, you're a scientist. You recognize the situation. We don't have enough data. Either we get more data, or you are going to have to go on gut feeling. Lets walk back. We need to find out about this Raul. Maybe Roland can help." Matt stood up, and lifted Kiren gently to her feet.

After dinner, Matt called Roland and explained the situation. Roland was upset and they discussed options. Roland finished by saying that he should be able to find the telephone recorder and trace any incoming calls. He concluded:

"Matt, we may have exceeded our logistic envelope. I'm sure we can keep your operation in Alaska in the secret packet, but I find it hard to believe that we can hide a large operation with a lot of plants growing out in the open."

"Agreed. Are you saying we should bag this now?"

"Quadratic negative! We're in this space shuttle together and there are no parachutes in space. We're together for the whole ride. We may have to bury the virus for a few years to let things cool down. What's the chance you can make enough virus in Alaska to get the infection in South America started? Get me some answers and I'll put a trace on this Raul person.

For two days Kiren cycled between being angry at having Ralph used as a weapon and then tearful thinking about him lost in the jungle. Time was spent discussing how much virus could be extracted from the plants they had and if it was enough to start a scourge in South America. Kiren was working on the calculations when the call from Roland came in. Matt turned up the speaker so all could listen.

"Hey my scientifically-challenged types. Here's what I found. This Raul didn't seem too worried about being traced or he may not be very sharp. The telephone answering machine was in a vacant apartment in Los Angeles. It was being checked from a phone in Cancun, Mexico. The phone is in the villa of one of the major drug smugglers known as Raul. I assume he sent it and had the letter postmarked in Colombia."

"So, what did you find out about him?" queried Kiren.

"There are so many small fish out there that they slip through our net and we don't even know anything about them until they get to be pretty big. Also, they are constantly coming and going, appearing and disappearing. The big guys have professional plastic surgeons and are very good at changing appearances. When one of them disappears, we don't know if he was eaten or just changed his name and face."

"Roland, that's the wrapper, give us the cookie inside," Matt pushed.

"Well, Kiren, as a friend and not a fat government type, here are the facts as I read them. If I thought your brother might be out there in the jungle I would be the first to say so. If I sound negative it's not that I am trying to get you to continue, clear?"

There was a pause and Kiren replied: "yes".

"Well, from what we found out about Raul, this letter is chronologically flawed."

"Why?" Vitz interjected.

"We know your brother worked out of Bogota and the Southern Caribbean. We know he was in jail for a year. Sounds as if he was running one of the smuggling operations in that area. From what you said and what we know, he never worked out of Mexico."

"So?" Matt was waiting for Roland to make his point. Roland did this just the way that he would eat a large chocolate pastry. He would spend hours nibbling around the edge and then when you were about to take it away from him, pounce on the middle.

"Seems Raul has always worked out of Mexico. Raul came to our attention about the time your brother disappeared. Also we found out who was in jail with your brother. Two are in jail in the US and the two others are high level cartel people we know to be living in Colombia and neither fit Raul's description. Want to know my guess?"

"Go on."

"Speaking from my speculative pulpit, I say Raul is a top dog directing things from Mexico. Possibly used a different name back then. Maybe it was his airplane your brother was flying. I'm not saying he sabotaged the plane, it's just hard for me to see how Raul and your brother could have been such good buddies that Raul would still keep going to the jungles looking for him."

Kiren walked out of the room and Matt ended the phone call.

"Roland, thanks. Kiren is going to need a day to digest this but we'll get those virus numbers to you tomorrow."

Kiren was sitting on "her" boulder overlooking Matt's landing strip. After a while, Matt walked over and standing behind her, began rubbing her shoulders. Kiren waited a while and then turned around and put her arms around him with her head on his shoulder.

"God, Matt, it just isn't fair. Life isn't fair. Now I'm going to have nightmares thinking about Ralph trapped in some jungle village. Oh, I know Roland is right. It makes me hate those ass holes even more. Why did they try this?

"They are afraid. Just like you are afraid— aren't you?"

"Of course. When I started, I knew the cartel would not like what I was doing, but I thought I would do my work in some quiet place, give the virus to Roland — and go back to my life. This scares me. What that letter said scares me."

"I wouldn't blame you if you want to bag it, and make the call to Raul's answering machine. Roland left it intact for you. If you do, there will be a lot of dumb stuff on the news for a while and then it will die out. But you will be in it alone. Roland needs to keep Vitz and me clean for other projects. So we would have to deny any involvement."

"Lynx person, I wouldn't name my two big brothers. You know that. Scared or not, I want to settle the score. Do you think Raul killed my brother?"

"Kiren, we'll never know. Life is very short in the drug business and if your enemy doesn't shoot you in the back today, your best friend will shoot you in the front a week later. I'd like to think he died like all good pilots want to– 200 miles per hour into a stone wall."

Matt was holding Kiren tightly and they stood under The Mountain for a long time until Kiren reached up kissed him. As Matt was beginning to make the transition from a warm loving kiss to a deeper kiss she pulled away and said:

"God, I'd like to pull out your chest hairs one by one, but there's work I've got to do later today." They walked back to the mine together. Kiren found Vitz' bottle of Jim Beam, poured three glasses and sat down facing Matt and Vitz.

"First things first! I feel like calling that answering machine and telling Raul to fuck himself but that probably wouldn't be wise."

"Not really." Matt nodded.

"Either ignore them, or call and leave a message continuing our original cover. You might say you desperately want to find your brother and when you get back from the South Pacific that you want him to contact you. After we get done here we can have Roland sneak us out from Elmendorf Air Force base. We could go to Samoa and lie on the beach and mail a lot of cards back home. We could appear here and there for a month and then come back. We could both use the vacation on Roland's dime and it would keep them confused. After that, we are going to have to take it one day at a time, but we will keep some security for you."

"More time away from Mr. Copper?"

"Afraid so."

Kiren took a sip out of Vitz' glass of Beam just to annoy him and took her paper pad. The calculations were based on simple assumptions and estimates: how many virus particles could be isolated from the hundred remaining plants they had at the mine if they infected all the plants with the final re-engineered DNA? What would be the yield of partially purified virus they could obtain? If the virus was diluted and spread here and there in the major coca fields, what was the minimal amount that would be needed? The results indicated that if everything went their way they would have more than enough to begin a virus infestation in the major coca areas. While it might take a few years to spread, it would nonetheless have the result they intended.

Several days later the samples arrived at the Anchorage Airport Fedex building and Matt flew down to pick them up. Matt and Kiren were impressed that when asked to work day and night, her people did exactly that. In several weeks they would be able to isolate the new coca-killer viruses from the plants and be able to go back to doing what they had before the whole project began.

There were days when Kiren seemed intent on orchestrating a sexual rivalry between Matt and Vitz. One day she began by flirting with Vitz, then after getting some work started she announced that she and Vitz had to go off for a hike – and that Matt could keep watch on the plants. They returned two hours later with Kiren patting Vitz on the rump while tossing comments at Matt intended to further tease: "We wanted to give you some privacy to phone home to Ros" or "Catch up on your latest Playboy magazine while we were gone?". Matt ignored her behavior the best he could, but the twinge of jealously was there knowing that Vitz could be counted on to exploit any opportunity Kiren might offer.

Several rainy days had passed and they were getting along well. Kiren was absorbed in finishing work with the new virus and had recruited Matt to help. Their closeness pleased Matt and made him wish that they could have time alone without Vitz around—although there was no reason to believe that she would be willing to grant him any more intimacy than she had so far.

The next morning the sun broke out and in her elated mood Kiren reminded Matt of a Jack Russell terrier puppy. Here, there, bite at this, snap at that – "everyone stand back" he said to himself. Thinking that a hike up to the glacier might help her burn off some energy and give them a chance to be together, he was about to suggest this when she grabbed Vitz by the hand and turned to Matt:

"Vitz and I are going to climb up the hill and cuddle. We'll be back in 2 hours. Can you handle making pancakes for us? Vitz is going to be very hungry when we get back." And off they went, Vitz towed out the door with a grin on his face.

Matt was irritated, but a call from Roland came in and nearly two hours were spent clearing up matters from a previous project. Apparently Roland had gone over budget and some reasonable explanations needed to be fabricated. He had just finished when Kiren and Vitz returned. Vitz made pancakes while Matt sat outside ignoring them. Breakfast done, Kiren announced that she had made a bet with Vitz — that in two hours he could not climb as far up the hill on the opposite side of the valley as they had climbed on their side of the valley. He claimed that without her holding him back he could do that and more.

Breakfast done, a heavy load of pancakes in his stomach, and the .243 rifle pressed into his hands by Kiren "for your protection, my love– and shoot a shot when you are at the top." Vitz went out the door.

Kiren turned to Matt singing "Macho macho-man – well, I got rid of him for the rest of the day. That hill is twice as far away as it looks and twice as steep. We've got the day together just you and me. Let's climb up on the hill and lie in the sun together."

Matt stood dumbfounded. After jerking his emotions around all morning she was offering just what he wanted.

"Afraid of little me?"

Matt stabbed his finger in the air at her as he grabbed a soft pack sack, and tossed in a bottle of wine and pair of binoculars. Holding Kiren in the left hand and his .300 Weatherby rifle in the right, out into the sun they went. The .300 Weatherby had been a gift to him from his father when he turned 16. He had wanted one badly but they could not afford one built by the Weatherby company so his Dad found a pre-world war II Winchester model 70 .300 H and H magnum and had it re-chambered in Anchorage for the more powerful .300 Weatherby cartridge. Its recoil was so unpleasant that Matt's father refused to shoot it. The length of its stock made it far too clumsy for Kiren to try which pleased Matt as he was very possessive of the gun.

The temperature was in the low 70's and sun was strong, making the breeze flowing up the valley refreshing. As he climbed Matt wondered why he allowed himself to be manipulated by this woman who was obviously toying with him for her amusement. They hiked for an hour before reaching a plateau just below the crest of the ridge. A large rock outcropping afforded a perfect spot for lying and watching out across the valley and Matt knew this spot well.

Kiren wore her hiking shorts, cut well above the knees. Her legs really bothered Matt. They were slim but well muscled from riding, and her calves were shaped in a way usually seen in European women who had grown up walking everywhere. He knew her shorts had been selected to provide the best view, but could not resist frequent glances. Fifty percent of the human race was drug-addicted he would tell people. The drug being testosterone.

Sprawled out on the rock shelf, Matt took out the binoculars and started to scan the far hillside for signs of Vitz. After a minute Kiren leaned over him holding her two hands over the binocular lenses and pushed her face close to his:

"Are you looking for Vitz to protect you or are you going to let me kiss you?"

In a playful mood, Matt turned the binoculars around so that he could peer at her through the wrong end, and scanned them over her face. He then lay them aside on the rock and pulled Kiren to him. While he had kissed her once before, that kiss has been unexpected and far too short to have been satisfying. Now, he would have the time and position to enjoy her much more fully. As the rocks were cool he pulled her over on top of him and stroked her cheeks and head as he kissed her. The kisses moved away from her lips and wetted her forehead, the tips of the ears and throat. Every time he ventured lower she would move them back to full lip-to-lip kisses. Matt held her more and more tightly to him and squeezed and stroked her back. Each time he would start to move his fingers under her blouse she would move his hands away setting the rules for the moment. Finally, Kiren pulled herself away and holding both of his hands she rolled over beside him.

For some time Kiren didn't speak but would rub his face lightly or make a purring noise. Matt felt very happy being close to her and was more than willing to let her set the pace. Finally she rose up and pulled the wine out of the pack and filled the two plastic glasses they had carried along.

"You looked so sad when Vitz and I returned, you really didn't think that I have a thing for him do you?"

"Of course not. I was worried about Roland's allergic reaction to a chocolate bon bon. If we lose him the three of us are left on the moon without a ride home."

"You were jealous! Vitz is just a big sheep dog. I don't find him sexy."

"Well then, you're one of a kind, or so I hear from Vitz."

"Yah, yah, to hear Vitz tell it, the only woman who he hasn't had is Madonna and that is only because she is still working her way through the LA Lakers."

She reached over kissing him lightly. "Lynx person, tell me about the Arctic lynx. We've never seen one."

"Big, about 180 pounds, and they wear dark glasses. No— they are all over this area, I glimpse one now and then, but you have to know what to look for. They are light colored, a mix of gray and white; long fur tufts on their ears, and enormous paws. A big male might be 50 pounds. You'll never see one in the open. Very solitary, live mostly in the forests and eat rabbits, mice, birds. Never known to hurt people and I doubt they could take a moose calf."

They lay in the sun for a while.

"Matt, I'm really frightened about where this project is going. When I started it seemed so simple and easy. And there weren't any people attached to it. But now, there's you, Vitz, and Roland who could get hurt and while I haven't seen any of these drug people, other than that guy who was following me, we know there's a bunch looking for us. I'd just like to give this virus to Roland and go back to my lab."

"I hope we're close to that, Kiren."

"Yah but after I'm back in the lab the trouble will just begin for Vitz and I worry that Roland is going to keep you involved too."

"Not me, its back to the lab for me too. Vitz, yes, but remember, this is what he lives for and dreams of. He needs a periodic rush of danger to keep himself emotionally centered."

"You sound like Ros."

"That was Ros' analysis of Vitz, not mine. We'll be fine, hold my hand tight and we'll get through this."

Matt kissed her lightly this time, feeling how finely boned and delicate she really was. The 3 shots from the far side of the valley roused them and scanning the opposite ridge they spotted Vitz. He was much farther down the valley than they expected, having traded a hike down the stream for a shorter climb up. Exchanging a final hug they headed back to camp.

Brian called Henry with enthusiasm. "Henry. Have Raul transfer those funds! I've been hit by even more than my usual bri bri bri brilliance!"

"Great because we are stuck, and Raul is fit to kill."

"How did the letter turn out?"

"No reply, what's up?"

"OK, as a lawyer you know that certain things are a matter of pu pu pu public record —like grant applications."

"So?"

"So, I checked and found out that she had applied for a grant from the National Institutes of Health, the NIH six months ago. I got the gra gra grant application number, title, abstract and all. I even found it was close to the pa pa pa payline but just shy of getting funded."

"So what?"

"So simple. I'll call her departmental manager, give them these grant numbers, title, and tell the manager that I am her pro pro pro program officer at the NIH. That's the person who is responsible for handling this grant application. That should wake them up."

"Guess so, but I still don't see how you use this to get to her."

"I will tell them that we, the NIH, just got a bo bob bo bolus of extra funds and that I would like to pay her grant, but I must have a revised bu bu bu budget signed by her, FAXed to me within 24 hours, or I will give the money to the next person on the list. I will tell them to come up with a bu bu bu budget that is twenty percent less than what she asked for. The important thing I need from her, I will tell them, is an original signed sheet even if it is handwritten— accepting the funding. Exactly what a program officer would do."

"Ah, — beginning to follow—".

"Right, she will have to find some place very close by by by by and FAX a signed revised bu bu bu budget to me. I'll make it clear that it cannot come from her departmental manager bu bu bu but only from her. I'll arrange for a phone in Be Be Be Bethesda, Maryland that will have the same first three numbers as the NIH exchange. When the FAX comes in, it will also come with an origination number telling us where it came from. How ab ab ab about that."

"Brian, true genius! Raul is going to be very happy and a bit poorer. Need any help arranging this?"

"No, I have a friend in D.C. who can help me. I'll rent a one room office in Bethesda for a week or two. Should be re re re ready in a week, ten days at the most."

It didn't take long for Brian to arrange things. A week later the go ahead signal was given and Brian made the call to Kiren's business manager. It worked extremely well as the manager was more than anxious to accommodate an NIH program officer and to do anything to ensure that Kiren's funding came through. The call from Brian came in first thing in the morning and she anxiously awaited Kiren's normal lunch time call. When it came, she explained what was needed and urged Kiren to find a FAX machine and provide a signed authorization for the reduced budget. Kiren went to Matt with a "this has to be done now and you make it happen" attitude.

"Matt, this is the first real legitimate funding I will have gotten all by myself. You know what that means to my chances of getting tenure and started with regular NIH funding."

"Oh, I understand. Getting tenure now days requires that you prove you can get funding. I also understand that if they give the money to someone else you may have a black mark against you the next time a chance comes around. I just don't like the idea of having to FAX something ASAP. Our phone was not set up for FAX's and Talkeetna is the closest place that has a FAX machine. Given the four hour time difference we need to take off within thirty minutes to get to Talkeetna and a FAX machine in time to get this to the NIH today. Just wish we had more time, then Roland could check on this to be sure it was legitimate or could get the NIH people to go ahead without your signature. Give me a few minutes to call Roland. If we don't get him, I'll fly you to town."

Matt tried to get a phone call through to Roland but he was gorging himself in one of Georgetown's best cafes. Matt had no choice but to fly Kiren to Talkeetna.

They landed at Talkeetna, and found a FAX machine at one of the flying services. The FAX contained the details of its point of origin.

Brian called Raul. "Raul, I hope you have that money re re re ready. The FAX just came in and you won't believe where from."

"Shit. Finally someone with a brain. Brian-the-brain! I have the cash right here. Where did it come from?"

" Tal Tal Tal Talkeetna, Alaska. I had to find an atlas and then search for fifteen minutes to find it. Talkeetna is a ti ti ti tiny town just south of Mt. McKinley. I'll be be be bet there are only a few hundred people there."

"Oh fuck, this doesn't sound right. They are supposed to be in some secure research laboratory making a virus, not climbing some friggin mountain. They are jerking us around."

"Not really, Raul. Clever-clever. Remember the sun is up almost around the cla cla cla clock in the summer in Alaska . Great place to gr gr gr grow plants! They would have to make a greenhouse to keep the humidity and temperature up, and it would help if the altitude was a few thousand feet abu abu abu above sea level to resemble Colombia. Have you ever see the pi pi pi pictures of the hundred pound cabbages that grow in there in the summer? No, I don't think we are being jerked around at all."

There was a long pause until Raul responded. "Maybe you are right. Money is yours as long as they are really there. I'm going to get a group together to go up and track them down. We may need your help but I'll let you know."

"Ah, I don't know abu abu abu about that." Brian replied.

"An extra fifty grand for a couple of days of playing tourist and asking a few questions?"

"Just questions that's all."

CHAPTER THIRTEEN

ESCAPE TO ST. LAWRENCE ISLAND

The call from Roland came at the usual time.

"So Roland, this place is turning into a world class center for blueberry picking and pie making. Why don't you come on up and help us fold things up. Bring a suitcase full of chocolate and we can invent a new blueberry-chocolate desert."

"You three vacationers seem to be in an anxiety vacuum. Leaving me to do all the worrying as usual. Give me the day's round up of events. Details details please. There was a note you called."

"Rooo-land, not a hell of a lot here. Oh, right. The call. I would have appreciated your help. Kiren got a message from her NIH program officer. Had to have a signed revised budget by today if she was to get the money. We flew to Talkeetna for her to FAX it to him. I didn't like to do it but things are about wound down and getting onto the NIH bandwagon is the most important thing in her life."

"So you idiots sent a FAX from Talkeetna to Washington D.C. with her name on it?"

"Rooo-land, I'm sure it was fine."

"Who was the program person? Who-who-who? This sounds subterranean!"

Matt called to Kiren then responded. "She said it was a Dr. Rollins in the virology program."

"Give me the phone and FAX numbers and I'll check. Anything else?"

It was less than an hour later when the call came back.

"Matt. We're swimming in a pond of crocodile dung. This Raul person now knows where Kiren is. What are you going to do about this? This is very anxiomatic."

"What do you mean? What's happened? What did you screw up?"

"What did I screw up, you clowns! You have just given the whole project away and wasted all the money I have spent on this."

"Roland. From the top. Slow. My blood pressure is starting to rise here."

"I checked into your Dr. Rollins. There is no such person, so I had my man check the FAX number. It was put in a week ago in an empty office and was pulled out not more than a couple of hours ago. Someone very clever discovered how to irradiate your dials. I assume that figuring out where you are once they get to Talkeetna will take them ten minutes given what they have done so far."

Matt shut the door to the room and grabbed a pad of paper.

"Roland. We could be in deep shit here fast. You're right– we've been traced. It was my fault. Now, Jesus. Here's the time table. We need a week to ten days to finish this work and then we can sanitize the place. Once we are out of here with your virus, then they can only guess. Could sit on the virus for a couple of years if need be. Got to figure out how to keep them off our backs for another seven to ten days."

"Why that much time? Can't you pull out now and bring the stuff back?"

"No, unfortunately no. Based on what we calculated, we infected all of our plants with the engineered DNA. It is going to take a week to ten days before we can isolate the new virus. If we were to try to extract the virus now we would not get enough. We just have to wait a week at the minimum. Then it will take about two days to grind up the plants and split."

"Matt, you've pulled off some miracles before but this may be asking the fat man to bag Thanksgiving. I won't hold you or Kiren to any promises if you guys want to tear things apart and high tail it out now. For all I know, they may be on route to Alaska. Of course my bosses may fire me or send me to some place where chocolate is illegal."

"Rooo-land, this is what you pay me for. Things are just beginning to get interesting. Think of it as a chess game in which getting checkmated is forever. Give me fifteen minutes to think of something. I'll call you with what I need and we have Vitz– he loves this kind of stuff. You should fly up here to be closer to the action."

Slipping out of the backdoor, Matt walked a hundred yards, sat down cross legged and leaned forward placing his head on a large rock. This was Ros's favorite meditation position and he had discovered that it shut out everything around him. Fifteen minutes later he got up, and briskly walked back to the mine house. He called Kiren and Vitz to the phone and got the connection through to Roland. Kiren and Vitz were still in the dark as to what had happened.

"Roland. Matt back. Kiren and Vitz here. Now from the top. Apparently Raul and his friends traced us through a fake FAX. Cute, but our mistake. There are too many people in Talkeetna who know of the mine and who have seen me with Kiren. If we are going to keep them away from here for a week, we are going to have to blaze a trail that Inspector Clouseau couldn't miss."

Kiren grabbed Vitz and stood staring at Matt who seemed very calm as if he was chatting with Roland over what kind of food to bring to the next spy potluck dinner. Matt continued.

"Here's what I need. That turbo Goose in Homer the Forest Service has – I need it and a credit card number for fuel and supplies. Have it delivered to Talkeetna by tomorrow morning. Also locate all helicopters of Jet ranger size or larger around the Nome to Kotzebue area. Get the FAA to put an immediate freeze on any short term rentals. I'm going to leave a billboard saying that we are all alive and well on St. Lawrence Island. Should take a while for them to catch up with us out there. Could be fun. Got that? Check into the Captain Cook Hotel in Anchorage. The restaurant is four star. I'll have Vitz call you back in a few minutes with a shopping list of his own. Have it ready for us at the Air Force base in Fairbanks."

Matt turned to Kiren and Vitz:

"We got snookered! Bad! That FAX was a fishing lure and we bit. Here's the timing. It takes a full day to get here from The States. Further, it will take them at least a day to get themselves in gear. So we should have two full days before they arrive in Talkeetna. Our game is to keep them away from here for a week. After that we can extract the virus in a day or two and split."

Kiren complained: "Fine, but everyone in Talkeetna knows you. Someone is going to tell them about this place."

"Exactly what I was telling Roland. I will prime everyone in Talkeetna with the story that we come here now and then for mail but that we are working out of Gambell on St. Lawrence Island."

Vitz shook his head. "Where is this St. Lawrence Island place?"

"You will see." Chuckled Matt. "Think of it as a short trip to the beach, yah, like the Florida Keys of Alaska. A little vacation to the beach. I have some favors I can call in and I promise you, its a place where these dopers will be on my turf."

Kiren looked upset. "This scares me. I'm out of control here. I don't like that. Don't I have any choice?"

"Sorry, not unless you vote for burning this place down and calling that phone recorder."

Kiren changed her expression as if she had been slapped in the face. "No! Tell me what to do."

Vitz piped in. "No way we give up! I've been hanging around months just for the chance to rip some one's trachea out."

"We're not quitting, but not because Vitz here needs his fix of human body parts. Damn you Matt, I am going to have to trust you. I don't like that at all. So what do we do?"

Matt smiled. "Kiren, set aside the equipment we will need when we return. Put your notebooks, and personal stuff in a pile. Pack some equipment we won't need that can be used to create a fake lab. I will fly it to Talkeetna and load it into the Goose. That goes. All the rest of the stuff here, in particular anything that might tie us to virus work, Vitz you throw down the mine shaft. We need to be able to return, spend two days extracting the virus and then leave the place the way we found it."

He turned to Vitz: "Roland can get you anything you want within reason and have it ready in Fairbanks. I assume that you know how to use something other than that .243 relic of yours."

Vitz smiled: "Can I have a hand held nuke?"

"No, but anything up to that. Remember, we've got to stay light."

Vitz called Roland with his list.

The sun was up until 9:30 PM and it remained light until nearly 11 PM. Matt made several trips to Talkeetna with their gear. They slept for several hours and as the sun poked back up around 4 AM, piled into the 185, Kiren asked:

"Matt we're coming back aren't we? There's so much of me tied up in those plants."

"Damn right we'll be back! We're just off for a week's vacation at the beach."

Kiren seemed encouraged and asked about St. Lawrence Island.

"Is this place a resort? With beaches? I didn't bring a swimming suit. I'll buy one there."

Matt smirked to himself. "I'm sure we can find something."

The temperature swings in central Alaska at this time of the year are large. August temperatures in the Talkeetna environs can reach 85. A turn of bad weather however can drop daytime temperatures into the 50's. They had been enjoying high temperatures the past week, so the idea of lying on some sun warmed beach with a large rum drink seemed possible, even for Alaska.

The Goose was waiting and while Matt and the pilot went over operating details, Vitz and Kiren loaded their equipment aboard. There was more than enough room as the interior had 8 seats in addition to the pilot and copilot's seats that were forward. There was a cargo hatch on the nose of the Goose and more cargo space at the back.

The Grumman Goose was built during World War II as a coastal patrol aircraft. A smaller version called a Widgeon opened each episode of "Fantasy Island" on TV. The Goose has a single wing on top of the fuselage, and was originally equipped with two 450 hp Pratt and Whitney engines. Its belly is that of a boat with a keel, and has a sculpted nose and sides so that when the wheels are pulled up into their wells, the Goose is a boat. After the war, these sturdy aircraft found great utility in Alaska, British Columbia and the Yukon. Their ability to land on lakes, shores, or rough gravel runways was ideal for these areas. The Goose flies at a leisurely 180 mph and is very noisy inside. A number of businesses were dedicated to their upkeep including Griffco in Seattle and another in Portland that specialized in conversions to turboprop engines. The turbo conversion gave significantly more power and replaced the heavy bulky radial engines with light aerodynamic ones.

Before leaving, Matt walked around Talkeetna explaining to everyone he knew that it was likely that some people would appear looking for them. They were to say that while Kiren had been seen here with a local pilot, they were working at Gambell on St. Lawrence Island. Craig and the mechanic who worked on Matt's airplane were rehearsed several times and understood clearly that they were to give the information about St. Lawrence Island freely. It was mid-day when the Goose rumbled along the paved strip at Talkeetna and headed for Fairbanks, 200 miles, give or take, to the north. The sky was clear and the view of McKinley was spectacular. Following the highway north, McKinley was to the left and 9000 foot peaks– brightly colored with iron deposits lay to their right. Leaving The Mountain behind and flying north, they passed over McKinley village and the entrance to the National Park. The dirt road from the park entrance winds through forest, tundra, and alpine country, over Polychrome pass, eventually arriving at the base of The Mountain and Wonder Lake. When The Mountain is "out," that is cloud free, the fortunate visitor is able to stand, humble before the tallest wall of ice and rock in the world. If you cross the marshes from Wonder Lake and hike to the base of the mountain you arrive at a point where the top of McKinley is only 8 miles away in a lateral distance –but is also over 17,000 feet above you.

The Parks highway follows a narrow valley, and not far beyond McKinley village the world opens up in every direction as you leave the big mountains and enter the true Alaskan North. Behind, the rivers and streams know where they are going and flow with a fierce intensity homeward. To the north, the streams frequently seem lost with no idea of where they should go, meandering here and there, carving nearly complete circles in the earth. To the south, the lakes are long, narrow, and deep, filling mountain valleys carved by a recent glacial advance. To the north, the lakes describe perfect circles, appearing as an endless field of water-filled bomb craters. The lakes to the south have more individuality. Some like Kenai Lake, which is fed by glacial streams have an opalescent radiant green color –due to the refraction properties of the fine rock silt suspended in the water. For Matt, these lakes were always calling to him to stop and visit and each had a distinct name, Beluga, Strand Line, Skilak, Chakachamna. The lakes to the north were rather nameless. This was not always the case since the mountains would again offer lakes with personality. But for the large part, in the endless open expanses the lakes seemed of less interest.

Ahead, lay Fairbanks. Following the highway, they flew along the Nenana River to where it joined the Tanana River. Looking out they could see Fairbanks nestled against some low hills that formed a crescent. The Tanana River followed this crescent and the city had built itself upwards into the hills rather than across the river into the marshy lands of the Fort Wainwright Military Reservation. Eielson Air Force base was a major factor in the Fairbanks economy and Matt had arranged permission to land there. Roland had used his contacts to fill Matt's and Vitz' shopping lists of supplies and equipment they would need in Gambell besides food and fuel for the Goose. Lowering his wheels, Matt found his first landing of a Goose in some time easy, given the very long paved runway of the Air Force base. He hoped that he could repeat this when it came to the shorter and more demanding strip at Gambell. He had logged a lot of "Goose time" but that was years ago with only occasional flights since then. Oh well, he thought, it would come back to him.

The military truck arrived as they were getting out and three soldiers greeted them and chatted with Matt over the list of equipment as Vitz helped load. It included oil heaters, several large tents, one bright red, warm sleeping bags, clear plastic sheeting and an assortment of odds and ends that would be needed for setting up a summer camp on St. Lawrence Island.

Another military truck had arrived and Vitz took on an air of excitement they had yet to see. He inspected one device after another and finally, after Matt's complaints over weight, settled on two large fiberglass boxes. One held several automatic pistols and rifles and an M203A which is a combination of an M16 rifle and an M-79 grenade launcher. It can be used as an M16 but can also fire a 40mm grenade which has an effective range of 200 meters. The other box was much heavier and contained ammunition as well as grenades.

All this took no more than an hour and Matt lifted the Goose off for the dozen mile flight back to Fairbanks. Calling approach control, he requested a landing on the float pond adjacent to the paved runway. The float pond provided home to a swarm of small float planes.

In the interior, float planes are working tools. Matt held pilots who fly year around in the interior with the highest level of respect. In the 'Old Days' and in the interior, the real bush pilots flew with almost no navigational gear other than a compass. And in this country where magnetic declinations from true north run thirty degrees and stray almost that much place to place, a compass was at best, a rough point in the right direction. Real bush pilots were the guys who flew airplanes when engines blew up all the time and one was constantly flying with one eye picking out the next crash site. Matt was thinking about this as he happily headed toward the float pond.

On short final to the float pond the controller in the tower who had cleared him for landing suddenly screamed at Matt.

"Goose November-six-one Charley abort your landing! Repeat abort your landing! Fly current heading and climb to fifteen hundred! Verify please."

Matt immediately added power, trimmed for nose up, and climbed on his heading, leveling out at fifteen hundred feet and repeated the instructions to the tower. When he was established, he called the tower again.

"Tower, Goose November-six-one Charley, instructions please would like another approach to the float pond."

"Roger six-one-Charley, but please decide whether you want to land on the float pond with your wheels down or on the pavement with your wheels up. Can you think about that and give me your choice?"

Matt pounded himself sharply on the side of his head. He had left the wheels in the 'down' position after leaving Eielson, since it was such a short run. Had he landed on the water wheels down, they would likely have flipped the Goose on its back. A wheels up landing on the pavement would have been less of a disaster since the strong steel keel provides a reasonable skid. He called the tower:

"Tower six-one-Charley. Heh guys, really appreciate that back there, haven't flown one of these in a while. Better make a check-list. If you will clear me, I would like a wheels up landing on the float pond, six -one Charley."

The landing went well with Matt cross checking himself three times. They pulled to the dock to get fuel and were given one of the most rundown International Travelalls Matt had ever seen to drive to the grocery store. With snow on the ground by the end of September, salt is applied to the roads nine months of the year in Fairbanks. The carnage on cars is brutal and this Travelall had lost large slabs of its exterior sheet metal.

As Matt was waiting for the groceries to be rung up, Kiren appeared with a handful of sunscreen lotions. He was about to suggest that she put them back but Kiren seemed in a vacation mood and why break the spirit now? Vitz noted that this store could have been any supermarket in America except, possibly, for the fact that any one could pick up ammunition for their rifles with the same ease as tossing in a box of bran flakes. While Anchorage at 250,000 people is largely self sufficient and gives the air of ignoring the people who live in the outlying areas, Fairbanks with a population closer to 50,000 calls itself the 'Gateway to the North' and is just that; the last city before the beginning of the great north.

Before returning to the float pond, Matt gave Kiren and Vitz the ten cent tour of town, pointing out the University of Alaska built on hills overlooking town, the museum with wonderful archeological finds, and downtown Fairbanks. By the time they loaded the Goose and took off, it was mid-day and they had many hours of light left for the long flight ahead.

Leaving Fairbanks, and clearing the tops of the hills west of town, they were greeted by their first glimpse of what lay ahead. The Minto flats consist of miles and miles of scrub black spruce trees, muskeg and small round lakes. At this latitude, the elevation above which trees will not grow is only a few thousand feet, and those that do are seldom more than 20 feet high. The land between the lakes is wet and filled with ponds and provides one of the world's largest breeding grounds for millions of ducks, geese, and bugs. Matt referred to it as the "great mosquito desert". Its name was derived from its inhospitality rather than resemblance to a desert as it was generally water-logged. The term mosquito needed no explanation other than the telling of stories of how a Baptist preacher from South Carolina came to believe that the bugs were sent by Satan and stripping himself naked, ran out into the muskeg to combat the devil himself. He was found dead an hour later drained of the last corpuscle of blood.

It was not all flat as they flew west, small hills and 3000 foot 'mountains' lay here and there, almost a joke considering the massive wall of rock seven times as high that they could see in the distance to the south. Crossing a set of these hills, the Chitanatala Mountains, Kiren exclaimed as she could see out ahead. This was the Nowitna National Wildlife Refuge. In the distance was the great Yukon River and the 60 miles between them and the river was one of the flattest stretches of bog, ponds, and meandering streams that Matt had ever seen. The Nowitna River almost defined the term confused. The land was so flat that instead of going in a generally straight direction, the river would curve smoothly in one direction for three-fourths of a circle and then in the opposite direction the same amount. Frequently the river would curve so much that it would cut itself off forming a full circle which in time was left behind as the river found some other path. Thus although not that wide themselves, the rivers occupied a swath of land two or three miles across filled with worm-like left over fragments. Even from the vantage of the air, it was nearly impossible to trace a clear path for such rivers.

Reaching the Yukon River, they flew over the town of Ruby where the Yukon River was over a mile wide. Certainly the largest river of the north and rivaling the Mississippi, it cuts a straighter path through the flat Arctic land and flows in a generally southwest direction. The river is spotted with small towns of fifty or a hundred people and numerous Indian villages. At this point the Yukon swerves to a more westerly direction, and Matt followed its course pointing out Galena and Koyukuk. People who live along the river are a mix of Eskimo, Indians, and whites. While the Eskimo traditionally lived only along the coast, they did follow the big rivers inland as the salmon that migrate up the river provide food for them and their dogs. The classic inhabitants of the central portion of Alaska are Indians with a different language, appearance and customs.

Kiren walked forward and rousted Vitz from the copilot's seat.

"Matt, I get very discouraged at times over thinking about being a molecular biologist. It seems that we have to work so hard and are constantly having to prove ourselves. You seem to be enjoying what you are doing and have a more relaxed attitude about your career, how long did it take you to get to that point?"

"You know, I've felt that we've spent too much time discussing science's problems rather than its good side. A couple of times I almost called you up to tell you that things will work out. We yak about why your chairman is an unfeeling ass, why the dean didn't meet his promise, and why it is so hard to get funding for research unless you have done the work already. But, trust me, it's very much worth it."

"Trust me. Right. That makes me suspicious already."

"Now wait. Look at the good aspects of being a molecular biologist. First, by the time you are a full professor, you will be pulling in a very good salary. Add to that retirement which the university pays, good benefits, and for some universities–free tuition for your kids, and that amounts to what many MD's make after they pay their own retirement, insurance and so on. Further, for good or bad, the university tenure system provides a level of job security that is matched by no other profession I know of. An airlines captain makes a lot, but the day he can no longer pass his first class medical, he is out. Show me a shrink in private practice who can take a paid sabbatical to France for a year with his family. The frontiers of the 19th century were on the plains, and a matter of bravery and hard manual work. The frontiers of the 21st century involve challenges to our minds —to understand nature and to subtly change it to our benefit."

"Molecular biologists are gifted with the ability to follow their whims, to direct their lives as they choose, and are paid to do it. Also, the people you will get to know in your lifetime are extraordinary people: for example, Nobel prize winners, –I know over 20 myself, or neurobiologists who are also world renown mountaineers, or molecular biologists whose hobbies range from serious music and art, to racing cars. Your students will become your family, and you will keep in touch with them and will always be part of their lives. Possibly one of the nicest aspects is the respect you get from others. I know many lawyers who are sincere, warm, and highly moral – but I sure wouldn't want to face a lifetime of lawyer jokes."

"But we always seem to be worrying." Kiren commented.

"Every professional worries, Kiren, but in my opinion, of the lot, molecular biologists are in general happy people. Sure, we are driven and work hard. Most anyone with a salary over fifty thousand does. The difference is, I known a lot of molecular biologists who retire at 70 and continue going in to the labs half days for no pay, just for the pleasure of learning. Discovering something that no one has ever known is incredibly rewarding. When I was a kid here in Alaska, one of the most exciting things I did was to hike into the mountains and find a small mountain valley where I told myself that no human had ever been before. I explored the valley knowing I might find a 1000 pound gold nugget, the largest meteor yet found, or a cave full of diamonds. I never found such things, but I explored a lot of areas where it was very likely that no one had ever been before. When I do molecular biology I feel the same way. In the narrow area of viruses I work on, I am considered to be one of the half dozen world's experts. There are areas of virus studies where I know more than anyone else in the world. Think about that, there are over 2 billion people out there and I know more about my little valley than any of the 1 billion, 999 million, 999 thousand, 999 rest." He concluded:

"That's why I enjoy doing science. You don't have to be brilliant, just dedicated, and devoted to learning all you can about one specific area, and thinking about it most of the time. You are in a stressful period, and trust me, you will get through it like I did."

Kiren responded so quietly, that he had a hard time hearing her, and wondered if she might be choking back a tear. She squeezed his hand.

"Thanks."

At Koyukuk, the river takes a sharp southward turn and Matt continued west. It would be another 100 miles of muskeg and another row of hills before they reached the Pacific coast and Norton Sound. Vitz and Kiren peered to one side and the other. She would walk to the rear and look out of one window or the other and then come forward and sit on a raised ledge between the pilot's and copilot's seats and ask Matt where they were. Tired with this, she would roust Vitz from the copilot's seat. Getting bored with the endless muskeg she came forward and explained to Matt that she needed to learn to fly the Goose in case he had a heart attack.

"And pray tell why am I going to have a heart attack?"

"Because Vitz and I are going to make love sitting right here in the copilot's seat and you will be so jealous you won't be able to stand it. That's why."

"Heart attack no, but falling asleep out of boredom likely." Matt replied.

"OK, give me a primer on flying this or Vitz and I are going to do it right here, right now." Kiren replied.

"Its your call Vitz, but if she discovers you are impotent, your rep in Fort Bragg is going to crash. I say go for it." Matt joked.

Kiren sat on Vitz' lap facing him and began to unbutton his shirt and tug at his chest hairs with her teeth. At this moment Vitz shifted himself in the seat pushing Kiren against the steering wheel putting the Goose in a nose-dive. By the time Matt had recovered, Vitz was swearing and Kiren laughing announced:

"Well, Vitz is just like the rest, over so fast you don't know it ever happened. So do I get my lesson?"

"Kiren, you just discovered boinking." Matt laughed.

Kiren placed the Bad Easter Rabbit on the dash in front of the copilot's seat and Matt let her play with the Goose. Now and then she peeked back at Vitz and seeing that he had drifted off in one of the aft seats, turned the Goose sharply in an effort to roll him out of his seat. With Kiren flying, Matt took the opportunity to walk back and move Vitz' ammunition box into the aft baggage compartment to help balance the airplane which he felt was nose heavy. These activities kept their attention until Norton Sound was made. It would be 120 miles more with a short over-the-water segment until they reached Nome where they would land to refuel. Noting that a gauge which indicated outside temperature was sitting at 30 degrees, Kiren turned to Matt.

"It's freezing outside, and it's been getting colder and colder ever since we left Talkeetna. You said we would be at this island resort by the end of the day and that's only a few more hours. It had better start getting warm fast. Besides this doesn't look like sunny resort landscape to me."

"Now Kiren what did I say? I said that we are going to a lovely island, and that is true. Trust me. We will be on the beach. That is true, trust me. I did not say that it would be ninety degrees, now did I? Trust me, you will enjoy our vacation."

"Trust me, trust me, trust me! That's all you ever say and every time I trust you, look what happens. Shit! I knew I would be miserable. Just where the hell is this island?"

"Just off the coast from Nome a bit. Trust me, it's very quaint and different. You'll like it."

"Horse shit! Trust me, horse shit!" She fussed.

They followed the south shore of the Seward Peninsula watching the 2000 to 5000 foot mountains in the distance. Along the shore were scattered clusters of houses and approaching Nome, a lone road was spotted going a short ways inland.

If one imagines the shape of Alaska as a face seen from the side, then the Seward Peninsula is the nose and Nome is situated at the opening of the nostrils. Nome began as a port of entry to the high Arctic, one of the last places along the coast where the ocean was free of ice for a short time in the summer. During the gold rush, gold was discovered in the mountains in the interior of the peninsula bringing thousands of fortune seekers here. Now with gold mining in the past, Nome provides the last true outpost to the high coastal Arctic. How many months of 'summer' there are, is arguable, and whether there even is a summer is discussed. The ocean is free of ice for a couple of months and there is little snow on the ground through June, July, and August. Unlike the interior, Nome's weather is dominated by the Bering sea and the vast sheets of ice that lie for thousands of miles not that far to the north.

Matt made a wheels down landing at the Nome airport and refueled. A flight plan was filed and they left around 5 in the afternoon. They would have dinner in Gambell.

The flight from Nome to Gambell took somewhat over an hour and was one that Matt didn't enjoy. There were clouds at all levels, some nearly on the water. The flight path was west and slightly south. St. Lawrence Island is 100 miles long and 25 miles wide, with its long axis pointed east to west. Matt flew toward Savoonga which is in the center of the island rather than to Gambell which lies at the far western tip. Missing Savoonga by a bit they would still intersect the island, while missing Gambell to the west would mean landing on the far coast of Siberia. As it is, Gambell is 200 miles out into the Bering sea from Nome, but only 20 miles from the international date line and less than 50 miles from the coast of Siberia and the Russian town of Providenija. The weather in this region where the Bering sea meets the Chukchi sea to the north and where thousands of years ago the Bering land bridge joined Asia and America is routinely awful —grading on horrendous. Kiren and Vitz were quiet. It was clear to them that they were bound for the North Pole and the only respite was the thought that the South American drug dealers wouldn't consider venturing this far into the Arctic.

Fortunately, the clouds had broken up as they approached Gambell. Matt had not been relishing a single pilot approach to IFR minimums. As it was, he did a respectable wheels down landing on the runway and taxied the Goose back to the parking area. His friends knew of their arrival and it seemed that half the village had turned out to meet them. Staring out of the window of the Goose, Kiren was the first to break the silence once the engines had wound down.

"Where in the name of hell are we and who are all those people dressed up in bright table cloths?"

Matt decided that a short explanation was due, if for no other reason than to keep Kiren and Vitz from making asses of themselves.

"Well guys, as I said, trust me. We are in the hands of some of the most wonderful, protective people in the world and there is no place where the people will do more for you if you are honest with them. We are at Gambell. Gambell, is as I told you — on the beach. There, there is the beach right out there. Now just beyond us a few miles is the coast of Asia and Siberia. We don't do Siberia today. When I was a boy, I spent a couple of summers here and know these people. Furthermore, I did them a favor a couple of years ago and they think they owe me one. As long as they know that you two are under my care, you will be under their watchful eyes. We are going to stay in town at the Inn and then tomorrow go down the coast a bit to set up our research camp. Tonight is celebrations, stories, no drinking– sorry Vitz– and sleep. Tomorrow we will see the rest of the island. Oh, you asked about what they are wearing. They are all wearing fur parkas, but for the summer to keep the fur clean, they put cotton parka covers over the outside and the brighter and more colorful, the better. Let's get out and say hi to some old friends."

Vitz pushed Kiren out first as if offering a virgin to the wild natives and he was holding a machine pistol. Matt snatched it away from him, whispering in Vitz' ear:

"They are such good shots that if they wanted to they could vasectomize you from 150 yards while you were pole vaulting. Leave the gun."

Gambell has a small steady population, nearly all Eskimo. It is one of the hardest towns to get to and as such has also been a settlement which has held more firmly to the traditional ways of the

Eskimo than many of the villages on the mainland. Here, for centuries the villagers lived in houses that were dug into the ground for protection and insulation. The ceilings of these dwellings were made from whale ribs and covered with sod. Life was hard. The ocean was frozen much of the year and they went out over it hunting or fishing. When the ice broke up, small one-man kayaks or larger umiaks were used to hunt sea lions or whales that migrated through the straights between Gambell and the coast of Siberia. This kind of hunting involved life and death for all. Killing a few whales and harvesting the oil, blubber, and meat could feed the village for the long winter and promise life to all for yet another year. At the same time, hunting with primitive harpoons thrown from the fragile umiaks covered with walrus hide and filled with a half dozen men was extraordinarily dangerous and had to be done at such close range that the chance of being turned over by the thrashing whale was high. Falling into the water at those temperatures spelled death unless one was quickly pulled out. In the days told about in the traditional oral stories, many umiaks did not return.

Now, hunting is highly regulated and employs high powered rifles. Nonetheless, by the standards of the deer hunters of the "South 48" this kind of hunting is so dangerous that only these Eskimo have the nerve to go out to keep their traditional ways alive. While hunting provides a major source of food, gathering berries, bird eggs and hunting small shore birds provides summer work for the women and boys. Now life is much different with excellent schools and health care provided by the State and Federal governments and the Native Corporations. Food is brought in by ship in the summer or by air. Traditional ways however remain important and hunting and gathering continue as an key activity. Houses are made from wood frame and heated by oil burning stoves. There are almost no trees on the island and every piece of wood is put to use since at one point it had arrived by ship or air.

Matt went from friend to friend trading hugs and handshakes. Kiren and Vitz stood to the side. The villagers seemed delighted to stare at Vitz, whose enormous size and blonde hair poking out from under his green cap contrasted with their short stocky build and dark complexion. Kiren's inch and a half carrot red hair was hidden by her floppy hat. Matt pulled them over and began introductions.

Lodging was in the Inn, and James joined them for dinner. Kiren inspected the dinner laid out for them: cod, canned peas, potatoes all familiar, but the fresh sausage caught her eye.

"Huh, Eskimo wiener schnitzel. Looks good but what's inside? Sled dog pate'?"

James laughed, and catching Matt's eye he responded.

"No no, this is caribou sausage, actually caribou and reindeer are the same. Reindeer sausage is made in Nome. Good stuff. When I was a kid it came in wrapped boxes and we all hoped to get the box with the grand prize." Kiren took the bait.

"So what was the prize, a heated beach ball?

"No, no a bright red reindeer nose." Vitz howled and Kiren sneered at Matt and James.

The dinner was most welcome after a day which had begun in Talkeetna and had crossed a distance equivalent to from flying from Illinois to Colorado. The evening however had just begun.

Following dinner, James Ahgupuk, a long time friend of Matt's and a respected senior member of the village arrived and explained that an impromptu dance had been arranged on their behalf and that it would begin in an hour in the recreation hall of the Presbyterian church. Kiren objected.

"I'm too tired to dance, and I do not dance with wolves!" She said, pointing a finger at Vitz and Matt.

James looked amused and replied. "You are welcome to dance if you wish and have a tale to tell, but why don't we begin the dance with traditional tales first. You will like it."

Kiren looked confused but Matt smiled, said they would attend and turned to Kiren:

"You will love it. Trust me."

An hour later, they walked to the church. On the way Matt explained, but only because Kiren was threatening not to go.

"We are being given the honor of a traditional Eskimo dance. They do the dancing, not us. Each dance tells a story, usually about a successful hunt, some escape from danger, or a visit by the raven god. I've seen them many times and I have a hard time following some of the stories. Sit back and enjoy, it will be something that few outsiders see. These people love their dances. These are not ones cooked up for a bunch of tourists, what you see is for us, but really it's for their enjoyment as well.

The room was crowded. When Kiren removed her hat the room echoed a collective gasp as everyone stared and chitter-chattered in Eskimo. Few had seen such a punky bright red haircut other than in fashion magazines. The Eskimo still use the traditional language on a day to day basis and it is not considered impolite to talk in Eskimo in front of whites. Soon things returned to the business at hand and a number of men arranged folding chairs and cleared the people from the center. The lights were turned down and men with skin drums sat in the chairs forming the circle. Everyone else either stood or sat in chairs in subsequent rows. The drums were made from round hoops of wood or whale bone over which was stretched a thin layer of seal skin pulled tight. The drum was struck with a wooden stick held by the same hand holding the drum. A chant arose from the men and into the ring sprang a man dressed in a fur parka who began dancing while the chant continued. The dancing was done in a flat footed posture, feet apart, knees bent with the arms held apart. The arms were used to gesture, to describe things, to indicate animals, hunting postures and so on. Although what was being related verbally was unclear, they could see that a story was unfolding and that the other Eskimo were enjoying it and knew what was to come. It was, Matt thought, not that different from Italian opera— it makes more sense if your speak Italian, but even if you don't, it is enjoyable to watch. Over the course of two hours, different Eskimo entered the circle and portrayed their tales. The room was warm from the crowd, and the noise from the drums and chanting was at times deafening.

Vitz had become more and more interested in the dancing and finally entered the circle doing an excellent job of following their format with his moves, gestures, and facial expressions. Later he explained that the Indians in Brazil had similar dances and that this was one he had learned from them. Elated, Vitz went from group to group in the room laughing and with relish, sampled treat after treat of muktuck, herring oil and berries, and other Eskimo favorites. Finally James noted that Kiren and Matt were looking exhausted and called a halt to the festivities promising that in a few days there would be more. As the four of them walked back to the Inn, Kiren thanked James and asked him about his background.

"James, I really appreciate your doing this for us. I dance too, something we call ballet. I took ballet dance classes. I can see a lot of similarities in the two forms. Different music but dance all the same. This dance we call ballet also tells a story. Tell me about your background. Were you born here?"

Matt jabbed James. James shook his head at Matt and replied.

"Ballet, yes. Frankly I tend to like the classic works when Vaslav Njinski and Sergei Diaghliev were at their peak. The post war Russian school under Balanchine perfected many moves to a pinnacle, but I feel that is more a technical advance than true art. Of course every Christmas we rerun the Nutcracker that Nureyev and Gelsey Kirkland danced—that even brings tears to the eyes of this old walrus hunter."

Kiren shut her eyes, hung her head, responding: "Got me. Sorry. I just don't know anything about you people out here. How did you get interested in ballet? Let's start there."

James and Matt jabbed each other and Matt whispered to him:

"Give it to her straight, she's so gullible that pulling her leg is no sport."

James smiled: "I was born here. Stayed through high school, then went to the U of A in Fairbanks for two years. Met Matt when I transferred to Stanford. Did a B.S. in electrical engineering. After Stanford I stayed in California for a few years and then came back home. Life in The States is sure easier, but it isn't the traditional way. Somehow I felt it wasn't time for me to be away from the old ways. Maybe in a few years— but not now."

"So what are you doing here?" Kiren asked.

"Oh, a mix of things, I maintain the radio and navigational equipment for the airport, in the summer I do some work for the Air Force in their radar stations. I teach in the school. I do a lot of work with the church. Still do the traditional hunting. Keeps me busy."

All three turned in. That was good, the next few days would be long.

Brian's discovery spurred Raul into action. Raul insisted that he himself take charge and organize a group to go to Alaska and collect the needed evidence and do whatever had to be done. It was an odd mixture. Brian had been bribed with a large sum of cash to come along. Henry also came, but unhappily. Raul flew his Cessna Citation, suspecting they would need their own transportation. The Citation was one of the later models, a corporate jet with two jet engines on the aft fuselage. The interior had been stripped and fitted with the simplest removable seats. It had been painted an extremely flat, dull gray-blue color. The identification numbers on the side were of an off white color such that against the gray-blue color, they were nearly impossible to read and in fact to determine what country the aircraft was registered in. The overall appearance was sinister. Raul brought six others along in the Citation. Brian and Henry flew to Anchorage on Alaska Airlines.

In addition to Estaban, he had garnered three of his own personal guards and Thanh. Thanh was in his 50's and had played both sides against each other in Viet Nam, for the purpose of continuing his transportation of heroin from Cambodia to the large cities of Viet Nam. There, he had been a major supplier for the middle men who sold to the street people. He was physically large for a Vietnamese and was strongly muscled. His English was good by the time he left Viet Nam. Raul was concerned that Estaban might be more loyal to The Colombian and having Thanh along who had worked only for him made him feel better.

Raul's three bodyguards (his wolves) were not capable of acting independently as were Estaban or Thanh but were much more dangerous, and highly skilled in the use of all kinds of weapons. They would be, as Raul said "tied like dogs to the Citation until they were needed".

Two pilots, Roy and "Coyote" were engaged and completed the roster in the Citation. Both had strong drug connections. Roy was 50ish, and had transported tons of drugs and hundreds of illegal

Mexicans across the border. Coyote was a cowboy from Wyoming. In his 40's, he made a living shooting coyotes for bounty in Wyoming and Montana. He did this by flying a Super Cub low with the doors open using an assault rifle. He also had been involved in a number of projects for the cartel. Two days later they arrived and they met in one of the outlying motels in Anchorage. Raul called a meeting to order.

"Get one thing straight. I am in charge. We have a lot of fire-power but it won't be used until I say so. If anyone, in particular Estaban here, thinks differently then fly back tonight."

All heads nodded while Raul pecked at Estaban's hand with his snake mouth. Estaban nodded with the rest.

"Fine. What we need is evidence of work on this virus. Get the evidence. With the evidence we can give it to Brian's reporter girl friend and she will do the rest. No blood on our hands. If some-body gets killed by accident, that's not my problem,— as long as we have the evidence. Clear?"

Brian asked: "What do you spe spe spe specifically need?"

"That Mr. Professor is why we are paying you fifty grand. What do you think we need?"

Brian leaned back in his chair and closed his eyes for a moment and then spoke slowly.

"Laboratory notes spelling out what they ar ar ar are doing would be excellent secondary evidence. Photos of their la la la lab-oratory– also good secondary evidence. But in today's climate of grocery st st st store magazines with photos of Elvis screwing some European princess from the 12th century, no no no notes and photos would be considered suspect. What would nail them would buh buh be samples of the virus itself. I could ge ge ge get a testing lab to analyze it and show that it was a virus that would infect co co coc coca plants and that it contained new genetic information that had be be be been added by someone unnaturally. That is what we should go for."

"You guys got that? That's what we are here for."

The group broke up as they went in twos and threes for dinner. Brian and Henry sat together. Henry spoke first.

"I got you into this. I'll feel even worse if things get out of control. You've made a good pile of cash already. If you can get the virus sample, Raul will set you up for life. I've never seen him like this before. You understand viruses, is this really the end of cocaine?"

"Could be. If these people are gu gu gu good, it could knock the hell out of the plants. You know, no virus is going to ki ki ki kill everything, and with selective bre bre bre breeding one can find resistant plants. If we were talking corn, the government scientists would get to to to together and make a resistant species and then give it out to all of the major se se se seed houses and in a couple of years everything would be back to normal. Problem here is that the growing is be be be being done by peasants with no knowledge of plant horticulture, and the government scientists are not likely to be helpful. So, in the time frame measured by the lifetime of your drug dealers, ye ye ye yes it could be the end of their careers."

At an adjacent table Estaban and Thanh were conversing. Estaban had his head nearly in his soup and seemed to be talking at the same time he slurped the soup.

"Raul. Fuckhead! Hijuperta! If the big guys in Medellin didn't love his butt, I cut his throat. He knows I– (slurrp), hate snakes. He (slurrp) - watched two Mexicans I know die from his (slurrp) fucking snakes and he laughed. (slurrp) Fucking snakes. I say kill these scientists. My friends in Medellin want me to finish things the right way."

Thanh whispered. "Raul, he know that?"

"Fuck no. You tell him, I (slurrp) cut your throat you fat gook."

"Indian shit, try it and I will stuff a baby cobra up your ass while you sleep." Thanh mimicked Raul's snake mouth pecking at Estaban's butt. Estaban cringed. Thanh continued.

"No, I not tell Raul. But I work for him for long time. I never see him so angry about things. If Mr. Raul tells me to cut your throat, I will do it."

Blaah— Estaban blew some of the soup into Thanh's face. They stared at each other for a moment and then laughed.

The next morning the group – minus Raul's three wolves who remained with the Citation, rented a car in Anchorage to drive to Talkeetna, not wanting to make note of their arrival in such a serious looking airplane. Brian, Henry, and Raul fanned out asking questions about Kiren, leaving Thanh and Estaban and the others at a roadside cafe. Brian went to the air service where the FAX had been sent. He was surprised at the rapidity at which he was given a full accounting of Kiren and her whereabouts.

Within thirty minutes Raul, Brian and Henry converged on the Sled dog motel for lunch and shared their findings. Brian commented:

"Sounds like we know where to guh guh guh go. Now all we have to do is find out where this island is. I assume it's not far from here. Let's ask the wa wa wa waitress,— Ma'am–."

The waitress pushed his plate aside so that he could look at the plastic placemat which displayed a map of Alaska. She allowed a drop of syrup from Brian's knife (he had just finished pancakes) to fall onto the west end of St. Lawrence Island on the map. Brian commented:

"Jesus, that's out in the middle of the ocean." Raul screwed his nose up and shook his head.

"Why the fuck out there?"

"Well," Brian continued, feeling that he had become the expert on the virus group, "Clever, clever. The sun is up a lot more out there (he was confused since the sun is up more and more as you go north not west), and I'll bet there is no one out there."

Raul shook his head.

Henry broke in. "Wait a minute, we've been told all along that they were doing research for the Navy on some South Pacific island and that it had to do with mutant viruses created by A bomb tests. What if they are not making cocaine viruses at all! What if we just got the north pacific mixed up with the south pacific!"

Brian exhaled strongly. "Whew, a pos pos pos pos possibility guys, look at this map! This island is close to Siberia! Recall that before the test ba ba ba bans, we were shooting in the South Pacific but the Ruskies were popping H H H H H H bombs in the Siberian Arctic."

Raul broke in. "That fuckers, would make me very very happy. We could all go home and sleep. Now back to reality. What do we know? We know this Kiren bitch talked about coca viruses. We know that some of our coca plants got dug up and shipped to the US. We know that she is no where to be found. Now we know she is on this god damned island."

Brian nodded. "A lot of co co co coincidences but not enough to con con con convict them. Got to tie the co co co coca plants to them. That's the key."

"Well, back to Anchorage, we've got a long trip ahead of us." We have too many to fit in my Citation and it needs longer runways than some of these bloody villages around here offer. I figured this might happen and have a short term lease set up on a Beechcraft King Air. It hold more people and lands short but, damn, sure is not as fast as the Citation. Great drug delivery vehicle however," Raul concluded.

The rest of the day was spent returning to Anchorage and loading their gear into the King Air 350i, a rather fat looking low wing aircraft sporting twin 1,000 hp turboprop engines for the 700 mile flight to Gambell. A King Air can easily handle a 3000 foot runway and with full fuel, has a 1500 mile range. With three quarters fuel Raul felt it could carry himself and his 9 passengers since they did not have a lot of baggage and the "wolves" were of slight build. The density altitude in Alaska was also in their favor, increasing its takeoff performance. They were not sure exactly what they should do when they arrived. After talking to a number of tourist agents in Anchorage, it was decided that once at Gambell, they would explain that they were from a US oil company and that they were touring some of the potential oil fields along the northern Siberian coast. The Russians have been anxious to promote tourism and cooperative ventures since the breakup of the USSR, and local flights back and forth between the US and Siberia are frequent –and permission easily obtained. They left Anchorage early the next morning.

The first full day at Gambell began with moans from Vitz. Midway through the night he had acquired a severe case of the Eskimo version of Montezuma's revenge. The herring oil may have harbored some unpleasant bacteria, but more likely the treats were fine but his system was just not ready for such a large amount of very unusual and oily foods. Matt felt sorry for Vitz and worried that he might become clinically dehydrated given his state, and it was decided that Vitz would stay in Gambell for the day in case medical intervention was needed. At Vitz' suggestion, his armament would go with Matt and Kiren as Vitz would follow in an ATV later. The ATV is a 4 wheeled motor scooter with large tires which can carry one or two people over rough terrain.

Matt had the Goose unloaded and arranged for a tractor to pull a large sled filled with their gear from Gambell fifteen miles east along the coast to a site between two hunting camps, Naskak camp and Apatiki camp. The site was on the inside of a lagoon, Nikrakpak lagoon, which was nearly closed off by a spit of land except for one opening to the Bering sea which lay to the north. Matt felt that this was an ideal site since it was part way between Gambell and Savoonga, which lay to the east on the north shore and at the point of Kookoolik cape. Matt had arranged to borrow a couple of ATVs.

The weather was typical for that time of the summer. Mid 40s, windy, a mix of fog and clouds, high humidity that cut to the bone and made it feel even colder. As they left Gambell, they could look out in all directions. The tundra is an extremely fragile layer of living matter only a few inches thick and it takes years to regenerate once it has been disturbed. Even with the inclement weather, Kiren and Matt were in good spirits and Kiren would zoom ahead on her ATV and then fall behind as she would stop to watch this or that bird or inspect the flowers.

The flowers on the Arctic islands at this time of year make the tundra appear like a pointillist painting created by an artist bent on using every hue and shade on his palate. Indeed all summer the tundra is ablaze, but mid August is the peak and the visitors were being treated to the best the island could provide. The color could be enjoyed from afar in which the colors blended into patches and whorls of color, each blending into another. They could also be seen nose to petal, inspecting a flower in all its delicate beauty.

Matt called to Kiren: "See that humungus mountain over to our south, it's the second tallest mountain on the island. Called Poovoopuk, yah that is poo–voo–puk, mountain. All of fifteen hundred and seventeen feet above sea level. Pretty impressive after McKinley isn't it!"

Kiren called back. "So where is the tallest one?"

"Oh, over by Savoonga, Atuk mountain. It's about 2000 feet. We're going to a spot near Olngooseenuk, Oln–goo–see–nuk mountain. I think it may be 1000 feet." He pointed in the general direction they were traveling. Here, unlike the area around McKinley where mountain peaks rose tens of thousands of feet and the ground was sharply cut and angled, St. Lawrence Island was very smooth, polished by centuries of winds. It was created not by the uplifting of continental plates clashing, but rather by the passive rise of the ocean level to create an island out of what had been the rounded top of an ancient Arctic mountain. It was mid-morning when they reached the site on Niyrakpak lagoon. James had ridden along with them and took them a few hundred yards inland to show them a sacred ancient village site. All that Kiren and Matt could see at first glance were depressions in the ground arranged in a helter skelter way. Each depression was the site of a house that had been dug into the ground. In a few, a segment of whale rib stuck out, a left over from the ribs that helped form the ceiling. James explained that if one was to dig into these house sites ivory and bone artifacts from the old life could be found but that now days these sites were off limits to digging and that for anyone –in particular a white– to dig was a very serious matter. Kiren promised to look but leave them alone and James appreciated Matt's sensitivity in these matters.

Several young men from the village arrived on ATVs and helped set up four large tents. Supplies were placed in one, another set up for cooking, a third harbored the "scientific equipment" and a bed for Kiren. The fourth had two more military folding cots for Matt and Vitz. Clear plastic sheeting was laid out over sections of the tundra as if to protect the plants underneath. By the end of the afternoon Matt stood back and announced to James:

"Damn, looks like we have been here all summer. Now remember my promise. If we pull this one off, Roland will send an Air Force transport out this Christmas to pick up all these young guys and take all of you free to the "Great Alaskan Shoot Out in Anchorage." James nodded with a smile. The shoot-out is a several day basketball tourney hosted in Anchorage which features the best University teams from the"South 48".

James' entourage left and they strolled down to the beach and stood talking while seeing who could skip flat stones the most number of times.

"So Matt, the last time we talked, you had a theory of wars. Is that still on the stove?" James asked.

"Damn right. For the last few thousand years the major reason governments existed was to protect their people against dying prematurely at the hands of their neighbors– be they Egyptians, Gauls, Vandals, Germans or now terrorists. Until our very own generation, if you asked people what was the major reason that people died before they got old, it was wars. Certainly my parents could recite a long list of people– usually young men– who died in WWII. But now for the first time in the history of civilization, that's no longer the case. What people are dying of in this country is not national conflicts but diseases– cancer, AIDS , smoking related diseases and so on."

"And cocaine related crime." Kiren added.

"Right, also crime. But now in the US, the single most common cause of death for men over 20 is cancer and heart disease." Matt continued.

"I know this, so where are you going?" Kiren snapped.

"Where I am going is that we are now fighting a very different war. Our governments should be turning their attention to protecting the people under their care from premature death due to disease– not the Visgoths or Barbarians. Disease is the world war of the 21st century."

"I'll buy that. So what you were saying as I recall was that the governments are still building early warning systems for invaders they know will never come." James commented.

"Right, we should be creating an early warning system against the appearance of pandemic flu viruses that might spread through our urban population and wipe out more people than any H bomb ever could."

Kiren broke in. "Can you imagine what would have happened if the AIDS virus could have been spread by casual contact like flu? We could have lost 50 million people in one year. Makes losses from the nastiest wars look mild, doesn't it. Recall that one third of the people in Europe died of the Bubonic plague. One third of Europe now days is a lot of people."

"But could that really happen?" asked James.

"Maybe, maybe not, but we sure are losing a lot of young people from diseases. I have absolutely no doubt that if our government was to make a stable investment into fighting these diseases and making major advances in biotechnology that we would be saving a lot more lives."

"So Matt, as I hear you, you are not just talking about old viruses spread by terrorists?"

"Not at all, I doubt that any terrorist group could grow enough small pox, for example, and disburse it to kill millions. Maybe a rogue nation could, but we are watching a lot more closely now. What we do not seem to be doing well is watching for are entirely new viruses."

They walked along the shore for a while, quiet, then Matt returned the discussion to old friends and after some time James bid ado.

Matt started the cooking stove. Over coffee and a ham and eggs dinner he explained the plan.

"I figure that the soonest our drug dealers can get here is mid day the day after tomorrow. Vitz should be back with us tomorrow. By that time we will have subtracted four days from the minimum seven we need, and our plants are doing their part back at the mine. Now, every eye on the island is watching for them. I made the ultimate offer. Basketball tickets to the tourney. Only tickets to the Final Four are worth more, and I doubt that even Roland could manage that. Once the drug people arrive, James will keep in touch by radio. No one in town will give them ATVs, so they will be on foot. They may spot us flying in, depending on whether they fly themselves or not. Still it's going to be damn slow to get to us."

"What about their using boats?" asked Kiren.

"Good point. Nobody will give them an umiak, but they might bring inflatable Zodiaks. But if they do, they have to come through that small opening on the lagoon and we will see them. A fall back plan is to have James offer to take them in an umiak– but only after he stalls them for a while. If they come in from the water we can zip off in our ATVs, get to town and fly the Goose off to the next spot on this little chase about Alaska."

"What do you mean?" Kiren asked.

"Oh, I figured we needed one more secret camp just to be sure. So tomorrow morning we are going to use these paint cans and write "base camp/Homer Ak" on all the boxes. When they find this camp, it won't take a village idiot to figure out that they might look in Homer. And how about that! The Goose will be there ready for the next wild goose chase!"

"Helicopters, what if they fly in here in helicopters?" asked Kiren, still fretting about not being in full control.

"Roland will see to that. First, few chopper pilots would be willing to fly one across 200 miles of the world's shittiest open water. Since the only place they could come from is Nome, Roland had the two that were capable of such a trip grounded for an FAA safety inspection."

As dinner was finished and Matt broke out a bottle of sherry, Kiren asked:

"You spent summers here a long time ago but these guys seem to hold you in a lot of respect. What gives? You said that they owed you some favor."

"Well, I don't consider it a favor, just looking out after my friends. You see, there has been a lot of disagreement out here over quotas set by the damn white environmentalists on hunting seals, walrus, whales. These quotas are fine if one considers hunting a sport, but for these people, the hunts are a matter of gathering food in their traditional way. One way or the other, it's a very few animals we are talking about. Well, a few years ago I found out through Roland that some Feds were planning a sting on the islanders, to trap them into going out on a hunt for pay and taking more animals than the quota allowed. If it had succeeded it could have put half the village in jail."

Kiren asked: "So what happened here?"

"Absolutely nothing. I found out from Roland who the agents were and when they arrived, everyone was very polite and recited quota laws to them. They did get a tourist ride in an umiak. Damn thing sunk, and they almost drowned."

More sherry was poured and they toasted an enjoyable stay in their camp which Kiren had named Poopoovoovoopukpuk camp. It was getting late but at this time of the year, this far north, it was still light out. Matt helped Kiren arrange the sleeping bag in her tent, and possibly warmed by the sherry and their closeness, he felt a burning desire to hold her while falling onto the cot and her sleeping bag. Kiren reached up kissing him with a quick wet kiss on the lips and brushed his thigh with her hand. Caught off guard Matt started to pull her to him, but she ushered Matt out the tent door stating that she was tired and had to wash up.

Matt stood outside for a minute weighing the consequences of what he wanted to do and then shook his head and retired to his tent where he washed his face, stripped to his shorts, opened up the sleeping bag into a large comforter, and pulled it over him. He spoke to himself:

"Jesus! I'm a tenured professor at Johns Hopkins, right? So why am I running from the Cocaine Cartel, reenacting some camping trip from my childhood, and lying here feeling like a school boy over a woman with a red bottle brush haircut?" He rolled over on the cot and continued to ponder his situation. "Well, its only been games and frustration to this point. Go any farther down this path and good bye Rosalind. But damn, I think Ros and I are history anyhow. Never quite connected. Damn again. I haven't been this way over a woman in a long time. Yah –Yah, its the situation, the closeness, her dependence, her damn legs—it is those damn legs."

Matt rolled back face up. "Nothing will happen here, she just likes snapping men's jock straps for fun."

Kiren entered his tent draped in her L.L. Bean jacket but possibly little else. Her slim bare legs were exposed to where the jacket stopped mid-thigh. She held a glass in one hand and with the other, she wetted two fingers in the sherry and reached down running them over Matt's lips.

"I can't figure out how to turn the lights off," she stated.

Matt had risen to his elbows allowing the sleeping bag to pile up in his lap and grinned.

"You can't. I have to hold your eyelids closed. I'll show you." He reached up and pulled Kiren down on top of himself. As she giggled, Matt rolled her over on the cot and holding her down he first closed one eyelid and then the other with his fingertips.

"See simple– one eye and the other for lights-out time." Matt started to pepper her forehead, cheeks and throat with small kisses, approaching her lips and then receding. He could feel her squirm under his weight and her two legs separated and then clamped down tightly on his left leg. Matt raised up for a second to look at her from a much closer distance than ever before. "Oh God do I love this woman," he thought to himself as he released his fingers from her eyelids, took both of her hands gently in his and squeezing them, pulled her arms up around the back of his head as he focused a deep long wet kiss to her lips.

Kiren reciprocated twisting and wiggling, allowing Matt to remove the jacket and discover nothing under it other than Kiren herself. For Matt this was an intense sensory overload. Over the past several months he had inspected her in fine detail but from a distance: her sharp nose, the upward twist where her lips came together at the edges, her sharp pointed collar bones, her slim but muscular arms, on and on– and suddenly all of it was his. He pulled the bag over them for warmth.

Matt stroked her arms and back for some time before turning her over and venturing lower and lower with his kisses. Kiren was becoming more active as she hugged him, returned his deep kisses and ventured lower with her hands. At one point he feared he would lose it all before the time and had to move her hands away to slow the pace. Kiren however seemed determined to get on with it and have him enter her as she helped pull him fully on top and maneuvered him into position.

Matt prided himself on his ability to hold himself in check until his partner was close to her climax. But he was so aroused that once he entered her he felt helpless to do more than enjoy the feeling even though he had little control over himself. He didn't let his orgasm stop him and continued working with Kiren until she too climaxed. Finally they both began to relax and continued with light delicate kisses. Matt held and caressed her for a long time and then arranged the bag so that it would keep them warm for the night.

The next morning, Kiren awoke, kissed Matt quickly and retired to her tent to get dressed before he had a chance to initiate morning sex, which frankly was his preferred time. The sun was out and temperatures warmed into the mid 50s so that even with the breeze it was pleasant to be out as long as one had a jacket. By noon, the camp had been arranged, and Homer had been written on the boxes. Matt held Kiren for a moment now and then as they did their chores. Kiren asked him:

"So, are real scientists better lovers than socials scientists like your Ros?"

Matt laughed loudly and replied: "A thousand fold at least."

"Good, then tell me. The scar on your chin, I find it sexy, give me the truth now, what's the story?"

"Happened in high school. My fault really. You know teenagers. We were playing chicken. Get way back from each other. Face off. When the flag drops, let go of the brakes and go straight at the other guy. The one who turns away is chicken."

"So who turned away?"

"Neither of us. Head on collision."

"God, must have been awful!"

"Was. Took several hours just to get us untangled. Had to cut things apart. Never do that again."

"You were badly hurt?"

"Just the cut on my chin from the sled. My sister bailed off the back of her dog sled before the dogs teams ran into each other. Dogs had more fun rolling around all tangled up in their harnesses."

Kiren began to chase Matt but they stopped, hearing the sound of two ATVs approaching. Exiting the tent they saw Vitz who started talking even before his ATV stopped.

"You won't believe it! If I get these sightings verified it could get a mention in the bird watchers journal. Amazing! This little hawk back there is one of the rarest birds ever seen on the North American continent! Normally seen along the Siberian coast! Jesus there are dozens of Asian birds out here!"

Vitz explained that for an American bird watcher to collect (sight) 1000 different species in North America in his or her lifetime was the pinnacle of bird watching. To do so within the continental US was extremely difficult, and one option was to add 'easy sightings'. A favorite place for this was the Pribilof Islands four hundred miles to the south in the Bering sea. Many birds that are found there are Asian birds, not American. Matt found this amusing and Kiren was entranced as the ferocity of Vitz' interest. As Vitz jabbered on she laughed:

"Our big bad Vitzie is a bird watcher. Isn't that sweet! What a contrast, in the morning pull someone's testicles off with your bare hands and then in the afternoon go watch a gold crested water goblet – or what ever it was he called that little peeper."

Matt just smiled and shook his head. Vitz looked drained and still had to retire over the hill at frequent intervals with a roll of toilet paper in hand but kept dragging them here and there to look for yet another bird and verify his sightings. Matt was not concerned, as he guessed that it would be the next day at the earliest when their company arrived, and he was carrying a hand held radio with which James would alert him to any intrusion. So watching Vitz watch birds seemed a highly reasonable way to spend the afternoon. Kiren kept getting bored and in spite of Vitz urging not to talk she kept asking Matt about the island and his friends.

"James. A bright guy. So why did he come back here and not stay in California?"

Matt shook his head. "People like you assume that quality of life is measured by the number of silver grapefruit spoons in your pantry, or how many cable stations you get on TV. For someone who grew up in the old ways, the traditional ways, all of that is as meaningful to them as how many different names they have for snow– is to you. There are things, feelings, sights, climactic changes, closeness to the animals they hunt, that you and I could never begin to sense. Tasting muktuk– the raw cartilage from the flipper after killing a walrus. That elicits thousands of years of collective memories to James, all handed down orally like we saw the other night. You've been sanitized from such feeling. It has been cut out of your soul by years of living in apartments, by not taking the time to bid the sun good night every night and asking it quietly if it would please come again the next day, of believing that the raven carries knowledge from the beyond— on and on. People in modern America don't have a shred of that left in them. I consider that the ultimate tragedy of modern life. That's one of the reasons I'm drawn back every year– to remember the tales of my father and his ancestors. And I'm much more like you than any real Indian or Eskimo. For James, I don't think that there ever was a doubt as to where he belonged. Sure he's bright. He's damn bright! One of the best grade point averages of his class at Stanford. But what does that have to do with the arrival of the first whale in the spring? Does the raven who knows more than he does care about his degree? I think not. James is caught in two worlds. Of course he enjoys ballet (Matt watched her wince), he danced some himself and had dinner once with Nureyev (jab-jab) and I know for a fact that he was as wild as the other students. It would have been easy for him to stay there. He had a good job. But he has taken a harder task of coming home and helping provide a bridge for his community helping it learn how to come to grips with deciding how much of the new ways they can adopt while not losing the old ways."

Kiren nodded and pointed back to the camp. She was feeling chilled in the breeze and Vitz seemed to be increasingly annoyed at their lack of excitement over his birds.

As dinner was about to be served, James arrived in his umiak and another plate was prepared. James was anxious to hear about Matt and Kiren's research. They took turns describing their research and Kiren was surprised at the depth of James' knowledge of molecular biology. Finally James bid them ado and Matt broke out a bottle of Jim Beam he had hidden, feeling sensitive not to be seen drinking with any of the Eskimo, even close friends. Matt and Kiren looked at each other and Vitz spotting the glance, began teasing them.

"So lovie-dovies, what went on when I was gone? Are you two planning to name your first born after me? Could call him Vitz the twenty-third."

"Fuck you!" Kiren blushed bright red and left for her tent. Vitz looked squarely at Matt, realizing that he may have pulled the golden straw out of the pile by accident and asked:

"Anything you want to tell me Kemo Sabe?"

"Go to bed or I will burn every shred of toilet paper in this camp."

It was mid-day the following day when the King Air radioed Gambell it would be landing. It was not uncommon that an aircraft would stop in at Gambell, then arrange via radio for permission to cross into Siberian airspace and fly up the Siberian coast before crossing back to the Alaskan side and return to Nome. Raul and his group climbed out and asked if they might find something to eat. They were directed to the Inn. James had seen them arrive and met them as they walked into town. He sized the group as being one of the oddest mixes he had seen. While the whites seemed not that different from various tourists and businessmen, the two dark skins as he referred to Estaban and Thanh, had eyes of the weasel, and the three who remained with the King Air were children of the wolverine. As coffee was being served, Raul asked James:

"So, Mr. Ahugupuk, one of the reasons for stopping is we may have some friends of ours working here on the island."

"No oil people I know of." James replied.

"Well, they are more like environmental scientists. A couple of biologists, work on plants. Worked for our parent company for a long time, real friends of mine, in particular the woman. Her name is Kiren Moore, she's now a professor at Duke. Quit our company a few years ago. Anyhow I was told she and some others had a summer project out here and if they are around I sure would like to stop in and see if they need anything."

James had rehearsed the reply. "Oh, her. Short red hair? Yah and a couple of guys. They have been in and out all summer. Doing some research on the north shore past Poovoopuk mountain. I can show you where they are on the map. Hard to get there. A whole day's walk. I suggest you stay in the Inn and start in the morning. I can guide you if you want."

"So they are here and have been here all summer. How about that! So we've found our friends! Great! I'd like to see where they are on the map. I'll chat with my friends here and see if we want to take the time to go out. A whole day's walk huh? Any faster way, car, truck, some of those big wheel things the kids were running around in?"

"Oh, no. Sorry you must walk or get a permit to take a gas powered vehicle out there. It's all in the Gambell Traditional Historic Preserve and no motor vehicles are allowed out there. To go would put you in jail."

"Damn, we don't have that much time. How does one get a permit?"

"You write the Department of the Interior in Washington D.C. Takes about six months."

"Right. Not surprised. Shit! Well, we'll think it over. Check with you after dinner. Thanks."

James radioed Matt explaining what had transpired. Matt suggested that he might have to offer to take them in an umiak but that they would have to wait until the end of the next day for the weather and waves to quiet down. At the end of dinner James stopped back and Raul asked about boats. James provided the answer and explanation and Raul replied:

"Fine, we will be back in the morning day after tomorrow. You can have the boat ready then."

All this was relayed to Matt who was delighted they had bought an extra day for the viruses to grow.

That evening Raul walked to the King Air and spent several hours on the radio. They flew out after dark.

As morning broke, Vitz ate a quick breakfast and finally appeared to be fully recovered from the herring oil episode. The previous day had been quiet with everyone keeping to their own space. Matt had caught up on a good bit of reading, Kiren took hikes to look at flowers, and Vitz had collected nearly twenty new birds. Vitz had repeatedly checked his weapons and coffee cup in hand, laid the pieces out on the floor. He picked up the M203A grenade launcher. It was his favorite weapon. The other items included a machine pistol, a fully automatic assault rifle and a variety of grenades. Vitz noted that the rocket launcher was not loaded and asked Matt:

"Where did you put the red box with the ammunition?"

Matt stared at Vitz, then threw his head back.

"Oh, Jesus H Christ! I left it in the aft hold of the Goose. It never got loaded on the sled."

"You mean we are here with Vitz to protect us– but he has no bullets?" Kiren exclaimed.

"That's about it. Look, Vitz, it's an hour back to the Goose and an hour back in the ATV at full speed. Take the hand held radio and check in with James. When you reach him maybe he can send someone to meet you and save a bit of time. We'll be exposed for a short time and the people in that jet may not show up for another day."

Vitz grabbed a machine pistol and the unloaded rocket launcher and sped off in the ATV. Trying to seem calm, Matt continued reading about viruses while Kiren worked on a fake notebook that would be left behind. Matt watched her and asked:

"What is that book that you are copying things from?"

"Oh that's the real notebook with all my data. I didn't want to leave it at Talkeetna and needed to do some calculations and clean up some of my notes. This little book contains the guts of everything we have done this summer."

"Fine, but be damned sure you bring it back when we leave."

"I sleep with it, –well, not the other night."

Vitz had picked up the red ammunition box and was returning when the large black Russian helicopter flew over, passing in the same direction he was going.

CHAPTER FOURTEEN
KATMAI AND THE SHOOT OUT

Matt's hearing was tuned to the sound of airplanes. The 'whup-whup' of a large twin blade helicopter combined with the hum of the turbine engines created a very distinctive noise which he recognized long before the helicopter came into view. Responding to his alarm, Kiren snatched her knapsack and the .243 rifle as Matt grabbed his .300 Weatherby. They donned their jackets and ran up the hill to the ancient village site where there would be some protection in the depressions of the old house sites.

"I thought you said that they couldn't get a helicopter over the ocean!" Kiren yelled as she too could distinguish the sound.

"I did! But that sounds like a Ruskie chopper and a twin blade turbo job!" Matt yelled as they dove into one of the holes and peeked over the edge at their camp now 200 yards away.

Kiren held her head in her hands. "We didn't remember that we are only fifty miles from Russia now did we— where an American dollar can buy anything you want, now did we —Mr. Perfect- plan trust me person!"

"Well, only minor perturbation, we are still right on schedule. They come by air, they come by boat, big shit deal!"

"Right, but they can also fly around in that thing and blow our butts into little pieces if they find us. We sure can't outrun them in those motor scooters! The moment they saw us in them we would be toast. " Kiren yelled back.

The helicopter was making a criss cross search pattern looking for the camp. James had given them a general idea of where it was but that still amounted to a large area to cover. Once the helicopter was within a mile of the camp, it veered sharply and flew directly toward the tents. The helicopter was dark, nearly black, and landed several hundred feet from the camp.

Inside the helicopter Raul was rehearsing Henry and Brian as to what they were to do. On the assumption that the camp and work was legitimate, and related to the A bomb testing, they did not want to rush the camp with guns blazing. "No", Raul urged, Brian and Henry would amble over with no weapons and chat with the occupants. If the people were hostile they were to run back toward the chopper in which force would be met with force. If they spied any coca plants or guessed that coca viruses were being made then they were to leave ASAP. Finally if it did seem legitimate, then they were to be friendly and leave with smiles. Brian and Henry exited the chopper dressed in their new parkas and walked to the camp expecting at any moment to be either shot or met by an offer of hot coffee. Neither Brian or Henry were happy about this, yet they felt that there was a high chance that the A bomb virus work would be verified and that all could go home with no shame and everyone happy including Brian's investment broker.

It seemed odd to Matt that only two emerged from the chopper which sat with its blades idling and that the two who did, walked slowly to the camp as if to offer the inhabitants a subscription to The Reader's Digest.

Having failed to raise anyone by repeated hello's, Henry and Brian poked their heads into each tent. Brian called:

"Henry, over here, this is where they have been doing some work."

They looked here and there examining everything in turn. Brian shook his head:

"Shit if I know, this is all stuff I see in my lab everyday and could be used for almost anything including measuring bacterial counts in baby crap. I sure don't see any co co co coca plants. Was there anything out there under the clear plastic?"

"Nothing, just weeds."

Brian sat down in one of the folding chairs and looked around him.

"Henry, su su su something isn't right here. What does this lu lu lu look like to you?"

"Hell, I don't know – a lab I guess."

"Yes, bu bu bu but no. Everything here is fresh. I don't see a single bro bro bro broken glass, a discarded pipette tip, it's like the equipment is here bu bu bu but nothing has been done. Most scientists can crap a place up in a few hours of real work. This place is virgin– no scientific garbage."

Henry and Brian sat looking about until Henry spotted a pair of notebooks that appeared to have been tossed into a corner in haste. Picking them up, he handed them to Brian who sat reading one, putting it aside and then the other which was much more detailed and filled with page after page of notes. Suddenly he stood bolt upright.

"Well on the gu gu gu ghost of Gregor Mendel, this is it! I can't be be be believe it! Do you know what I am holding?"

"What?" "The notebook! I mean the notebook! Their ve ve ve very notebook with all of the details of making a virus that will knock out co co co coca plants. I'll bet it's all right here! Let's get back to Raul and see what he wants to do. Maybe this is enough!"

They ran back to the chopper. Matt noted this, commenting that this did not bode well.

Raul was shown the prize and examined it in detail. He sat swearing over and over.

"Fucking little bitch, god damn her! Hijeputa! I thought we had scared her out of doing this –or she wasn't doing it all. Fuck it anyway."

"So who do we kill?" Estaban seemed to be smelling blood.

"Evidence! Stupid asshole! We all go back to those tents and we find the virus! Remember stupid, what Brian told us. Any nut case could cook up a nice looking notebook like this one. I don't see her signature in here and she could say it was faked. We need some test tubes with this virus in it. Then I will decide what we will do. Bring your guns."

Raul's three guards remained in the helicopter but the rest fanned out and went back to the tents. Matt counted: "Five- six, a whole bunch this time. Maybe more in the chopper. I sure don't want to get into a shooting match, although at a distance the .300 Weatherby gives us some advantage."

Inside the tents Raul was furiously throwing things here and there looking for something that might be a tube filled with virus. He would take this item and that to Brian who would inspect it and shake his head. Finally he yelled at Brian.

"Brian what the hell is going on here? This is just a few tents, not a lab. I don't even see a generator. This is supposed to be some hot shit lab where viruses are being cooked up. I don't see any plants. All I see are boxes marked "Main camp" and "Homer". Where the fuck is that?"

Brian replied. "No idea, bu bu bu but I told Henry the same thing. This place is odd, they were here, bu bu bu but I sure don't see any evidence of any work going on. Also it's far too cold out here to grow coca plants."

Roy broke in: "Homer, I saw it on the map, it's on the Kenai Peninsula south of Anchorage."

Raul shook his head. "Fuck us all! We've been led all the way to the middle of the god damned north pole to keep us away from this Homer place. All the crap we got in Gambell about not being able to get here except by walking sounded too weird. But these fuckers are here, I can smell them. Their airplane is back there and their god damned coffee is still hot. Get back in the chopper and find their butts."

There was a mass exodus to the chopper. Matt whispered:

"This doesn't look good. Let's cover ourselves with as much dirt as we can. If they spot us, I will run to distract them and keep them busy with my rifle. Kiren, what ever happens you stay put."

Matt covered Kiren the best he could, but was pessimistic about being able to hide as there was little cover. From the air they would eventually be spotted.

The black chopper lifted off and started swinging back and forth over the area keeping a hundred feet off the ground. For a moment, it appeared it might be going far enough away so that they could run to the beach where there might be better cover but then it returned. The chopper slowly scoured the area around the camp. Finally right over Matt, he was spotted and it moved back a hundred yards and hovered. A man with a gun poked out of the opened side door and started yelling at them to come out but it was hard to hear him over the noise of the helicopter. Matt yelled to Kiren:

"If they come any closer or start shooting, I'm going to shoot back. You stay down."

At this point the man reappeared with a short barreled automatic rifle and raked the area around them with shots. Matt pushed the dirt away and began returning carefully aimed shots.

Kiren responded by doing the same with the .243 and for a moment it seemed that the more accurately placed shots from the two rifles would keep the helicopter at bay. Unfortunately neither Kiren or Matt had a large supply of ammunition.

The chopper moved back and hovered again while several men began firing their automatic weapons. While these weapons were highly inaccurate, they were nonetheless, sending a large volume of bullets that kept Kiren and Matt from returning fire easily and in time would hit their targets if only by random.

Just as Matt was loading his last 4 rounds into the Weatherby and was getting up to run, a bright streak of light appeared several hundred yards to the left of the helicopter. It arced toward the chopper and erupted in a ball of fire exploding on the ground fifty yards short of its target. As the helicopter rotated around to face the new intruder, a second grenade appeared this time exploding much closer, rocking the helicopter which flew off hovering over the beach.

Vitz came into view standing up on his ATV, waiving his M203A. Matt and Kiren ran to him and Kiren hugged him while Matt let out a great sigh and then turned to watch the helicopter.

Suddenly Matt's radio which Vitz was carrying came alive.

"Matt, you there?" It was James.

"Hell! Yes! They're here in a big black helicopter. Vitz just ran them off for the moment. They were shooting at us. Where are you?"

"We saw the chopper coming across from the Siberian coast and I'm just now entering the lagoon with a dozen umiaks. We'll spread out and start shooting. They aren't going to want to take all of us on."

"Great, start firing even if you are out of range!"

A dozen umiaks powered by Evinrude outboards suddenly came into view and standing in each were several men firing high velocity bolt action hunting rifles. The clatter of the bullets on the chopper caught the pilot's attention who jammed power in, and swung the helicopter back, this time disappearing from view.

Matt, Vitz and Kiren ran to the umiaks as they pulled up on the beach. As the boats ran out of Niyrakpak lagoon, the black helicopter reappeared but stayed several miles away.

Running in the open Bering sea James called to Matt.

"Matt, someone cut the tires on your Goose last night. I assume it was them when they left in that King Air."

Matt nodded, replying: "Let's hope she has a strong stomach."

It was an hour's run in the boats to Gambell. There, everyone got out and watched as the black helicopter hovered and then sat down about 500 yards away on a small rise. Matt, Vitz, and Kiren stood with the rest watching. Shaking, Kiren asked:

"What do they want? "

"Us, bunny, I assume they are watching to see what we are going to do now that they have flattened the tires on the Goose which as you see, is sitting several hundred feet from the water like a dead duck– or dead Goose that is. They sure don't want to come closer or get into a fire fight with these guys." Matt nodded here and there as nearly every man including Matt was holding a telescopic sighted hunting rifle.

At this moment the crowd froze. A man exited the chopper and began running toward them and it was only as he came closer that a small girl emerged from a lower rise between them also running. Before anything could be done, the man grabbed the girl. They were 250 yards away, and the man stood facing them holding a pistol and the girl.

Matt looked at James and raised his .300 Weatherby. James put his hand on Matt's shoulder and pulling the barrel down, said:

"No, it is Irigoo's daughter —he must do it." Matt looked to the side as a short stocky man raised a Winchester model 70 chambered for the .257 Roberts cartridge, a favorite for long range seal hunting. Irigoo took a breath and watching the man hold his young daughter said loudly:

"He is only a seal," and shot.

The 100 grain hollow point copper-clad Nossler bullet had less than 40 grains of cordite powder behind it, but its speed kept its trajectory nearly flat across the 250 yards where it entered the side of the man's nose expending its energy fully within his cranial chamber. The man fell limply to the side as James and the others called loudly in Eskimo for Irigoo's daughter to lie on the ground and not move. Matt covered the 250 yards at full tilt not caring whether or not he was being shot at. The helicopter began to sizzle from the barrage of bullets hitting with great accuracy. Matt was in more danger of being shot from behind than from the front as he dove next to the girl and watched the helicopter lift off and fly out over the Bering sea toward the Siberian coast. Matt carried her back handing her to her father.

"James, we need to get out of here fast before they come back with others. I'll call Roland and get him to scramble a jet to give us cover for a while and send a turboprop with soldiers and some fire power. They can stick around and keep you company for a few days and clean up our mess back at the lagoon. I have a feeling that these guys are getting angry and we need to get to Homer before they do. If you can get a few strong young men on each wing tip, I think I can get the Goose off. Fortunately we fueled up when we landed."

Matt hugged James and a number of others, and then helped Kiren and Vitz into the Goose. With men holding the wing tips level, he raised the wheels so that the Goose was now resting fully on its keel on the gravel. It was about 100 feet to the beach and another hundred feet downhill to the water. The turbine engines running, Matt applied power slowly and with screeches and sparks, they began a tortuous skidding ride to the beach where it finally picked up speed— shedding the men on the wing tips. The Goose has pontoons that extend below each wing tip to provide stability in the water and bouncing from one pontoon to the other, the Goose made an enormous splash as it plowed into the water and finally floated. Matt was afraid that he might have punctured the hull with all of the scraping and immediately applied full takeoff power and ignoring the fact that he had a fifteen mile an hour tailwind, picked up speed and raised it onto the step of the hull, which is the forward running surface. This reduced the drag and allowed it to assume a flat "step" attitude and after crashing its way through a few more waves, Matt horsed the Goose into the air. With the airplane flying properly, Matt turned to his two comrades:

"So Kiren, I hope you enjoyed your beach vacation. I thought I selected a rather nice place. Sure beats the Bahamas– that place is dull city."

Kiren was sitting on the ledge between the pilot and copilot's seats and reached out and held Matt's hand.

"I've never seen a person killed before. It was so simple. Just bang and he fell down. You saw him — he was dead?"

"Went right up his nose. The Eskimo are the finest shots in the world. A seal will poke its head out of its breathing hole for just a few seconds. The hunter may be unable to get closer than a couple of hundred yards. Unless you hit the seal in the head just right, its lungs will collapse and it will sink– and no food and one less seal. But what Irigoo did was beyond me to imagine."

Vitz broke in: "Give me another 'trust me' and I'll shove a canoe paddle up your nose. The plan, now that these guys are smelling our asses, what's the plan?"

"Trust me– trust me –trust me, no one ever trusts me. You are beginning to sound just like Kiren. You seemed rather somber back there, did a bit of blood bother you?"

"Fuck no, I was just depressed that I didn't shoot first, haven't scored on a goon in a couple of years."

"Right, with that .243. At that distance you would have been lucky to have not missed the sky."

"That's why I didn't shoot. Wish they had been closer, my grenades would have cooked their butts. Shit! That guy was something else. Your joke about a running vasectomy wasn't a joke."

"I never said it was a joke." Matt replied. "Oh the plan. Simple, just keep these people who ever they are, chasing us for a couple more days and then while they are looking elsewhere we slip back to Talkeetna, extract the virus, burn the evidence and be done with this business. Or at least Kiren and I are done, you will just be on your way."

"That doesn't sound like a very detailed plan to me." Kiren complained. "Give us some details."

"OK, We are heading out across Bristol Bay for Brooks Camp on the Alaska Peninsula. We'll get there in about three hours and spend the night. The reason for going there is that this Goose belongs to the Feds and it spends a good bit of time at Brooks. Its appearance won't turn any heads. In the morning we go on to Homer which is another hour's hop. That will give us a day to spread a bit of scent around and then Kiren and I will drive back to Talkeetna while we leave Vitz in Homer to keep these guys running in circles. How's that for a hundred dollar plan."

Kiren broke in: "Why Vitz?"

"I'm trained to do this, unlike Mr. Trust Me here. Maybe I'll even have a chance to crack a few necks." Vitz replied.

Matt shook his head. "Now, friends, we've got an hour plus out over Bristol Bay before we hit the coast. I need to radio Roland and I'd suggest you two get a nap. Been a long day and it may be late before we find some beds."

The call to Roland in Anchorage took a good bit of time. Matt wanted him to do all he could to find out where the King Air was, and if it requested entry back into US airspace, Roland was to instruct the customs people to ask it to land in Nome and they were to hold it as long as possible for a routine search. The weather over Bristol Bay was clear but there was little to see. Had he turned southwest from St. Lawrence Island, he could have flown nearly 1000 miles over the Bering sea before crossing over Attu island, one of the outer islands of the Aleutian chain. These distances continued to amaze Matt. If the map of Alaska is placed over the map of the continental 48 states, then Attu Island in the Aleutians is at Bakersville California, St. Lawrence Island is in eastern Nebraska, Homer is at the southeast corner of Kansas, Talkeetna is near St. Louis and the southeastern islands of Alaska fall of the eastern coast at the Georgia/South Carolina border.

It was late in the afternoon when they intersected the coast near Hooper Bay. Inland lay the great Yukon Delta Wildlife Refuge. This is an area of tens of thousands of square miles of land that is so boggy and laced with ponds and small lakes that it is not clear if there is more water or land. Through this delta the Yukon River spreads wider and wider, finally meeting Bristol Bay. Another large river, the Kuskokwim, parallels the Yukon to the south making the land between the two rivers low and wet. The delta provides nesting grounds for tens of millions of ducks, geese and other water fowl. Matt considered this area to be the core– of the "great mosquito desert" To be cast out there without professional level bug gear, was to be drained of every blood cell in your body in less than a minute.

As they began crossing this area Vitz and then Kiren came forward and watched out of one side and the then the other. Matt held 6000 feet which gave them good view of this land below which harbored no more people per square mile than the deserts of the American southwest. Crossing the Kuskokwim, they climbed to 8000 feet to clear a row of 4500 foot mountains– the Kilbuck Mountains. Matt doubted that one person in one hundred in Alaska had heard of these mountains and probably only one in a million in The States. The next row of mountains however were well known to Alaskans and many southerners who had traveled to Alaska for fishing. The Wood River Mountains are low but rugged and create a series of lakes: the Wood River-Tikchik Lakes. This is a chain of a half dozen large lakes, each pointing east to west and stacked one north of the other in a zig zag fashion and joined one to the next by a short river or waterway. The combination of fabulous trout and salmon fishing in these rivers and the ability to travel from one lake to the next by boat has made this area for fishermen what Graceland is to Elvis fans. The area is also high enough that the bugs are less of a problem. He turned to fly over Dillingham, a working fishing town serving as a gateway to the Wood River area. At Dillingham they were still 100 miles from Brooks camp in the Katmai National Park.

A quick stop was made at King Salmon to refuel. King Salmon had both a sea plane base and a hard surfaced runway so that if there had been any damage to the hull of the Goose during their exit over the beach, they could have left the Goose and flown out on a commercial flight. Landing in the water because of the flat tires, no damage was found and in twenty minutes they were on their way to Brooks Camp twenty five miles away.

As they approached Brooks camp and The Katmai National Park, the scenery changed back to that typical of the Mt. McKinley area. In the distance were several large lakes, the largest, Naknek, was 20 miles long. Beyond Naknek Lake, high mountain peaks could be seen jutting 6000 feet into the air. These peaks had a snap to them being clad with snow and sharply pointed. They said to all "we are volcanoes and when you are around us, take care". Brooks Camp is situated on a narrow finger of land that separates Brooks Lake from the larger Naknek Lake. Katmai National Park is one of the least visited national parks. The only way for the tourist to get there is to fly into King Salmon and then take a float plane or amphibian to Brooks Camp. The camp is constructed of several rows of sturdy log cabins that will sleep a family, a large communal building that provides meals and a number of outlying buildings that host lectures by park service personnel. The most that can be accommodated is a hundred at a time.

Brooks Camp serves as gateway for three enterprises. One is fishing in the river along which the camp is built. In the summer runs of several different species of salmon trailed by voracious trout flood the river with more fish than any fisherman from the continental states could dream of seeing in a day.

The fish are the reason for the second enterprise which is watching giant Kodiak brown bears gorge themselves on salmon. These bear are the Alaskan coastal variety of the inland grizzly. Same bear, just a lot bigger, pushing a thousand pounds. They migrate to the streams in mid to late summer to fill themselves with salmon. These are not zoo animals and a number of humans in the Brooks area have been badly hurt or killed over the years from encounters. However the park service people know their bears and do a splendid job of keeping the bears and tourists happy and separated. At night however the land belongs to the bears who frequently tromp through camp. During the day, visitors are led down a mile long trail through the woods to a viewing station overlooking Brooks falls, a 50 foot high waterfall with a pool at its base. Some days the pool is shoulder to shoulder Kodiak bears engaged in fishing. Many of the famous photos of bears catching salmon are taken at Brooks falls.

Brooks Camp also provides the only reasonable means of visiting the Valley of Ten Thousand Smokes, the third thrill of this land. This is one of the great wonders of American scenery. Matt would shortly describe its origin to Vitz and Kiren.

The Goose skimmed low along the shore, settled onto the water and taxied to the shore where it took its place nosed up on the bank along side a half dozen float planes. Matt had radioed ahead and arranged lodging in one of the cabins. After they had carried their gear to the cabin and argued over who slept in which bunk, it was after 6 o'clock. They adjourned to the main log building for dinner. Kiren was tired and somber and picked at her trout filet until Vitz finished his and began taking bits of hers which caused her to take her plate and sit by the fireplace to finish her dinner. Vitz commented to Matt:

"Stuck in my guts for a while myself. Bet this is the first time she saw someone drop dead. But that asshole got his due. She'll be OK. You two have the top bunks, I won't watch."

"Oh, fuck, Vitz, you define disgusting at times. I'm going over to console her, and not how you are suggesting."

Matt sat beside Kiren and after a few moments, not saying anything, held her hand and rubbed it gently for a long time before she spoke.

"I just have to tell myself that man who was killed back there was part of the cocaine machine responsible for Ralph's death. It was so easy to want to see people like that pay for his death but now that it is starting to happen it scares me."

Matt put an arm around Kiren and held her tightly until they had to rescue Vitz from a female tourist twenty years his senior who was telling him in detail about her grandchildren in Fargo, North Dakota. After bedtime chores had been taken care of, Matt carefully barred the door from within with the large bolt that was provided for the purpose and commented that one must take a flashlight when venturing out into the night. He had been careful not to mention bears to Vitz.

Just before the sun rose Vitz woke and walked to the Goose to retrieve a book he had left inside. All was well, and he returned and finished several chapters before the others arose. It was 8 AM by this time, and after washing their faces and dressing, Matt explained the "plan of the day".

"OK troops, here is where we are on the "world's greatest Goose chase" as I call it. We need to get out of here pronto. I treated us all to a good night's sleep since we are safe here and we got a head start on the King Air crowd. My guess is that they flew the chopper back to Providenija in Siberia since that is the closest place they could have left their plane. I imagine that the chopper had a lot of new holes in it and they may have had some trouble getting out of there. I also asked Roland to have the King Air detailed at customs if it appears back in US airspace. Nonetheless, we need to go on the assumption that they will be able to get to Homer by the end of the day today. We need to be there ahead of them. As I told you yesterday, we will let Vitz play the role of a local and point them toward the boondocks during which time Kiren and I will drive back to Talkeetna. So dudes, lets grab a quick breakfast and be gone."

The three were just finishing pancakes and coffee when one of the park rangers burst in and ran to Matt. "Do you want the bad new or the awful news first?"

"Oh shit, the Goose sunk?"

"No, it's where you pulled it up on the beach, but someone left the main cabin door open. That's the good news."

Matt knew that he had carefully turned the door handle and cross-checked it. He looked at Vitz who hearing this, looked straight down into his plate picking at the leftover blueberries. Matt turned back to the ranger.

"Water got sprayed inside?"

"No, maybe you guys should come see for yourselves and decide what to do." The ranger smirked. He was relishing what would come.

The four hundred feet were quickly covered. Holding his finger over his mouth to indicate silence, he motioned them to approach the side of the Goose and peer in one of the windows. Vitz strode over in a "take command" mode since he had left the door open and poked his face against the glass.

"God damn it! A god damn bear!" Vitz spun and ran at full speed back to the main cabin. Matt noted that the ranger was carrying his bolt action .458 Winchester–a large bore hunting rifle, and pulled Kiren by the hand to look into the window.

Lying happily on his back in the aisle with his feet resting on the seats, an extremely large Kodiak male was asleep having taken up residence in the main cabin of the Goose. After watching for a few minutes Matt, Kiren, and the ranger retreated a safe distance and Matt shook his head.

"Right. This, dudes, and trust me on this one – is not good news! Is this fur rug friendly or hostile?"

"Well, if he is the one I think he is, he has been hanging around for the last week. One night he slept against the door of the main building and we didn't have breakfast until almost noon. My guess is that he filled up with salmon yesterday afternoon and should wake up by mid day. If we keep our distance, he should eventually leave. I'd tie that door open to give him a clear path out."

"Fine but we don't have all day. We are on a get-our-asses-out-of-here schedule and could be in deep shit if we don't."

Vitz had reappeared and they formed a circle. Kiren was full of ideas.

"Can't you just bang on the airplane and scare him out?"

"Yes miss, but there's a 50/50 chance he would exit through the side of the Goose and then come looking for us. When I was a kid one of these monsters woke up from hibernation mid-winter and while peering into a cabin covered to the second floor in snow, the bear fell in through the window. Tore the cabin to the ground trying to get out."

"Well, you rangers must have tranquilizer guns. Shoot him and Vitz can drag him out."

"Yes miss, we have tranquilizer guns. Guys in The States frequently use Sernylan– that's fast but dangerous to the bear. Sernylan is "Angel Dust" or PCP, and the bears wake up with a lot of weird behavior. I like to use, ah – – about 80 cc of Ketamine, and I toss in 2 cc of Rompin and maybe 4 cc of Valium to soften the side effects. Works great but takes about 17 minutes for a bear of his size to go down. Seventeen minutes is a long time to deal with a pissed off bear."

"Maybe Vitz could wave a dead fish through the open door and lure it out."

Vitz muttered something akin to "like fuck" but the amused ranger replied:

"Miss, that bear may have eaten fifty pounds of fish yesterday. One more fish isn't going to do much."

By this time there was a large contingent of onlookers and the ranger was having a full time job keeping them away. Several of the float plane pilots appeared and one by one pushed their craft from the beach and paddled some distance before starting their engines. None wanted to have the bear exit the Goose and tear into them. Matt was getting very anxious to leave and they had already lost an hour. After waiting another hour, he slowly opened the doors on the nose of the Goose and slipped into the baggage compartment from which he was able to crawl head first part way into the cockpit. He turned on the radios and called Roland.

"Roland – you up yet? We have hit a bit of a snag. Over"

"Matt, yes! A chocoholic rhapsody! I had breakfast here at the Captain Cook and am enjoying a wonderful chocolate desert left over from last night. A snag, let me guess. I'll bet that your Goose airplane is serving as a hotel for a giant brown bear. How's that for clairvoyance?"

"How the what ever did you find out— over?"

"I am omnivorous. I was monitoring general aviation frequencies and heard the whole thing on the radio. Some pilot saw it and it's the talk of the airwaves."

Matt realized that if the King Air was airborne, they would now have a fix on his location.

"Roland this is not good. Have your heard anything from the King Air? over—"

"Not a peep. Either they are still out of US airspace, or have slipped back in on the quiet. Since they never officially checked out, they may not feel anxious to check back in –over"

"I'd better find some other way out. We really need to get to Homer."

Before Matt could say "over", he heard a grunt and found himself looking at the bear who had roused and come forward to investigate. Matt carefully laid the microphone down and was about to pull himself out when he saw The Bad Easter Rabbit on the dash of the Goose. He reached up, grabbed it and slid out backwards into the nose compartment and then bailed out over the side into the water.

Matt was greeted with claps from the onlookers. He walked to Vitz, stuffed The Bad Easter Rabbit into Vitz' hands and turned to the crowd:

"Its his. He can't go to sleep without it." Approaching the ranger he said:

"We really need to get on our way. Can't tell you the details. I saw Burt Kasiloff's Heliocourier over at King Salmon yesterday. I'd like to use your phone to see if I can get him to help us."

A few minutes later Matt reappeared and told Vitz and Kiren to collect their gear which fortunately they had taken to the cabin from the Goose after they landed. He showed the ranger a federal agent's badge Roland had supplied for such occasion and explained.

"I know we normally would need a back country pass for camping in the valley, but I am going to ask you to overlook that and have one of your helpers drop us off at the end of the road at the overlook to the valley. I'll tell them we will be out there for a week. How we get out of there is our business. Don't worry about us."

The ranger nodded and then spun around looking at the sky as a King Air made a low pass over the camp and then pulled up sharply and headed back toward King Salmon.

Vitz wanted to stay and fight.

Matt countered. "Look, I'm not against taking these people on, but don't you think that shooting jets out of the sky with rockets in front of a hundred tourists is going to get the press interested? A good fight, fine, but where we choose and sure as hell not in the middle of a National Park."

Matt grabbed one of the summer students explaining that she was to drive them to the overlook in one of the camp Suburbans. Driving off, it was clear that the girl was not used to washboard roads. Washboards are dirt roads with deep crosswise wave-like ruts generated by the traffic and lack of grading. The ruts resemble moguls on a ski slope and are navigated at either slow speed– at which the vehicle goes up one side of a bump and then down the other, or at a velocity at which the vehicle skims along, bouncing from the top of one to the top of the next. Matt took over and found that for this road, 55 mph provided the appropriate speed and all held on. Kiren did her best to engage the girl in discussion. The drive would have been spectacular under any other condition. The road winds 15 miles up along Margot creek which is an optically clear stream with many waterfalls. As the drive continues, the elevation increases so that the view to the back includes both Brooks and Naknek Lakes. To either side were rough 4000 foot mountains and in the distance they could begin to see a series of white topped volcanoes.

Reaching a wind swept overlook and a small cabin, they thanked the girl and urged her to tell anyone who asked that she had dropped them off at the overlook and that they would be back in several days. Once she departed, Matt stood at the edge of the overlook and provided an explanation of the wondrous moonscape below them.

"Dudes, you are looking out over one of the most violent wonders of recorded history. Below is a valley 25 miles long and several miles wide that hardly has a speck of life in it. The only feature down there other than a several hundred foot layer of yellow sand-like volcanic ash is that deep gorge in the middle cut by the river that begins with the glaciers on Mt. Katmai behind. Now, look up at the head end of the valley. See that mile high mass of rock and snow?" Matt pointed to Mt. Katmai.

"Looks like it hasn't changed in a thousand years doesn't it?" Kiren and Vitz smiled and nodded.

"Wrong-wrong-wrong, dudes. Only a split second ago– geologically speaking — that wall of rock generated one of the four largest volcanic eruptions in the last 5000 years. In fact I find it rather interesting that if one measures volcanic eruptions by the volume of solid material ejected, then the biggest in the last 5000 years was in Eastern Oregon. It ejected 9 cubic miles and desolated what is the entire eastern half of present day Oregon. After that eruption, things were quiet for four thousand eight hundred years other than tiny puffs in the sky like Vesuvius. Then in 1815, Tambora in Indonesia blew. It ejected 8 cubic miles of rock. Then in 1883, Krakatau, also in Indonesia, blew out another 5 cubic miles. Then a mere 29 years later the mountain in front of you let loose 3 cubic miles of rock into the air. To give you an idea, friends, Mt. St. Helens in Oregon ejected zero point one– or one thirtieth as much as Katmai. The eruption covered the town of Kodiak one hundred miles away with over 12 feet of ash. There was so much matter ejected into the atmosphere that it changed the world's temperature by several degrees."

Kiren and Vitz pulled back from the edge of the overlook as if to distance themselves from Katmai. Matt continued:

"The ash and debris totally changed this valley. For tens of years after the eruption, hot steam forced its way up through the several hundred foot thick layer of ash and formed thousands of steam vents. Hence the name "Valley of Ten Thousand Smokes."

"I don't see any now." Kiren commented, scanning the valley with her binoculars.

"No, they finally died out. But stand here and think about two things First, the unbelievable energy of what happened, one of four volcanic eruptions in the last 5000 years that stands out way ahead of all others. Got that?"

Vitz and Kiren were standing transfixed.

"Right. So. Point two! Think of it. Four biggies over 5000 years. Now the first was 5000 years ago and the last three have occurred over the last 180 years. Two of them came close together in Indonesia. The last was right here. Know what this tells me?"

"Ah, noooo." Vitz shook his head.

"Simple. It means that we just entered a period of geologic madness. Three this close together after 5000 years is not random. Further if two were close together in Indonesia, my guess is that there will be another really big one and it will be within sight of where we are standing right now. Could be a hundred times Mt. St. Helens. Might cover half the state. What do you think about that?"

Matt watched Kiren and Vitz through the corner of his eye knowing that there were many holes in his "theory of volcanic eruptions" but also noted that Kiren and Vitz were noticeably uneasy.

Kiren turned to watch a pair of marmots playing in the sun a hundred yards away. Suddenly the two dove for their burrows and the Parka squirrels, an Alaskan ground squirrel with a high pitched squeak, also became still. A few seconds later, an unusual looking single engine airplane buzzed 50 feet above their heads. As the pilot turned to take a look at them, Matt waved and the pilot wagged the wings in response, turned away for a minute, and then flew directly back at them along the dirt road. Matt pushed Kiren and Vitz off the road as this odd craft with giant wings and tail flew slower and slower, finally settling down on the road and came to a stop in less than a couple of hundred feet.

Matt started carrying their gear to the cargo door and was greeted by the pilot.

"Damn, Bub, every time I see you it's some emergency."

"Burt, you are for me and I am for you, that's the way it is. But I sure owe you on this one, some very ugly guys are real close to our asses and we got ambushed back at Brooks by one of the blonde guy 's pet bears."

Vitz muttered something and helped Kiren into a rear seat. As soon as Burt and Matt were in, Kiren pulled herself over so that she could talk to the pilot:

"Is this the STOL airplane that was designed at MIT?"

"Roger, mam, a Heliocourier. Three hundred horse engine and the biggest, fattest wings they could design. Big gangly tail too. I can horse it off in a couple of hundred feet if I need to, and can fly at fifty miles an hour all day."

Burt turned the Heliocourier around on the dirt road so that they had about six hundred feet before the road turned sharply to the right. If the Helio was not airborne by that point, it would pitch nose over and tumble nearly a thousand feet to the valley floor below. Kiren's eyes were wide as Burt held the brakes, ran the engine to full rpm, released the brakes and sat back.

As the Helio lifted off with three hundred feet left, Burt turned around to Kiren and yelled:

"In the Air Force, I once started from a dead stop inside a hangar and was flying as I went out the door."

Matt poked Burt and made a motion with his hand indicating that Burt was to fly down into the Valley of Ten Thousand Smokes and then up over Mt. Katmai. The flight was one that caused Kiren to squeeze Vitz' hand to a point that his fingers finally went numb and he had to change hands. With the story of the Katmai eruption, and the steaming valley still fresh in their minds, the flight was nearly surrealistic as the Helio flew only a hundred feet above the valley floor devoid of any color besides the yellow volcanic ash. The only break was where the river cut its deep canyon into the ash. At the base of Katmai, Burt circled the Helio around and around as they gained altitude, climbing up and up. At the head end of the valley, Katmai rose a mile straight up and at an angle that averaged forty five degrees. The effect of this wall of rock and ice and the knowledge of what the mountain had done just a few geologic seconds before was frightening. Clearing the edge of the 6700 foot peak by the least possible amount, Burt cut the power and allowed the Helio to drop down into the crater which was two miles wide and filled with crystal blue water. Even Matt grabbed the door handle as Burt smirked and then ran the engine up and circled the crater lake before climbing back up and clearing the far edge.

They were a hundred and fifty miles from Homer and Burt's path took them along the eastern shore of the Alaska Peninsula past volcano after volcano. Each was majestic on its own, but there were so many that Kiren quickly quit asking Burt for their names and sat back gazing at the peaks to their left, and below them, coastal bays painted green making cupped hands that held the blue ocean. Eventually at Augustine Island, another volcano that lies in the mouth of Cook Inlet, Burt turned west out over the open water to make the crossing to the south tip of the Kenai peninsula and Homer. They landed at the Homer airport and after Matt and Burt had exchanged a few stories of old comrades from their days of growing up together in Talkeetna, Burt left and Matt turned to Vitz:

"Well, big blond bud, this is where we split up for a few days. Kiren and I are going to rent a car and drive part way to Talkeetna tonight. Before we leave, we'll go over to the office on the lake and introduce you to the people who will keep an eye on the Goose after it is flown over later today. When the King Air crowd comes looking for the Goose, you can tell them that you have done some work for us and give them directions that will keep them running in circles for a few days. Improvise. Then pick up a car and sneak back to Talkeetna. Craig will fly you over."

Vitz nodded and they piled into a rental car. Vitz and his gear including his "war boxes" as he was now calling them, were dropped off at a nearby motel. Matt phoned Roland from the room.

"Roland, those jerks in the King Air nearly landed on top of us at Brooks and I had to call in a favor from an old high school bud in King Salmon to sneak us out. Hopefully they will waste a couple of days chasing around out there before going on to Homer, and if Vitz can keep them confused for another couple of days we will be home free. Kiren and I are heading north and will call from Talkeetna. See any reason to get together face to face in Anchorage?"

"No, deceptively speaking, you are still transparent and seeing me might break the cloud cover. Call from Talkeetna. Is Kiren holding up?"

"Scared to death but anxious to get the virus purified and go on with a nice month's vacation in Fiji with me to let things cool down– at your expense of course."

"Only if you name your first child after me." Matt laughed, and hung up.

Vitz walked to the car with them and as Matt was starting to get in, Kiren grabbed Vitz and have him a very long, very wet kiss then turned back toward Matt with a smirk on her face.

As they headed out of Homer, Matt asked: "I assume that was necessary?"

"Soldiers going to war are due one last kiss. Besides he saved my life after you put me in mortal danger. It was the least I could do."

Matt realized that he had been hit with a twinge of jealousy and a mile later, to make a fresh start on the drive, stopped at the top of the bluff overlooking Homer and Kachemak Bay.

"Kiren, god, I wish we had the time to poke around here for a few days. Maybe we can come back sometime. Look at the view. Out in the distance you can see the great chain of volcanoes stretching almost to Japan. Down there is Kachemak Bay, one of the most beautiful places in Alaska. Here on this side, the land is soft, green, and there are farms. Across the bay– wow some of the most lovely, rugged coast in the state with glaciers, bays-within-bays and giant fur trees growing right to the water's edge. The town is a bee hive in the summer with the tourists, but in the winter it reverts to a quiet fishing town. Great weather for Alaska, the ocean keeps things a lot warmer than inland. I think of it as being what Carmel by the Sea in California looked like in the 1920's. That narrow finger of land stretching five miles out from Homer into the bay is called "The Spit" and at the far end are the docks where all the boats tie up. I wish we could take a day and go to the other side of the bay. There is a nearly enclosed bay called Halibut Cove where some of the best artists in Alaska live. Great place with great people. It was developed by an old Alaskan family who boated the restaurant over on a barge and have made the place what it is. They even bring horses across in the summer. Some time ago a harbor seal who was the town pet passed away and everyone came out for a wake in which the seal was placed on a small boat they constructed along with a burning torch and sent out to sea. Damn, I really would love to have you see the place and meet all of them."

Kiren gave him a quick kiss. "Sometime. But unless we get this project finished we may not see next week. I know you love this place. But right now I am saturated with unbelievable scenery. Every sight I have seen the last few days has been better than anything I have ever seen before. It must have been hard for you to leave this state."

He nodded, shook his head, and began their drive north. They drove to the Alyeska ski resort just south of Anchorage. At the front desk of the hotel he handed them his credit card and asked for a single room with a king size bed, watching out of the corner of his eye to monitor Kiren's response. None was made and with a warm smile to himself, they adjourned. In the elevator going down for dinner she commented:

"Well, you just assumed that I would go along with the one-room-one bed routine now didn't you, Mr. Trust me Lynx-cat person."

"Just going by the federal regulations for keeping beautiful princesses out of trouble in times of danger."

"Yah, right." Kiren reached over and gave him a warm kiss.

That night they made love again. This time Matt took command, and after it was over he felt that it was different than before. While he was covered with fewer drops of testosterone this time, it felt deeper with more communication and warmth. "More love and less lust" he thought to himself. "Don't want to swing too far this way" he mused as he gave her one last kiss before they settled into their respective pillows.

The next morning after sourdough pancakes at the Bake Shop, they drove to Talkeetna, and slipping in quietly, pulled the Moose Gooser out, left Craig a note, and flew to the mine.

The week had begun poorly for Raul and was beginning to shape up as the worst of his recent life. When they arrived at Talkeetna and found that Kiren and whoever she was with were on some far out North Pacific island and Brian had made the connection with Russian H bomb tests, he had been elated, feeling that this whole affair might be for naught and that they would be able to go home and call off the whole stupid trek. Landing at Gambell and finding that Kiren was in a camp along the shore that could only be reached on foot, Roy suggested that they arrange a helicopter in Providenija since he had been there a year earlier and used one to run some cocaine to the oil crews on the North slope. Raul opted for crossing below radar and spreading some cash after they landed to pay for their failure to request permission. The chopper was a large military one and it came with a former Russian Air Force pilot who spoke some English.

After searching along the north shore of St. Lawrence Island for a while they located the camp and Raul pushed Brian and Henry to go in first in a friendly way to take a look. At this point Raul had relaxed assuming that they would return with stories of mutant flowers resulting from dirty Russian H bombs. He exploded when Brian handed him Kiren's notebook with the details of virus growth, coca plants, and all the rest.

They ransacked the camp but found nothing and Brian convinced Raul that the camp was at most a few days old and due to the lack of any "scientific garbage" no real science had been going on. Raul ordered everyone back to the chopper. Inside his rage grew.

"Fuck it!" He yelled as he banged his pistol against the side of the chopper. "They must be around, their coffee was still hot! Get this thing in the air. I want them spotted and if we can get them alive –fine, they will be forced to give us the virus. If not, fuck them, and we will find it anyway."

The fight that followed their discovery of Kiren and Matt would have had its intended result if Vitz and his grenades followed by the Eskimo flotilla had not arrived. They finally retreated to the top of the hill overlooking Gambell, and watched the incoming umiaks. Raul was ranting.

"Jesus H Christ! Here we are in a modern war machine and we can't fight a bunch of yo-yo's with B-B guns. This is a fucking joke!"

"So what do we do?" Estaban had asked, looking at his 9 mm short range automatic Mac 10 and not wanting to take on the dozen men armed with hunting rifles, let alone whoever it was with the rocket grenades.

"Shit if I know! We wait and watch. If it gets late we go back to Russia. I sure as hell am not going to spend the night here with all of them out there." Raul was realizing that they were badly out gunned at this range. At this moment Roy had spotted the girl picking berries and yelled.

"A hostage! I'll grab her! We use her as a trade!"

Raul pushed him out of the helicopter and watched as Roy grabbed the girl and holding his pistol, stood facing the Eskimos, as if to exhibit his captive, expecting that in a few minutes someone would walk to him –hands in the air —asking for a trade. Raul was moving his binoculars from the Eskimos to Roy and the girl, and had just moved back to Roy when he saw Roy's head snap backwards. At the same moment bullets began hitting the chopper and he dove to the floor yelling to the pilot to pull out fast.

Brian yelled to Raul. "We can't just le le le leave Roy there, he must be hurt! What will they do do do do with him?"

"He's just taking a fucking nap. You stupid academic shit head, he just got a bullet in his face! One more minute and we could have lost an engine— and our asses."

The flight back to Siberia was short, but it took a large amount of cash to pay for the damage to the helicopter. They refueled the King Air and spent the night so they could fly back to the US low and in daylight. The next morning all looked strained from the previous day, and Brian chatted with Henry about quitting right there. Henry recommended not:

"Raul is madder than I have ever seen him. If we can get him what he wants, you can retire from science. I'm afraid that if we run out now he might track us down and we would find ourselves retiring early. Just ride it out for another day or two. All we need is that virus sample."

Raul arranged for some coffee and sandwiches, then held a conference.

"So what the hell do we know? Besides the fact that Roy's plan had a fatal flaw. Stupid shit head. That was a real bright idea. Grab a girl in front of fifty of her relatives armed with hunting rifles. Got what he fucking deserved."

"Well, I think we found out wh wh wh where they really are." Commented Brian.

"And where is that?"

"Some town called Homer. It was written all o o o over the stuff ba ba ba back there, all the boxes had shipping labels marked 'Homer, Alaska' This morning I found it on the ma ma ma map– – south of Anchorage and looks like a lot be be be better place to grow plants than up here. I'll be be be bet it has a livable climate."

"I think he's right, Raul. I don't know what they were doing out there but there must be some place where they are growing their plants and doing some science, Homer sounds like the place." Henry reinforced Brian.

"So, off to Homer. Find that Goose, then find them. Can't be that hard." Raul began plotting the trip to Homer.

They had been in the air over an hour and were just crossing over the Yukon River. Raul was playing with the radio, monitoring this channel and that when on a frequency of 122.8 MHz, he happened to overhear a pilot explaining with great glee of a bright yellow turbo-goose that was sitting on the shore at Brooks Camp with a giant brown bear asleep inside. Raul was elated.

"Hey back there. We just got a god given break. No shit! I just heard that the Goose is at some place called Brooks Camp and they can't fly it because it has a bear sleeping in it!"

Raul dialed Brooks Camp in on the GPS and was given a magnetic heading of 290 nautical miles at 157 degrees; "love them computers", he thought. Approaching Brooks, he realized that they would have to land at King Salmon but opted for a low fly-over to be sure the Goose was still there–which it was. They returned to King Salmon and found the least respectable pilot they could, who had a beat to hell De Havilland Beaver on floats. Raul's three guards remained with the King Air. They were able to just stuff everyone else in the Beaver for the short trip.

As they arrived Raul admonished his group.

"Now look shit heads, this is a national park and these rangers are empowered as police. So no show of force unless we need it. We are just here to walk around a bit and say hello to our friends in the Goose. Got that?"

The bear was still in bruin slumber land and Raul was able to chat up one of the rangers watching the Goose and keeping the visitors at a safe distance.

"The guys who came in on the Goose, any idea of where they are? One of them is an old friend."

"Yah, they gave up and went camping. Said they would be back in a couple of days. We've got an extra cabin that opened up, a last minute cancellation, stick around if you like."

"Thanks, but any idea where they are camping?"

"Somewhere past the end of the road up the valley. Ask that summer student over there in the hat, she drove them out."

Raul paid the girl well to take them to the overlook where she left them for the rest of the day with a promise to pick them up at dinner time.

Raul and the others walked around taking in the scenery and peering in all directions. Finally they all sprawled out in the sun which had warmed the temperature to the mid 70's. Early afternoon a bus pulled in with a load of tourists who walked down to the river gorge and then returned. Raul and his group returned to Brooks camp, spent the night and paid the girl again to take them back out the next morning. The rangers and girl had emphasized that there was only one way into this area and one way out and that was via the end of the road and the overlook. So, simple, Raul assumed, wait here and they will walk right back to us. He had posted Estaban, Coyote and the others at different overlooks so that Kiren and the two men would be seen first. It was just after lunch when Raul began getting anxious and paced back and forth along the dirt road at the overlook. Standing looking at his feet he suddenly yelled to Coyote.

"Coyote get the fuck down here!" Coyote arrived out of breath and asked:

"Where are they? Did you spot them?"

"Shit no, but stand right where I am and tell me what you see."

"The valley, a mountain–"

"No shit head, look at the road, look at those tracks– are they car tracks?"

"Oh no, tundra tires, and big ones!"

Coyote was down on his hands and knees inspecting the tire tread and then carefully measured the distance between the two parallel tracks.

"Way too big for a Super Cub. Tail dragger, see the tail wheel marks, width too wide for a cub or Cessna 180 or 185. Had to have been something substantial– beaver sized I would guess."

It was not hard to follow the tracks to where they turned abruptly around and then pointed back the way they had come, suddenly becoming a series of hops and skips and then disappearing. Coyote concluded:

"Fresh, recall it rained here a few days ago. Either yesterday morning or at most the day before. About the time our guys were here. What ever the bird was, she was big."

Raul was furious and began a forced march of his group back down the road. As it was, they were still miles from camp when they were picked up. Raul called back to King Salmon but the earliest he was able to arrange for a pick up was the next morning.

As they were about to depart in the Beaver the next morning, a US Forrest Service Officer walked over to the Goose which had finally been vacated by the bear and settled into the pilot's seat. Raul ran over and asked.

"I say, hello, ah, the guys that flew this in here, any idea where they are?"

"No idea, all I was told was to come over and ferry it back to Homer."

"Is that where it is based?"

"Well, it's been here and there, but most of the summer – been in Homer, yeh."

"Can you tell me where?"

"On the lake at the base of The Spit, can't miss it."

They landed the King Air at Homer and hired a station wagon. He drove to the lake and told the rest to stay inside while he did some checking. The Goose was there and Raul walked over to the building nearby, and walked in. The woman at the desk pointed to a tall blonde man reading a magazine in the other room.

As Raul began his questioning, the man stood up and Raul sensed that this man was not quite what he seemed to be and felt that he was being sized up at the same time. He wondered if this man might have been one of the two with Kiren. Fortunately at Gambell Vitz had been too far away and too bundled up for Raul to have gotten a clear look at him.

"I was told that you, ah, can tell me about where I could find some friends of mine, a woman and a couple of men, ah, they have been using that Goose. The woman is about 35 and has very short red hair."

"I might, why?"

"Friends, that's all, here on vacation. Hear she was working on some project around here."

"Been here all summer."

Vitz led Raul to a map of Kachemak bay that covered one wall of the office and jabbed his finger on a spot on the other side of the bay.

"Grewingk Glacier. That's where I take stuff for' em. Gotta tent camp on the lake by the glacier and are doing some experimental farming or something."

Raul smiled, feeling that finally he had closed in on Kiren and the others. He asked:

"So, my friend, how does one get there? I don't see any roads."

"Nope, no roads on that side of the bay. When the lake is clear of icebergs we can land a floatplane. But there's a good trail from the beach and it's only 3 miles in to the lake and another 2 or 3 around the left to the camp next to the glacier face. Start of the summer we took the big load over in a twin chopper, but now there's not too much stuff so I go over in a boat and carry it in. They pay me and if it's not raining, I like the walk."

Raul nodded and thanked Vitz. He said that it seemed a bit far and they would have to see if they had time or not.

Back at the King Air, Raul held a conference. "They seem to come and go by floatplane or by boat and then walk to the camp. I don't have a float rating and damn it, Roy was the only one of us who did— and look how he fucked things up. Damn him! We can't hire a local and ask him to watch while we go kill someone. So, tomorrow. We get a boat."

"You really need us?" Henry asked unhappily.

"Yep. Remember we need to find the evidence and get this woman to spill the details. You don't have to carry a gun, that's what I brought my three wolves for."

The next morning they examined the map of Kachemak bay in detail. The Grewingk Glacier and lake were 15 miles away, across the bay. While the Homer side of the bay was relatively flat and the area dotted with farms, the far side of Kachemak Bay slopes upwards from the water into a line of high mountains from which glaciers flow back down. None of the glaciers make it all the way to the bay as they did hundreds of years ago. They now stop several miles inland and are in retreat. Grewingk Glacier is one of the larger ones. Its path back from the ocean is marked by a flat area several miles wide and several miles long filled with gravel and brush and ends in a large lake on whose far side the wall of ice meets the lake. The lake drains through a series of criss-cross streams that wandered across the wide flat area. On either side of the flats are low ridges and a trail from the beach goes up the flat area to the edge of the lake. Another trail continues around the left side, and over a small hump to the glacier face. Vitz had set up the tent camp past the hump and near the ice face. The face is several miles wide, and all of it rises from the lake created by ice melt. From there the glacier is a maze of crevasses and jumbled ice slowly becoming more organized as it reaches the top of the mountain 15 miles in the distance. Raul and his group rented a boat in Homer and took it to the beach where the trail began.

Vitz was delighted at making direct contact, but was not certain that there were enough of them to generate any serious conflict. He had gotten a good look at Estaban and Thanh in the car and felt that they at least were reasonable adversaries. As soon as he had spoken with Raul, Vitz loaded his equipment into a Zodiac boat and left for the glacier. The glacier site had been selected after he had paid a local to give him a sight-seeing ride in a float-plane just after he arrived in Homer. Hiking in, he was warmed by opportunities he saw for ambush. He set up two tents and climbed up on the glacier. More sites for mortal combat appeared as he wended his way over ice ridges, valleys, and past very deep crevasses. From up here he had a perfect view of the tents, lake, and ridges beyond.

The next morning at 5 AM as the sun rose and warmed the area, Vitz collected his battle gear, ammunition, and some supplies and carried them up the glacier to a place that gave him a perfect vantage. It was equi-distant from the edges of the glacier and almost a mile from the tents. His 'spot' was in the center of a maze of deep crevasses such that there were few direct routes in or out.

After several hours of hiking, Raul stopped his group at the top of the hump as they looked ahead and spotted the tents. It was decided that they would wait there with a hand held radio while his three wolves with their weapons would sneak close to the tents, and if there were people inside or close by, rush them, killing all but Kiren.

As the three approached the tents, Vitz waited until they were within fifty feet of the "camp" tents and stood up in full view of them and fired several bullets from his M203A. At that range there was little chance of a clean hit, but the bullets struck close enough and the volley echoed across the ice, causing them to dive for cover.

Vitz moved from one hiding spot to the next popping up now and then to fire a shot. He had placed several brightly colored shirts here and there so that from this distance even with his binoculars, Raul was unsure at as to how many were on the glacier. Raul decided that somehow word of their approach had gotten there ahead of them and that it was likely that Kiren and the men she was with were hiding on the glacier. Possibly the giant blonde man they had encountered the previous day was their bodyguard and he was the one who was shooting.

Raul radioed his three wolves that they were to go for him first and kill anyone else Kiren was with – but under no conditions harm her as they needed her intact for the moment.

Guiding them by radio, Raul watched their progress to the edge of the glacier and then slipping and sliding, up the glacier as they headed toward Vitz. Even this close to the edge of the glacier several of the crevasses were at least a hundred feet deep and their sides were so sheer and slick that to fall in would be lethal. If the fall itself did not kill you, the ice-blue, ice-cold water at the bottom of the crevasses would in a short time.

Vitz monitored the progress of his adversaries by listening to their grunts and the noise of ice fragments they dislodged. At one point he was fearful that they might have given up and he tossed some rocks in their direction– mostly to see if he got a response. The echo in the form of several bursts of automatic rifle fire cheered Vitz up as he awaited their arrival.

It took nearly an hour for the trio to work their way into position where they would be in range of Vitz given their armament which consisted of short range Mac-10 machine guns and a grenade/

rocket launcher similar to Vitz'. They had fanned out so that one was to Vitz' left and the other two were close together to his right.

Raul watched their movements and fussed to Estaban.

"God damn it! These idiots of mine always dress up like teenage Ninji turtles! Look at them. They are in all black! Great for stalking someone at night in New York City! But fuck it all to hell,– not on a god damned white glacier in bright sunlight!"

The black clad man to Vitz' left made the first move. Vitz could hear him coming and worked back and forth along a flat ice shelf which gave him a good vantage point and the ability to duck down behind the back of the shelf for protection. He checked the M203A and nodded to himself.

Raul could see Vitz now and moved his first pawn forward. Just a bit farther and his man would be able to stand up and face Vitz from a distance of fifty feet. Raul gave the word when he saw Vitz turn to watch in the opposite direction as Raul had given the other two instructions to throw pieces of ice up the glacier as a diversion. The ploy would have worked had Vitz not heard a closer piece of ice tumble down the glacier, dislodged as the first man rose up. Looking face to face at each other over their grenade launchers, they fired at the same second. The grenade aimed at Vitz passed a few feet to his left and arced out over the glacier exploding in the distance. Vitz smiled as he purposely fired low so that his grenade would hit the ice in front of his target. The round hit ahead of where Vitz had aimed but the force of the explosion threw the black clad man in the air and his body fell back within feet of the edge of a very deep crevasse behind him. Vitz watched carefully for signs of life and saw none. He wished that the the man had fallen into the crevasse, but this would do for now. Besides there might be some useful information on the body that could be retrieved before he was pushed into the crevasse.

Raul swore loudly. "Oh Jesus H Christ. Now I'm out Roy and one of my own men and son-of-a-bitch, that idiot had a clean shot!"

The second man was moved into place. Vitz knew roughly where he was, since without the ice climbing crampons that Vitz was wearing, they had to kick the ice with their boots to gain footholds and this frequently gave their position away. There was an ice shelf thirty feet to Vitz' right which overhung a deep water-filled crevasse. It was slightly higher than the flat area where Vitz was hiding. He suspected that the man was working his way to the edge of the shelf where he would be able to peek over and down at Vitz, and would have an excellent vantage point for shooting.

Vitz slipped into a narrow crack in the ice and waited, listening and watching the lip of the overhung ice. Smiling to himself as he saw a piece of ice at the edge dislodged, Vitz fired the M203A so that the grenade impacted under the overhung ice shelf just below the point where he knew the man to be. The explosion had its intended effect of collapsing the overhang. The man screamed as he– together with hundreds of pounds of fractured ice were suspended for what seemed seconds in the air before falling in a disorganized mass onto the sheer side of the crevasse and then into the water below making a thunderous echo. Vitz could hear the man yelling and splashing in the water for several minutes before things were still.

Raul again screamed and held his head in his hands.

"I paid thousands to have these idiots trained for man-to-man combat and look what happens the first time I need them. I should have brought my fucking 60 year old cleaning lady! Shit!"

The third man took advantage of the noise of his compatriot thrashing in the bottom of the crevasse to move into position where he was directly above Vitz on an ice overhang under which Vitz had taken cover. It was now a game of waiting and listening. What Vitz did not see was that the first man whom he assumed was dead had only been rendered unconscious and was slowly awakening and was in clear sight of Vitz as well as his comrade.

Vitz placed his ear against the ice, suspecting that his third adversary was above him. Through the ice he could hear breathing and movement back and forth. Vitz worked his way to a spot just under the man who was now lying flat on the ice. Vitz dislodged a piece of ice which tumbled down giving his position away. The man raised up, pulled the pin from a grenade and reached over the lip of the ice shelf to drop in at Vitz' feet.

Vitz saw the hand and the grenade and reached up, took the grenade with one hand and the man's arm with the other. He tossed the grenade out over the glacier. Vitz pulled with all of his might as his third combatant fell down on top of him.

The man had a knife which he was trying to use on Vitz, who had no weapons immediately at hand. The two rolled over and over on the ice– several times starting to slide as a pair into the crevasse before Vitz dug his crampons in and stopped their progress. After this tumble, Vitz managed to dislodge the knife which fell away and the man broke free, scurrying up under the ice overhang where he turned and pulled a pistol from his belt. Vitz dove on top of him and pushing the pistol away, looked up to see a massive ice sickle that had formed under the ice ledge and was inches to their right. He pushed the man under the point of the ice sickle and slammed the side of it with his forearm. The several hundred pound ice dagger broke free, and plunged down splitting the man's chest. Vitz pushed the ice away, and rolled the body over. Spotting a grenade in the man's shirt pocket, he pulled the pin and pushed the body down into the crevasse. Vitz called:

"Here's some help from your friend." The explosion in the bottom of the crevasse created a thunder which was echoed in the sound of thousands of small ice shards falling back into the water each adding its splash to that of the others. There was an incredible silence.

Raul was watching and just as he was ready to turn his head yet again, he looked to the left side of Vitz and saw his first man raise up slowly, then stand aiming his grenade launcher at Vitz who was beginning to get up, a smile on his face assuming that he had yet again vanquished the opposing army.

The recoil from the launcher caused the man — who was still dazed and unsteady to fall backwards on the ice, gain speed and tumble into the deep water filled crevasse behind him where he yelled and yelled to Raul for help before drowning. Vitz however was unaware of any of this. The grenade had hit near him and threw him into the air. He landed on the back of his head where his body lay on the flat ice shelf.

Raul was beside himself. He had lost all three of his men just to take out one of theirs and they were no closer to finding Kiren and the virus. Brian and Henry were nearly sick and Estaban and Thanh wanted to climb up onto the glacier and push Vitz' body into a crevasse. Raul insisted that they wait for one hour to see if any others who might be hiding would appear and then if not, go to the tents and look for evidence. After an hour they walked to the tents, Estaban first with an automatic rifle. He returned to explain that there was absolutely nothing in the tents and that it was clear this had been a trap.

Raul held another conference.

"I am going to kill the next six people I see. We have been jerked around for the last week and I'm ready to fire bomb a convent! As I see it, we started with a good lead here from Brian at this Talkeetna place.

But then every god damn person in town was standing there with their fingers pointing to the north pole– so off we go to the north pole. Next we find this camp, catch sight of what must have been them but nearly get everyone killed when their Eskimo buddies and someone with rockets arrive. But what do you know, there is another signpost telling us exactly where to go to find them again. This time we think we get lucky but lose a couple of days watching bears while they sneak out the back door. Now here, everyone says they are here– but the only one we found was grenade-man. Now look. I lost three good men taking him out and we still don't know where they are."

Coyote and Thanh shook their heads. Estaban commented.

"They lead us around. They – long ways from here. That big guy, he was working for them. If the rest were around he wouldn't have done this stuff."

"He's right, Raul, I still think that the only clean tra tra trace we had on them was the one I made in this town of Tal Tal Tal Talkeetna. That one was just too good to have be been a trap. I bet they are back there, not down here." Brian commented.

"Right, Raul. That's the only thing that makes sense."

"But why the hell lead us all over the god damn state?"

"They want to keep us away far from there." Concluded Brian.

"OK, so we fly to Anchorage, leave the King Air and find a couple of airplanes better equipped for tracking these people down." Raul stood up and they began the hike back to the beach and the boat ride to Homer. Later in the day they landed at Merrill field in Anchorage. Posing as oil company representatives and pilots, they spent a lot of money arranging for a turbocharged Cessna 185 and a Super Cub for the following morning.

As Raul and his group headed back toward the beach, Vitz regained consciousness. He felt shocks of pain from many places but couldn't find any broken bones. There was only one problem. He was blind. He sat up, realizing that he had no idea which direction would take him off the glacier. What if he got to the glacier edge and fell off the cliff into the ice cold lake?

Vitz felt a strong surge of nausea and began to panic. He took a deep breath and talked to himself: "Spook and you are dead."

The nausea subsided for a moment and he was left with a splitting headache. Feeling the side his face he realized that he had likely impacted on his temple and that was the cause of his blindness. Vitz talked loudly again.

"I'm not afraid of dying, it's just that I don't feel in the mood today. It's Monday. I don't die on Mondays. Promised mom that years ago. I sure as hell don't want to become an MIA in Alaska's first undeclared drug war. So let's sit here and maybe in a bit my vision will clear. But for now, I should paint a few pictures."

Vitz sat quietly on his jacket and turned this way and that until he knew exactly where the sun was. So where had the sun been in the sky moments before? Recalling that, and where it was relative to Kachemak Bay, he turned facing down the glacier and toward the bay. Good, he thought, marking that direction in the ice beside him with his knife. Vitz then painted a picture in his mind, going over it first with broad sweeps and then adding in more and more detail. He had practiced this many times in the jungles of South America for fun. He would hide in a tree in the late afternoon and after the sun went down, spend the whole night recreating the landscape around him in his mind. In the morning he would see how well he had done.

The afternoon came to an end and the wind shifted as the sun began to lose its warmth. Vitz had painted as much as he could and not gaining his eyesight, he made more marks around himself and then scooted this way and that collecting as much of his equipment as he could. There was an extra sweater in his pack and it would help somewhat, but he began to shiver badly. Maybe it was just the cold, but maybe it was the blow to his head. Were he to go into shock it would certainly be a one way trip. He continued to talk to himself.

"Since I can't see I guess there's no sense of waiting for daylight is there? Now what do animals do that can't see? They get around. Bats? Whales don't see in the deep ocean. Sonar, sounding. I need sonar or radar of some kind."

He took his woolen cap off and with some sorrow unwound the yarn to create a line fifty feet long. At the end he tied a rifle cartridge. Vitz could toss the cartridge and line ahead. If there was a crevasse or drop-off in front of him he would be able to feel it as he retrieved the cartridge and could try another direction. Yes, that would help, and he could mark the ice with his knife every few feet so that he could back track or recognize that he had been there before.

The cold began its work and the wind was growing stronger. The fits of nausea came and went and he kept having to remind himself which direction the sun had been in the sky and which direction he had decided he needed to move. Vitz tried to stand but was dizzy and felt sick. He sat down. He might have to wait the night out, but would like to make some start toward the edge of the glacier. In his mind picture there was a large flat area fifty yards down and to his left and on the uphill side was an ice cliff that would afford some protection from the wind. That would be his goal.

Pulling his pack with him, Vitz moved slowly toward the flat area. He was able to identify the crevasse that was directly below him by the feel of the line and cartridge and also by tossing ice chips he dug out with his knife. If they clattered to a stop that was OK. If they continued to slide or ended in a plop in water that was bad. Another fit of shivering and nausea hit and he threw up. It seemed like hours before he was able to move again and he felt confused as he kept reaching points where further progress seemed to end in an abrupt drop off. Was he lost or going in circles? At least he could smell the mess he had left behind and knew that he was slowly moving away from that. Vitz was about to quit and huddle in the growing wind when he realized that the flat area must be just ahead. Unknown to him there was a steep ramp leading to the flat and as he pulled forward he began to slide. Vitz fought the panic as he dug his knife into the ice and broke the speed as best he could as he slid down the ice ramp onto the flat area. Recovering, he found protection from the wind against the uphill ice cliff.

The night deepened and his greatest enemy was not the crevasses but was from within — hypothermia. Even though he was not physically active, his breathing would begin to race in short gasping breaths and he felt very sleepy. Vitz fought to stay awake and to control his breathing. Time seemed suspended. Was it night or just late evening? Was there any chance that it was early morning? The howl of the wind over the ice ridges was gone and night must have deepened. Another bout with breathing. Realizing that he was gambling with limited rations, he took two candy bars from the pack and slowly ate half of one, waiting to continue until he was sure that it would not come back up. At least the worst of the nausea had gone.

He was losing the battle against hypothermia. He had drifted off several times and this time his dreams had become muddled and were rapidly changing as his breathing was more and more shallow. The dreams jumped this way and that, frequently replaying episodes from his youth, dreams of searching for his father. As his heart began to falter, there was a piercing shriek next to him that caused him to sit up. This elicited more shrieks from a pack of ravens that had alighted nearby to investigate. Morning had arrived and although it would be several hours before the sun would clear the horizon, the ravens were up for the day having watched the fight the day before from their nests along the ridge.

The warmth of the sun brought Vitz away from the edge of hypothermia, and the noise of the ravens and the seagulls in the distance made him feel less alone. Seagulls, yes, that would be the direction of the bay, and if he could only get off the glacier he could follow their sound to the beach and listen for a passing boat. Good plan. Now just one minor thing. His mind picture of the glacier had a series of deep crevasses with knife-like ice ridges separating them and he would have to cross this area to get to the hillsides beyond. He had to get off the glacier. Even with the sun, he was feeling exhausted and knew he could not survive another night.

The nausea had gone but his eyesight had not returned. At least the headache was subsiding. Vitz organized things and reestablished directions. He moved quickly to the edge of the flat area and stopped for a while to listen. In the distance he could hear the young ravens playing near the nesting area. That would provide a foghorn.

The first ice ridge left Vitz near panic. He knew that he would have to straddle it and pull himself along. He had crossed that way coming up. With his pack on his back he would start to lose his balance, and tossing the line and cartridge seemed to do little good now as it dropped off in every direction. He could hear ice fragments falling into the water on both sides. He had left the M203A behind but had his .45 automatic pistol. He could end it now– no, better drown. Besides, in 500 years his frozen body might be found and some scientist like Kiren could open him up. He was beginning to question whether his mind was playing with him. Maybe he was lying paralyzed back where the fight ended and had never moved at all. Maybe all of this was not being played out at the speed he felt, but was just the last few moments of life. A raven screeching close by jarred Vitz out of these thoughts and brought him back to the task at hand.

The sharp ice ridges seemed to go on forever. He would pull his way along one and then reach an impasse where it seemed to drop off into a large pool of water. Vitz would backup and try another track but after what seemed like at least a half an hour, he would come to yet another brink and the same impasse. He was not making any forward progress, and he was getting anxious and irritated. Finally after another failed approach he stopped for a while and reviewed the picture in his mind. He should be heading toward the edge of the glacier and the trees, but he had not found any rocks on the ice, an indication of the glacier edge and it seemed as if he was barred from progress by some long pool of water. But to his memory there were no crevasses that large with water at their bottoms in the direction he had been moving. So, what did this tell him? He talked to himself.

"OK, so what do I see from a distance? I see the glacier. I see the hillside. I see the trees and ravens. Fine, what else? Well, the lake at the face of the glacier of course, but I should have kept well above that, farther up the glacier. Vitz, Vitz, Vitz, where is Vitz? He is near some water. OK, oh Jesus, what if the water is the lake, then where is Vitz?"

He tipped his head down and took a breath.

"Son of a Bitch, Vitz is at the edge of the cliffs overlooking the lake. So what do I see? Oh shit, I see a lot of broken ice in every direction. I see that to get off Vitz will have to go a long ways back up the glacier and then traverse across to the hill. God damn, Vitz has let himself move straight down the glacier too much."

The situation was deadly and he knew it. Even if he had had his eyesight, it would have taken some time to work his way off since he would have had to climb back up close to where he had started and then begin his cross-wise traverse. Vitz sat still and then began talking again as if he was an observer.

"Vitz has lost energy and needs food. It does not seem to this observer that Vitz can survive another night on the ice. Vitz felt the sun pass overhead maybe an hour ago. That does not give Vitz time to start over. So fans, it's do or die time for Vitz, how about that! Let's go over to the edge and see what he can find out."

Vitz pulled himself along the ice ridge until he was at the brink and could drop ice chips nearly straight down and hear the water splash. He then measured the distance with the line and found that it was about 30 feet. Next Vitz cut ice pieces and began throwing them harder and harder listening for a splash. Finally, teetering, he stood up and threw ice chunks as hard as possible. Most clattered onto the glacier or made a distant splash. A few others however aimed in the general downhill direction from the ravens made an occasional thud. That had to be the shore, and recalling his ability to throw baseballs 50 yards, he guessed that to be how far he was from the beach.

He sat down and thought. He knew that circumnavigation of the ice ridges and crevasses could not be accomplished before the sun set. The ending of that story was clear. So, what was left? A frontal approach. He had to jump into the water and swim to the shore. Vitz began to talk to himself again.

"So, a swim in damn cold water. Fifty yards – not much under normal conditions but damn cold water and I've got to go in the right direction. Also stay in the top two feet of water, it will have been warmed a bit by the sun and anything will help."

He shifted his gear into the pack, ate the three remaining candy bars and gave himself ten minutes for them to provide extra energy. He took his pants and shoes off, putting them in the pack and reeled in the yarn and stuffed it in his shirt pocket and buckled the pistol holster around his waist. It would provide a 3-shot SOS signal if was able to reach Kachemak bay. Vitz fired once in the air. As the ravens responded loudly he jumped, holding tight to the pack.

The shock of the cold water was fierce and bit into his bare legs and the skin on his head. As soon as Vitz surfaced he stopped and listened for the ravens. They were still squawking and were behind him, not in front – so he had apparently turned as he fell. Vitz swam hard toward their sound. It seemed to take forever and at one point he was near panic and considered letting go of the pack. Another burst of swimming ended in complete exhaustion. His arms quit functioning and the birds seemed a long ways away. Gasping, he allowed his legs to fall downwards. He found himself standing on the bottom. Vitz yelled and waded ashore.

Shivering, Vitz stumbled ashore and onto the warm rocks where he fell asleep. When he awakened, the sun had dropped behind the mountain peaks and the air was getting colder. Donning his pants and shoes, he made his way along the shore to where the lake ended and then followed the outlet stream as it emptied the lake and flowed toward the bay. At several places reaching out, he found himself grasping blueberries and stopped for nourishment. In the middle of the night he reached the beach and found a protected spot to sleep. The next morning hearing a passing boat, he fired 3 shots. He was spotted and taken to the hospital in Anchorage where his vision returned.

The next morning Raul flew the Cessna with Thanh, Brian and Henry, and Coyote flew the Super Cub, a two place airplane with Estaban in the rear seat. The Super Cub was fifty knots slower than the Cessna which had to fly frequent circles to avoid getting too far ahead. The slow speed of the Super Cub is due in part to a very large thick wing and tundra tires. A low speeds however the wing is extremely stable and provides great lift allowing a skilled pilot to fly one at 45 to 50 mph with one notch of flaps while turning circles. These characteristics have made the Super Cub the favorite aircraft of hunters like Coyote who track and shoot from the air, or of legitimate hunters who wish to land on out-of-the-way sandbars, lake shores or mountain meadows. It was early when the two aircraft landed at Talkeetna. Raul and Coyote stopped the airplanes at the far end of the runway and parked them out of sight of the air service cabins and hangars. Brian and Henry stayed with the airplanes while Raul, Thanh, and Estaban went hunting for a straight story about Kiren and her friends. Raul talked as they walked:

"We got the fucking run around the last time we were here and asked about Kiren. I assume we'll get the same treatment this time. Let's start by asking about that guy she was with. Maybe they will be a bit looser tongued."

Raul entered the cabin of one of the flying services and spotted a sleepy fellow making coffee.

"Hello there, I'm Brad Fearrington from Washington D.C. Park Service publicity. Trying to track an old friend down. Should be around here somewhere. He was with a redheaded woman. He's about 6 feet, brown hair. Seen him around?"

"Oh, him, yeh, he was here a day or two ago with her. Dunno where he is at, but Craig over there in that hangar knows him." The fellow pointed to a hangar at the edge of the row of buildings. Raul nodded, thanked the fellow and rejoined Estaban and Thanh. Turning to Thanh he smiled.

"They were just here and know some guy in that hangar over there. Think we may have hit gold, amigos?"

The three walked to the hangar and peered in. One man was there, working on an airplane. Raul went over quickly.

"You Craig ?"

"Why, yes, can I—"

The gun barrel of Raul's 9 mm H&K was rammed hard into Craig 's stomach and then slowly drug upwards until it was pressed against his throat.

"You know a couple of people who flew out of here a day or two ago. I need to find them. None of your business what about. You tell us where they are and we all walk out of here with smiles on our faces —you and us. All friendly."

"No idea of what you are talking about."

"Wrong answer asshole, wrong answers get you killed. Try again."

Thanh walked over and side cocked Craig knocking him to the ground. Craig looked up at the three realizing that he would be shot if he ran, and might be shot if he did not. Before he could think of a plan Raul pointed to Estaban.

"Bring that can of aircraft brake fluid over," he sneered at Craig.

I am only going to explain this once. You are going to drink enough of that brake fluid so that unless you get to the hospital in Anchorage in two hours time, you will die a horrible death over several days of liver failure. Real ugly. Now after you have swallowed this, if you don't tell us what we want to hear, we will whack you on the head making it look as if you fell down and you will never wake up in time to get to the hospital."

Pointing to Estaban and Thanh, they held Craig down and forced his mouth open pouring the entire can of brake fluid down his throat.

Craig was gagging as he was dropped to the floor.

"The Kanikula, they are at the base of the Kanikula Glacier, forty miles west of there. Please don't hit me."

Raul nodded to the others and the three ran to the airplanes leaving Craig behind.

As the Turbo 185 and Super Cub began their takeoff rolls, Matt and Kiren were tossing scraps of pancakes to the ravens prior to wrapping things up at the mine. Kiren continued to fret over the failure of Vitz to appear on time.

"Matt, this really upsets me. Isn't there any way that Roland can track him down?"

"Not without exposing him to more danger. I'm worried as much as you are but remember, this is his profession. Getting killed cancels his vacation pay."

The previous three days had been ones of day and night work. The plant leaves had to be removed and then mixed with a solution of salts and ground up in a Waring blender they had borrowed in Talkeetna. The green "soup" was then filtered through pieces of cotton table cloths that Kiren had raided from the cafe in Talkeetna. Next the filtered soup was centrifuged in a small table top clinical centrifuge. Finally the clear liquid from the centrifugation was mixed with a high molecular weight polymer and more salt and allowed to sit for several hours before being centrifuged again. The virus now resided in the gooey paste that was at the bottom of the centrifuge tubes. It was scraped out and placed in screw cap plastic vials. The bottleneck had been the centrifugation steps and this had required that they operate the centrifuge day and night taking turns doing the different steps.

The remainder of the morning was to be taken up in several final centrifuge runs. Matt had tossed plant remains and the equipment they were done with down the mine shaft and had begun making a pile of the things that they would take out with them. After much discussion as to how best hide the vials until they were handed over to Roland, Matt decided to fill them one third of the way to the top and then drop them down the gasoline filler holes on the top of the wing of The Moose Gooser. By filling them only part way up, they would float in the gas tanks and could be retrieved once they arrived back in Baltimore.

Matt had just filled the last round of vials and was writing labels on paper slips stuffed inside the vials with the virus paste when the sound of two single engine airplanes making low passes over the mine caused him to run out to investigate. It was apparent that the two airplanes were not from the Talkeetna flying services which had distinctive markings, and their failure to radio ahead suggested that they were not interested in relaying their plans. Kiren snatched the .243 and her knapsack as they ran out the back of the greenhouse and hid behind a pile of large boulders, watching the Turbo 185, and then the Super Cub land. The 185 nearly ran into The Moose Gooser before stopping, but then gunned the motor and turned back pointing outwards – blocking The Moose Gooser from taking off. The Cub floated in using less than 300 feet to stop. It motored up just ahead of the Turbo 185, and also turned around pointing back for a rapid departure. Out of the airplanes came six men. Raul led the way wearing a hooded jacket, top pulled over his head and dark glasses, making him impossible to recognize. Thanh, Estaban, and Coyote followed carrying automatic rifles. Brian and Henry trailed behind, timid and unhappy.

Inside the mine house the hot pancakes and coffee signaled that Kiren and her comrade were close by. Nobody spotted, the six moved to the greenhouse. Brian was the first to enter the room with the plants, and reeling from the White Flies, called for Estaban to verify that the plant stems lying around and the few plants left growing were indeed coca plants. Estaban entered and began chewing leaves and inspecting the stems. Henry photographed the rooms, plants, and equipment, while Raul and Coyote stood guard. Brian was the first to find a handful vials with labels inside marked "extracted coca virus, fraction #1." Brian collected some of the vials.

"Raul! This is it! The vi- ru ru ru us! We ha ha ha have it!"

Matt and Kiren watched helplessly and considered their options. The valley around the mine for more than 5 miles was treeless and open. Matt felt that if both the Super Cub and the 185 were to start searching for them by air, it would be impossible for them to hide for long. The only real hiding places were at the mine, but in time they would be found. The Moose Gooser was blocked from taking off so that route of escape was out. Matt's rifle was in The Moose Gooser and all they had was the .243.

Matt whispered to Kiren:

"We've got to split up. Take the .243 and climb up the ridge above the mine house and hide. I'll watch for a break and then run to the Super Cub and disable it. I'm really afraid of the Cub. It can fly so slow just feet off of the ground, that if we are spotted from the air, a good shooter in it could pick us off."

"What about the other airplane?" Kiren asked.

"A lot more sluggish at slow speed. If we can get the Cub out of the picture and my rifle, or if we can get off in the Moose Gooser we may have a chance." Matt countered.

"We really need to get your airplane out of here! It has all of our virus hidden in the gas tanks and they might burn it just to be mean! What are you going to do?" Kiren asked, not understanding what he had in mind.

"As soon as you have hidden, I'll look for a break and run to the Cub. From there I may be able to get to The Moose Gooser and my rifle."

"And what if you don't get a break?" They are going to find you here!"

"Just do as I say. In that case keep climbing up the hill and hide the best you can." Matt whispered.

"I can cover you." Kiren replied.

"No, don't shoot! That will give you away. If I get to the Moose Gooser, be ready to run back and dive in. Now go!" Matt urged seeing nobody in sight.

Inside, Estaban found a 5 gallon container of fuel oil and used it to douse the area where the plant work had been done. The fire started, they ran back to the mine house to continue searching for Kiren and her accomplice.

A few moments later, Kiren reached an outcropping on the hill and looked down. She realized that Matt had no chance of getting to the Super Cub without some diversion and began yelling and shouting.

Thanh spotted a lone person on the hill and returned the yelling with fire from his assault rifle. Kiren fired 2 shots, one of which passed through Thanh's shirt burning his side, and caused him to retreat out of sight. Seeing his chance, Matt sprinted to the Super Cub. Lifting the cowling, Matt used Leatherman Model One to cut the starter wire and throttle cable to the carburetor. He jammed the throttle full open, ran to a large boulder near the Moose Gooser and hid.

With the shooting, Raul and the others ran to the door of the mine house. Raul yelled at Thanh who was holding his side.

"God damn it! Now listen! When I say go, Estaban and Coyote, you take the Cub and you will be the shooters. The rest of us will be in the 185 and we will do the spotting. Go go go!"

The six were briefly out of sight of Kiren as Estaban ran and dove into the back seat of the Cub and Coyote jumped into the front with their assault rifles. Coyote switched on the magnetos, put the throttle to idle, and turned the starter switch. The lack of any response after several tries, and a quick check that there was battery power, led him to jump out and raise the cowling. It took one look to spot the severed starter wires. Looking inside the cockpit Coyote checked that the mags were on, and that the throttle lever was set to idle. By this time, Raul had the Turbo 185 started and was yelling for him to get in and off.

Coyote flipped the propeller with all his might to execute a hand start of the engine– which he assumed would run at a low idle. The engine caught, but with the throttle jammed open, it reached 2600 rpm in two seconds. The Cub leapt forward, and within 3 propeller revolutions, Coyote's head and left arm had been severed from his torso. With Estaban in the rear seat and not able to grasp the stick, the Cub rapidly attained flying speed, lifted off, assumed an increasingly nose high attitude and then stalled, snapping over on its back and impacting straight down in the gully below. The impact rammed Estaban's head forward onto the back of the front seat, creating a G force that ripped his brain from its tethering inside his skull.

The four in the Turbo 185 were stunned to see Coyote flung into pieces and then watch Estaban's death. This only strengthened Raul's anger. Raul gunned the engine of the Turbo 185 and took off, climbing out away from the mine, temporarily unable to see what was happening behind them.

Matt recognized that his window of escape had just opened for a brief moment and stood up yelling at Kiren to run down and get in. With the Moose Gooser running and the passenger door open for Kiren, it seemed like a replay of a slow motion picture. Kiren was running down the hill holding the rifle in one hand and her knapsack in the other. It was as if she was suspended –almost frozen and the Turbo 185 which was climbing out and away was slowly, nose up, beginning to reach a point where it could roll around and come back– zooming in on them. Matt yelled and yelled for Kiren to drop her things and run faster but she shook her head and lurched on.

Just as the Turbo 185 was making its turn back toward them, Kiren pulled herself in and Matt added full takeoff power. As soon as they were airborne, he pushed her head down out of view and reached over and closed her door which was flapping open. Seeing the Turbo 185 begin to descend from above, Matt pointed their nose down and skimmed over the brush into the gullies below the mine. The other pilot would have no choice but to make a slow turn and then try to catch up.

Matt yelled to Kiren: "Keep your head down. If they can't see you, they will think I'm the only one in the airplane and may give up and go back to find you. If they want to play chase, they are going to have to fly in my backyard and there are some things up there they may not be ready for!"

Matt had climbed up and away so that they were now higher than the Turbo 185 which he was trying to lure across the black ice of the Tokositna Glacier, and the narrow 3000 foot ridge that separates the Tokositna and Ruth Glaciers. Crossing the ridge, he turned up the Ruth Glacier and toward The Great Gorge 10 miles ahead. His hope was to outdistance them or induce them to give up following once they saw what was ahead. If they did not, and the Turbo 185 caught up, then one of them with a rifle could well blow The Moose Gooser out of the air.

Inside the Turbo 185 Raul was fussing.

"Damn it to hell! Now we've got him in the airplane and her back on the ground. I want this fucking guy ahead of us god damn dead! Lets deal with him first and then go back and find her, she can't go very far and we can spot her from the air!"

As the two airplanes flew up the Ruth Glacier equi-distant from the canyon walls, and 500 feet above the ice, Matt was slowly gaining distance. Thanh yelled at Raul to add more power.

Raul yelled back at – Henry in the right seat beside him, and Thanh in the back seat along with Brian:

"Look ass holes, we're at full power. That 185 is probably not turbocharged, but he is a lot lighter than we are. We took on full fuel in Anchorage, and there are four of us. He may not have a lot of fuel, and there's just one aboard. We're just too fucking heavy."

Thanh grabbed the back of Raul's head turning it around and asked, with his face six inches from Raul's:

"So how much too heavy?"

To which Raul replied: "We're one person too heavy, seeing how they are pulling away– but the more altitude we gain, the better off we will be, since the altitude will start hurting them unless they have a turbocharger."

The side windows in Cessnas are pop-outs, so that in an emergency they can be kicked out, and Thanh had already pushed his out to be in position to shoot. With no warning, Thanh grabbed Brian's head and slammed it hard against the window on Brian's side causing it to be thrown clear. He unbuckled Brian's seat belt, and with Brian still stunned, began shoving him out.

Kiren was peeking back through the rear window of The Moose Gooser and watched as she saw a person forced head first out of the Turbo-185, until all that kept him from dropping was his feet. She screamed to Matt, who swiveled back to watch the Turbo-185 roll sharply lowering the wing to the side where the man was dangling, and then snap straight as the man fell, spinning, 500 feet to the Ruth Glacier.

Henry turned around to see the Brian's feet disappear, and over the noise of the air rushing through the airplane yelled at Thanh:

"Jesus, what have you done?"

Thanh leaned forward and replied: "I cure his stutter!"

Matt knew that they may have just lost their advantage and trying to gain altitude on a Turbo 185 would be a losing game. By now, the two airplanes were less than 1/4 mile apart, with Matt 100 feet higher. The Turbo 185 continued to close on them as they climbed up The Great Gorge.

Inside the Turbo 185 Thanh started to lean out of the airplane to shoot but Raul yelled:

"Dumb shit! Fuck man, you might hit our propeller! Don't shoot until we are side-by-side."

Matt could play cat and mouse in the Ruth Amphitheater, but having to circle around and around, the others would eventually be in position to shoot. He did not know who the other pilot was, but he was not a local, and hopefully not skilled in Alaskan mountain flying. If so, he might chicken out flying up a very tight canyon.

To the west side of the Ruth Amphitheater lies an extremely steep, curving, narrow mountain pass called 747 Pass. Its bottom is filled with glacial ice. It is formed by 3000 foot walls that rise to its apex at 7000 feet. Matt had flown it numerous times, as it provides a route between the Ruth Glacier and the top of the Tokositna Glacier. If he were to fly the pass, he would end up at the top of the Tokositna Glacier where upon flying back down, they would return to the mine. That was not what he had in mind, but figured that the other pilot might not realize that it was a pass and would not follow Matt all the way up — but would turn around and wait for Matt to come back down.

Circling the Amphitheater with the Turbo 185 closer and closer on his tail, Matt saw a cloud layer close to 7000 feet but it looked as if the pass was open at the top.

Matt swung around the Gateway to the Amphitheater and headed into the pass. He hoped that the pass would be open and that the other airplane would back out. If the pass was not open, or the other airplane kept on their tail, he would have to position himself so that he could turn back around. The prime requirement, Matt saw, was to fly as close to the right side of the canyon as possible, just scraping his wings on the rocks, to give himself the greatest room to turn when he rotated to the left.

Behind them, Raul glanced at the map and saw that it was a tight pass. He shouted to Thanh and Henry —who given Brian's unexpected departure and their proximity to the cliffs, was holding onto his seat as if he would be ejected next.

"We have them! I'll be on their butts just as we top the pass and when I come along side, start shooting!"

Just at they approached the narrowest point in the pass, Matt saw that the top of the pass was fogged in and they would have to turn back. They were 200 feet above the ice below. Just ahead, and on their left side was a rock finger that protrudes hundreds of feet out from the wall. Matt knew that past the rock finger there would be just enough room for him to turn, but that he would have to avoid hitting the back side of the finger, and start the turn from the far right. Any miscalculation would be lethal. Just beyond that was the fog bank.

The radio came alive on the unicom frequency. It was one of the flying service airplanes in the Amphitheater.

"Hey 185's going up 747! Careful, it may be fogged in at the top."

Matt turned to Kiren: "Damn, we've got to turn around pronto cause if they do first, then they will be ahead and we will be behind that that's the wrong place to be. I need to get them to follow me just a bit farther."

Kiren replied: "Maybe I can buy a few seconds."

747 Pass

She grabbed the hand held microphone beside Matt and replied to the unicom call.

"Roger-roger, this is the lead 185, it's open up there now, we're going up and over, thanks much for the concern!"

The radio came alive again but this time much louder.

"185 ahead of me, who the hell are you? Who's in there? I thought it was just one guy there!"

Matt had passed the rock finger and saw that he was within seconds of his turn-around point. He spoke rapidly to Kiren.

"Unbuckle your belt and lean forward under the dash but don't hit the pedals! I need your weight as far forward as possible. Do it now!"

Matt pushed her forward and as he did, Kiren fired off one last message in the radio before disappearing under the dash.

"It's Kiren and Matt –assholes! Leave us alone!"

Matt almost touched the rock cliff on the right, pulled 20 degrees of flaps, chopped the power to 17 inches of manifold pressure, and rotated the nose down and around to the left using the G force he felt in the seat of his pants as an indicator of how tight a turn he could make without entering a spin. Watching the airplane rotate around and the approaching back side of the rock finger, Matt felt that he may have entered too soon, and might not be able to complete the turn before hitting the rock wall. If he turned any harder he might lose it and spin. Yelling "now" to himself, he pushed full power in, and skimmed just feet above the glacier floor, turning steeper. Their wheels seemed to scrape the wall as they rounded the nose of the rock finger and headed back down and out of 747 Pass.

Behind them, Raul assumed that as long as he followed Matt, he would be in no serious danger. Shortly before reaching the rock finger he saw the fog bank ahead, and heard the radio call from the flying service aircraft. He was not sure of Matt's intentions. Looking at the map, he saw that the pass curved such that flying straight ahead through the fog would be impossible. He guessed that Matt might be tempting him to do that, but that Matt would turn around shortly. Raul recognized that he may have been given a checkmate move. If he turned now he would be ahead of them and exiting the pass, they would have to come along side. He was about to begin a turn when he heard Kiren's call. Stunned, he froze for a moment.

Kiren's ploy generated the few seconds needed to lure Raul into a situation where the weight distribution in the Turbo 185 now put him at a deadly disadvantage. With more weight to the aft of the airplane, he was much more likely to enter a flat spin in such a tight turn than was Matt who was carrying less weight and all of it forward. Raul began to panic. The canyon was very narrow and the fog bank was not far ahead. He was in the dead center of the canyon.

As Matt stuffed his 185's nose down, turned to the right and then left, and disappeared under him, Raul followed, but part way through called over the radio:

"Kiren, tell Ben and Ma I'm sorry!"

The Turbo 185, carrying Raul, Henry, and Thanh failed to complete the turn. Glancing back, Kiren saw its right wing hit the rock wall splitting it into a shower of bodies, engine parts, and aluminum sheeting. This all fell onto the steep bottom of the pass creating an avalanche of snow and debris that nearly overtook Matt and Kiren as they flew down the pass and into the Great Gorge. Kiren began screaming hysterically:

"No! No! No! No! it's not possible! No! Please no! Don't let this happen! " And then sobbed, "The pilot, it was my brother Ralph!"

As Matt flew up and out of The Great Gorge, away from the mastiff, he cradled Kiren's head to his shoulder. Behind them a large cloud mass moving in from the north engulfed The Mountain. They headed down the Susitna valley toward the Chugach Mountains and Prince William Sound where his fishing camp lay hidden. There Kiren could wander the endless beaches accompanied by his ravens. While Matt Lynx was a scientist, he still held many of the traditional Indian beliefs and deeply felt that the wisdom of the ravens would provide Kiren's best hope for an acceptance of what had happened and enable her to move on.

Mt. McKinley

17423499R00201

Made in the USA
Charleston, SC
10 February 2013